SOME REMARKS ABOUT THE SHERLOCK HOLMES ADVENTURES RELATED BY HUGH ASHTON:

"...one of the best writers of new Sherlock Holmes stories, in both plotting and style".
The District Messenger, newsletter of the Sherlock Holmes Society of London

"...I am always delighted by the way Hugh Ashton can make me believe the the story was penned by ACD himself."
Paperartzy – Amazon review

"... a magnificent emulation of the writing style of Sir Arthur, the language, syntax and grammar are exactly as one would expect from the man himself."
Nick T – Amazon review

"...stories which would fit seamlessly into the original Conan Doyle accounts. [Ashton] has picked up the cadences and language use which make them hard to distinguish from the originals."
Drstatz – Amazon review

"Hugh Ashton is the premiere Holmesian pastiche writer today without exception."
Maineiac – Amazon Review

Adventures from Watson's Third Box

Adventures from Watson's Third Box : Previously Undiscovered Tales of the Celebrated Consulting Detective Mr. Sherlock Holmes

Hugh Ashton

ISBN-13: 978-1-912605-80-4
ISBN-10: 1-91-260580-5
Published by j-views Publishing, 2023

Many of these stories have previously appeared in various volumes of the *MX Book of Sherlock Holmes Stories*, and the author and publisher wish to express their gratitude to MX Publishing for permission to reproduce them here.

This is a work of fiction. Names, characters, places, brands, media, and incidents are either the product of the author's imagination or are written in respectful tribute to the creator of the principal characters.

j-views Publishing, 26 Lombard St, Lichfield, WS13 6DR, UK
info@j-views.biz

DEDICATION

These stories are dedicated to those who, like me, feel their spiritual home to be in the London fogs swirling around Baker-street.

I would like to pay special thanks to my wife, Yoshiko, who patiently supports me through my writing. Also to David Marcum for his continued friendship and support, as well as the foreword to this book. And lastly to Victoria Yardley, whose sharp eyes and attention to detail have resulted in the elimination of many spelling and typographical infelicities.

"Somewhere in the vaults of the bank of Cox and Co., at Charing Cross, there is a travel-worn and battered tin despatch-box with my name, John H. Watson, M.D., Late Indian Army, painted upon the lid. It is crammed with papers, nearly all of which are records of cases to illustrate the curious problems which Mr. Sherlock Holmes had at various times to examine."

Contents

Noted Pasticheur
by
David Marcum

 FIND it recorded in my digital notebooks that I first became aware of Mr. Hugh Ashton, the noted pasticheur of Japan, and later Lichfield, England, in February of 2012. He came to my attention during one of my routine and regular virtual rambles through the twisted alleys and passages of Amazon, seeking more and more new Sherlock Holmes adventures.

Back in those long-ago days of 2012, there weren't quite as many pastiches as there are now. We are truly living in a Sherlockian Golden Age, and part of that reason is because of the prolific Hugh Ashton and his high-quality adventures.

In February 2012, I found Hugh's first Holmes book, *Tales from the Deed Box of John H. Watson, MD*, and of course purchased and read it immediately, as I do all traditional Canonical pastiches. That's what I want to read, and that's the only type of Sherlockian effort that I support. I found the book to be excellent, and that Watson's voice, as filtered by Hugh's editorial skills, was spot-on.

The year 2012, when Hugh first obtained and then shared a treasure trove of Watson's manuscripts, was a prolific period of publishing for him. In that year alone, he produced:

Tales from the Deed Box of John H. Watson, M.D.
More from the Deed Box of John H. Watson, M.D.
Secrets from the Deed Box of John H. Watson, M.D.
The Darlington Substitution
During that same year, Hugh also published a couple more

new Holmes stories, but initially as stand-alone e-versions only. I only ~~buy~~ lease e-books when forced to, in cases where they aren't published as real books. Not knowing for sure if these would be released at some point as real books, I purchased these two, read them, and enjoyed them. And on October 18, 2012, I wrote Hugh a fan letter, basically encouraging him to include these stories in another physical book, and also noting that I had written my own collection of pastiches published the year before, and discussing one of his stories where he included Holmes's sister, Evadne. I posited that she was in fact a cousin instead of a sister.

Hugh graciously and immediately replied the same day with an informative email, stating that there would be another physical volume soon, and stating, "*You may, of course, be correct in your assumption that Evadne Holmes was a cousin, rather than a sibling. We have only Watson's word for this, and his accuracy was not always of the highest, as we know.*"

The next volume, published in late 2012, was a very handsome hardcover, *The Deed Box of John H. Watson, MD*, containing both previous stories and those that had only been previously electronically released. A similar hardcover, *The Dispatch-Box of John H. Watson MD*, came out in 2016. Over the years since, he's followed with quite a few other Holmes collections and novels:

Notes from the Dispatch-Box of John H. Watson, M.D.
The Reigate Poisoning (Concluded)
Further Notes from the Dispatch-Box of John H. Watson, M.D.
The Death of Cardinal Tosca
Without My Boswell
The Last Notes from the Dispatch-Box of John H. Watson, M.D.
Notes on Some Singular Cases of Mr. Sherlock Holmes
The Adventure of the Bloody Steps
The Adventure of the Lichfield Murder

I continued to communicate with Hugh by email, and during that time, his excellent Holmes adventures kept a great many Sherlockians who were hungering for more Canonical tales, including me, happy. By then, the new publishing paradigm where authors could directly reach readers instead of going through the tired, broken, and highly restrictive old-school publishers was firmly established and successfully in use, particularly by

Hugh, and also by MX Publishing founder Steve Emecz, who recognized both the importance of the print-on-demand model, as well as the existence of many Sherlockian authors and readers who were all frustrated at how the old system limited publication.

I'd written and published a couple of Holmes books with MX, and in early 2015, I had the idea of assembling and editing a collection of Holmes short stories, mostly as a push-back against recent disturbing and subversive Holmes iterations wherein the character is Holmes in name only, usually instead presented as a broken addict or a high-functioning sociopath and murderer while set in modern times. I wanted to remind people about the correct True Sherlock Holmes – a hero and not a loser or villain. I'd thought that possibly I'd get a dozen stories at best, and with this uncertainty, I emailed every pastiche author that I could think of. Of course, Hugh was one of them – and he was on my initial list of who I wanted to include when I first broached the idea to Steve Emecz, because the Holmes he writes about is a hero.

The idea of *The MX Book of New Sherlock Holmes Stories* grew from a theoretical small paperback to three massive simultaneously released hardcovers, published in Fall 2015 with over sixty stories – including a new one by Hugh. Afterwards, I was asked by a number of the contributors, as well as newly interested authors, about the next book, and when should they send their stories. I hadn't planned for a next book, so this took me by surprise, but Steve Emecz and I discussed it, and since all the heavy-lifting decision-making was already in place, we charged ahead, initially thinking of having one new volume per year. However, there was so much interest, and so many new stories arriving, that the single volume became multiple volumes released both in the spring – an Annual edition – and in the fall, with themes such as Christmas adventures, Untold Cases, Impossible Cases, etc.

Since the beginning, all of the series' royalties have gone to support the Undershaw school for special needs children. The school, initially called "Stepping Stones", is located at Undershaw, one of Sir Arthur Conan Doyle's former homes. The series, now up to over 850 stories in 42 volumes (with more in preparation) from over 200 contributors worldwide, have raised over $116,000 for the school, and interest in the series and the traditional Canonical stories they contain is higher than ever.

Throughout the course of these books, Hugh Ashton has been a great supporter, providing many new stories. Most of these have remained uncollected – until he realized one recent day just how many of them he'd written, and that he had enough to make a really great new book of his own – this book that you now hold.

I've only had the chance to meet Hugh once, and I regret that I didn't make more of it at the time. On October 1, 2015, I was able to visit London for my second Holmes Pilgrimage, with the main reason being to attend the grand launch party of the first three-volume MX anthology. The event was held at Heron Tower, (also known as Salesforce Tower), 110 Bishopsgate, and a number of the first MX contributors attended. Hugh, living in Japan at that time, flew to London and was there that night – and I had the chance to meet him in person and talk for just a minute. I very much regret that it wasn't longer, but the entire evening was something of a whirlwind for me, briefly meeting many people. I do hope to see Hugh again on some future Holmes Pilgrimage.

For those interested in seeing a few photos of the event, including Hugh and me in attendance, the Sherlock Holmes Society of London's photo album of that night can be found at: *https://www.flickr.com/photos/shsl/albums/72157659282048780*

I'd like to believe that Hugh came halfway around the world just to support the first MX anthologies, but actually I think he was also scouting around England with the intention of moving back after so many years in Japan, because he and his wife did so the following year, settling in Lichfield, Staffordshire. Since then, he's stayed busy and continued to write – both Holmes adventures and otherwise – and he's also become very involved locally, serving as a City Councillor since 2019 and a District Councillor since 2023.

Hugh doesn't just write about Holmes. He's authored the adjacent Sherlock Ferret series, several stand-alone novels, with some of them being alternative history. He's continued

E.F. Benson's *Mapp and Lucia* series, and in 2017, he tried his hand at a Father Brown pastiche, "The Persian Dagger". As I wrote in my Amazon review: *"Ashton has already proven himself to be a master of bringing us new Sherlock Holmes adventures by way of Dr. Watson's Tin Dispatch Box. I hope that he never stops editing those for publication. But now I want him to find more and more of these Father Brown narratives as well. In fact, I hope that he has found the equivalent of Father Brown's Tin Dispatch Box, and that it's very deep and very full. Good job, sir!"* In 2023, Hugh contributed a Holmes and Father Brown story to *The Detective and The Clergyman*, and again, I want to encourage him to send us some more new Father Brown tales – but not at the expense of writing more Holmes pastiches!

Over the course of his trips to Watson's alternately named Deed Box and Dispatch-Box have continued, Hugh has made something of a specialty of writing about Holmes's Untold Cases – those investigations mentioned in The Canon relating to such interesting topics as the Darlington Substitution Scandal, the vanishing of James Phillimore, and the Giant Rat of Sumatra. Hugh has now written over four dozen Holmes pastiches, many of which provide his versions of these Untold Cases – but there are actually over 140 Untold Cases, which leaves plenty more of them for Hugh to relate. As a fan of both Canonical Holmes adventures and Hugh's writing of them, I challenge him to chronicle the rest of the Untold Cases – and I'll be first in line to read them!

David Marcum
August 2023

PREFACE

 HAVE been editing Watson's accounts of Sherlock Holmes's adventures for over ten years, ever since that famous tin box deposited in the vaults of Cox & Co. was passed to me by a friend.

Even when I was sure that the box was empty, another box appeared, and yet another. The stories I have retrieved from this last box have made their way into print courtesy of MX Publishing, who took up the suggestion of eminent Sherlockian David Marcum to collect and publish many tales of Sherlock Holmes which were previously unknown to the public. David, who acted as editor for the first and all subsequent books, and whose Foreword is included here, has been a mainstay and a support for all the authors, including me, whose stories have appeared in this series. Many thanks to him and to Steve Emecz for their efforts in promoting traditional pastiches over the years, and for their encouragement of the authors around the world who have contributed to the series.

These collections, starting with Volume I in 2015, and all known in their various volumes (now up to volume XL) as *The MX Book of New Sherlock Holmes Stories*, have raised substantial sums of money for Doyle-related good causes, with the authors waiving their fees and royalties. It is a cause that I am proud to have been associated with.

Some of these stories have appeared elsewhere as "stand-alones", either in paperback or ebook format, but I make no apology for including them here. However, two of the " MX stories" (*John Vincent Harding* and *The Deceased Doctor*) have been published in the collection entitled *Mr. Sherlock Holmes – Notes on Some Singular Cases*, and are not included here.

Some have been edited slightly and corrected from the

originally published editions, and the names of a few characters have been changed.

So here, then, are the stories which go to make up the
contents of the third box. You will notice that they are all titled as "adventures". I never forget the words of a wise critic
who pointed out that "Other detectives have cases: Sherlock
Holmes has adventures".

The majority of these adventures are the "untold" stories of
Sherlock Holmes, as collated by the late Philip Jones, who was
a source of great encouragement to me when I started on my
Sherlockian journey.

The plots are a little complex at times – perhaps over-com-
plex when compared to the Canon, but perhaps more
suited to modern readers who have grown up on more fully
psychologically developed criminals than to those readers who
first encountered Sherlock Holmes in print. Perhaps Watson
felt that his audience was not ready to enjoy these more complex stories, or that his editor and agent, Sir Arthur Conan
Doyle, dissuaded him from sending them for publication.

There are other reasons why some of these may have been
suppressed, or at least remained unpublished: political, moral,
or going against societal norms of the day.

Not all of these stories deal with a crime, let alone murder, and in some ways, these stories are more satisfying than a
criminal investigation.

Anyway, they have been fun to edit and polish (lightly!) for
publication. I trust they will be fun to read.

Hugh Ashton, Lichfield 2023

ABOUT THE ADVENTURES

THE ADVENTURE OF THE FUTURE FUNERAL (P 1)
"...his arrest of Wilson, the notorious canary-trainer..." (BLAC)

The rather macabre idea of someone ordering a funeral well in advance of the deceased's death has always had a fascination for me. Interesting to see it used by a criminal as a device to help achieve his evil ends. It was also fascinating to see how the ' canaries' make an appearance.

First published in MX Vol. X (2018)

THE ADVENTURE OF THE
GROSVENOR–SQUARE FURNITURE VAN (P 21)
"... ...the little problem of the Grosvenor Square furniture van." (NOBL)

A locked room mystery, but without a body – rather, the vanishing of a body which is very much alive from the locked room, and its reappearance elsewhere. I have the feeling that this case amused both Holmes and Watson.

First published in MX Vol. XIII (2019)

THE ADVENTURE OF THE SILVER SKULL (P 41)
"I heard from Major Prendergast how you saved him in the Tankerville Club scandal." (FIVE)

What sort of scandals would reverberate around a London club of those days ? Card scandals, of course. And in fact I found a stick with a similar head in a curio shop, though it lacked the special features of the stick in this story.

First Published in MX Vol XI (2018)

THE ADVENTURE OF THE RETURNED CAPTAIN (P 67)

"... the facts connected with the disappearance of the British barque Sophy Anderson." *(FIVE)*

Dead men return from the deep to haunt Holmes and Watson. There's nothing supernatural about them, or the *Sophy Anderson*, but evil deeds are afoot all the same.

First published in MX Vol. VI (2017)

THE ADVENTURE OF THE LICHFIELD MURDER (P 91)

"...and there was Henry Staunton, whom I helped to hang" (MISS)

Set in the Staffordshire city where I have lived since 2016. Good to read that familiar buildings and places I know were visited by Holmes and Watson. A nice little bloody mystery with a fair bit of forensic CSI in it.

First published in MX Vol. I 2015, subsequently as a paperback (Inknbeans Press and subsequently j-views Publishing)

THE ADVENTURE OF THE BLOODY STEPS (P 113)

"Suppose that I were Brooks or Woodhouse, or any of the fifty men who have good reason for taking my life..." (BRUC)

No canonical reference other than the name of the villain. The Bloody Steps legend is real, as are the events that triggered the legend, though occurring long before Holmes's investigation. However, it had sufficient appeal enough for Watson to use it as the title of this adventure, though Rugeley appears to be far from being his favourite place. Of course, Doyle was also involved with the Edalji case, not ten miles from Rugeley, and probably had no love for the area or its people.

First published by j-views Publishing, paperback, 2018

THE ADVENTURE OF THE HOLLOWAY GHOSTS (P 149)

No canonical reference

Recast by me from the original rough Watsonian notes as an audio drama, initially published in print, and later recorded by the late Steve White. It involves politics and international intrigue, which would be familiar territory to Sherlock Holmes, given the activities of brother Mycroft, though clearly this was a reason for Watson to suppress publication.

First published in MX Vol. XVII (2019), then as an audiobook (MX) and Kindle (j-views Publishing, 2020)

THE ADVENTURE OF VANAPRASTHA (P 177)
No canonical reference

A rather bloody little adventure, with a very strong Indian element to it. India definitely exerted its influence over late Victorian society to a great degree. I wonder if this is one of the adventures that Doyle persuaded Watson to suppress, given its relationship to Eastern religions.

First published in MX Vol. VII (2017), subsequently as
an ebook by j-views Publishing (2018)

THE ADVENTURE OF THE CHOCOLATE POT (P 203)
*"Old Baron Dowson said the night before he was hanged that
in my case what the law had gained the stage
had lost." (MAZA)*

Hanged for a chocolate pot ? Collector's mania can lead to excesses. And when the objects collected are valuable in their own right... Happily, Sherlock Holmes displays his talents to ensure justice is done.

First published in MX Vol VII (2017)

THE ADVENTURE OF THE MURDERED MEDIUM (P 227)
No canonical reference

Although Sir Arthur was a Spiritualist, I don't think Holmes ever would have been, and this definitely goes against Doyle's views. This is set after the Great War, and tells us of Holmes and his place with the Government following the Armistice.

First published in MX Vol. XXXIII (2022)

THE ADVENTURE OF THE DEAD RATS (P 257)
*"I believe that my late husband, Mortimer Maberly, was one of
your early clients." (3GAB)*

It took a little effort to discover the link between this early adventure and Watson's published work. I like the idea of a seemingly trivial, somewhat grotesque, start to a case, which may either grow into something serious, or may remain trivial. However, I feel that Watson (or perhaps Doyle) felt that the opening scene might be too much for delicate stomachs.

First published in MX Vol. XL (2023)

The Adventure of the Nonpareil Club (P 275)
"...he had exposed the atrocious conduct of Colonel Upwood
in connection with the famous card scandal at the Nonpareil
Club.." (HOUN)

The "Devil's picture book" again – the cue for this story came from the name of the club. What sort of members would belong to a club with this name ? And what sort of tensions might arise between them ?

The Adventure of the Green Horse (P 297)
No canonical reference

An examination of the relationship between classes, specifically servants and their employers. And an interesting side to Holmes at the end. I think it is fairly obvious why Watson did not publish this adventure.

The Adventure of the Murdered Maharajah (P 313)
"The whole question of the Netherland-Sumatra Company
and of the colossal schemes of Baron Maupertuis." (REIG)

This appears to have been intended as the first part of a novel-length adventure in which Sherlock Holmes confronts the Baron. Sadly, the adventure appears to be incomplete, but there is still hope that the rest may be discovered. Maupertuis would seem to be a more Blofeld-type character than is Professor Moriarty, and the crime investigated here is worthy of a place in this collection.

An Unnamed Case
No canonical reference

Discovered on a scrap of paper pinned to the back of the previous adventure. The bulk of this is in Watson's hand, and the final sardonic addition is almost certainly the work of Holmes – certainly not ACD's distinctive handwriting. This is definitely not an adventure.

ADVENTURES FROM WATSON'S THIRD BOX

PREVIOUSLY UNDISCOVERED ACCOUNTS
OF SOME CASES OF THE
CELEBRATED CONSULTING DETECTIVE
MR. SHERLOCK HOLMES BY
JOHN H. WATSON M.D.

EDITED BY

HUGH ASHTON

WITH A FOREWORD BY
DAVID MARCUM

AND PUBLISHED BY
J-VIEWS PUBLISHING, LICHFIELD, UK

THE ADVENTURE OF THE FUTURE FUNERAL

I T must be admitted that Sherlock Holmes thrived on occurrences of the unusual, not to say the macabre, which would turn the stomachs of most men. I have elsewhere recounted his exploits in the case of Black Peter, where he carried a blood-stained harpoon through the streets of London, following his tests on the carcass of a pig in order to determine the strength that would be required to pin a large man to a wall like a butterfly in a collector's cabinet. Nor was he averse to viewing the most grisly of mortal remains, some of which would have sent my medical colleagues scurrying to a place of greater comfort.

It was hardly a surprise to find him interested in the story of Mr. Nathaniel Urquhart of Southwark, who visited us in our rooms at Baker-street one bright spring morning. Mr. Urquhart himself was of some interest to the discerning eye, being tall and thin, the sparseness of his figure accentuated by the severe black of his clothing.

" 'Nathaniel Urquhart and Sons, Undertakers, Southwark,' Holmes read from the card that had been sent up. "Ah yes, I believe it was your firm that had the making of the special coffin in which the Lady Frances Carfax was to be buried alive."

" On my honour, sir," replied our guest, " I had no knowledge of the matter until after it was all over."

" Oh, no blame attaches to you, Mr. Urquhart," Holmes reassured him. " I myself was completely unaware of the nature of the business until I was almost too late."

" Thank you, sir." Nathaniel Urquhart produced a large red and white spotted handkerchief which formed an incongruous contrast to his sober black attire, and mopped his brow. " But seeing as how you solved that case, I wonder if you would be kind enough to listen to my story and give me some advice, if you can."

" I can but listen," Holmes told him. "A cigarette ? " he offered.

" No thank you, sir. I find they make me cough something terrible, and there's nothing so disturbing as the undertaker coughing his way through a funeral, wouldn't you agree, sir ? "

" I would indeed," agreed Holmes, straight-faced. " Now, to your story, Mr. Urquhart."

" Well, sir, it was last Tuesday that this gentleman came to see me. Well, not quite a gentleman, perhaps, though he spoke well enough, there was something about him that didn't quite ring true."

" His boots, perhaps ? " suggested Holmes.

Our visitor started. " Why, that was exactly it," he exclaimed. " I was just about to say that it was his boots that gave him away, as you might say, and you put the words into my mouth. Well then, this man–"

" He has a name ? " Holmes asked.

The other smiled. " He gave me the name of John Blenkinthorpe, and requested that I collect the body of his wife."

" Hardly an unusual occurrence, I would have thought ? " I interjected.

" Indeed not. It is, after all, the way in which I earn my living," replied Nathaniel Urquhart. " In such cases, we naturally enquire what time will be the most convenient for us to make the collection. In this instance, I was given a date and time a year from now."

Holmes raised his eyebrows. " Indeed ? That would seem to be an unusual development."

" Not merely unusual, Mr. Holmes, absolutely unheard-of. Why, you can imagine the state of a body after a year, can you not ? "

" Indeed so. Most singular. There is more ? "

" Yes, the whole business is confoundedly queer. I was taken aback by his request, but asked for the name of the deceased. He thereupon informed me that he was unmarried at present."

" And yet he had asked you to collect his wife's body ? "

" That is correct."

" You would appear to have been the victim of some form of practical joke," I suggested.

Our visitor smiled. " It goes further than that," he explained. " As you may guess, I had been given an address from which to collect the body of this non-existent wife, before I had even been given a date on which to perform the operation."

" And the address was a false one ? " suggested Holmes.

" Not quite. When I passed by 23 Belvedere Gardens some

time later on my way home from my business premises, I noticed that a sign proclaimed that it was to let. Out of curiosity, I went to the nearest letting-agents and enquired regarding the lease of the property, describing to them the man who had given his name as John Blenkinthorpe. Not only was the name unknown to them, but they had no knowledge of a man who answered the description which I presented to them, and, even stranger, the property was not to let through them. They recommended several other agents in the vicinity, given that I had expressed an interest in the property, but I likewise failed to obtain any information about Blenkinthorpe or the property."

" Most curious," remarked Holmes. " But I fail to see where my services may be of value to you. In what capacity do you wish to engage me ? "

"Why, none, sir," replied our visitor. " I knew that the unusual held some interest for you, and remembered you from the time of poor Lady Frances, and thought you might find my story to be worth the hearing."

Holmes threw up his hands in exasperation. " I am a busy man, Mr. Urquhart, and even though your story may be interesting of itself, unless you set the puzzle for me to unravel, with a definite solution and goal to attain, I consider the telling of it to be a waste of time. Goodbye to you." With these words, he turned away, and thereby brought any further conversation to an end.

Urquhart turned to me, but while Holmes was within earshot I was unable to offer him any advice, or to do other than to usher him silently to the door.

" I have no doubt that Mr. Holmes has an interest in your story," I told him, when I judged us to be out of my friend's hearing. " However, it is hardly reasonable to expect him to take on any kind of investigation without a definite end in sight. I can assure you that it is not the financial aspect of the matter that is of concern – I have known him to take many cases without fee – but it is the intellectual challenge that stimulates him to action. I therefore wish you a very good day."

I saw him down the stairs and returned to the room.

" Thank you, Watson," Holmes remarked to me, without

turning or raising his head. "You have an admirable gift of tact on occasion, a gift which I all too often seem to lack."

"And what of our visitor's story?" I asked.

"Do you believe it?" my friend asked me in reply.

"Why, yes. What possible reason could he have for telling us such a fable?"

"I can conceive of at least three reasons why we have heard this story," Holmes told me. "You surely have not forgotten the story of Mr. Jabez Wilson, with the remarkable head of red hair. His story to us seemed too preposterous to be true, but it ended in the very satisfactory capture of Mr. John Clay, who had been a thorn in the side of Scotland Yard for some years. Could not this story be a similar ruse to lure Mr. Urquhart from his business?"

"And the other two reasons?"

"I am reminded of a case in Baden in 1865, where a Herr Hufschmidt made a similar request for a coffin for person or persons unknown, to be filled in the future. The motive in that case was to deflect any suspicion of murder, for what murderer would signal his motives in advance in so brazen a fashion? In this instance, the murderer is himself the maker of the coffin to contain his future victim."

"But surely you do not consider Mr. Nathaniel Urquhart to be a potential murderer?"

"All men, even you, Watson, may be said to be capable of that crime, given appropriate circumstances and motivation. However, I do not say that I consider this to be a likely probability, merely one of several possibilities."

"And the third?"

"That Mr. Urquhart is not of sound mind, and has recounted a dream or some other delusion to us, in the sincere and firm belief that this incident really occurred."

"That last should be easy enough to check," I laughed. "It is a simple matter of making our way to Belvedere Gardens and examining the premises."

"And if they turn out to be empty, pray, what would that tell us? Merely that Mr. Urquhart has passed an empty house in his everyday journey and had remarked the fact that it was empty somewhere at the back of his mind. He then proceeded to spin an elaborate fable around the fact."

I sighed. " It is a shame that we are not able to take the case further."

" Case, Watson ? Case ? There is no case. There is merely a procession of bizarre and *outré* events related to us by a stranger, which may or may not have a basis in reality."

" At all events, I propose to take myself to view the premises in question."

" By all means do so, though I fail to see what you will discover of interest there. In the meantime, it is of importance to me that I should finish these notes on the derivation of harmonies in the motets of Lassus."

I therefore took myself off, and proceeded to Belvedere Gardens. Number 23 proved to be at the end of a red-brick terrace, and presented a forlorn aspect. One of the front windows, bare of any curtains or hangings, was cracked, and the paint was peeling from the front door.

Since the house stood at the end of the row, it was a comparatively simple matter for me to make my way to the rear of the building, where I entered the back yard through an unlocked gate. The back of the house was, if anything, more unprepossessing than the front, but it was noticeable that the handle of the back door appeared clean and free of grime.

On a whim, I turned the handle, and to my surprise, found I was able to open the door, which moved easily and silently on its hinges, allowing me to enter the small room that served the house as a primitive kitchen. Though I am well aware that I lack Sherlock Holmes's powers of observation, it was clear to me that this place had been used in the very recent past. There were vague imprints of feet on the dusty floor, and there were signs that the range had been in use not too long before. A half-burned scrap of newspaper bore a date of only two weeks before.

There were few other signs of occupation, and on my trying the door that led to the other rooms of the house, I discovered that it was locked. I was therefore forced to the conclusion that whatever had taken place in this house had taken place only in this room.

I returned to find my friend engaged in looking through the voluminous scrapbooks that formed such a large part of his working tools.

"This case is almost unique in the annals of crime," he remarked, glancing up from a page of newspaper cuttings. "I now recall a similar event in Brussels in 1876, and the one in Baden in 1865, as I mentioned previously, but as far as I am aware, this is the first time that such a thing has occurred in this country."

"You believe there to be a case, then?"

"Indeed I do. Regarding its precise details, I am as yet unable to say, but we may take it as certain that some devilment is afoot, and that of a strange nature. But tell me, what have you discovered?"

I informed him of the nature of the house and its internal arrangements.

"Indeed, most singular," he commented.

"What, then, are we to make of this funeral ordered for a year hence?"

"For me to answer that, you must inform me of what the neighbours had to say about this house and its inhabitants."

"I fear that I did not talk to any of them."

"Tut, Watson. Was there no twitching of the net curtains, as a stranger walked through Belvedere Gardens?"

"I did not observe."

"And you entered only the kitchen from the rear of the house?"

"That is correct."

"You have been most confoundedly careless about the whole business. No matter. Prepare to leave here in twenty minutes."

"Where to?"

"Why, Belvedere Gardens, of course."

"You regard this as significant, then? I have discovered a clue?"

"In the sense that you have discovered some parts of this business which have whetted my appetite, yes. In the matter of clues leading to the solving of this mystery by the forces of justice, no. I must therefore conduct this investigation myself. I can ill afford to take time away from my investigation of the

Duchess of Hampshire's diamonds, but the case is almost at an end, and I believe that even Lestrade will be able to apprehend the criminal with the hints that I shall give him." So saying, Sherlock Holmes turned to his writing-desk, and proceeded to write a few lines on a scrap of notepaper, which he folded and sealed in an envelope before ringing for Billy, our page, with instructions to hand it to Inspector Lestrade personally.

"And now," he announced, entering his bed-room, "I shall make myself ready to visit Belvedere Gardens."

It was precisely twenty minutes after Holmes had announced his intention of visiting the house that we caught a cab to Southwark. I guided Holmes to the back of the house, where I once more entered the back door into the kitchen.

Holmes cast a quick eye over the scene, as if to confirm for himself what I had previously communicated to him, and made for the door connecting the kitchen to the rest of the house.

"It is locked, as I told you," I informed him.

"No matter," said he, and indeed, his ever-present picklocks were already in his hand as he spoke. "Ha!" he exclaimed as the lock sprang open.

The hallway likewise was bare of furnishings and furniture, presenting a dismal aspect.

"Curious," I remarked.

"Let us look further," Holmes answered me, and led the way to the other rooms on the ground floor. These, too, proved to be empty of all furniture, with bare floorboards. "And upstairs," Holmes added, bounding up the bare boards of the staircase. The rooms at the front of the house on the first floor were also bare and empty, but those at the back were furnished, albeit meagrely, with a bed and washstand, and on my drawing my finger across one of the ledges, it appeared to me that these rooms had been used and cleaned relatively recently.

Holmes bent over one of the beds, and removed something from the pillow, which he placed carefully in an envelope.

I observed a strange crunching feeling under the soles of my boots, and on closer examination, I discovered that a part of the floor was covered in places with small round globes, less than one-tenth of an inch across. I picked up one of these, and examined it, but could make nothing of it. I therefore picked up a few of these, and folded them in a piece of paper torn from my notebook, and passed them to Sherlock Holmes for his perusal.

Holmes examined them carefully through his high-powered lens before bringing the paper to his nose and sniffing cautiously.

" Birdseed," he pronounced.

" Birdseed ? " I repeated incredulously. " I see no trace of any birds here."

" In that case, Watson, what would you make of this ? " he asked me, smiling.

" I cannot tell," I answered. " This is most curious – I have never encountered anything of this nature before. To find a house with but a few rooms unfurnished, and with some birdseed on the bare boards, it passes all understanding."

" Well, well," smiled Holmes. " Shall we pay a call on the neighbours ? "

We left the house by the way in which we had entered, Holmes carefully re-locking the door leading from the kitchen to the hallway, and made our way to the front.

" See, Watson," said Holmes, gesturing with his stick towards the windows of the house we had just left, " there are no curtains in the window, and no sign of habitation from the street, and would you not swear, from this aspect, that the house was uninhabited ? "

" I would indeed."

" And now," said Holmes, knocking at the door of one of the houses opposite. " Let us see what we can discover."

The door was opened by a maid, who listened to Holmes's request to talk to the mistress of the house. This personage transpired to be an elderly lady, who regarded Holmes through a pair of thick spectacles.

" Excuse me, madam," Holmes addressed her. " I have a rather delicate question to ask. I am a complete stranger to London, but I am the only nephew – indeed, I believe I am the only relative of my aunt, who passed away two days ago. I received the telegram this morning, sent by her neighbour, Mrs. Parker, and came from Hampshire right away, together with my friend here."

" I am sorry for your loss, Mr..."

" Johnson, madam. I apologise for not presenting you with my card, but in the heat of the moment..."

" I quite understand, Mr. Johnson. As I was saying, I am sorry for your loss, but I fail to understand what your aunt's death has to do with me. Do you know of some connection between her and me ? "

" No, no, no. It is nothing of that nature, I assure you. My query is a more general one, though of a delicate nature, as I say. It is the matter of the funeral. I have no knowledge of the undertakers in this part of the world, and I was wondering if you had any knowledge of firms who provide these services ? "

" My dear husband passed away some years ago, and his funeral was arranged by the firm of Nathaniel Urquhart whose business is not far from here – on the Kennington Road, in fact."

" My condolences on your loss, madam. Thank you for the information." Holmes bowed slightly by way of thanks.

" However," our interlocutor told us, " if you would like to know more about these things, you should ask over there," and she pointed towards the house from which we had just come.

" Indeed ? " Holmes raised his eyebrows.

" Well, it's a strange thing," she went on in a conspiratorial whisper, " but that house hardly ever seems to have anyone entering or leaving it, and as you can see, it is marked as being to let, and appears empty, but there have been at least three funerals from there in the past eighteen months. I am not sure, but I think there may have been four."

" That does seem to be an excessive number," Holmes agreed. " And you have no knowledge of the undertakers who carried out these services ? "

" I couldn't tell you that, but it did seem more than a bit strange to me that there should be so many funerals in such a short time."

" Perhaps they were children who had succumbed to some common malady," I suggested. " Diseases such as chicken-pox can be very contagious, and often prove fatal to young infants."

She shook her head. " These were not children's coffins. I had half a mind to tell the police about it, but then I said to myself that I was just imagining things. It does seem strange, though."

"I agree that it is more than a trifle peculiar," Holmes confirmed. "I thank you for your information regarding Urquhart. I will take your recommendation. Thank you for your time, and goodbye."

"What in the world did you hope to gain from that conversation, Holmes?" I asked, as we walked away.

"We have been informed, have we not, that there has been an extraordinary spate of funerals conducted from that house."

"But that is impossible," I expostulated. "We have seen for ourselves that no one lives there."

"Indeed they do not. But we should consider the possibility that they die there, or at least, that their bodies are taken from there."

"I begin to understand you, Holmes."

One aspect of our findings continued to puzzle me until we returned to Baker-street, and I asked Holmes, "By the by, what do you make of the birdseed that I discovered on the floor of the room?"

"Oh, that is common birdseed, such as is used to nourish caged birds. There is little remarkable in the seed itself, merely in its presence."

"Caged birds? In an empty house? There were no feathers or any other sign that there might have been a bird in there. At any event, I observed none."

"Then, my dear Watson, I would recommend that you secure the services of a good optician." So saying, he leaned across and plucked something from the back of my right shoulder, which he proceeded to scrutinise.

"What is it?" I asked.

"A feather. I believe it to be a wing feather from a specimen of *Serinus canaria*, the common domestic canary. I can only assume that it escaped your notice as it drifted onto your coat."

I was more than a little crestfallen that I had failed to observe what was clearly an obvious sign that a bird had, in fact, at some time been present in the room. "You are certain it has come from a canary?" I asked Holmes.

"I am as positive as I can be without a microscopic

examination," Holmes told me. "The shape of the feather, its colour, and the barbs on the tips are almost conclusive, however."

"But how would a canary find its way into an empty house ?" I asked.

"I do not believe that it found its own way. The presence of the food on the floor would seem to confirm that. I fear, Watson, that we are about to find ourselves rubbing shoulders with one of the more detestable specimens of the London criminal. Would you be good enough to reach down the volume of the Index that deals with the letter 'W', and read for me what you find regarding Edward Wilson."

I perused the scrapbook in question, and under the relevant entry, read out the following words, which had been written in the sprawling and near-illegible hand that Holmes used for such matters, " Edward Wilson, born–"

"Yes, yes, Watson," Holmes exclaimed impatiently. "The meat of it, the nub."

I read on and reported, "You have written here that he is one of the most vile men plying his trade at present. This is strong language, Holmes."

"Indeed so. I have my reasons for believing this. Read on."

"His offences are such that he has so far escaped the attentions of the police, it would seem."

"So they have, but I have had my eye on him for quite some time now. This may be what I need to arrange the fate for him that he so richly deserves."

"Good Lord, Holmes, you have written here that his business, at least as far as the law is concerned, appears to be breeding canaries, and training them to sing. But you have good reason to believe otherwise ?"

"Indeed so. I believe him to be one of the most villainous of all the criminals in London at present. He will stop at nothing to achieve his ends, which are, I believe, evil incarnate."

It was unlike Holmes to use such terms to describe those against whom he had set himself, and I could not help but enquire further.

"Ah, Watson," was his reply, uttered in tones of sadness and compassion. "He preys on vulnerable young women, of the poorest and most defenceless kind. They are shamelessly exploited in ways I do not care to expound on, and when they appear to be of no further use to him, they are disposed of, brutally, and without remorse. These he also refers to as his 'canaries' and he treats them as if they were indeed beings of a lower standard than humanity."

" He is a man to be avoided, then ? "

" On the contrary, Watson, I wish to meet him, and put an end to his activities."

" Why is this villain still at large, and why is he not behind bars ? " I expostulated.

" He is damnably cunning, and uses his skills to cover his tracks in such a way that none of his tricks can be traced to him. Young Stanley Hopkins has had his suspicions for some time, ever since I informed the police of his activities, but even he has been unable to find the proof that would satisfy a jury, and Hopkins is one of the best of the bunch at the Yard. However, this hair here that I removed from the pillow in the house, while perhaps not constituting a legal proof, may yet form a strand in the noose that winds itself around Wilson's neck."

" How do you mean ? "

" I told you that Wilson cynically refers to the young women whom he exploits as 'canaries'. This is partly an allusion to their caged nature, but also, I have heard it said, that all of them are fair-haired, or blonde, as our French cousins would have it, if not by nature, by artifice. And so," he added, bending to one of the microscopes that graced the table by the window, " this hair, naturally dark, has been treated to give it a fairer appearance."

" So you believe the man who ordered the funeral a year hence from Mr. Nathaniel Urquhart was this Wilson ? "

" I believe that to be the case."

" And his purpose for doing such an extraordinary thing ? For showing his hand, so to speak ? "

" Ah, that is something that at present I have been unable to deduce. There is something confoundedly mysterious here, Watson, and I am unable to determine it."

For a few days, I was busy with my practice, and Sherlock

Holmes was engaged on other cases, but it was with some excitement that I received a telegram from my friend, requesting me to call on him at the rooms at Baker-street.

"I believe we are to attend another funeral from Belvedere Gardens," he remarked. "We are not invited, but I feel we should at any rate view the *cortège* as it leaves the house."

"Wilson?" I enquired.

"Indeed so. Word has come to me through sources that I prefer not to reveal at present, that one of his 'canaries' has departed this life, and he is ready to dispose of her."

I shuddered. "There is something monstrous about this, Holmes."

"I agree."

"But why does he not dispose of the bodies in Whitechapel?" I asked.

"I cannot tell, but I agree with you that this business of carrying them across the river to Southwark seems a deucedly long-winded way of doing his foul business. But come, are you ready?"

We set off on our journey, and paid off our cab as soon as we had crossed Blackfriars Bridge.

"It is best if we proceed on foot from now on," Holmes told me, but failed to provide a reason for this.

We reached Belvedere Gardens, and took up our positions opposite the house where we had discovered the birdseed and the other mysteriously furnished rooms.

A hearse, drawn by a pair of black horses, was already standing outside.

"There is no coffin inside at present," I whispered to Holmes. Indeed, not only was there no coffin, there was a complete absence of undertaker's mutes or any other person who appeared connected with the funeral.

"Indeed, strange," muttered Holmes. "By whom and for whom was this ordered?"

"It was ordered by myself, for your benefit, Mr. Holmes," came a rough voice from behind us.

I turned, to behold a face, the likes of which I hope never to see again. The brow was bestial, beneath which a pair of dark eyes glared, and the lips curled in an animal's snarl exposing jagged and crooked teeth.

I started, and even Holmes seemed taken aback.

" I surprised you there, I think, Mr. Sherlock Holmes," the apparition said, with an unpleasant chuckle. " But I had been expecting you as soon as I was told you had visited my little hideaway." He nodded towards the empty house. " I can see you are still wondering who I am and who informed me of your doings."

" Not at all. You are obviously Edward Wilson, and the woman who told us of the funerals here was in your pay."

The man threw back his head and laughed. " You have me placed to rights," he said. " I'll give you that, Mr. Holmes. But you are mistaken if you think I would pay money to my dear old mother for her work in helping bringing you to meet me. Now, if you don't mind, you two gentleman are going to pay me a visit at my crib, and we will have a little talk." He had hardly finished speaking when two roughs came from the shadows, and before Holmes and I had fully grasped what was happening, our arms were twisted behind our backs, and I could feel rope being placed around my wrists, binding them together.

" In you go," Wilson said, gesturing to a baker's van. " We're going for a short ride."

The two bravos pushed us into the closed vehicle, and Wilson presumably acted as driver, or sat with the driver. We could see nothing of the road as we rattled and swayed our way through the streets of London. I started to speak to Holmes, but was instantly checked by a heavy hand on my shoulder and the gruff words, " It'll be better for you if you say nothing. Try to speak again without being told you can, and you'll regret it."

I held my peace, as did Holmes. For my part I was racked with apprehension regarding our possible fate, but as far as I was able to judge in the semi-darkness that surrounded us, it appeared that he was unconcerned.

After what I estimated was about forty minutes, the jolting and rattling stopped, and the doors of the van were opened after a short time. Holmes and I were unceremoniously escorted by our gaolers to what appeared to be a warehouse, where

Wilson was already seated behind a rough table. A faint sound of birdsong was audible from a darkened corner of the room.

" So, Mr. Sherlock Holmes," Wilson sneered. " I hear that you have been looking into my affairs, and as you might imagine, since you have the reputation of being an intelligent man, I am somewhat averse to others poking their long noses into the business of my canaries without my permission."

Holmes smiled wanly. " I can quite understand that," he remarked in an easy tone of voice.

" My problem now is how to proceed. Your reputation does not lead me to believe that a financial inducement will cause you to drop your interest in my canaries."

My friend seemed to be seized with a fit of coughing. "You are correct," he spluttered out, in the midst of his paroxysms.

" In that case, I must take measures to ensure that you do not meddle any further in my business, or indeed, the business of anyone else. That goes for your friend here as well," he added, nodding in my direction.

Holmes, who was still coughing, nodded. To my horror, I heard him say, " I quite understand your position, Mr. Wilson. I would probably feel the same way myself were our positions to be reversed. However, may I trouble you for a trifle ? "

" Why not ? "

" My handkerchief is in my pocket. Would you permit me—" here his coughing interrupted his speech for a full thirty seconds. " Would you permit me," he resumed, " to have my hands untied so that I might at least be a little more comfortable as regards my throat ? "

Wilson laughed, not altogether pleasantly. " See to it," he ordered one of his henchmen. " Slowly, and no tricks," he warned Holmes, as my friend rubbed his hands together, and slowly extracted his handkerchief from his pocket. " Excellent."

Holmes raised the handkerchief to his face, and coughed twice. " Thank you," he said, removing the cloth from his face briefly, before replacing it.

The room was suddenly filled with the noise of the police whistle, concealed in the folds of the handkerchief, which Holmes was blowing with all his might. Before Wilson or his bravos could react, the door crashed open, and four police constables entered, truncheons drawn, with Inspector Stanley Hopkins at their head.

The scuffle which ensued was brief, thanks to the element of surprise enjoyed by the guardians of the law, and Wilson and his men were quickly overpowered and handcuffed. Hopkins himself released me from my bonds, and I thanked him sincerely for his efforts.

"Search the place," Holmes instructed the police-agent. "You are likely to find some canaries, and not all of them will have feathers."

That evening, Inspector Stanley Hopkins called at Baker-street, where Holmes greeted him warmly.

"My congratulations, Inspector, on a remarkably fine piece of work."

Hopkins shook his head. "The credit is all yours, Mr. Holmes," he said to my friend. "We needed you to allow us to enter his premises and search the place. We cannot thank you enough. Over twenty of Wilson's 'canaries' are now free to live their own lives, poor things, and I feel that Wilson and his men will not see the outside of prison for many years once they have been sentenced."

I was still in the dark. "It is clear that you baited the trap to catch Wilson with both yourself and me," I said, "and that you knew that all this was going to take place."

"I apologise, Watson," said Holmes. "Though I never feared for our lives, I did expect a certain amount of discomfort in the time that Wilson had us in his power."

"But you knew that he would be there to meet us?"

"Of course. Consider the facts, Watson. Though the house was marked as being to let, our friend Nathaniel Urquhart was unable to find any letting-agent, and I was likewise unsuccessful. The notice was therefore a blind, to persuade the neighbours that the property was unoccupied. As you and I discovered, Watson, this was not the case. The place was used by Wilson's 'canaries' to carry out their trade. Their customers would use the back door. You will note that the front rooms of the house remained unoccupied, and all comings and goings were through the rear of the house."

"But the funerals that we were told took place there?"

" Tush. Pure fiction, as I suspected from the first. Wilson's mother—"

" Whom we now have in custody," Hopkins added, " as an accessary to Wilson's crimes. She acted as caretaker and guardian to the 'canaries'. She has already told us that she was installed in the house some months ago, and told to report the story of funerals to anyone who asked about them."

" It was clear to me that no funerals had taken place from that house," Holmes said. " What undertaker would ever have calmly removed a body from an empty house without asking questions ? And as you yourself wondered, Watson, if Wilson were to dispose of bodies, why would he take the trouble to take them over the river ? Indeed, why would he pay for a funeral ? I therefore started my investigations following our visit to Belvedere Gardens with the conviction that that the woman who had informed us of them had been less than truthful in her account. I therefore made enquiries of all the undertaker's businesses in the area, and, as I had expected, there had been no such funerals."

" And then ? "

" I had little alternative but to consider that the story was a trap designed to ensnare me. The order for a funeral in one year's time presented to Mr. Urquhart would almost certainly bring the mystery to our door sooner or later. We explored the house, and I am sure that the birdseed and possibly the canary feather that attached itself to your coat were left there deliberately to lead us to Wilson. The account of the false funerals would confirm the suspicions in my mind."

" And then Wilson spread the rumour of another such funeral in order to lure you to the spot ? "

" Precisely. I did not, as you saw, go unprepared. Once again, though, I must apologise if the results of my actions caused you any discomfort, or seemed to place you in any danger. I had previously alerted Hopkins, who was waiting with his men in another house, unobserved by you or by Wilson. As soon as we left in the baker's van, he followed at a discreet distance, and stationed himself outside the warehouse to which we were taken, awaiting my signal."

"Remarkable," said I. "You would appear to have anticipated Wilson at every move."

Holmes shrugged. "The credit shall all go to Hopkins here. I was merely the bait, he the hunter who snared the prey."

"Uncommonly good of you to say so, sir," said the police inspector. "We have wanted this villain behind bars for some time now, and I am sincerely grateful to you for your help."

"And I am sure that gratitude is shared by Wilson's ' canaries'," I added. "You have performed a noble service, Holmes."

"However," my friend added, "I trust you will not give this account to your adoring public. The details of the crime are too unsavoury for general consumption."

However, I have secretly recorded the events of this case, which had such a strange beginning, and will place it carefully at the bottom of my dispatch-box to be deposited at some future date with Cox & Co. It may be that in years to come, it will be discovered, and felt to be interesting enough to justify its introduction to a wider audience.

THE ADVENTURE OF THE GROSVENOR-SQUARE FURNITURE VAN

HARING rooms with Sherlock Holmes often involved my being exposed to strange, even bizarre events. Few that I can recall surpassed in this regard the case in which he saved a prominent member of the peerage from exposure to ridicule at the very least, and possibly also a premature end to a promising political career.

I was opening the morning post at breakfast, prior to dividing it according to the rules laid down by Holmes. The first, and largest, pile of letters was one that he called "Fire". These were either begging letters demanding money, or requests to solve problems that he regarded as trivial, such as the tracing of missing dogs or errant husbands. Unless there was something out of the ordinary in these letters, they were consigned, unread by Holmes, to the fire burning in the grate.

The next, which Holmes had named "Enquire", contained details of potential cases requiring further investigation before a decision could be reached as to whether or not to take on a case. This group was significantly smaller than the first.

The next group, dubbed "Hire" by Holmes, were those where he would take the case without any further ado. On most days, no letters met the exacting requirements that would justify their inclusion in this category.

On the day that I am describing, just one fitted the bill to allow it to make its way into the "Hire" group. I placed it beside Holmes's plate, and awaited his arrival wat the breakfast table.

" Halloa ! " he commented, as he remarked the crested envelope. " The Duke of Staffordshire requires my services ? That coat of arms is familiar enough. Or rather," he added as he examined the envelope more closely, " the Duchess, if the handwriting is to be my guide in this matter."

" Indeed so," I confirmed.

I should add here that Holmes, though his clientele ranged from Dukes to dustmen, preferred to deal with the upper classes. Not only were they more remunerative (though he claimed to pursue his profession for its own sake, it must be confessed that he often exacted large fees for his services from the more affluent of his clients), but, he claimed, the solutions to the problems that they posed demanded a higher level of intellectual activity than did those of the lower classes.

He opened the envelope, and extracted the letter. " You have read this, Watson ? " he enquired, having seemingly perused its contents.

" Indeed so."

" And what do you make of it ? "

" If the events she describes are indeed true, then it is clear to me that she is in need of your assistance."

" I would agree. It is not in any way usual for a man such as the Duke to shut himself in his room for hours at a time, without food or drink. Moreover, he is a member of the Cabinet, though I cannot imagine that he will retain that honour for long unless his habits change in the near future. The letter also hints at other matters of a mysterious nature, which piques my curiosity."

" I remember reading in that letter that the Duchess would prefer you to visit her in Grosvenor-square, rather than her visiting us here in Baker-street."

Holmes smiled. " She will meet us here in the first instance, or not at all. I prefer to meet my clients in surroundings which are familiar to me but not to them. Much may be learned in the first instance from a client's adaptation to strange surroundings." He waved a hand to encompass the furnishings of the room, some of which, such as the jack-knife securing unanswered correspondence to the mantelshelf, the Persian slipper which acted as a tobacco-pouch, and the initials of our sovereign tastefully picked out in bullet pocks on the wall, might well be classified as " strange".

He picked up his pen, and wrote on a page of his notebook before ringing for Billy, our page, to whom he gave the paper with instructions that it be given to the house in Grosvenor-square, with instructions that it be given to Her Grace, the Duchess of Staffordshire. Billy, suitably impressed, set off with a smile and a sixpence for his pains.

" What did you write to the Duchess ? " I asked my friend.

" I merely mentioned that I was indisposed, and would welcome a chance to speak to her here."

I laughed. " May I suggest, then, that you dispose of, or at least conceal, some of those foul-smelling chemicals which have been your principal means of recreation for the past few days ? I can scarcely imagine that our visitor will find them as congenial as do you."

" Very well, Watson. You remind me often of one of the principal reasons why I have never contemplated matrimony."

" That being ? "

" In a marriage, it is essential that one maintains at least the semblance of affection – an attitude that it is hard to maintain when one partner continually imposes her or his wishes on the other. Friendship demands no such obligation."

I could not think of a suitable rejoinder, and sat reading the newspaper's agony column out loud to Holmes as he busied himself tidying away the flasks and reagents which had polluted our air for the past few days.

" Heigh-ho," he remarked as I came to the end of my recital. " There seems to be little of interest in London these days. I trust that Her Grace will provide some respite from this *ennui* which engulfs us."

I had been observing the street as I read the newspaper to Holmes, and espied a carriage bearing the same arms as had appeared on the morning's envelope. " She has arrived," I announced.

" Excellent," he said, throwing himself into a chair and instantly assuming an air of languor, which was in complete contrast to his frenetic activity of a minute before. " Remember, Watson, that I am indisposed. A matter of a slight chill, maybe, or a touch of influenza, perhaps ? " he smiled.

" Very well," I said.

In a minute, Mrs. Hudson knocked on our door to announce the arrival of the Duchess, and Holmes waved a negligent hand to indicate that she should be admitted.

I was not acquainted with the appearance of the Duchess of Staffordshire, and I was not expecting the somewhat stout lady of a certain age, though dressed fashionably and well, who made her appearance in our room. She glanced around her, using her lorgnette, and a faint smile came over her face as she remarked the singular features of the furnishings to which I alluded earlier in this narrative.

Her glance fell on Holmes, and her manner changed to one of what appeared to be genuine concern.

" I am sorry to trouble you when you are unwell, Mr. Holmes." she told him. Her voice was marked by a highly pleasing musical tone, which contrasted with her almost coarse appearance.

" It is nothing," my friend informed her, in a weak voice which hardly resembled his usual ringing tones. " Watson here," indicating me, " is not only a good friend, but an excellent physician, and I am confident that with his assistance, this slight indisposition will be gone in a matter of days at the most."

" I am glad to hear it." There was a genuine warmth in her manner.

" Please be seated and tell us what has brought you here," Holmes invited her, and I helped her to the chair in which our visitors took their ease as they unfolded their mysteries to my friend.

" Why, it was you yourself who brought me here," she answered him. " I wished you to visit me at Grosvenor-square, so that you might see for yourself the impossibility of the situation, but your illness prevents this. However, if you will allow to describe the circumstances, I am hoping that you may be able to work your magic at a distance, and solve the riddle."

" There are few things in this world that one might describe as 'impossible'," Holmes replied. " Many may appear so, but on close examination, and the application of reasoning, it is almost always the case that there is a rational explanation."

" Then perhaps, Mr. Holmes, you can examine these facts, and apply your reasoning to them. My husband, the Duke is, as I am sure you are aware, one of the foremost in the land. He holds high office in the present Government, and up to a few weeks ago, he was most conscientious in his duties in that regard." She paused and looked significantly at Holmes and me. " I am telling you all of this in confidence, you understand ? "

" Naturally," Holmes murmured.

" Very well, then. Starting about two months ago, Gerald informed me that he was not going to attend the Cabinet meeting that morning, giving no reason."

" Perhaps it was a subject on which he felt he had nothing to

contribute, or perhaps one to which he had some antipathy?"
I suggested.

"I confess that I take little interest in politics, so I cannot
tell you if that is correct or not. In any event, he went to his
study, and locked himself in for the whole of the day."

"If I might venture a guess at the reason you ascribed to
his reluctance?" Holmes smiled. She nodded her assent. "You
probably considered that he had taken a violent personal dislike to one or more of his Cabinet colleagues, and therefore
wished to avoid meeting them."

"You are correct in your assumption of my reasoning, Mr.
Holmes. However, this did not seem to be the case. Only two
days after the incident I have just described, he proposed
holding a dinner at Grosvenor-square, to which all members
of the Cabinet were to be invited. All accepted the invitation,
and I observed closely for signs of hostility or dislike between
Gerald and the others. I flatter myself that I have some skill in
discernment in these matters, and I can assure you that there
was nothing of the sort. Some of the junior Ministers, indeed,
were obviously a little envious of the success of their elders,
but there was nothing that I could see to indicate anything
other than a body of able men, united in a common cause, and
with a genuine liking and respect for each other. No, that was
not the answer. Since that time, my husband has refused to attend meetings of the Cabinet several times, averaging twice a
week, I would judge."

"Then we should fall back on the idea that he has some antipathy to some of the ideas expressed in the Cabinet at the
meetings he does not attend," Holmes remarked. "In all honesty, Your Grace, I had expected something a little more— interesting, shall we say?"

"I have not yet begun to tell the full story," the Duchess
continued. "Last Tuesday, the Duke disappeared, and then appeared again." There was a smile on her face as she noted the
effect that her words had on Holmes, who instantly drew himself into a posture of alertness, and fixed his eyes on her with
a new intensity.

"Pray continue," he urged her. "Watson, you are taking

notes, I trust ? Your Grace, was this disappearance and reappearance witnessed by yourself ? "

She shook her head. "Allow me to explain. As I mentioned earlier, my husband locked himself in his study when he decided not to attend Cabinet meetings for the first time. This has been his practice on all such occasions since then. However, on the day that I referred to, that is, last Tuesday, the Prime Minister sent a message that the Duke should attend him at Downing-street on a matter of the utmost urgency. I therefore determined to inform him of this myself, rather than letting a servant be the bearer of the message. I knocked on the door of the study, and requested him to open it. There was no response, and I repeated my request, this time informing him that this was all at the request of the Prime Minister. There was still no response. It is the custom at Grosvenor-square for a spare key to every room to be kept in the servants' hall, where it may be used in cases of emergencies, such as a fire in the building or the like.

" I judged that this was such an emergency, and availed myself of the key to the study. I knocked once more, and receiving no answer, unlocked the door, assuming that maybe Gerald had fallen asleep. You may judge my astonishment when I discovered no trace of my husband within the room. Not only had he vanished, but his clothes – that is to say, his jacket, trousers, waistcoat, and shirt – were folded neatly on a chair next to the desk. I hardly knew what to believe." She stopped as if to catch her breath. " I called Jeavons, the butler, swearing him to silence on the matter, and together we searched every possible place in the room where he might have been hiding, for whatever reason. There was nothing."

"And there is no other door leading from the room, of course ? "

" None."

" You did not call the police ? "

"Jeavons was all for following that course of action, but the resulting publicity would have been distasteful, and I forbade him to do so. We must have searched for at least thirty minutes, at the end of which time we left the room, and I relocked the door behind us. I retired to my room for about an hour, when I heard my husband's voice downstairs. I fairly ran down those stairs, Mr. Holmes, to behold Gerald, dressed in the clothes in which I had seen him dressed earlier that morning. On my enquiring of Jeavons where he had appeared, I was informed that he had come out of his study, having used his key to unlock the door."

" Curious indeed," remarked Holmes. " Has there been a recurrence of this ? "

" There has been no such urgent summons that necessitated his presence, but on one occasion when the Duke had locked himself in his study, on Friday last, I took it upon myself to knock on the door on some pretext – something which I had never done before. There was no answer, but I did not enter. To tell you the truth, Mr. Holmes, I was afraid."

" Understandably so," I said to her. " There is something almost of the supernatural about this, would you not agree, Holmes ? " I added this last in an attempt for him to persuade the Duchess, using all the force of his reason and logic, that such an explanation was not to be considered. I was not disappointed, and the Duchess expressed her relief that the supernatural was not to be reckoned with in this case.

" There is one further development, which sounds so trivial that it hardly merits a mention," she added. " Yesterday was Collins, my maid's, day off, who returned to the house yesterday evening in a state of some excitement. She swore that she had seen the Duke coming out of a house in Holland Park at two o'clock precisely. She was sure of the time, as the clock of St. Barnabas struck the hour. At that time, I had every reason to believe that my husband was locked in his study, having retired there following luncheon."

" She was possibly mistaken in the identity of the man whom she saw ? "

" I fear not. Collins is an exceptionally intelligent and observant woman, and it is unlikely that she would make such an error, especially in the case of a man whom she sees every day. In any event, though it is not generally known, the Duke suffers from a slight limp in the left leg, as the result of a bout of infantile paralysis. The man whom Collins saw had just such a limp, though he was dressed in what she describes as rough tradesman's clothes. I am satisfied that she saw my husband, but at the same time, I firmly believe that he was in a locked room in our house, from which there is no exit, and I am at a loss as to why she describes him being dressed in that way."

Holmes rubbed his hands together. "This is a most singular turn of events," he said. "When may I come to visit the scene of the disappearance? Obviously such a visit must be made in the Duke's absence."

"But you must not consider that, Mr. Holmes. You are ill, are you not?" She spoke with what seemed like genuine concern in her voice.

"I find the stimulation of such a problem to have a remarkably curative effect," he smiled.

"In that case, Gerald mentioned to me that he intended to attend a Cabinet meeting this afternoon from two o'clock. You may call at any time from then for the next two or three hours."

"Excellent. One more small matter. Did your observant Collins happen to remark the address of the building from which she claims to have seen your husband emerging?"

"She did indeed, and I have it written here." She pulled out a small slip of paper, and passed it to Holmes.

"Number 1 Holland Park-road," Holmes read out. "Thank you."

"I may expect you this afternoon, then?"

"Without a doubt," Holmes assured her, and on that note she took her leave of us.

"Well, Watson, what do you make of this?"

"If it were not for the disappearance from the room, I would suspect a vulgar intrigue being carried on at the Holland Park address. Her Grace is certainly not the most alluring example of female beauty."

"Nor was she ever," remarked Holmes. "However, as Viola Simmons, she possessed one of the most beautiful mezzo-soprano voices ever to go on the stage at Covent Garden, before the Duke married her. Her reputation was one of complete honesty and probity, unlike that of many others of that profession, and I believe the Duke was not the only contender for her hand. I believe that everything she has told us today is the truth – at least, as she sees it."

" I am puzzled about the disappearance of the Duke from a locked room, and his reappearance in another part of London."

Holmes smiled. " I am sure there will be a perfectly rational explanation for this. Your suggestion of an intrigue may well be the correct explanation of the Duke's appearance in another part of London. It may well be that his change of attire is the result of his wishing to pass unremarked, which would also bolster the idea of an intrigue."

" But how," I asked, " could he leave a room, the only exit from which was locked ? "

" The answer is, of course, that he did not."

" Then I am puzzled. The Duchess told us, did she not, that she had examined the room carefully, and found no other means of exit other than that locked door ? "

" If you care to cast your mind back, she did not tell us that."

I racked my brains, and consulted the notes that I had made. " I still fail to follow your reasoning, Holmes."

" Be that as it may, let us take a trip to Holland Park before we present ourselves at Grosvenor-square."

I assented. It was a fine spring morning. The night's rain had washed away much of the grime and soot, and London presented a sparkling face to the world. On our arrival at the house at which the Duke had been identified, we observed a furniture van outside the house. " Are the inhabitants moving house ? " I wondered aloud.

" It is easy enough to discover," Holmes answered, striding forward to engage one of the workmen in conversation.

" Is that Miss Katherine Thornton's furniture that you are loading ? " he asked. " I'd heard that she was leaving Town." I saw the glint of gold as a coin changed hands.

" No, sir. This is the gentleman who has the flat on the first floor. A Mr. Armitage, and he's not moving. These are just a few pieces which he's sold to the Dook of somewhere."

" The Duke of Staffordshire ? " suggested Holmes.

" That's the one, sir. Now, if you'll excuse me, we've got to get these to him before this evening. It's a pleasure talking with you, sir," he said, displaying the half-sovereign that Holmes had slipped into his hand, " but work's work."

" Indeed it is," replied my friend, returning to join me.

"Who is Katherine Thornton ? " I could not help asking.

"A dainty creature. Sadly, she is merely the product of my fancy," he asked. "It is always easier to find a man ready to contradict you than to supply you with a straight answer to an open question."

"So you have discovered that Mr. Armitage who lives here is selling furniture to the Duke ? "

"That is certainly what our friend there believes."

"And you do not ? "

"I will reserve judgement until more facts are forthcoming. In the meantime, let us make our way to Grosvenor-square."

We were admitted by a footman, who took our names and disappeared with our cards. In a minute, a man entered the hall, who from his dignified bearing could only be Jeavons, the butler.

"Mr. Holmes. Dr. Watson. This way, if you would, gentlemen," he greeted us with a slight bow. We followed him to a drawing-room where the Duchess was reclining on a couch.

"No, pray do not disturb yourself," Holmes said to her, as she prepared to rise. "I am sure that Jeavons can conduct us to the room in question, and when I have examined that, I would like a word with Collins, if I may."

"Certainly. Jeavons, be good enough to take these men to His Grace's study. I hope that they will be able to solve the mystery that has puzzled us."

"Very good, Your Grace," he answered. He led us through the hallway to a large room at the front of the house, before making as if to leave us.

"No, stay," Holmes ordered him. "Tell me, what were your feelings when the door was opened and the Duke was nowhere to be seen ? "

"Well, sir, I have to say that I was shocked. And then when we found his clothes, I was struck all of a heap, as they say. You'll laugh when I tell you this, but I thought he might have been taken up to Heaven by an angel or something like that. They don't need clothes up there, do they ? "

Holmes laughed. "Such theological niceties are beyond me," he said. "But in any case, he came back, did he not ? "

"He did, sir, and in its way that was just as shocking as him disappearing."

"I can well imagine that to be the case. It was you who searched the room with Her Grace, was it not?"

"Yes, sir, and we found nothing."

"Did you search the room together?"

"No, sir. She searched that half of the room," indicating the side with the windows facing the street, "and I searched the other part."

"And it was you who discovered the clothes?"

"It was, sir. On that chair there. Now if you will excuse me, I hear the furniture van outside. His Grace has ordered some furniture, and I must supervise its delivery and unpacking. Please ring for me when you are finished here, sir, and I will arrange for Collins to be sent to you as you requested."

"A very helpful servant," I observed as Jeavons left us in the study.

"Indeed. He told us a lot."

I was surprised at Holmes's words, since I considered we had learned very little from the butler.

"We have little enough time," Holmes told me, "so let us begin our search."

"What do you expect to find?"

"Anything that is out of the ordinary. Anything that you feel is surprising in a room such as this."

Puzzled, I moved to the window, and commenced an examination of the floor, walls, and window, together with the furnishings."

"No, not there," Holmes said. "Her Grace has already examined that side."

"But Jeavons has examined the other," I objected.

"So he tells us," Holmes said. "Come, join me."

After a few minutes' searching, Holmes let out a sharp exclamation. "Watson! Here, look!" He had rolled back the Persian rug that covered the floor behind the desk, to reveal what appeared to be a trapdoor. "Here is the solution to the mystery of the vanishing Duke!" He pulled at the ring let into the floor, to reveal a flight of wooden steps leading down to what must be the cellars of the house. "And look!" He pointed to a suit of clothes hanging on a hook let into the wall of the staircase. "Let us examine them."

The garments turned out to be a brown tweed suit of the sort worn by a tradesman who has fallen on somewhat hard times, together with a shirt and tie to match, and a brown bowler hat, to which Holmes applied his lens. Beside them was a shelf with a candlestick holding a half-burned candle. Holmes also examined this last closely, and pronounced that from the absence of dust, it had been used in the recent past.

"Where do these steps eventually lead ? " I asked.

"Time enough for that later," Holmes answered. "Come, let us restore order, and talk to the maid Collins."

We replaced the candle and the clothes, and closed the trap-door, replacing the rug over it before ringing for Jeavons, who appeared.

"The furniture has arrived safely ? " Holmes asked him by way of making conversation.

"Indeed, sir. It is now in the hall awaiting His Grace's orders as to its disposition."

"New furniture ? "

There was what sounded like an audible sniff. "No, sir. Old chairs and chests and the like. Maybe hundreds of years old. If you want my personal views, sir..."

"Yes ? "

"I wouldn't give such things house room. Very dark and gloomy to my way of thinking. I hope you won't tell Their Graces what I have just said," he added hurriedly.

"Of course not," Holmes assured him.

"Thank you, sir. In that case, I'll just go and fetch Collins. You will talk to her in here ? "

"If I may."

"Very good, sir."

In the few minutes while we awaited the arrival of the maid, Holmes amused himself by examining the spines of some of the books on the shelves.

"This is Collins, sir," announced Jeavons, ushering in a pleasant-faced middle-aged woman.

"Ah, Collins," Holmes greeted her. "I won't keep you from your duties for long. Thank you, Jeavons," he added, dismissing the butler. " Now, Collins, I just want to ask you about the man you saw the other day in Holland Park."

" It was His Grace, sir. I'd know his walk anywhere."

" You see, Watson ? " Holmes turned to me almost triumphantly. " I have maintained for a long time that a man's gait is as distinctive as his face, and may be used to identify criminals, but those blockheads in Scotland Yard..." He broke off. " I am sorry to interrupt."

" That's all right, sir," she smiled.

" What was he wearing ? "

" A shabby brown suit. Not the sort of thing one of his position should be wearing in Town, if you ask me. More like a pawnbroker or something like that. And he had this brown billycock on his head which meant I couldn't see his face that clear, but I know it was him, sir. I know his boots, seeing them being cleaned often enough, and it was those boots that this man was wearing."

" Would you happen to know what size of hat His Grace wears ? "

She seemed surprised at the question, but answered, " I couldn't tell you offhand, sir, but I could find out for you quickly enough."

" Please do so." She left the room on her errand.

" It seems clear to me," I said, " that this mysterious figure in Holland Park is the Duke, wearing the garments that we have just discovered."

" I agree. The hat will be the conclusive proof."

" Then you will tell the Duchess of her husband's infidelity ? "

" I do not believe that to be the case here."

Before I could reply, Collins returned, bearing a silk hat. " I must give it back soon, sir. Please do whatever it is you have to do quickly."

With a word of thanks, Holmes took the hat and examined the interior minutely before handing it back.

" Thank you. That has been most helpful. You have been in this household for long ? "

" I was with Her Grace before her marriage. I worked as her dress– her maid, sir. And now I must go and return the hat, if you will excuse me, sir." She bobbed a curtsey and left us.

" So she was Viola Simmons' dresser," mused Holmes. " Well, well. I believe we have discovered all we need in this place. Let us go."

We left the room, and entered the hallway, which indeed was occupied by a number of pieces of carved dark oak furniture which appeared to date from the beginning of the last century. As Jeavons had said to us, the overall impression was one of gloom. Holmes bent to examine one or two of the chairs and chests, and stood up with a look of satisfaction on his face.

Jeavons joined us. " Will you be leaving now, sir, or will you wish to see Her Grace before you go ? "

" We will leave," Holmes told him. " Please thank Her Grace from me, and please inform His Grace on his return that I would very much appreciate it if he were to call on me tomorrow. He may find me at this address." He took one of his cards, and wrote a few words on it before handing it to the butler. " If he can let me know at what hour he intends to visit, I shall be much obliged."

We took our hats and sticks, and walked into the street. Rather than taking the turning for Baker-street, Holmes led the way to the mews at the back of the house. " There," he exclaimed, pointing with his stick to a dusty door which appeared to lead to the house's cellar, reached by a set of steps. " That will be the door by which the Duke emerges in his disguise, unseen by anyone at the front of the house."

As we walked back to our rooms, Holmes was humming a tune to himself, which I recognised as " *Si vuol ballare*" from Mozart's *Figaro*. It seemed to have a certain appropriateness under the circumstances.

That evening brought a message from the Duke, informing us that he would call the next morning at nine.

At the appointed hour, the Duke made his entrance to our rooms. Although I was familiar with his features, which had been reproduced often enough in the illustrated press, I had not seen him in the flesh prior to this meeting, and was struck by his bearing, which seemed to be that more of a common man than of one of the foremost peers of the realm. Following our introductions, Holmes waved him to the chair which had been occupied by his wife the previous day and offered him a cigar, which the peer accepted.

" I have heard of you, Mr. Holmes," he said, opening the conversation. " I have heard that you are a man of discretion."

" Thank you," my friend replied. " It is one of the more flattering descriptions that has been applied to me."

" I believe you know something of Mr. Armitage of Holland Park ? " was our visitor's next question.

" That is correct," answered Holmes.

" How much do you know ? "

" Other that he wears a brown tweed suit with a matching bowler hat, rents a first floor flat in Holland Park, and displays a keen interest in purchasing furniture of the early eighteenth century which bears particular symbols, very little, I confess."

Our visitor's face was a picture of astonishment which appeared to be mixed with fear as Holmes recited these details. " Upon my word, I had no idea that the man was so well-known outside certain circles."

" I may also add," said Holmes, " that he is married, seemingly very happily, to a charming lady, and spends his nights and much of his days at their house in Grosvenor-square. Some of his days are spent in Westminster, or in Downing-street."

At these words, the Duke's face turned pale, and I had a momentary fear that he was about to faint. Seemingly with a great effort, he spoke in a faint voice. " You say you are a man of discretion. How much must I pay you to assure myself of that silence ? ? "

Two spots of colour stood out on Holmes's pale cheeks. " Upon my word, sir, I fear that you are utterly mistaken if you believe that my silence is to be purchased in the marketplace like some– some article of furniture. I have seldom been so insulted in the whole of my professional career. With all due respect, sir, I must ask you to leave immediately. My regards to your charming wife. Good day to you, sir." It was clear to me that Sherlock Holmes was as angry as I have ever seen him.

The Cabinet minister rose to his feet. " I apologise wholeheartedly," he said in contrite tones. " I will no longer inconvenience you. Good day to you both."

I could see that Holmes's mood was not one in which he was

willing to answer questions, and I refrained from making further enquiries about it until some time later, at which time he was involved with the affairs of Lord St. Simon, an account of which I have given previously in a piece entitled 'The Noble Bachelor'. He mentioned in passing that there was no mystery in the case, and that that the whole business had been obvious from the beginning. Indeed, he added, that there had been so little work for him to perform that he had not charged the Duchess for his services. Instead, he had sent her a note, reassuring her that the mysterious absences of her husband were by no means due to the agency of some supernatural force, and had nothing of the sinister or criminal about them, but for reasons of professional etiquette, he found himself unable to provide her with the precise cause, and recommending her to seek the details from her husband.

However, I was still in the dark regarding the solution. Accordingly, when we found ourselves in a train to Dorking to investigate a case of suspected forgery of a will, I took the opportunity to ask Holmes of his conclusions regarding the case.

He drew thoughtfully on his pipe. " Quite frankly, Watson, I am surprised that you have not worked out the details yourself."

"You made it clear that the Duke of Staffordshire and this mysterious Mr. Armitage were one and the same person. We could deduce that from the description given by the made, and the clothing we discovered in the passage under the trapdoor in the study."

" Correct. Proceed."

" But what I do not understand is why the Duke as Armitage was selling this old furniture to himself."

" He was not," Holmes answered shortly. " I have no reason to believe that money changed hands between 'Armitage' and the Duke."

" But why the deception ? "

Holmes sighed. "A strange mixture of vanity and reticence. The values of the Duke have always been somewhat at variance with those of his class – witness his marriage to a woman who was neither a beauty in the conventional sense, nor the possessor of great wealth. He is, however, proud of his descent from those noblemen who supported the Old Pretender in the Jacobite Rebellion of 1715. In his study in Grosvenor-square, I noted several shelves of books devoted to that particular episode in history.

" At that time, several of the great families of England, particularly in the Midlands and in the North, who resented the imposition, as they saw it, of the Hanoverians on the country. Much of this resentment was also in connection with religion – the Stuarts, as you know, being inclined towards Catholicism, and the Hanoverians being staunchly Protestant. The Duke's family have been Catholics since time immemorial. It was common for such families to display their allegiances, both religious and political, in physical form, albeit discreetly."

" Such as carvings and decorations on furniture ? " I hazarded.

" Precisely so. When I examined the chairs and chests in the hallway at Grosvenor-square, I discovered several crowned thistles – one of the Stuarts' badges, along with symbols associated with the Church of Rome. It is not without the bounds of possibility that many of these pieces originally belonged to the Duke's family, prior to its near-bankruptcy at the hands of a later ancestor's profligacy towards the end of last century."

" So far, I follow you," I said. " But what of the assumption of the person of Armitage ? "

" Ah, there I wander a little into the realm of supposition, though I have little doubt that my theories match the facts. Firstly, the Duke would not want to draw attention to his purchases. A Minister of the Crown showing what might be regarded as excessive interest in an armed revolt against the government would hardly advance his political career. And there is another, somewhat farcical, possibility that strikes me. Most of these items that he acquired would be purchased through professional dealers, rather than through private dealings. I am sure that such merchants would double the price on their items should they suspect that their future owner was a duke. As Mr. Armitage, however, His Grace doubtless derived a great deal of amusement from dealing with these people on their own terms. The flat that he rented in Holland Park was, of course, the address to which the items were to be delivered."

" One thing still puzzles me, however," I said. " Why did you insist on searching that half of the study which had not been searched by the Duchess ? "

" Oh, it was clear that Jeavons was fully cognisant of the whole business. He had been in service with the Duke from an early age, and no doubt his master's sympathies had transferred themselves to him. It would be he, after all, who acquired the garments for the disguise, and who maintained them, and provided the candles and so on to allow the Duke to present himself secretly to the world as Armitage."

" It all seems so simple now that you have explained it," I commented.

" It was childishly simple," he replied. " I am sorry that the Duke misjudged my motives in the way that he did. I find myself admiring his sense of humour and his ingenuity."

" Maybe an opportunity will present itself to set matters straight," I told him.

As it turned out, it was a matter of a little over a year when such an event occurred, and the Duke, clearly willing to let bygones be bygones, called on us with a problem in his Ministry to which he required Holmes to provide a solution. Though I am not as yet at liberty to provide full details of this case, let it be known that on this occasion His Grace and Holmes worked together in harmony to solve the problem, and at the conclusion of it each regarded the other with trust, and even affection.

The Adventure of the Silver Skull

HAD spent a holiday of a few days in France, and had consequently not seen my friend Sherlock Holmes in that time. However, as I sat down to breakfast on the day before I was due to return to England, the manager of the Biarritz hotel at which I was staying handed me a telegram.

"THANK GOODNESS I HAVE FOUND YOU AT LAST STOP RETURN TO ENGLAND AND PROCEED DIRECTLY TO BAKER-STREET, WHERE I AWAIT YOU STOP HOLMES STOP".

"Will there be a reply, *monsieur* ?" the manager asked me solicitously. "It is pre-paid."

I scribbled the words, "Coming at once," on a leaf torn from my memorandum book, and handed it to the manager, together with the few francs which he and the rest of the hotel staff seemed to expect for every service. "I will be leaving this morning," I told him and ordered a cab to the station.

After enduring a seemingly interminable journey on the French railways and a squall which disrupted the Channel crossing, it was a positive relief to set foot on English soil once more.

On my arrival at Baker-street, I was not a little discommoded when Mrs. Hudson, answering the door, informed me that Sherlock Holmes was not in the house.

"He went out this morning," she told me, "and said he'd be back for dinner. I'll just let you into the rooms, sir, where there's a nice warm fire, and you can wait for him to return."

I passed the time waiting for Holmes attempting to deduce for myself what sort of case had prompted this imperious demand for my return, and at the same time had called Holmes away. A pile of newspaper clippings stood on a small table beside the chair where Holmes typically sat. I was surprised by their source, which was evidently the popular press, and their subject, which was the circumstances surrounding the scandal involving the card-room at the Tankerville Club, rumours of which had reached me even in France.

As I had heard the story already whispered in the smoking-room of the Hôtel de la Plage, the Earl of Hereford, Lord Gravesby, had won heavily at cards a few evenings previously. His opponent at that time was one of the Royal Dukes, Prince

____, and in the usual way of things, this would not have been of any great import.

However, the rumour was that His Royal Highness had, not to put too fine a point on the matter, accused Gravesby of having been less than honest in his play, and that he had been backed up in this accusation by his equerry, a certain Major Lionel Prendergast. Lord Gravesby, faced with this accusation, had hotly denied any such wrongdoing, and had consequently challenged Prendergast to a duel, etiquette prohibiting the participation in an *affaire d'honneur* by a member of the Royal family. Prendergast had declined to fight, instead demanding that the matter be brought before the Membership Committee of the Tankerville Club.

Opinion within the Club, it appeared from my perusal of the newspaper clippings lying beside Holmes's chair, was divided on the matter. On the one hand, there was talk that Gravesby had won more at cards than might be reasonably be expected from a player of his ability, and that the act of challenging the man who had made the accusation, regardless of any Royal privileges, was unworthy of a true gentleman. On the other hand, there were those who believed that Lord Gravesby had done no wrong, that His Royal Highness was stepping outside the bounds of decency by making his accusations, and that Prendergast was a coward and a poltroon for refusing the challenge.

My reading was interrupted by the arrival of Sherlock Holmes, who glanced at the clippings that I had been perusing.

" Well, Watson, what do you make of it all ? " he remarked, in a conversational tone.

" I knew Prendergast well in my time with the Army," I replied. " I cannot believe some of the things that are written about him here."

" I am well aware of your acquaintance with him," replied Holmes. " That, after all, is the reason for my summoning you from your sojourn in foreign climes. I take it Biarritz was not too much to your liking, by the way. I would feel a little guilty should it become apparent that I had dragged you away from some budding romance or a similar situation."

I felt myself blushing. " Nothing of that sort, I assure you,"

I told him. "But I fail to see how my acquaintance with Prendergast may be of use to you."

"Major Prendergast has retained my services to determine the truth of the matter and to make it public. He will be visiting me here in a few hours. In the meantime, I would value your comments as to his character."

"I knew him to be a solid character and a good soldier, albeit at times what one might term a rough diamond," I told Holmes. "I firmly believe that, if he gives you his word, it is to be trusted. When may we expect his visit ?"

"In approximately half an hour," Holmes told me. "While we are waiting, perhaps you might care to tell me of whatever you know of Baron Maupertuis, who was staying in Biarritz while you were there."

"I hardly know the man," I protested. "I was introduced to him by a mutual acquaintance., and I fear that my impressions of him were hardly favourable. To be frank, he struck me as a common swindler."

Holmes chuckled. "As always, my dear Watson, your instincts, at least as regards personalities, are infallible. The Baron is indeed a swindler, though hardly a common one. He is, in my estimation, and that of half the police forces of Europe, one the of most accomplished members of his accursed breed. It would provide me with great satisfaction were I to be the one responsible for bringing him before a court of justice. His schemes are on a large – one might even say colossal – scale, and have been the ruin of many men and women whom I would otherwise have regarded as being intelligent."

"He has not been arrested, then ?"

Holmes shook his head. "Sadly, no. He is a sly one, and usually works his nefarious deeds through confederates or cat's paws. Nothing can be traced to him – nothing, that is, that would serve as evidence in a court of law. In addition, he always contrives to be resident in a country other than the one in which his current scheme is operating. This presents several interesting conundrums from the legal standpoint." He broke off. "From the sounds downstairs, I believe our visitor is arriving a little early."

Mrs. Hudson knocked on the door, announcing that Holmes had a visitor.

"Show him in, Mrs. Hudson," Holmes replied, throwing himself into his armchair.

The man who was admitted to the room bore little resemblance to the strapping young officer I had known in India. While, as I had explained to Holmes, Prendergast had something of the bluff soldier about him, our visitor was epicene, almost effeminate in the delicacy of his features and the exquisite nature of his dress. A frogged frock-coat and a somewhat gaudy waistcoat and neckcloth formed the foundation of his appearance, which was completed by a top hat with an exaggerated curl to the brim, and a lacquered walking stick with a curiously worked silver handle in the shape of a human skull.

"Major Prendergast, I presume?" Holmes greeted him.

"Indeed not," was the reply, uttered in a fluting tone of voice. "I take it you are expecting him to pay you a visit?"

Holmes inclined his head by way of answer.

"I must request you not to entertain any belief in anything he may say to you."

"Indeed? And may I ask your interest in making this request?"

"I make this request as the result of the earnest wish – one might even term it a command – of the gentleman whom I have the honour of serving."

"This gentleman would be one who has an interest in this case, I take it?"

"Indeed so. You would be wise to take due heed of his wishes in this matter, given the rank that he holds and the influence that he exerts."

"I will treat your words and the wishes of your master with the consideration they deserve," Holmes told him. "May I have the pleasure of knowing with whom I am speaking, by the way?"

"I am merely a messenger. My name is of no relevance here. I bid you good day, sir." He sketched a faint half-bow as he left the room.

"Well, Watson," said Holmes, after he had watched our

visitor's carriage pull away from outside our house. "What do you make of that?"

"It would seem that Prendergast knows something to the discredit of the Prince, does it not? But what will you do?"

"It is evident that our recent visitor and his master, whom we may well assume to be His Royal Highness, are unaware of the influence wielded by certain persons known to me within the government. Their power, though wielded discreetly, is nonetheless of sufficient potency to put a mere prince of the blood in his place. It will be interesting, at all events, to discover what Prendergast has to say for himself when he arrives here."

In the event, we had not long to wait. Prendergast entered the room, little changed from the time when I first knew him, save for a touch of grey about the temples, but appearing flushed and in a state of high excitement.

"My dear Watson," he exclaimed. "This is indeed a pleasant surprise. I am more than happy to see you again after all these years. And Mr. Holmes, sir. Delighted to make your acquaintance. I look to you as my saviour."

"I hope that I may be of assistance to you in your troubles," Holmes said to him. "The problem would seem to be a relatively simple one."

"Alas, I fear that the issue has compounded itself since I first requested your help." Holmes did not reply, but raised his eyebrows in response. "I assume," Prendergast went on, indicating the newspaper from which I had been reading prior to the arrival of our previous visitor, "that you are acquainted with the facts of the case, as far as they have been made public." Holmes inclined his head. "There has been a shocking development. Lord Gravesby was found dead at the Tankerville Club yesterday. The newspapers have yet to be informed of this development."

"Dear me," Holmes tutted. "And the cause of death?"

"I can only repeat what I have overheard, which may or may not be accurate. I heard that he was found with a pistol ball through his brain – a pistol of an antique type, used for duelling, that is – with the weapon lying nearby."

"An antique pistol?"

" Indeed so. One of a pair owned by His Royal Highness."

" The case certainly would appear to have its points of interest," Holmes remarked. " May I enquire what part you play in all of this ? "

" The other pistol of the pair, as the police will shortly discover, if they have not done so already, is to be found in my room at the Tankerville, together with powder and ball."

" How did it come to be there ? "

" Following the accusations of cheating at cards made to his late Lordship, you will be aware that a challenge was issued. His Royal Highness, had he accepted this challenge in person, rather than by proxy as he did, would have had the choice of weapons, and he felt that this privilege would be extended to me. He therefore made me the loan of these duelling pistols, which apparently are a family heirloom. Both pistols were in my room when I left it this morning."

" And now ? "

" As soon as I heard the shocking news of his Lordship's death, I hastened back to my room at the Club where I am staying while I am in Town. I had been performing an errand of a somewhat confidential nature for his Royal Highness and was only informed of Gravesby's decease on my return. There I discovered the pistols' case opened, and one pistol missing, along with the powder-horn. There also appeared to be fewer balls than I remembered. My first instinct was to take the remaining pistol and its accoutrements and fling it into the Thames, but I considered that the Club servants might have remembered seeing it, and its disappearance would raise more questions than it would solve problems."

" Very well considered," remarked Holmes. " To my mind, you have done the right thing if, as I conjecture, you wish me to clear your name. Tell me, do you know if the police are on your trail ? "

" I do not know, but I strongly suspect that they are," replied my unhappy friend. " How can they not be ? "

" Before I proceed further in this matter," Holmes told him, " I would like to inform you of a singular event that occurred shortly before your arrival here." He proceeded to inform Prendergast of our visitor, and the warning that we had received. Prendergast heard Holmes with the greatest attention and sighed heavily at the end of the recital.

"Your visitor, I may inform you," he told us, "rejoices in the name of Sir Quentin Austin. He is a long-time intimate of His Royal Highness, and enjoys his full confidence."

"As do you?" Holmes suggested.

Prendergast shook his head. "You do me too much credit, sir. I was not brought up alongside the Prince, as was Sir Quentin, nor do I share some of their mutual tastes. No," he held up a warning hand. "I am not about to inform you of the nature of these tastes. Though they may appear shameful to some, they are within the letter of the law – in the majority of cases, at any event. In any event, loyalty to my Sovereign and her family, if not to my employer, would prevent me from providing you with further details."

I was intrigued, as I believe was Holmes, but we both refrained from making any further comment. At that moment, Mrs. Hudson entered, and announced that Inspector Lestrade was downstairs and wished to visit.

"By all means show him up, Mrs. Hudson," Holmes said affably. "I fancy we can guess the errand that has brought him here."

Lestrade gave a visible start when he entered and beheld Prendergast. "I was not expecting to find you here, sir," he exclaimed. "Though on second thoughts, perhaps it is a natural progression of events. I am sorry to have to do this, Mr. Holmes, to one of your guests, but—"

"Stop!" Holmes commanded him. "There is no urgency about this, I am sure, and I will stand surety that Major Prendergast here will be available if you need him in the future to assist you with your enquiries."

"As will I," I told Lestrade. "Major Prendergast is an old comrade-in-arms. Our friendship goes back many years, and I can assure you that he is a man of his word."

"Very well," said Lestrade. "I will refrain for now from making the arrest. But you are incorrect on one point, Mr. Holmes."

"Oh, and what may that be?"

"There is a great deal of urgency attached to this. Orders

have come to us from the very highest levels that this case be solved and dealt with at the earliest possible opportunity."

"Then it is lucky that you have me on your side, is it not, Lestrade ? " said Holmes, smiling. " I believe that between the two of us, we will be able to satisfy the demands of the Palace in very short order, do you not agree ? Pray take a seat and join our conversation. Watson, refreshment for our guests ? "

I busied myself with the decanter and soda-syphon, and the conversation resumed.

" I must warn you, Major Prendergast," Lestrade began, " that anything you say now in this room may be used as evidence in court, in proceedings against you or others."

" I understand that."

A silence ensued, broken by Holmes enquiring of Lestrade, " You have discovered both pistols, of course ? "

" Naturally. This, after all, is the reason for our suspecting Major Prendergast here."

" And there is no doubt in your mind that Lord Gravesby was killed by the pistol found nearby of which Major Prendergast has informed us ? "

" None whatsoever in my mind."

" And that it is not a case of suicide, rather than murder ? "

" With a bullet through the brain and the pistol on the other side of the room, some feet away, suicide would seem to be an unlikely possibility, Mr. Holmes," Lestrade smiled thinly.

" I see. And the place where he was found ? "

" It is the Club room where he had been playing cards with His Royal Highness and Major Prendergast here on a previous evening."

" The game ? " Holmes asked Lestrade.

" I beg your pardon."

" What game was being played ? "

" I never thought to ascertain that," Lestrade confessed. " Is it of any relevance ? "

" It was bridge whist," Prendergast informed us.

" Then it is indeed of relevance," said Holmes. " There are four players required for the game, one of whom at any one given time will be dummy. Since the dummy was obviously not Lord Gravesby who was being accused of foul play, rightly or wrongly I cannot say at this juncture, the accusation was made by His Royal Highness, who felt compelled to drag Major Prendergast, who presumably held a hand on this deal, into all this, there is a fourth person involved, who was presumably acting as dummy on this hand, and may well have been the one who first raised the alarm. Furthermore, I would assume that this person had the interests of His Royal Highness rather than Lord Gravesby, at heart."

Major Prendergast started. "You are absolutely correct, Mr. Holmes. The fourth was Sir Quentin Austin." His voice appeared to me to quaver a little as he informed us of this.

" Indeed ? " Lestrade asked in apparent surprise. " He was the source of the information about the pistol in your room, Major Prendergast. He was in the Club when I called to investigate , and he provided me with the information voluntarily."

" The snake ! " exclaimed Prendergast in a voice of fury. " It was he who brought the pistols from His Royal Highness to my room at the Club. Naturally he would know where they were. But for him to inform the police of this – why, it is hardly the act of a gentleman. And together with his visit here earlier today—"

"What is this ? " Lestrade enquired. Holmes informed him of the events prior to Prendergast's arrival.

" Before today, what was your relationship with this man ? " Holmes asked my friend. "You have told us a little of his relationship with His Royal Highness. Can you tell us a little of his character ? "

"I frankly confess that I have never liked the man," Prendergast told us. " He would not have lasted long in the Mess, Watson, I can tell you that. There has always been something about him that gave me the cold creeps. Nothing, I hasten to add, that can be precisely defined in public, but there is that in his nature which I find to be repellent. And indeed it was he who called attention to the alleged irregularities in play. You are perfectly right in your recital of the facts, Mr. Holmes."

" And you are unable to tell us whether those allegations made by His Royal Highness have any basis in fact ? " Holmes enquired.

Prendergast moved uncomfortably in his chair. "I would prefer not to answer that question," he answered at length.

I noticed Holmes and Lestrade exchange glances. "You may be compelled to do so under oath when this case comes to court – either as the defendant in a criminal trial, or as a witness," Lestrade told Prendergast.

"Nonetheless I would prefer not to answer the question at this time."

"Very well, then. I think we may be able to infer something from Major Prendergast's answer, eh, Mr. Holmes?"

Holmes said nothing, but merely nodded his head.

"I fear I have said too much," Prendergast complained. "I pray you both that any conclusions you may have chosen to draw will go no further."

"I fear we are moving in deep waters, do you not agree, Mr. Holmes?" the police agent said with a touch of anxiety evident in his voice.

'Deep waters indeed. Perhaps we may view the scene together, Lestrade? Has the body been moved from there?"

"It was moved by the Club servants before we were called in," Lestrade told him ruefully. "If I have learned one thing only from you, Mr. Holmes, it is that evidence should be left undisturbed as far as possible until the investigation is complete. Other than the body, we have left the room as we first entered it, and gave strict instructions to the Club that no one was to enter, let alone move any object inside it."

"I am pleased to see that some of my seeds have fallen on good soil," Holmes smiled. "However, even without the body, it is possible that some useful data may be obtained. Major Prendergast, I do not think that your presence will be required at this stage, but undoubtedly I may wish to ask you further questions, without Inspector Lestrade here being present, as has been my practice in several past cases."

"I cannot say that I am happy with this arrangement, Mr. Holmes, but I am content to let you do so. You have always played fair with us at the Yard, and I do not believe this will prove to be an exception," Lestrade answered.

"Thank you. Watson, Lestrade, your hats and sticks, and then we shall be off to the Club together."

At the Tankerville, we were greeted by the Club Secretary, Brigadier Hetherington, who conducted us to the place where the body had been discovered.

"Who discovered Lord Gravesby?" Holmes asked him.

"Kenning, one of the waiters here. If he is here now, would you like to speak with him?"

"If it is possible, certainly I would." Hetherington called a Club servant to fetch the man. Holmes cast his eye about the room, where three chairs still stood around a card table. The fourth was overturned. "I take it that this is the chair that was occupied by Lord Gravesby?"

"We have every reason to believe so. The body was found on the floor beside it."

Holmes dropped to his knees and used his lens to scrutinise the carpet. "Do you happen to know if Lord Gravesby smoked cigars?" he asked Hetherington.

"Indeed he did."

"While he was playing cards?"

"Usually that would be the case, but I have every reason to believe that on the night which concerns us – that is to say, the night of the unfortunate incident in which His Royal Highness and Major Prendergast were involved, he did not."

"Oh?"

"His Royal Highness was suffering from a cough, and made it clear that he did not wish others to smoke in his presence."

"And on the evening when the body was discovered?"

"I cannot say. It may be that Kenning will be able to provide further information on that score."

"I see. And one final question on the subject. Do you happen to know if Lord Gravesby smoked Trichinopoly cigars?"

"Good heavens, no. He smoked Cuban Coronas. The Club used to keep a stock for his exclusive use. Ah, Kenning," he added as the waiter entered. "This gentleman here, Mr. Sherlock Holmes, would like a few words with you."

The waiter appeared to be ill at ease as he stood facing Holmes, his hands visibly trembling. "I didn't do it, sir," he stammered. "All that happened was, I came in here, and found him on the floor just there," pointing to a spot near the overturned chair.

" No-one is accusing you of killing his Lordship," Holmes assured him. " I simply wish to know how you discovered him, and what you did then ? "

"Well, sir, I had just finished tidying the smoking-room, putting the newspapers back on their racks and so on. Then I thought it was time to do this room, the second card-room, so I came in here and saw what I've just been telling you."

" You have two card-rooms ? " Holmes asked Hetherington.

" We have three, as it happens. His Royal Highness always used this one, and we were careful that it should not be booked for use by any other members when he was in Town. He often used to come here with no advance notice."

" I see," answered Holmes. " Kenning, what did you do after you discovered the body ? "

" Well, sir, I thought he might have dropped off to sleep and slipped off his chair, like, or else, begging your pardon, that he'd had a bit too much to drink, which has happened in the past, sir, if you'll excuse me saying so, but there was no glasses or decanter on the table."

" No ashtray or signs of a cigar or matches ? "

" No, sir. The table was bare. Nothing on it. I'd take my oath on that." Here the man paused, clearly relishing the importance that his recital was bestowing upon him. " Well, I bent over him and had a closer look, and he was stone dead, sir. His face was set all rigid, like, and when I turned him over, there was a hole in the back of his head, just there." He pointed to a spot on his own head. " I could see that at a glance, sir."

" Ha ! You are familiar with dead bodies, then ? "

" Indeed, sir. I served my time with the Gloucestershires before coming here, and I've seen my share of dead men. Good friends, too, some of them."

"Yes, yes." Holmes's tone was a little impatient. "And then ? "

" I called for help. Nichols came, and I told him to go and fetch Brigadier Hetherington."

Hetherington nodded in confirmation. " Nichols brought me here, and I could see at a glance that his Lordship was dead. I told Kenning and Nichols to carry him discreetly to one of the bed-rooms, and I sent another of the servants to call the police."

"How long was it before the police arrived?" Holmes enquired.

"There was a constable outside the door who arranged for Inspector Lestrade to come here."

"I arrived as soon as I could, with Sergeant McIver – you remember him, Holmes, in the affair of the emerald earrings? – I would estimate I was no more than fifteen minutes from the time that I received the message," Lestrade told us.

Hetherington coughed discreetly. "Inspector Lestrade was here within twenty-five minutes of the alarm being raised, Mr. Holmes."

"And during that time, no one entered this room?"

A flush stole over the Club secretary's face. "I am afraid I am unable to answer that question, Mr. Holmes. My attention, and that of the Club servants, was taken up by Lord Gravesby, and the necessity of concealing the fact of his demise from the other persons in the Club at that time."

"There were many members, then?"

"Indeed there were many people there that night. The Worshipful Company of Confectioners were holding their annual dinner, and the usual number of members were present."

Holmes turned his attention back to Kenning. "The pistol here," gesturing to a flintlock pistol that appeared to date from the last century lying on a table at the other side of the room, "was it there when you entered the room and discovered Lord Gravesby?"

"I'm afraid I couldn't swear to that either way, sir. You see, I was more concerned for His Lordship than anything else."

"Naturally." Holmes turned to Lestrade. "The cause of death is the bullet, I take it?"

"Surely you are joking, Mr. Holmes? A man is found dead with a bullet wound and a pistol in the room, and you question the cause of death? I know you have your fancies and your theories, Mr. Holmes, but this beats all."

"Then I take it that the bullet has not been extracted? The post mortem examination has yet to take place, Inspector?"

"This afternoon, Mr. Holmes. I take it that you and Doctor Watson here would like to attend?"

"Who is performing the autopsy?"

"Sir Greville Patterson, if I recall correctly."

"Then there will be no cause for me to attend. Pray let me have a copy of Sir Greville's report as soon as it becomes available."

"As you will, Mr. Holmes, but I do not believe that it will shed any new light on the matter."

"My thanks." Stepping cautiously, and keeping to the edges of the room, Holmes moved to the side table near the door where the pistol lay. "With your permission, Inspector?" he asked, reaching for the pistol. Lestrade nodded silently, and Holmes picked up the weapon and raised it to his nose. "There is no smell remaining," he remarked, "such as I would expect from a weapon using black powder." He examined the flash pan. "There is no sign that the weapon has been fired in the recent past."

"What?" exclaimed Lestrade in confusion. "Are you telling us that this is not the means by which Lord Gravesby met his end?"

"Indeed I am," said Holmes. "You may verify this for yourself," he added, presenting the pistol for the police agent's inspection.

"Then we have more than one mystery on our hands, Mr. Holmes. Who placed the pistol here, and how did Lord Gravesby die?"

"As to the first, I strongly suspect Sir Quentin Austin, presumably to place suspicion on Major Prendergast. I believe we will have to await the results of the autopsy before we know the answer to the second."

We left the Club in company with Lestrade, who seemed to be more than a little disconcerted by Holmes's findings. "So you believe Prendergast to be innocent?" he asked.

"Innocent of shooting Gravesby with that particular pistol, at any rate. Indeed, consider the evidence we have just seen and heard. Can we indeed believe that Gravesby was indeed shot?"

"I am not entirely sure why you should say such a thing. He

is dead, at any event, no matter how he died," said Lestrade, thoughtfully. " I hope you are not disputing that fact. But, as you say, the post mortem examination may provide us with a few more answers."

" I think I will make my way to Barts and view the body before Sir Greville starts his work," said Holmes. "Watson, you will accompany me to the haunts of your youth ? Lestrade ? "

"Willingly," I answered him, but Lestrade declined the invitation.

" However, if you would be good enough to pass on anything you find, Mr. Holmes, I would be most obliged," he requested, and Holmes acknowledged this with a nod of his head.

We took ourselves to the hospital where I had trained as a student, and made our way to the room where Sir Greville Patterson plied his grisly trade.

"Ah, Holmes. Good to see you here. Shocking business, what ? Watson, delighted to have another pair of hands and pair of eyes on this case. Shall we start ? " He withdrew the sheet covering the cadaver. " I was informed that the cause of death was a bullet at the base of the neck. However, I perceive no exit wound. Watson, if you would, please ? "

He and I turned over the body to expose the back of the neck, where a small hole was to be seen, which lacked the superficial characteristics that mark wounds caused by projectiles fired from pistols or rifles.

" If I may say so, Sir Greville," I remarked. " That hardly appears to be a bullet wound. I have seen enough of such in my time with the Army."

" I agree," replied my medical colleague. " We can easily determine the truth or otherwise of your observation, Watson." A few minutes' work with the scalpel, and Sir Greville grunted. "You were perfectly correct, Watson. There is no exit wound, and no sign of any bullet in here. I detect some fracturing of the second and third cervical vertebrae, but it does not resemble that which would be caused by a bullet."

" As I thought," commented Holmes, who had been silently observing the proceedings. " We must seek another weapon. You are certain that this wound was the cause of death ? " he asked Sir Greville.

" Certainly this injury was the cause of death. I would put the immediate cause as the extreme compression of the spinal cord caused by the pressure of the fragments of the vertebrae being driven forward by— by whatever it was that caused this." His tone, at first the confident manner of one of the foremost pathologists in the land, weakened and grew fainter as his doubts grew, in an almost visible manner.

" That, my dear Sir Greville, is my province," remarked Holmes cheerfully. " Yours was to determine the cause of death, and you have done so admirably. Thank you so much for your work here." He turned to go. " You will let me have the full report in good course ? Come, Watson."

" In all my experience, I have never seen a wound like that," I said to Holmes as we walked away from the hospital.

" No more have I," he told me. " This has the makings of a most ingenious case, Watson. The only possibility that suggests itself to me is that the murderer held in his hand an object similar to a dagger, but with no edge, and a slightly blunted tip – you observed the distinctive characteristics of the wound, did you not ? – and used it with sufficient force not simply to break the skin, but to crush the vertebræ and the spinal cord. Death must have been painless and instantaneous. There is a certain diabolical ingenuity here, as well as a powerful motive."

" I cannot conceive of such a weapon, or indeed, of the man who would wield it."

" Indeed. We would seem to be searching for a man of powerful build – a man of action."

" I hope that you are not suspecting my friend Prendergast," I told him.

" At the present time, no one and everyone may be suspected. But let us see Prendergast, in any event. It is best that we do not acquaint him with Sir Greville's findings, though."

We returned to the Club through the Park, and secured a quiet corner of the smoking-room in which we awaited Prendergast.

On his arrival, I noted his drawn face, which exhibited a curious pallor. " Are you unwell ? " I asked him.

" A bit worried, old man. What with the pistol missing from

my room and turning up next to the body. Enough to give anyone a turn."

" I quite understand your concerns," said Holmes. " However, I do not think you need to worry yourself over that matter. However, I would appreciate your providing more details on Sir Quentin Austin, specifically on his appearance. For example, does he usually carry a stick, and if so, what kind ? "

Prendergast appeared to be considering the question for a short while before responding. " I do not recall seeing him with such an article. I believe I would remember if I had done so."

" A lacquered stick, with a silver head in the shape of a skull, for example ? "

Prendergast started. " You are describing a stick that is the property of his Royal Highness. It is a most distinctive article, and one of which he is most proud. I have heard it said that there is some secret about it, but it is not one to which I am privy. It may have been a gift from one of his female friends, perhaps."

" Very well. Another question about Sir Quentin. I observed when he visited us, that he is a user of tobacco in some form. Perhaps you can enlighten me further as to the form in which he indulges the habit."

" He is often to be seen with one of those foul Trichinopoly weeds," smiled Prendergast.

Holmes clapped his hands together in an expression of delight. " Then the case is solved," Holmes told him. " When I have talked to the police, you will be freed from suspicion, and the culprit brought to justice."

" Sir Quentin ? " asked Prendergast incredulously.

" It may well be he," answered Holmes. " I would advise you, Major, to return to your rooms here at the Club and remain there until the police let you know formally that you are no longer under suspicion."

After Prendergast had left us, Holmes and I took a cab to Scotland Yard.

" But have you deduced that Sir Quentin killed Gravesby ? " I could not but refrain from asking my friend.

" I have," he told me. " No doubt you noticed his stick ? "

" Indeed so. I could hardly tear my eyes away from that grotesque skull that formed the handle ? "

" Tut. You did not observe the tip ? The silver ferrule was stained with some dark substance that was certainly not mud, and could not have been, since we have had no rain in a week. Furthermore, the shape of the stick at that end, and therefore the ferrule, was not round, but octagonal. When we arrived at the Club, I noticed a peculiar indentation on the carpet, within one of the areas that had been stained with blood. That, too, was an octagonal shape. The cigar ash that I observed is the final clue that points fair and square, or should I say fair and octagonally ? " Holmes gave a faint chuckle, " to Sir Quentin Austin as the murderer."

" I all seems too simple, Holmes. But you believe that that stick was the murder weapon ? However, Austin seemed to me to be of too slight a build to inflict a blow that could cause the injuries we observed at Barts."

" That point had occurred to me also, and I confess to being a little troubled by it," Holmes admitted to me. However, if we can convince Lestrade of the wisdom of interviewing Austin on the subject, I have little doubt that we will soon know the truth of the matter."

On hearing Holmes's words of explanation, Lestrade instantly sat up straight in his chair. " Why, thank you, Mr. Holmes. I will dispatch a constable to arrest him and bring him here immediately."

" It might be better if he were not arrested at this stage of the proceedings," Holmes suggested to him. " Let us hear what he has to say for himself first."

" Especially given his friendship with a certain personage," Lestrade added. " I see the sense in what you are saying, Mr. Holmes."

The constable was dispatched, and returned some time later with Sir Quentin Austin, dressed as we had previously seen him, and carrying the skull-headed stick on which Holmes had remarked.

Lestrade opened the questioning. " Sir Quentin, do you deny being in that card room at the Tankerville Club after the death of Lord Gravesby ? "

" I do deny it," came the toneless reply.

" Then how is it," asked Sherlock Holmes, " that your stick still retains traces of blood on its tip, which were imparted to it when the stick was pressed into that part of the carpet where a bloodstain was present ? " Sir Quentin looked down at the end of the stick with what appeared to be a genuine look of surprise and horror on his face. " Furthermore," Holmes continued, " traces of the cigar that you were smoking were present in that room, in the form of ash. We have established that while you were playing cards in that room on that night, you were not smoking."

Sir Quentin closed his eyes in resignation. " Very well, then. Yes, I was in the room after Lord Gravesby's death."

" For the purpose of placing the pistol that you had abstracted from Major Prendergast's room, for the purpose of implicating him in the murder ? " Holmes went on.

" Yes," came the answer in a hushed voice. " It was the work of a cad, I know, but the alternative was worse."

" Such as being hanged for murder ? " sneered Lestrade. " Sir Quentin Austin, I arrest you for—"

Holmes held up a hand. " Stop, Lestrade. Sir Quentin has not confessed to killing Lord Gravesby. With your permission, I would like to ask him a few more questions."

" Oh, very well," grumbled the police agent. " Since it is you."

" Sir Quentin," Holmes addressed the baronet, from whose face all colour had now drained. " However unpleasant or serious the consequences of your words, I strongly advise you to provide full and truthful answers to the questions I am about to ask you." The other nodded. " Very well. Imprimis, I believe that is not your stick that you are holding. Or, if it is, that it was only recently presented to you by another who was the original owner."

" The second of those statements is correct," was the reply.

" And I believe I know who presented it to you. Very well. Let us continue. Do you know the secret of this stick ? Why it was given to you ? " Lestrade and I looked at each other in puzzlement. Holmes's reasoning was beyond my comprehension, and from the look on his face, beyond that of Lestrade also.

" I believe I know why this was so," Holmes went on. " Will

you do me the kindness of passing me the object in question ? "
Wordlessly, Austin complied with the request. " Observe the
tip closely," Holmes requested us.

He held the stick horizontally, and we waited. Suddenly
there was a loud click, and what we had taken to be the ferrule
shot out from the tip of the stick to the extent of about two
inches, with the velocity and force of a bullet from the mouth
of a gun. " Imagine," said Holmes calmly, " that I had the tip
of this pressed against the back of my victim's neck. Watson,
what sort of injuries would result ? "

" Those that we observed on Lord Gravesby," I answered.

" But how does this return to its former state ? " asked
Lestrade.

" By the very simplest of methods," Holmes informed us. He
placed the tip of the stick on the floor and placed his weight
on the handle, forcing the stick downwards. After a little exertion, the tip retracted, and another clicking sound presumably
informed us that the mechanism was now locked into place.
" And hence, gentlemen, the bloodstains on the tip of this stick
when the murderer pressed the murder weapon into the carpet, at a point where it was soaked in the blood of the victim."

" What is this diabolical thing ? " I asked.

" Behold the *Totenkopfstock*. A few of these were created at
the end of the last century in Vienna for those involved in es-
pionage and in secret government work. I believed them all to
have been destroyed, but such is clearly not the case. The trigger to release this diabolical weapon is concealed in the eye-
holes of the skull."

" My God ! " breathed Austin. " I had no conception." His
face, formerly pale, was by now ashen. " To think I have been
walking around London with this— this monstrous thing in my
hands. So I have been in possession of the weapon that killed
Lord Gravesby without knowing it ? " he stammered.

" Why do you think it was given to you ? " asked Holmes. " As
a reward for placing false evidence to condemn an innocent
man ? No, it was to absolve your master of any complicity in
the crime. You are guilty, my man, of conspiracy to pervert the
cause of justice, even if you are innocent of the killing itself."

By now, Austin, slumped in his chair, had his face in his

hands, and appeared to be sobbing to himself. Between the sobs, we could make out the words, "I had no choice."

"I must warn you," Lestrade told him, "that anything you say will be taken down and may be used in evidence against you."

"No matter," replied Austin, recovering his posture, and addressing us with some dignity. "I am, as you may know, unmarried, and am likely to remain so for the rest of my life. I leave you to draw whatever conclusions you may choose from this statement. His Royal Highness drew his conclusions, and from then on, I was in his power, helpless to do anything other than what he commanded. The story of the card game at the Tankerville Club that you have read is a complete fiction. You have read, have you not, that His Royal Highness accused Gravesby of cheating?"

"That is so," Holmes affirmed.

"The truth is otherwise. It was Gravesby who accused His Royal Highness of double-dealing the cards. He, that is to say His Royal Highness, indignantly denied this, and he left the room, followed by Prendergast and myself, where we took counsel among ourselves."

"Was there any truth in the accusation against the Prince?" Lestrade asked.

Austin bowed his head. "I am ashamed to say that there was. It was not the first time that this had occurred. The Prince sent a Club servant to fetch a box from his rooms at ____ House.

"That containing the duelling pistols?"

"Indeed. When the servant returned with the case, His Royal Highness ordered me to talk to Gravesby, and prevent the facts from becoming public, as I am ashamed to admit I had done on previous occasions. In this instance, however, I was unable to do so, and reported as much to the Prince, who thereupon flew into a passion and stormed out of the room. He returned, some ten minutes later, informing me that Gravesby had challenged him in a duel. He had refused to accept, and had named Prendergast to take his place."

"Without consulting Prendergast? And did not Prendergast object?" I asked, incredulously.

Austin shrugged. "It is his way of doing things. Prendergast is a military man, and used to obeying orders. I believe that he would do anything in the world, if he were ordered to by a superior. His Royal Highness then dictated a note to me, addressed to Lord Gravesby requesting a meeting in the same card-room the next evening."

"That is to say, the evening that Gravesby died," Lestrade remarked.

"Indeed so. That evening, His Royal Highness and I made our way to the Club. While he made his way to the card-room where he had arranged to meet Gravesby, I, as I had been instructed, met Prendergast and requested him to deliver a letter to Lady Thruxton at her home in Grosvenor-square."

"The purpose of the letter?"

"I believe it was merely a ruse to take him out of the Club for a short time. I then waited in Prendergast's room, and His Royal Highness joined me a few minutes after Prendergast's departure.

"'Take this, and place it in the card-room where it will be found,' he instructed me, opening the box containing the duelling pistols, and handing me one.

"Naturally, I expressed some question as to why this was needed, and he turned on me with a look of fury such as I had never before observed.

"'Your instructions are clear. Do this, or else...' he hissed at me. The message was obvious. I would be exposed and shamed before the world if I failed to comply with his instructions. I therefore made my way down to the card-room, unobserved, and there beheld a sight such as I hope never to see again. Lord Gravesby was lying on the floor, blood seeping from a wound in the back of his neck. I could not think clearly, and merely deposited the pistol on the nearest possible surface. I left the room, and then realised that my master might have intended me to place the pistol in such a way that suicide would be suspected. I hastened back towards the room, but was prevented from entering by the sight of one of the Club servants moving towards the door. I therefore made my way back to Prendergast's room, where His Royal Highness awaited my return.

"'It is all done,' I told him.

" ' Excellent,' he said, " and that, Inspector, is when he pre-sented me with this devil's tool here," indicating the weapon that Holmes had named as the *Totenkopfstock*.

" We left the Club quickly, without meeting anyone. Already, it was clear that Gravesby's body had been discovered, but who, I asked myself, would suspect a Royal Duke of any misdoing ? "

" Who indeed ? " replied Holmes. " But not only does he ap-pear to have committed murder most foul to cover up his vil-lainy at the card table, but he has attempted to lay the blame at the door of not just one, but two innocent men. What say you, Lestrade ? "

" It's a puzzler, Mr. Holmes, and I don't mind admitting that the situation's a bit much for me. If it was anyone but His Royal Highness we'd have the darbies on him by now. As it is..." his voice tailed off. " As for you, sir," addressing Austin, " you're guilty of compounding a felony, obstructing justice, and I can probably think of some more if you give me a minute."

Holmes held up a warning hand. " Stop there, Inspector. Sir Quentin has given us an honest, and I believe a contrite, ac-count of events. I do not believe that society has much to fear from him in the future. Rather, he has much to fear from socie-ty should these events be made public."

" That is true," Lestrade grudgingly admitted.

" You must retire from public life," Holmes told Austin.

" I would recommend leaving the country. Paris, Aix, or Capri would be congenial, perhaps."

" He cannot leave England ! " Lestrade exclaimed.

" He must. It is in no one's interest that Sir Quentin remains here. Believe me, Inspector, if you bring this man to trial, let alone his master, you will set the country by the ears. He must leave." He turned to Austin. " You have the money to do this ? "

Austin shook his head. " I have little money of my own. His Royal Highness has been my chief financial support for the past few years."

" And he may continue to be so in the future, by the time we have finished with him," Holmes replied with a grim chuckle.

" What do you mean ? " I asked him.

" I have alluded before to these matters," he said simply, but refused to elaborate more.

A week later, we were sitting in our rooms in Baker-street, and I was reading the *Times*.

"It says here, Holmes, that His Royal Highness is to leave from Portsmouth next week to serve as Governor of Grenada. Is this your doing?"

Holmes smiled lazily. "Not mine, but the work of others with whom I have been in contact," he corrected me. "However, it is at my instigation. We have also arranged that Sir Quentin Austin is to receive a generous annuity from His Royal Highness as soon as he is settled in Venice, which he has selected as his destination. Also a consequence of doings by those in Whitehall and the Palace."

"But how did you know that His Royal Highness was responsible?" I asked.

"Your friend Prendergast, though he was obviously not telling the truth when it came to describing the card game and the events surrounding it, was clearly truthful in other respects, such as the discovery of the pistol in his room. Sir Quentin Austin was my first suspect. I felt sure that the account of Gravesby's death we heard from Prendergast was incorrect when I remembered the blood on the ferrule of Austin's distinctive stick that I had observed previously, and I believed that the victim had been battered to death. My first sight of the body dispelled that belief. The post-mortem puzzled me. A man of Austin's build and temperament could never have inflicted those injuries that we observed, but the evidence was strong that it was he who had placed the pistol in the room in order to falsely accuse Prendergast.

"Accordingly, I was forced to conclude that while he was not Gravesby's killer, Austin was in some way closely connected with the criminal, as you yourself will have remarked when you recall that he arrived in a carriage which bore the arms of His Royal Highness painted on the door. Prendergast appeared to have an easily checked alibi. His Royal Highness was the only possible suspect remaining, and when I heard that the diabolical *Totenkopfstock* was the property of the Prince, I was convinced. A man who retains duelling pistols in a condition where they are easily made available for use might also possess some other objects of an equally nefarious nature. I must admit that the motive puzzled me a little until we had heard Austin's story at the Yard. The idea that the tables had been turned, and that the victim was the accuser and *vice versa*, so to speak, had not occurred to me. The Prince was obviously not about to let his propensity for winning at cards at all costs to be made public – we may assume that a large sum was offered by Austin to Gravesby which was refused – and not content with personally eliminating his opponent, he attempted to cast the blame on others."

" Monstrous ! " I exclaimed. "Were it not for his rank..."

" Indeed, Watson. But we cannot live in the land of make-believe. However, we have at least ensured that we no longer inhabit the same land as His Royal Highness." So saying, he took his Stradivarius from the wall, and proceeded to play a tune of his own composition.

The Adventure of the Returned Captain

HE events I am about to describe took place in 1887. The bare facts of this dramatic incident were published in the newspapers, but the full circumstances leading to the loss of the barque commanded by Captain Winslow were not generally known, thanks to the efforts of the Government of the day to keep them from the public eye, in an attempt to prevent similar incidents from occurring.

As the world knows, the barque *Sophy Anderson* (often mistakenly reported in the Press as *Sophie Anderson* or *Andersen*) (captain James Winslow), was observed off Beachy Head one summer afternoon by a number of residents of the area, among whom was a retired Naval officer, Rear-Admiral Lionel Stokesey-Bradwell, whose testimony was most often quoted in the newspaper reports, presumably on account of his expertise in matters nautical, as well as his seniority and position in society.

According to the Admiral, the *Sophy Anderson* appeared to be making about five knots, beating upwind against a westerly breeze. She had just come about to starboard, when the Admiral observed a bright flash and a cloud of smoke, followed, some fifteen seconds later, by the sound of an explosion. From the time between observing the explosion and hearing it, he judged the barque to be some three miles distant. When the smoke cleared, a few seconds after the sound was audible on land, there was no sign of the *Sophy Anderson* visible to the naked eye, and even using the most powerful binoculars at his disposal, the Admiral was unable to discern more than a few shards of wreckage.

The Eastbourne lifeboat was launched as soon as possible, and headed straight to the last position where the barque had been seen, but all that was to be observed were some planks of wood, and some clothing, including a captain's cap (subsequently identified as that of Captain Winslow by his widow). The ship's boat was discovered a little way off, overturned, but there were no members of the crew, or their bodies, to be seen. A French trawler was already on the spot, the crew having witnessed the explosion, but they too had sought in vain for survivors. No trace of the Captain himself other than his cap, or of any of the twenty crew members who were listed as being on board, was ever discovered.

The *Sophy Anderson*, bound for Cadiz and then for Malta, was listed as carrying a cargo of assorted muslins and other fabrics. There appeared to be nothing in the cargo manifest that would account for such an explosion that had caused the ship to disintegrate so completely. The loss of the barque was a nine days' wonder, whose place in the public eye was soon taken by some proposed changes to the laws of cricket by the County Cricket Council.

It was some months following the incident just described that Sherlock Holmes and I were in the rooms at Baker-street. I was engrossed in the details of some financial investments that had been recommended to me by a friend, and Holmes was engaged on some chemical research which he pronounced to have no practical application, but was of great interest for its own sake.

"Aha! A knock at the door, if I am not mistaken," he pronounced without looking up from the table that served him as a laboratory bench. "Mrs. Hudson has admitted him, and he is mounting the stairs. A nautical man, if I am not mistaken."

"How—?" I began, but was cut short by the sound of rapping at the door of our room. I opened it to disclose a near-giant of a man, dressed in mourning black. The face appeared somewhat familiar to me, but I was unable to place it.

"Captain James Winslow, I presume," smiled Sherlock Holmes at our visitor.

The other appeared thunderstruck. "In the name of all that's damnable, Mr. Holmes, how could you possibly have guessed my identity?"

"There was no guesswork involved, my dear fellow. Pray take a seat." Our visitor, seemingly still confused, sat as Holmes continued. "Your gait as you mounted the stairs was that of a seafarer. Your face, albeit with a beard, was reproduced often enough in the newspapers following the loss of the barque. Your complexion is weather-beaten, other than for the parts where you have worn a beard in the past, telling me that it was removed relatively recently. Add to these trifles your physique, which was likewise remarked upon in the Press, and the nautical flavour of the tattoo on your right wrist, and it is clear that I am talking to a former mariner – one who has no intention of sailing the oceans, at least in the near future, if the lack of a beard is to be taken as any indication. Nor, I guess, does he wish to be recognised, if the turned-up collar and low-brimmed hat on a warmish day have any significance. Your mourning for your former shipmates does you credit."

"Well, you are indeed a magician, Mr. Holmes. Maybe you can say to me why I am here?"

My friend smiled. " My talents do not extend to discovering your thoughts, Captain. May I assume that your visit is connected with the recent loss of your ship?"

"You are perfectly correct. I now wish to God that I had never set eyes on that dratted Monsewer."

"A Frenchman?"

"A Belgian, damn his eyes! A Monsieur Malmaison, who promised me and my crew large sums of money in return for delivering what he described as 'a special cargo' to Morocco."

Holmes raised his eyebrows. " Have you any idea as to the nature of that cargo?"

The other sighed. " I fear I must tell you the whole story."

"That would seem to be advisable." Holmes leaned back in his chair, and half-closed his eyes. "Watson, if you would be kind enough to take notes, I would be much obliged."

Winslow sat up straight, his hands clenched in his lap, as he began to relate his tale. "The *Sophy* was coming to the end of her useful life. Her keel had been laid down some forty years ago, and she had been allowed to deteriorate over the course of time. Her owners, Hillbrook & Co. of Gravesend, had determined that she be sold off for scrap some time later this year."

"And your feelings with regard to this?"

"I am not as young as I was. It would be difficult for me to find another command. In addition, I had my crew to consider. They were all good men, hand-picked by myself, with two exceptions, these last being men who had been placed on board by the owners to replace those of my choosing who had died of fever in the West Indies on the previous voyage. If the *Sophy* was to be no more, I felt it would have been my responsibility to ensure that my men had employment in the future. I therefore refused to entertain the idea that the *Sophy* should be sold, and argued my case with the owners." Here he paused. " There is more," he stated, but failed to expound further, as he sat in our chair, his head hanging on his breast.

" Come," Holmes told him. " You must need my services, or you would not be here. But for me to provide my services, you must tell me all that is pertinent to the issues that beset you. Watson, let us offer our guest some refreshment."

After enquiring his preference, I served Winslow with a brandy and soda, which he accepted gratefully, and resumed his narrative.

" The suggestion put to me by the owners was that I should scuttle the *Sophy* at some convenient location offshore where the coast was close and the water deep, and take to the boats with my men. In that way, the owners would be free of the *Sophy*, and be able to collect the insurance on her, which would be significantly more than the amount they could expect to collect were she to be scrapped.

" I refused. As a man who has spent his life on ships, the idea that I should be party to the deliberate destruction of one was repugnant to me, as was the idea that I should take part in a fraud. I am a churchgoing man, Mr. Holmes, and despite what you may have heard of seafarers, we are for the most part a moral group of men."

" What recompense was offered to you, should you have decided to take part in this plot ? " Holmes asked him.

The other flushed a deep red with apparent anger. " Sir, that is an infamous insinuation." Holmes said nothing, but sat quietly, his eyes half-closed. " Very well," Winslow continued in a calmer voice, after a minute had elapsed. " I was offered an undisclosed sum, to be shared out with my men, were I to concur in this nefarious plot. I was given to understand that the amount would be considerable."

" And the leaden alternative ? "

" I do not understand you, Mr. Holmes."

" There is a saying in Spanish, commonly used in Mexico and other places, I believe. It is *plata o plomo*, which may be translated as 'silver or lead'. In other words, when requesting a favour of one who is unwilling to comply, there are two alternatives being offered – enrichment or punishment – in the case of this saying, the punishment being a lead ball fired from a gun."

" The proverbial stick and carrot, then ? "

" Precisely, Captain, but in a more direct form."

" No direct physical threat was made against me or against my family. I do not suspect Hillbrook & Co. of employing such tactics. However, it was made clear to me that if I refused to go along with their plans, I would no longer be in command of the *Sophy*, or any of their ships. Indeed, as a result of my refusal, the voyage on which the *Sophy* met her end was to be her last voyage with me as her captain."

"As indeed it was," remarked Holmes. " Now to this Monsieur Malmaison whom you mentioned earlier, if you please."

" It was to be, as I have just told you, my last voyage. Though I am not an improvident man, I do not have enough money saved to be able to support my family as I would like. Any chance of earning extra money, short of outright fraud, such as Hillbrook & Co. were proposing, would therefore be most welcome.

" I encountered M. Malmaison in a public house, the Hope and Anchor, near the East India Docks. He was in business attire, which caused him to stand out from the others there, who were for the most part officers of merchant vessels, and dressed accordingly. I had marked him down in my mind as being foreign, and when he came over to the table where I was eating and started to address me, I was in no doubt.

" The extraordinary thing was that he appeared to know my name, and many things about me, including the proposal to scuttle the *Sophy*, and the fact that I had turned it down.

" 'Might I suggest that it would be to your advantage to consider another proposal ? ' he asked me, in that strange English of his.

" Well, as you might imagine, I was prepared at least to listen to what he had to say to me, and invited him to share the last of the bottle.

" ' Captain Winslow,' he said to me in a low voice. 'Word has it that you are a discreet man.'

" ' Who told you that and how do you know me ? ' I asked him, but he merely replied that there was no need for me to be aware of these things.

" ' I can count on what I am about to say to you to go no further ? ' he asked me. I assured him on that point, and he continued. ' I am a Belgian, as you have probably worked out for yourself, and I am concerned about the plight of the blacks in the Congo, of which you may have heard.'

" I shook my head, and he went on. ' News is reaching us that they are being sorely exploited by some of my fellow countrymen since the establishment of the Congo Free State. I and a group of philanthropists are ready to help these poor benighted sufferers by supplying them with arms to use against their oppressors.'

" ' Very good,' said I, ' but I fail to see where I may be of use. My ship is not bound for Africa, and I have no intention of going there.'

" ' Ah, but you see,' said he, ' all we require of you is that you make a delivery to our agent in Morocco, who will ensure that the weapons reach their intended destination. You are bound for Malta via Cadiz, I believe ? ' I confirmed this. ' In which case, all that you need to do is to unload the crates and hand them over in Tangier. You will, of course, be paid handsomely for your services – enough to share generously with your crew, I might add.'

" He named a sum, which was considerably in excess of what Hillbrook & Co. had offered me to scuttle the *Sophy*, and I had been led to believe that the last was no mean amount, I can assure you.

" ' One quarter to be paid in advance,' he told me, ' and the balance to be paid on confirmation from our agent that the delivery was made satisfactorily.' Naturally, I wished to have some guarantee that the balance would be paid, and would you believe, cool as a cucumber, he brought out a contract, setting out the terms, and requiring only our signatures to be complete. I am no lawyer, gentlemen, but I have seen enough legal papers in my time, and this appeared to meet my demands.

" ' And what is it exactly that you wish me to carry to Tangier ? ' I asked.

" ' A hundred or so modern rifles on the Chassepot model, together with ammunition, and appropriate parts and supplies,' he told me. Well, that sounded to me like a cargo I was willing to carry, especially given its final destination, so I agreed with him that I would sign his contract to carry his rifles and deliver them to Tangier.

" Accordingly, we called over a fellow captain, who had been a shipmate of mine in the past, and whom I trusted absolutely, and he acted as a witness to our signatures. Here is my copy."

So saying, he withdrew from his coat a folded piece of paper, and handed it to Sherlock Holmes, who unfolded it, and raised his eyebrows.

" It is scarcely legible," he said.

" It suffered a bath in the Channel," explained Winslow. " It is possible, I assure you, to make out some words, and this was of great assistance to me, or so I believed at the time. Allow me to continue with my story.

" Malmaison paid me the agreed amount on the spot, in gold French napoleons. That very evening, a cart drew up at the *Sophy*'s berth, and the three men on the cart proceeded to unload the crates of rifles from it, and to carry them into the hold. I noticed, however, that they did not allow my crew to touch these boxes, but insisted on stowing them in the hold themselves, giving strict instructions that they were not to be moved from those positions.

" We set sail at the appointed time, and had soon rounded the Isle of Thanet and were beating upwind along the Sussex coast. At about the time we passed Beachy Head, I was at the helm, standing alone on the quarterdeck. There was a sudden flash and a deafeningly loud noise, and I knew no more, until I came to, floating in the sea. Of my poor *Sophy*, there was no sign other than a few shattered timbers, but some way off, I espied the ship's boat, seemingly in one piece, but capsized. I am no great swimmer, but by clinging to a plank I was able to keep afloat, albeit with some difficulty, owing to the gold I had received from Malmaison still being in my inner pockets, along with the signed contract, from which I had never taken it. I clung to the hope that some of the crew might still be alive, perhaps hanging onto the upturned boat, and so I hailed my shipmates, but there was no answer, and I was forced to the melancholy conclusion that whatever force had torn apart my *Sophy* had also claimed the lives of my crew.

" I do not know how long I drifted in this condition, but from the accounts of the wreck that I read in the newspapers, it cannot have been more than thirty minutes at most, though it appeared to be an age to me. A French trawler discovered me and took me aboard, but I was not keen that I should be identified as a survivor of the wreck. After all, I had performed a legally dubious act in accepting weapons to be transported, supposedly to a cause which might be approved by any human- itarian, but on reflection, I considered that in actual fact the ultimate destination might be to any group, perhaps even to Russian anarchists. Also, by accepting a cargo of ammunition and failing to inform my crew of its nature, I had placed them in danger. For all I knew, one of them might have been smoking in the hold, albeit contrary to orders, and set off an explosion of gunpowder.

" I therefore desired the trawler's captain to report that no survivors had been rescued, and to complete the deception, tore off my captain's cap and cast it into the water. The trawl- er crew, though bemused by my words and my actions, never- theless carried out my wishes when the lifeboat came on the scene, their deception being encouraged by the presentation of one of the gold napoleons I was carrying, and so it was that the newspapers told the public that there were no survivors of the *Sophy Anderson*.

" I was put ashore at Dieppe, and my first thought was to find Malmaison, and claim the missing portion of my fee. My first thought was to confirm the address in Brussels which I remembered seeing written on the contract, but on examin- ing the paper, I discovered, as you have just done, Mr. Holmes, that immersion in seawater is not kind to legal documents. However, I was in the end able to make out the address, and using some of Malmaison's gold, made my way by train to Brussels.

" There, my hopes were sorely dashed. There was no one by the name of Malmaison at that address, or in any of the houses in that street. Nor had anyone there any knowledge of a man resembling the description I gave of him."

" Is it not possible," I asked, " that you misread the name of the street, and you were enquiring in completely the wrong area ? "

Our visitor smiled. " I had indeed considered that possibility," he told us, " and accordingly I asked at the city offices if there were any other streets whose names resembled the one I had deciphered. They were kind enough to provide me with three such names, but my search in those was as fruitless as my first.

" I was nearly at the end of my tether. I had lost my ship, my position, my shipmates, and it appeared that I had thrown away my future. I therefore determined to return to England, and seek out a new direction for my life there. I had taken out insurance on my life some years ago, and I trust that my wife has been able to claim the sum owing to her from the insurance company."

" She is still unaware that you are alive ? " Holmes asked.

" I am worth more to her dead than alive, at least financially," Winslow replied simply. " My heart is aching to see her, but if she knew that I am alive, she would be duty-bound to return the insurance money, and she would be left with me on her hands, without a job, and without hope."

A long pause followed this last statement, during which Sherlock Holmes filled and lit his pipe.

" And yet you have come to me, Captain Winslow. How may I be of assistance to you ? "

" I have not yet come to the crux of my tale. I have been posing as a widower, having shaved off my beard, as you remarked, and unrecognised, save by you, up to now. I have been spending my time at the docks and in the vicinity, attempting, with no success so far, I may say, to establish the facts concerning this M. Malmaison. It was only yesterday, though, when I received the greatest shock to my system since the loss of the *Sophy*.

" I was turning a corner in Limehouse, when I saw, as plain as I see you now, Mr. Holmes, Jim Porter and Dick Sweethowe, the two members of my crew whom I had not selected personally, but who had been thrust upon me by the owners. Both appeared to be in liquor, and I am certain that they did not recognise me, but for my part, there was no mistaking them."

"And yet, you tell us, there were no survivors of the wreck other than yourself. Is that correct?"

"There were none that I could see, and I am certain if there had been any such, I would have perceived them."

"Well, well," chuckled Holmes. "Three dead men rise up from the deep and are walking the streets of London. Not an everyday occurrence, would you say, Watson?"

"By no means. But exactly what is it that you require of Sherlock Holmes, Captain?"

"I would like him to discover exactly how this pair come to be alive, and to discover this M. Malmaison. I can pay," he added.

"And then?" asked Sherlock Holmes. "Do you wish me to turn them over to the police?"

"I wish to pursue the matter myself."

"I trust, Captain, that you are not proposing to make me an accessary before the fact to a crime of violence,"

"I believe that if I do not furnish you with any details of my plans, no possible blame can attach to you," answered the other, coolly.

"Very well, then. This may well turn out to be a case where the problem and its solution provide their own reward," said Holmes. "I fear, though, that searching for two men in London is like looking for a needle in a haystack."

"These are somewhat uncommon needles, and the size of the haystack is limited to the areas around the London docks, I believe," smiled Winslow. "Porter and Sweethowe are quite distinctive in their appearance. Porter, for example, is of medium height, and a swarthy, heavily bearded appearance. When I saw him yesterday, he was wearing heavy hooped earrings. He is missing his left eye, which is usually covered by a patch, and the last two fingers of his left hand are likewise missing. Sweethowe is perhaps less distinctive, but he may be known by a picture of a mermaid tattooed on the left forearm, and one of Britannia on the right, as well as a scar which reaches from the outside of his right eyebrow to his right ear, the lobe of which is missing. He makes no attempt to hide it."

"Very good," said Holmes. "Watson, you have these particulars noted? Excellent. And Malmaison?"

"Dark, slightly long hair, and a waxed moustache. He wore pince-nez for reading and writing, but otherwise he did not need them. He had a habit of touching his nose at frequent intervals for no apparent reason." I duly noted these details as well. "I have a little skill as an artist," Winslow went on, "and I have with me some sketches of the men in question." He reached in his pocket and produced three sheets of paper, on which were skilfully drawn the portraits of three men, corresponding to the verbal descriptions we were given.

"Why, these are excellent!" exclaimed Holmes. "Would that all my clients possessed your skill and your foresight. This M. Malmaison – of what height and build?"

"Ah, I would seem to have forgotten to inform you of those points. He was about five feet or even a little under in height, and somewhat corpulent in build. His short stature should make him quite easy to locate, in my opinion."

"Quite possibly. And the address you were given in Brussels?"

"Rue de Flandres, number 27."

"And the address of Hillbrook & Co.?"

"I address my correspondence to their offices on Parrock Street. Number 4 on the second floor. I confess to never having met their principals, but have conducted my business with them chiefly through letters, though I have met their clerk Kendall on a couple of occasions."

"Thank you, Captain. Where can I contact you if necessary?"

"I would prefer not to say at present. May I call upon you again this time next week, and you can then report any progress."

"That is satisfactory," Holmes told him. "I bid you a very good day, and I hope to have some answers for you by this time next week."

As the door closed behind our visitor, Holmes started to laugh softly. "This is most gratifying, Watson," he remarked, rubbing his hands together. " I was beginning to despair of the English criminal, who has been showing a shocking lack of originality of late in his operations. A little housebreaking, some clumsy forgeries, and minor embezzlement have been my bread and butter for too long. It will be good to sink my teeth into something more substantial. I believe it is time for me to pay a visit to the docks in search of our friend's shipmates."

" You believe they are alive, then, and that the captain was not mistaken ? How could they have survived ? "

" I am sure he was not mistaken. As to the manner of their survival, I have a theory, but it needs to be verified. But I must change my attire if I am to make a visit to Limehouse." So saying, he entered the bed-room.

Knowing Sherlock Holmes as I did, I fully expected him to emerge in the guise of a rough-spoken mariner, and I was therefore amazed when he appeared, dressed in the style of a man of business, albeit one who was somehow indefinably not on the side of respectability.

" You propose going to Limehouse in that garb ? " I enquired incredulously.

For answer, Sherlock Holmes merely nodded before donning his hat and stepping out of the door.

As I awaited his return, I considered what we had been told. Assuming that he was not mistaken, how could Captain Winslow have seen the two crewmen in London, when all the reports were that no survivors from the barque had been seen ? I ruled out the possibility that the two men had been rescued by the same trawler that had acted as the saviour of Winslow, on the grounds that he would have seen them during his time on the boat. Nor, I reflected, was it likely that the Eastbourne lifeboat would have remained silent, had they plucked these two wretches from the jaws of death.

Furthermore, I pondered, it was a remarkable coincidence that the only two survivors of the wreck, other than the captain – that is, if Winslow's words were to be believed – were those whom he had not personally selected as members of his crew.

I fell to reading and re-reading the newspaper accounts

of the disaster, which had been clipped and placed in one of Holmes's voluminous scrap-books.

I had fallen into a semi-reverie when Holmes returned, a smile on his face.

"I placed my worm on the hook, Watson," he told me with an air of satisfaction, "cast it into the water, and I have caught two fine fat fish, with the confident expectation of landing another in the near future."

"You discovered the two men, then ?"

"Indeed I did, and a more unscrupulous pair of rogues you could never meet in a month of Sundays. Ready to cut throats or worse for the price of a bottle of rum. It will be a pleasure to see them in the dock."

"On what charge ?"

"Conspiracy to murder, and murder," he answered me. "But before that happens, we must pay a visit to Gravesend and reel in the big fish of which I spoke. You are with me ?"

"Always," I replied.

"Good man. I feel we will not need the services of your revolver, but it would be as well to equip yourself with a stout stick. I trust it will not prove necessary for you to use it, but it is always as well to be prepared."

Accordingly, the next morning we set off to the town of Gravesend, and made our way from the station to the offices of the firm of which we had been informed by Captain Winslow.

Holmes seemed in fine fettle as we strode the streets, humming to himself a tuneless melody which I eventually recognised as the theme from a Bach fugue. When we reached the address we had been given by Captain Winslow, Holmes remarked the polished brass plate at the entrance, proclaiming the existence of Hillbrook & Co., Ltd., Shipping Agents.

"Well-worn, you will observe," he remarked, pointing to it with his stick. "But lately removed to these premises, I feel. From what Winslow has told us, I feel that they may have come down in the world."

I noted the screws affixing the plate to the wall, which were markedly newer than the plate itself, and the tell-tale signs of another plate having previously occupied the space.

"Let us enter," Sherlock Holmes said to me, and fairly

bounded up the stairs to the offices, where an elderly clerk sat at a desk in the outer office, hunched over some papers.

" Do you gentlemen have an appointment here ? " he asked us, looking up and regarding us with some displeasure.

" Alas, no," replied Holmes. " The truth is that I am looking for a shipping agent with whom I might do some, shall we say, ' discreet' business, and I was recommended to this firm."

" Indeed, sir ? " replied the clerk, in a tone of voice that held more than a note of disapproval. " Might I ask who made this recommendation ? "

" I am afraid that he specifically requested that he not be named in this connection," Holmes told him. " However, he was most insistent that Mr. Hillbrook would be of assistance to me."

" I am sorry to inform you, sir, that Mr. Hillbrook is unable to be of any assistance whatsoever to you in this business," answered the other, with a faint smile.

" Indeed ? May I enquire why that is so ? "

" Because, sir, Mr. Hillbrook passed away some three years ago. The firm is now managed by his son-in-law, Mr. Nathaniel Jessop."

Sherlock Holmes allowed his surprise to show on his face. " Well, well," he exclaimed. " I would never have believed my friend to have been so mistaken. Why, as we were walking through the City two weeks ago, he pointed out a gentleman whom he identified as Mr. Hillbrook of this firm."

" It would appear, sir, that he was mistaken."

" If so, it was a strange mistake to make. The gentleman in question was quite short of stature, perhaps five feet or even a little less in height, and not of slender build, shall we say. Clean-shaven, and with neatly trimmed blond hair."

" You have just described Mr. Jessop, sir. Perhaps you confused the name of this firm with the name of the current principal ? "

" No doubt that is the case," said Holmes, shaking his head ruefully. " An elementary mistake. Perhaps Mr. Jessop would be available for consultation ? " he enquired, hopefully.

" He is not presently in the office, I am afraid, sir. However, he is expected to be here at two this afternoon, if you would care to call then. Alternatively, one of our other managers might be of assistance."

" I am afraid that is impossible. I must speak to the senior manager, or to no one, and must return to Town within the morning. I will write to Mr. Jessop this evening and request an appointment."

" Perhaps I could arrange such an appointment now, sir ? " suggested the clerk, " and save you the trouble of writing a letter ? "

" Admirable," Holmes answered him. " Would tomorrow morning at ten be convenient ? "

The other passed his finger down a ledger, and looked up. " Perfectly satisfactory. We may expect to see you tomorrow at ten o'clock, then, Mr.— ? "

" Jones," replied Sherlock Holmes. " Mr. Smith here will be with me."

If the clerk realised that the names he was being given were aliases, he did not show it, but merely inscribed the details of the meeting in the book, his face immobile.

" I bid you a very good day, then," said Holmes, tipping his hat to the clerk.

We walked down the street in silence until we reached the station, whereupon Holmes turned to me.

" I was not expecting to be able to land my catch so easily," he told me. " We must to London, and then I must return to the docks to meet my little fishes. And tomorrow will see some interesting developments, I am sure."

As he had told me, on our return to Baker-street, Sherlock Holmes donned the attire he had worn for his previous day's adventure, and returned, his eyes glittering with excitement. " It is all better than I had expected," he told me. " Champagne at this stage of the proceedings would be a little premature, but I think we can make merry at the opera tonight. What say you to a little Rossini ? "

It seemed that Sherlock Holmes had not a care in the world as he sat in his seat, seemingly entranced by the doings of Figaro and Count Almaviva. No-one who observed the languid figure in immaculate evening dress, idly beating time to the music, would ever have guessed that they were in the presence of the greatest mind ever to be dedicated to the detection and apprehension of malefactors. We finished the evening at a small restaurant in Soho, and the meal ended on a sombre note, as we raised our glasses.

"To the officers and men of the *Sophy Anderson*," proclaimed Holmes. "May they rest in peace."

"Amen to that," I replied, and drank.

The next morning saw us once again on the platform of Gravesend station, but to my surprise, we did not immediately set off for the offices of the shipping company.

"We are awaiting friends," said Holmes. "I expect them by the next train."

Sure enough, when the next train pulled in, two men of ruffianly appearance detached themselves from the crowd, and made their way towards us. I had no difficulty in recognising them as the two crewmen who had, according to Captain Winslow, been placed on his ship by the shipping agents.

"Do not be alarmed, Watson," Holmes confided to me in a low voice. "This pair of beauties is on our side – for the present."

We must have made a curious sight as we walked the streets of the town. Holmes, carrying his Gladstone bag, and flanked by a dastardly scoundrel on each side, led the way, with myself in the tail of the group.

On our arrival at the offices of Hillbrook & Co., the clerk appeared visibly surprised.

"Are these two men with you, sir?" he asked, indicating Porter and Sweethowe. "To see Mr. Jessop?" he added, with evident distaste.

"That is correct," Holmes answered equably.

"I will see if Mr. Jessop is available," said the clerk. He vanished through a door behind him, and we were able to hear voices, one of which was the clerk's, and the other, a deeper voice, seemed to be raised in anger.

The clerk returned. "Mr. Jessop regrets that he will not, after all, be able to meet you," he told us, apologetically.

"I think he is mistaken," said Holmes, pushing past the clerk, and followed by the two seamen and myself. "You have done your part. No blame currently attaches to you," he told the hapless clerk, who stood, seemingly paralysed, as Holmes opened the door and entered the inner office.

Jessop sat behind his desk. A florid face, red with anger, was topped by a head of sandy hair.

" How dare you ? " he shouted at Holmes. " I gave explicit orders that you were not to be admitted." His gaze fell upon the two seamen, and he gave a visible start. "And... and who are these two ? " he asked.

" Oh, I think you know them well enough," answered Holmes.

" Don't know him, though," grumbled Porter.

" Oh, I think you do," Holmes told him. " Mr. Jessop, may we try a little experiment ? " He opened his Gladstone bag, and from it produced a dark wig. " Would you please put this on ? "

" What manner of tomfoolery is this ? " cried Jessop. His face, which had been scarlet when we entered, now seemed drained of blood, and his eyes darted nervously about the room, as if seeking some means of escape.

" No tomfoolery," said Holmes. " Watson, would you please assist Mr. Jessop ? "

I thereupon held Jessop fast while Holmes adjusted the wig on his head. The change in his appearance was striking. " And now," said Holmes, producing a bushy false moustache, and holding it over the upper lip of the protesting Jessop.

The effect on the two mariners was nothing short of miraculous.

" Well, if it ain't the beggar who set us up on the *Sophy* ! " exclaimed Sweethowe with a foul oath.

" Blimey, Dick, you're right ! " said Porter, who turned to the now terrified Jessop. " You owe us some money, matey. We did what you told us to do, and went to meet you after, like you said, but you never turned up, did you ? That's one hundred pound each coming to us."

" Make that one hundred and twenty. We got wet, didn't we, Jim ? "

" That we did," said Porter. " I think you can manage another twenty for each of us, can't you, Monsewer ? "

It was now obvious to me that Jessop and the mysterious M. Malmaison were one and the same person. Not only had he persuaded Captain Winslow to accept the mysterious cargo, but he had been responsible for putting these two ruffians aboard, for whatever nefarious purpose he had in mind.

"I... I don't have the money here at present," stammered Jessop, who by now was visibly shaking with fear.

"We can wait an hour or so," said Sweethowe, ostentatiously taking out a large sailor's jack-knife and using its point to clean his fingernails.

"It might be a little longer than that," whimpered Jessop.

"Like how long?" enquired Sweethowe.

Jessop suddenly lifted his head, and a spark of defiance danced in his eyes. "Maybe never," he answered, with more than a little bravado. "After all, if the police were to know about the part you played in this little game..."

These were almost his last words. Sherlock Holmes's arm shot out to arrest Sweethowe's hand holding the knife, but he was too late. The blade entered Jessop's chest, and he sank senseless to the floor. Holmes had by this time seized Sweethowe's wrist in a grip of iron, and the knife clattered to the ground.

Porter started forward to free his comrade, but I stepped forward, my right hand still concealed in my coat pocket. "Move one step, Porter, and you are a dead man," I told him. "I am an excellent shot with a revolver – and I do not think you wish me to prove my words with deeds. Stand back, I say, and place your hands above your head," I commanded, and I was gratified to see him move to the wall, plainly terrified. "Now you, Sweethowe," I ordered, and he followed his companion's actions.

"Admirably done, Watson," said Sherlock Holmes, and raised to his lips his ever-present police-whistle on which he blew three short blasts. To my surprise, Inspector Lestrade entered a minute later, followed by two constables.

"Take this one," said Holmes, indicating Sweethowe, "on a charge of attempted murder, and the other on a charge of conspiracy to murder. That will do for a start. We will discuss the other charges later."

"And this one?" asked Lestrade, indicating the fallen Jessop, from whose mouth blood was now issuing.

"He needs an ambulance," I said. By this time, Sweethowe

and Porter now being guarded by the two constables, I was bending over him, administering what little aid I could to the obviously dying man.

"I will attend to that," said Lestrade. "Take these two to the station," he told the constables, and we were soon left alone with Jessop.

Sherlock Holmes stooped, and put his face close to that of Jessop. "Tell me, was it dynamite?"

Jessop's eyes flickered briefly, as he considered the question, and then he nodded feebly. "It was dynamite. Four hundred pounds." There was a rattle, all too familiar to me, and Jessop was no more.

"A pity," said Holmes, standing. "But he has gone to face a higher Justice."

"I do not understand," I complained.

"All will become clear when we are returned to Baker-street," he told me.

Once returned, and settled comfortably in our chairs, Sherlock Holmes began his explanation.

"It was clear to me, from the newspaper reports, and from Captain Winslow's account, that the *Sophy Anderson* had been destroyed by an explosion of some sort, sufficient to rend the ship to splinters, and to tear its crew to bloody shreds. Winslow, by his account the only man at the stern, was thrown clear, and survived through a freak, as is not uncommon in these cases. The *Sophy Anderson* was, as all reports had it, a sailing-ship with no auxiliary power, and we could therefore discount any such catastrophe as a boiler explosion.

"The explosion had to be caused by some explosive agent. It could have been some secret naval device that had somehow run amok and destroyed the ship, but having made discreet enquiries, I am assured on the highest authority that though such a weapon currently exists, the Royal Navy is not to blame in this case. Consider, though, we were told by Winslow that the cargo included guns and ammunition, carried and placed on board by men who were not members of his crew, and this was carefully located, with instructions that it be not moved. To my mind, that suggested two things. Firstly, that the crates contained something other than had been told to Winslow. This much was patently obvious. Secondly, that their location was of prime importance."

"Ammunition alone would not cause a large single explosion such as was described and witnessed," I pointed out.

"Indeed, nor would it. I suspected dynamite, or something similar, was contained in those cases. Hence my words to the dying Jessop, and he confirmed to me that this was the case."

"So it was Jessop who was responsible for placing the explosive on board, and for destroying his own ship?"

"Naturally. You have no doubt determined for yourself that Jessop and the mysterious M. Malmaison are one and the same person. We have already heard that the company wished to scrap the ship, or to commit an act of insurance fraud. This trick would bring more money than either, on account of the lives of the crew being insured, with the company being the beneficiaries. Naturally, such a plan required confederates."

"Porter and Sweethowe?"

"Precisely. In his guise as Malmaison, Jessop gave them a berth on the *Sophy Anderson*, and as himself, informed Winslow by letter that this precious pair had been assigned to his crew. Their task, given to them by 'Malmaison', was to set a timing device to explode the dynamite and complete the destruction of the *Sophy* and her crew. They were to escape from the doomed craft before the explosion using the ship's boat, which, you will recall, was found floating upside-down, apart from the main mass of the wreckage."

"And where were these rogues when the search was conducted?"

"Why, in the upturned boat, of course, breathing the air trapped underneath it. When the searchers had left the area, they were free to make for shore and claim the remainder of the money to be paid to them by the mysterious M. Malmaison. They were not to know that there was another survivor of the wreck, let alone that he was their captain, who was likewise seeking Malmaison.

"I discovered Porter and Sweethowe by going to Limehouse, and posing as an unscrupulous shipping agent who wished a criminal act to be performed for insurance money. It was not difficult to find such a notorious couple."

"The whole business is totally infamous!" I exploded. "To murder in cold blood nearly twenty brave souls, leaving widows and orphans to fend for themselves, and all for the sake of a few thousand pounds at the most!"

"I agree wholeheartedly," said Holmes. "I can only trust that the maximum penalty will be applied to them both once I have communicated the facts to the court. As to the amount, I have discovered that a few thousand pounds was indeed the whole of the sum that Jessop received."

"And even then, after receiving that money, he failed to pay his cat's paws for their foul deeds."

"Thereby hangs a tale. Quite apart from the debts owed by Hillbrook & Co., which were paid off through this means, Jessop also had personal matters of a delicate nature which claimed some of the proceeds."

"A young lady in the case?" I asked.

"As always, Watson, your instincts in this line are infallible. Not only a young lady, but an infant of tender years claimed a large proportion of Jessop's ill-gotten gains." He paused. "Watson, it is not often that I am puzzled and require an answer from you, but I find this to be one of those occasions. Tell me, did we not agree that you were to leave your revolver here when we went a-calling on Jessop?"

"We did," I smiled.

"Then why did you not do so?"

"My revolver has been here the whole time," I answered, indicating my desk drawer.

"Then with what did you threaten those two villains, if not with your revolver?"

"With this," I smiled, holding out my empty hand. "Concealed in my pocket, who was to know what manner of weapon it might be holding?"

Holmes regarded me with an expression of surprise for a few moments, and then fell to laughing heartily. "That is capital, Watson! Brave as a lion, resourceful as a serpent, as tenacious as a limpet, and as faithful a friend as a man could have."

It was not often that Sherlock Holmes bestowed such tributes on others, and these words from him meant more to me than they would have done from any other source. I blushed on hearing these words spoken by my friend, and it is with some embarrassment, I confess, that I write them now, as the concluding words of this adventure.

As a postscript, I would like to add that following the trial, the jack-knife with which Sweethowe killed Jessop somehow found its way into Holmes's possession, where it now skewers the correspondence on the mantelpiece.

THE ADVENTURE OF THE LICHFIELD MURDER

T the time that the events of which I am writing began, Sherlock Holmes was unengaged on any case. He had recently returned from the Continent, where he had been occupied with a matter of some delicacy regarding the ruling family of one of the minor German principalities, and now found time to hang idle on his hands.

He was amusing himself by attempting to discover a link between the Egyptian hieroglyphic system of writing, and that of the ancient peoples of the central American continent. This attempt, incidentally, proved to be fruitless, and the results of his researches never saw the light of day. The rain was falling, and few cabs and even fewer pedestrians were on the street, as I stood in the window of our rooms in Baker-street observing the scene below. " Halloa ! " exclaimed Holmes, who had laid down his pen with a gesture of impatience, and joined me at the window. "A client, if I am not mistaken." The corpulent man approaching our house certainly seemed to bear all the distinguishing marks of those who sought the assistance of Sherlock Holmes. The vacillation in his movements, and the nervous glances at the numbers displayed on the front doors of the houses of Baker-street had by now become almost as familiar to me as they were to Holmes. As we watched, he glanced upwards, and caught sight of us standing in the window, as we in turn observed him. Hurriedly ducking his head downwards, he quickened his pace, half-running to the door, and within a matter of seconds we heard the pealing of the bell. We returned to our seats as Mrs. Hudson announced the arrival of our visitor, presenting Holmes with his card.

" A somewhat uninspiring choice of name," he announced, after examining the card, briefly presenting it to his long aquiline nose, and presenting it to me, where I read simply the name " Henry Taylor" and the title " Merchant". " No matter," he continued, " the truth will eventually come out. Show him up, if you would, Mrs. Hudson."

The man who presented himself a few minutes later was clearly in the grip of a powerful emotion, in which fear appeared to be mingled with grief. " Sit down, please, Mr. Taylor,"

Holmes invited him. "You have come far today, and no doubt you are tired."

"Why, yes, Mr. Holmes, indeed I am." The words were uttered in an accent that betrayed our visitor as hailing from one of our more northern counties. He seated himself in the armchair usually occupied by Holmes's clients, and I was able to observe him more closely.

Clad in a tweed suit, more fitted for the country than the town, his large frame was still heaving with the exertion of having climbed the seventeen steps to our rooms, and to my professional eye, this, combined with his over-ruddy complexion, indicated some problems with his health. His left hand gripped a stout blackthorn, and the corner of a sheaf of papers peeked out from beneath his coat. His eyes were reddened, as though he had been weeping.

"Forgive my impertinence," Holmes said to him after about a minute had passed in silence, " but is your visit here connected with your recent loss ? "

I myself had, naturally, remarked the mourning band attached to his right sleeve.

For answer, Taylor raised his head, which had sunk to his breast, and answered in a lugubrious tone, "Yes, Mr. Holmes, that is indeed the case." Another silence ensued, broken only by the wheezing emanating from our visitor as he slowly regained his composure. At length, he spoke again, in a voice heavily charged with emotion. "Gone, Mr. Holmes. Gone. Struck down in the full flower of her beauty by a fell hand."

"Murder, you say ? " exclaimed Holmes in a tone of some excitement. The news seemed to arouse him from his languor. " How very fortunate— I mean to say that it is fortunate that I have no other cases on hand, of course. The police... ? "

"The police have their suspicions as to who may have committed this foul crime, but I believe them to be in error," replied the other. "This is why I have come to you. I wish to seek justice for my dear wife Martha."

"Tell me more," Holmes invited him, leaning back in his chair and regarding our client with that curious hooded gaze of his. "Watson, take notes, if you would be so kind."

" I am a merchant of cloth and other such goods," began our

visitor. "Some years ago, my first wife died of consumption, leaving me with two young children. As a busy man of business, I found I was unable to care for them as they deserved, and I thereupon lodged them with my sister in the town of Burton upon Trent, and made due financial provision for their support. Though my sister is a good woman, and took excellent care of them, I nonetheless felt that my children deserved to be with their father and his wife. In addition, living alone was irksome to me, and I therefore cast about for a wife. When I moved to the city where I currently reside, my eye was caught by Martha Lightfoot, the daughter of a neighbour, and after a brief courtship, we married, and my children, Stephen and Katie, returned to my home." He paused, and I took the opportunity to offer him a glass of water, which he accepted gratefully. "Well, sir, it seems I could not have made a better choice for a wife. Martha was devoted to my children as if they had been her own, and they, for their part, appeared to adore her in return."

"Excuse me," Holmes interrupted him. "May I ask the ages of the principals in this case ? "

Our visitor smiled, for the first time since he had entered our room. "I suppose that some would term our marriage – our late marriage, that is – a December and May affair. When we married, some two years ago, I was fifty-three years of age, and Martha twenty-two. Stephen was at that time twelve years old, and Katie ten." He paused and mopped his brow with a none-too-clean handkerchief. "We were a happy family, in so far as my work would allow it."

"What do you mean by that ? " Holmes asked him sharply.

"Well, Mr. Holmes, my work involves a good deal of travel, and obliges me to be away from home for considerable periods of time. I considered it to be somewhat of an imposition on Martha for her to care alone for two youngsters, but as I mentioned, she and the children appeared to have a harmonious life together. That is," he sighed, "until the events of a month ago."

"Pray continue," Holmes requested, as our visitor seemed to have sunk into some kind of reverie.

"I came back from an extended trip that had lasted for a

week, and discovered my Stephen in an uncharacteristically sulky mood, and with what appeared to be a bruise upon his face. I assumed that he had received a blow while scuffling with his playfellows, as lads will, but on my questioning him, he informed me that the blow had been struck by my wife. He refused to give the reason for this event, simply referring me to Martha. When I questioned her, and confronted her with the accusation, she admitted to striking the child, but claimed it had not been a deliberate action."

" No doubt she was able to give reasons for this assertion ? "

Taylor sighed. " Yes. She informed me that she had observed Stephen taking money from the maid's purse. A small sum, to be sure – a few pence only – but theft is theft, no matter what the amount, do you not agree, Mr. Holmes ? "

" Indeed so," answered my friend, with a half-smile.

" She remonstrated with him, and an argument ensued, during the course of which she attempted to retrieve the money, and struck the lad in the face. She swore to me with tears in her eyes that it was an accident, and she had never had any intention of doing him harm. He, when I questioned him later, admitted that he had taken the money in order to purchase some trifle, but claimed that Martha had deliberately delivered the blow to his face."

" And which one did you believe ? "

Taylor sighed. " I believed my wife, Martha. Much as I love my Stephen, he has proved himself to be less than truthful in the past, and I have had cause to admonish him. I fear that the sojourn at my sister's did nothing to improve his character. She is a woman whom some might term over-kind, and she indulged his whims while he was living there, at the expense of his character."

" I take it that relations between your wife and your son deteriorated from that time ? "

" Indeed so, Mr. Holmes. As I mentioned, I am often compelled to be away from home, and so it was for this past month. However, on recent occasions when I returned from my travels, it was painfully obvious to me that my wife and my son were on poor terms with each other. I confess that I was completely ignorant of any way in which this breach could be mended, and was forced to endure the spectacle of those whom I love in a state of mutual enmity. Mealtimes were a particular torment, where each seemed to find every opportunity to insult and belittle the other. If one could be banished from the table, peace would have prevailed, and as master of the house, I could remove one of the sources of conflict. But which one was to be removed, Mr. Holmes ? I ask you, for I could not resolve that riddle." He paused, as if for effect. " And then, Mr. Holmes, we come to the events of yesterday."

" It was last night that your wife died ? "

" Indeed it was only yesterday. I returned home to find Martha lifeless, stretched out in her own blood on the drawing-room floor. She had suffered a series of stab wounds to the body."

" And your son ? "

" I discovered him in the scullery, with a bloody kitchen knife. He was cleaning bloodstains off his clothes in an almost frantic manner. The water in the basin in which he was washing his hands and garments was a scarlet mess, Mr. Holmes. I never want to see the like again."

" And his story ? "

" He told me that he had discovered my Martha in the room, with the knife beside her. Despite his recent dislike of her, he is not at heart a bad lad. He believed that she was not dead, but severely wounded, and attempted to move her to make her more comfortable. It was during this operation that he determined that she was, in fact, dead, and it was at this time that his hands and clothing became covered in blood. He picked up the knife—"

" Why did he do that ? " I asked.

Taylor shrugged. " Who can tell ? "

" The mind causes us to act strangely and without rational motive under unusual conditions," remarked Holmes. " I can think of several similar cases in my experience. Go on, Mr. Taylor."

" He picked up the knife, as I say, and carried it with him into the scullery, where he started to wash his hands and to clean the blood from his clothes. When I encountered him, I immediately ordered him to cease what he was doing, and to come into the street with me, where I gave him over to a passing constable. It gave me little pleasure to do so, but I felt that justice must be served."

"Quite so, quite so," murmured Holmes, but his words seemed to me to lack conviction.

"I felt in my heart that it was impossible that he had committed such a base deed, but what other explanation could be given?"

"You mentioned a maid," said Holmes. "Where was she while this was going on?"

"It was her afternoon off."

"I see. And your daughter?"

"She was visiting a schoolfellow. My son and my wife were the only two people in the house when I returned."

"When you returned, was the house door to the street locked?"

"The police asked me the same question. Yes, it was. The door leading to the back yard was also locked."

"And there was no sign of entry through any other aperture? A window, for example?"

"To the best of my knowledge, there was no such sign."

"And the police?"

Taylor spread his hands. "What can they do, but believe that my son is guilty? What other explanation could there possibly be for these events? They are confining him, and I fear he will hang."

"Even if he is guilty, it is not likely he will be hanged," Holmes informed him, not without a certain sympathy in his manner. "The courts often show clemency to younger offenders, even in the case of serious crimes. However, I take it you will wish me to establish his innocence?"

"Of course, Mr. Holmes. But may I ask your fee? I am not a wealthy man, and I fear that I may be unable to afford your services."

"My fees never vary, save on those occasions when I remit them altogether," smiled Holmes. He scribbled a few lines on a card and handed it to Taylor. "I advise you to return to Euston and take the fastest train available back to Lichfield. Do you happen to know the name of the police agent in charge of the case ? "

"An Inspector Upton, I believe, of the Staffordshire Constabulary."

"Excellent. Pray give him this message, and inform him that I will be arriving soon. Thank you, Mr. Taylor. We will join you at your house. Where may we find it ? "

"Dam Street, on the way from the marketplace to the Cathedral. Number 23."

"We will find it, never fear."

Our visitor picked up his hat, and bidding us farewell, departed. I turned to Holmes in astonishment. "How on earth did you know that he lived in Lichfield ? "

"Elementary. When I see that not only his hat bears the label of a tailor in that city, but that his stick also bears the mark of a merchant there, I am forced to conclude that most of his purchases are made in Lichfield. Since he describes himself as a merchant who travels extensively, I consider it unlikely that he lives in a village, since Lichfield is a city well served by two railway stations. Lichfield therefore presents itself to me as his city of residence. In addition, today's weather being wet, I would have expected his boots and his stick to display splashes of mud if he lived outside the city. It is obvious, therefore, since they did not display such signs, that his journey on foot was conducted along paved thoroughfares. Hence my conclusion that he lives in the city. It is, by the by, a city with which my family has some connection. An ancestor, one Joshua Holmes, was an intimate of Erasmus Darwin and Anna Seward, and occupied a handsome property in Lichfield near to the Cathedral Close. Family lore has it that he engaged in the same line of business as do I." Holmes smiled.

"Returning to our client, you remarked that his name was uninspired. Surely a man has no choice regarding his name ? "

"Under certain circumstances, he may well be able to choose," answered Holmes, but did not expound further on this somewhat enigmatic pronouncement. "Did you not remark that the card he presented to us still smells strongly of printer's ink, thereby signifying that it has been produced very recently ? Not only that, but the initials marked in ink inside the hat were not HT, but HS ? Mr. Taylor, or whatever his true name may be, does not strike one as the kind of man who borrows others' hats."

" You see more than I do," I remarked.

" On the contrary, Watson, you see all that I do. I merely draw logical inferences from what I see, and you fail to do so."

" And those papers he was carrying inside his coat. What were they ? I had assumed that they had some relevance to his query."

" I, too," confessed Holmes. " Many of them appeared to be letters, from the little I could observe, and I fancy that at least one of them was a will."

" His late wife's ? " I asked. Holmes shrugged.

" Who can tell with certainty ? But we may assume so, I think. In any case, we must move fast, before the heavy boots of the local constabulary remove all traces of evidence from the scene. As you know, I have little faith in the abilities of our Metropolitan Police, and even less in those of the provincial forces." He rang the bell for Billy, our page, and wrote and handed him another note, to be sent as a telegram to the police inspector in Lichfield.

" You are prepared to stay in the Midlands for a few days ? "

" It is the work of a minute for me to be ready," I answered him.

" Good. If I recall correctly, there is an express train from Euston at fifty-three minutes past the hour, which will bring us to the Trent Valley station before the day is too far advanced. Be so good as to confirm it in Bradshaw."

I did so, and reported this to Holmes. " I confess that I am confused regarding our client's motives," I said to Holmes. " On the one hand, he appears to love his son with true parental feeling by approaching you in an attempt to establish his innocence. On the other, he seems keen to blacken his name, as shown by his confession that the child is not always truthful. Also, by immediately giving his son in charge to the police, Taylor seems to have assumed that he was indeed the culprit, without bothering to make detailed enquiries."

" Indeed, there are several mysteries about this aspect of the matter, which I believe we can only clear up by means of a visit to the scene. Come, let us make our way to the fair city of Lichfield."

We alighted from the train at Lichfield Trent Valley station, a mile or so from the centre of the city, and hailed a cab to take us to the market square. From there, we walked along Dam Street until we reached number 23, close to the Minster Pool, in which the famous Cathedral was reflected. A police constable was standing outside the door.

Holmes introduced himself to the constable, and requested permission to speak to the Inspector in charge of the case.

" I've read of you in the newspapers, sir," replied the policeman, " and I am sure that you will be welcome, but I have to talk to Inspector Upton first before I allow you inside, if you don't mind, sir." He went inside the house, and re-emerged a minute or so later, followed by a uniformed officer, who identified himself as the inspector.

" Mr. Holmes, sir, welcome to Lichfield. A pleasure to make your acquaintance, though I fear there will be not much for you to do here. We are pretty certain that the young 'un is the culprit."

" You received my telegram ? " Holmes asked him.

" Why, yes sir, we did indeed, and Taylor has presented your card to me. You'll be happy to know that the room is not significantly changed from when Taylor entered it and discovered his wife there, though of course we have removed the body. As I say, there is really no doubt that the lad did it. Shocking case. I can't remember anything like this happening here in the past. This way, sir."

He led the way into the front room of the house, which had been furnished in a good, if provincial style. Holmes stood in the doorway, and surveyed the room's contents, which included a desk by the window, and a chair lying on its side beside it. Some dark stains marked the carpet and the bearskin rug beside the desk.

" The front and back doors of the house were both locked, Taylor told us," we were informed by Upton. " All the windows appeared to be shut, and there was no other means of entrance into the house."

" Unless the murderer came down the chimney, or through the coal-chute, assuming there to be such a thing in this house."

" True enough, Mr. Holmes, as regards the coal-chute, but no such apparatus exists here."

" The case against the boy certainly seems strong, then."

" Strong enough, Mr. Holmes. It's a pity, as he seems like a nice lad. Just a sudden flash of temper, and—" The inspector shrugged.

" Where was the body located ? " Holmes asked. By way of answer, the police officer started to step forward to point out the spot, but was restrained by Holmes. " Please, Inspector," he implored the other, " let us not disturb any further the remaining evidence that will help us determine the murderer, faint as it may be by now."

" Very well, then," replied Upton. " Mrs. Taylor was discovered by Taylor lying on her back, over there by the desk, with her head nearest the chair."

" And yet she had been sitting at the desk, had she not, and the chair was overturned in the struggle with her murderer," mused Holmes to himself. " Strange. Taylor told me that the son, Stephen, had moved the body, but did not provide any details," addressing the policeman once more. " Do you know more ? "

" According to the son's statement, he discovered his mother – rather, his step-mother – lying on her side, and merely moved her onto her back, and at that time determined that she was dead."

" I see," said Holmes. " And where was the knife discovered, according to this statement ? "

" Beside the body, on the floor."

Holmes said nothing, but stood in silence for a moment before dropping to his hands and knees, and pulling out a lens from his pocket, with which he proceeded to examine the floor, crawling forward towards the desk as he did so. At one point he paused, and appeared to be about to retrieve something from the rug, but checked his movements and continued his appraisal of the carpet. The policeman and I watched him from the doorway for the space of about five minutes.

At length he stood up, and dusted his garments, before turning to the desk and using his lens to scrutinise its surface, and the inkwell which still stood open, as well as the pen and the blotter and other objects that lay upon it. "Your men have been busy," he said to Upton, "and have almost, but not completely, destroyed the traces of the events that took place. Nonetheless, some points of interest still remain. May we view the body of Mrs. Taylor?"

"She is at a local Inn, the Earl of Lichfield Arms, in Conduit Street by the market square," replied the inspector. "Though I fail to see that there is much to be learned from a further examination."

"There may well be more than you imagine," answered my friend. "May I advise you that no one is to enter this room until I have finished my investigation?"

I could see that the police officer resented this usurpation of his authority, but he assented to Holmes's request, and instructed the constable at the door to prevent any entrance to the chamber.

The inspector accompanied Holmes and myself on the short walk to the inn, where we were shown to an upstairs room, which had been cleared of all furniture save a deal table on which lay the body, covered by a sheet.

"There has as yet been no autopsy, of course?" Holmes enquired.

On receiving the information that this was the case, he requested and received permission to draw down the sheet and examine the body. There were several wounds to the abdomen, obviously inflicted with a sharp instrument.

"In my opinion," I said to Holmes, in answer to a query of his, "this wound here could well have reached the heart. Of course, without a post-mortem examination, it will be impossible to say with certainty that this is the case, but my experience with bayonet wounds leads me to this belief. Even without the other wounds, this alone could be the cause of death. Shock and loss of blood would also be a factor in the cause of death."

"Thank you, Watson," Holmes said. "As you rightly point out, this cannot be confirmed until an autopsy is performed, and it would be premature to certify this as the cause of death. But, dear me, this murder was committed in a frenzy of passion, was it not? I count at least five major wounds, and several grazes where the weapon has almost, but not completely, missed its mark." He bent to examine the ghastly wounds more closely. "Watson. Your opinion on the nature of these? Specifically, how they were delivered."

I, in my turn, bent to the cadaver. " Delivered to the front of the body, with the blade entering from the right and above for the most part."

" That was also my conclusion," said Holmes. " Mrs. Taylor appears to have been quite a tall woman, Inspector. Can you confirm that? "

" I believe she was some five feet and seven inches in height." Holmes made some notes in his pocket note-book.

" And the boy? "

" He is somewhat small for his age. I would put him at a little under five feet."

" And it would take considerable strength, would it not, Watson, to cause these wounds? "

" Indeed so," I confirmed. Holmes bent to the body once more, and eventually stood straight and addressed Upton again.

" What was the state of the boy's mind when the constable took him in charge, Inspector? "

" According to the constable's report, he was shaking. The constable judged him to be in a state of fear."

" That is hardly surprising," Holmes commented. " And he has not confessed to the murder? "

" He continues to insist that he entered the room and discovered his step-mother lying in her own blood. As to the knife, he says that he has no idea why he picked it up and carried it with him to the scullery where he washed his hands and clothing."

" Those in such a condition often are unaware of their actions," answered Holmes. " I think we may attach little importance to this. You are satisfied, of course, that the knife discovered with the boy is indeed the murder weapon? "

"Why, what else could it be?" asked Upton in surprise. "You may see it for yourself at the station. I take it you will wish to interview the boy?"

"If that is permitted."

"Surely," replied the inspector. "Though I fear you will be wasting your breath if you are attempting to establish his innocence."

"We shall see," answered Holmes. "By the by, where is Taylor now? He did not seem to be in evidence at the house."

"He has left the city for the day. He told me that he had urgent business in Birmingham to which he must attend, and I allowed him to go there."

"I have a feeling that you may never again set eyes on Mr. Henry Taylor," Holmes told him.

"Why, what can you possibly mean?" asked Upton in surprise and dismay. "Do you mean that he means to do away with himself in despair? Have I let him go to his self-inflicted death?"

"By no means," smiled Holmes. "The truth will prove to be at once simpler and more complex than that."

"You have me scratching my head," said Upton in puzzlement, and led the way to the police station, where he produced for our inspection the knife that had been discovered by the body.

Holmes produced his lens, and examined the blade, covered with now-dried blood, closely. "It is impossible to say with any certainty without knowing the exact position and location of the knife when it was found," he announced at length, "but it seems to me that this knife was not the murder weapon. Has it been identified, by the way?"

"Yes, Taylor recognised it as one of the knives used in the kitchen for preparing food. The maid, Anne Hilton, likewise identified it, as indeed does the boy Stephen. But why do you say that it is not the murder weapon. Surely it is obvious?"

"Too obvious," retorted Holmes. "Two factors lead me to this conclusion, which, as I said, must remain tentative for now. Firstly, the blade, as you will observe, is almost triangular in shape, with a narrow point, and widening towards the hilt."

" That is a common design," answered Upton, " and I fail to see how you can make anything of that."

" Ah, but the wounds on the body were performed using a narrower blade. Either that, or this knife was not inserted to its full depth."

" In which case, it could not have reached the heart, as I surmised," I interrupted.

" Precisely, Watson," he confirmed. " And in that event also, the blade near the hilt would not have been coated with blood, at least not to the even degree that blade exhibits. To me, this has all the appearance of a knife that has been deliberately smeared with blood, possibly not even human blood, and left beside the body, while the actual murder weapon is still missing."

" But no other weapon was found in the room or indeed in the house," protested the policeman.

" And there was no one else in the house other than the boy and his step-mother, according to the boy's story, and that of Taylor," Holmes added. " And the boy never left the house, it would appear."

" You continue to produce puzzles, Mr. Holmes. Do you wish to see the boy now ? "

" Thank you, yes."

I will not dwell for long on the exchange between the poor child and Holmes. The boy was clearly in a wretched state, and though he freely admitted the bad feeling that had recently sprung up between him and his late step-mother, and confirmed the story that had been told to us by Taylor, he emphatically denied her murder. The only new detail he added that we not had previously heard was his account of having heard some noises, as of something heavy falling, a few minutes before he entered the drawing-room. He appeared to be a somewhat nervous youth, of somewhat slender build, and undersized for his age.

Holmes produced his notebook, and asked the lad to draw a rough sketch of the room and the position of the body and the knife when he discovered them. Examining the diagram, he complimented the boy on his skills, for which he received a faint smile from the youth.

" And there were no papers on the desk or lying around the room ? " he asked the boy by way of concluding the interview.

Stephen Taylor shook his head. " Nothing like that, sir," he answered.

" Thank you," Holmes told him. " I am confident," he added, to Upton's obvious astonishment, " that you will be out of here very soon."

" What in the world did you mean by raising the boy's hopes with false promises like that ? " Upton asked Holmes, almost angrily, when we were walking back to the inspector's office. " That was indeed a cruel jest to play on the poor lad, was it not ? "

" No jest," Holmes told him. " I believe that we can have this whole matter cleared up in a matter of hours. May I make a request that you send word to Sutton Coldfield police station, and ask them to send a Mr. Henry Staunton to you for questioning in connection with this matter ? A house in Victoria Road, I believe, will find him."

" In the name of all that's good, Mr. Holmes ! " exclaimed the policeman. " What on earth can you want with such a person ? And how do you come to know of him ? "

" I feel that he will be most germane to your enquiries," Holmes answered him. " As to how I have knowledge of him, why, the answer stood as clearly before you as it did to me."

" Very well. If this request had come from any other source, I would have regarded it as the ravings of a madman, but your reputation, Mr. Holmes, precedes you, and I will do as you ask, though I fail to comprehend your reasoning on this matter."

" While we are awaiting the arrival of Mr. Henry Staunton," Holmes said to Upton, " we will find lodgings. I doubt if we will wish to be accommodated in the Earl of Lichfield Arms. I have heard The George spoken well of by an acquaintance who passed through this city once."

" The George is indeed a pleasant hostelry. I will send for you there once Staunton, whoever he may transpire to be, arrives here."

" Come, Watson," Holmes said to me, and we passed through the streets of this old city to the George, where we secured a

most comfortable room, and bespoke an early dinner, antici-
pating the arrival of Staunton.

Over the course of our meal, I attempted to interrogate
Holmes regarding what he had discovered, and the conclusions he had reached, but much to my chagrin, he refused to
be drawn, and discoursed instead on the life of Doctor Samuel
Johnson, a native of the city that we were currently visiting, whom he claimed had also been an acquaintance of the
long-deceased Joshua Holmes. I could follow his reasoning
with regard to the knife, and was forced to agree that the knife
that had been discovered by the body was in all probability not
the murder weapon. It also seemed to me that the boy was unable to have inflicted the wounds that had caused the death of
Mrs. Taylor, by reason of his under-developed physique.

We had just finished our meal when a uniformed constable
entered the dining-room, much to the consternation of the
hotel waiters, and informed us, with a strange smile, that Mr.
Henry Staunton from Sutton Coldfield was now at Lichfield
police station.

"Inspector Upton's compliments to you, Mr. Holmes," he
added with a broad grin. "He thanks you for your discovery of
Mr. Staunton, sir."

We followed the constable to the police station, where we
encountered the inspector who wore the same smile as his
constables. "Mr. Staunton is in the next room," he told us, and
opened the door – to reveal Mr. Henry Taylor !

"What is the meaning of this ?" I asked. "Are Henry
Staunton and Henry Taylor one and the same person ?"

"Indeed so."

Our client's face had turned red with anger. "How the devil
did you discover all this ?" he demanded of Holmes.

"You thought that by removing and destroying the letter
that your second wife had written to your first wife, informing
her of Mrs. Taylor's new-found knowledge of Mrs. Staunton,
you had removed any possible evidence of a motive, did you
not ? But you failed to notice that she had blotted the envelope. Your true name and address were clearly visible on the
blotter, reversed, naturally."

"My God ! " Staunton sank back in his chair.

" Bigamy, eh ? " said Upton. " Well, my lad, we can have you for that."

" And add to that the murder of Martha Taylor, as I suppose we must call her," said Holmes, " though I fear her actual marital status must be in some doubt."

" I never meant to kill her—" cried Staunton, and bit off the words as they came out of his mouth.

" Oh, but I think you did indeed kill her, and then worse," said Holmes. " In my whole career, I have hardly ever encountered such a cold-hearted diabolical piece of treachery."

" Your proof ? " taunted the other.

" It would be easy to prove to a jury that the blows that killed Martha Taylor were not inflicted by the knife found beside her body. The blows that killed her could only have been inflicted by a stiletto blade, as any wide blade would have been stopped by the ribs. Once that doubt had been established, your son would walk free. No other possible weapon was discovered in the house. You may have thought you were being clever by killing with one weapon and leaving another, more plausible instrument to implicate an innocent party – your very son – but you ignored elementary anatomy."

" That might prove my son's innocence, but it hardly establishes my guilt," protested Staunton defiantly.

" True," agreed Holmes. " However, there is the matter of the missing seal from your watch chain, the empty clasp of which I noticed when you visited us in Baker-street." Staunton looked aghast and grabbed at the chain in question with a look of horror on his countenance. " No, it did not fall off somewhere else. It is currently pressed into the bearskin rug in the front room of the house in Dam Street. Did your men overlook this, Inspector ? Pressed in there by the weight of a body lying on it, and covered with blood. It is impossible that in that state it was ever there before Martha Taylor was struck down.

Let me reconstruct the events for you, gentlemen. Mr. Staunton took a fancy to have more than one name, and more than one family. It happens to some men. I am myself not that way inclined, but I regard this aberration with an amused tolerance. As Mr. Taylor, he was widowed, and he removed himself to Lichfield, where he cast about for a new partner. Mrs.

Staunton is obviously not suited as the ideal sole helpmeet and companion of his life—"

" Leave her out of this, damn you ! " exclaimed Staunton, angrily.

" By all means," answered Holmes with an equable air. " In any event, Miss Martha Lightfoot fitted the bill, and she appears to have been a good match, and an excellent parent to the two children of the first Mrs. Taylor."

" The best," sighed Staunton, with what seemed to be genuine regret.

" But she became suspicious of her husband's frequent absences, which were not always as concerned with his supposed business as she had first thought. Somehow, perhaps by means of a private detective, or some other method, she discovered that her beloved supposed husband was maintaining another establishment in neighbouring Sutton Coldfield, and she decided to confront her husband with the knowledge. At this time, a coolness developed between her and Staunton's son.

" She told Staunton that she was about to reveal his double life, and confront his other wife with the knowledge of her existence. Frightened that he was about to be ruined, and quite possibly prosecuted, for his duplicity, when he returned home and saw his wife writing at the desk, he immediately guessed what she was about. He quietly let himself into the house and went to the kitchen for a knife. Entering the drawing-room, he confronted his wife, who was indeed writing the fatal missive. A violent argument ensued, during which he produced the kitchen knife, and in defence, she snatched up the long paperknife that lay in its holder on the desk. You really should have taken better note of that empty knife-holder, Inspector."

" Since we believed the murder weapon had already been discovered, it seemed to be of no importance," answered the abashed police agent.

" Well, well. Be that as it may. In the ensuing struggle, which took place in near-silence, the kitchen knife was dropped, and the stiletto paperknife passed from Martha Taylor to Henry Staunton, who in his blind fury used it to kill the unfortunate woman. It was at about this time that the seal was ripped from the watch-chain. The fastening is twisted on both the chain, and the seal itself, and I have no doubt that you will easily find a perfect match there, Inspector.

"You will remember Doctor Watson's characterisation of the fatal wounds, and also note the fact that Staunton here is left-handed. His son is right-handed, as I ascertained when I asked him to sketch the scene of the murder. The wounds could only have been inflicted either by standing behind the victim and stabbing her by reaching over her shoulder, stabbing downwards – a most awkward way of delivering the blows, and one which is contradicted by the position of the body's head relative to the chair – or alternatively if the victim was standing, by stabbing with the murderer facing his victim, using an overhand grip – less effective, perhaps, than the underhand grip, but ultimately fatal. Am I correct so far, Staunton ? " He received no answer, other than a silent, grim-faced nod, and continued.

" Being faced with the undisputed fact that he was now the killer of the woman with whom he shared his house, his principal object now was to avoid detection. He quickly snatched up the fatal letter in its envelope, which had only just been addressed and blotted before he entered the room. He knew his son was in the house, and his twisted mind instantly conceived a way in which he could escape blame, and transfer it to his own flesh and blood."

" A foul and heinous act," growled Upton.

" He secreted the stiletto, and smeared the kitchen knife with blood before letting the chair fall with a crash, to alert the boy and to draw his attention, before letting himself out of the front door and silently re-locking it. He disposed of the murder weapon, and I have no doubt that if you drag the Minster Pool at the end where Dam Street runs close by, you will discover it there. The rest you know."

" I never meant to kill her ! " wailed the unfortunate Staunton. " It was my intention only to prevent her from sending the letter."

" That's as may be," replied Inspector Upton in stony tones. " But instead of confessing to your guilt like a man, you attempted to fasten the crime on a poor defenceless young man – your own flesh and blood at that."

" I never meant him to go to the gallows," cried Staunton, in an agony of distress.

" Maybe you did not," answered the police agent. " But I will make every effort to ensure that you make that trip yourself. Thank you, Mr. Holmes. You have saved a young man's life, and prevented a grave miscarriage of justice."

" All I ask," replied Holmes, " is that my name not be mentioned in connection with this case. Inspector Upton shall take all the credit for the observations and deductions, and the bringing to justice of Mr. Henry Staunton. Come, Watson, our task is done, and I think that we shall sleep well tonight at the George before our return to London on the morrow."

" But why in heaven's name," I could not refrain from asking Holmes as we made our way from the police station, " did Staunton ask you to clear the boy's name, given that this inevitably would lead to the proof of his own guilt ? "

Holmes shook his head. " He believed that he had committed the perfect crime, and that suspicion would never fall on him," he said. " We may see his retaining me as an act of bravado and cocking a snook at the police. After all, who would believe that a man who had hired the foremost man in his field to clear his son's name would himself be guilty of any wrongdoing ? Unfortunately for Mr. Henry Staunton, he underestimated my abilities, as have so many others in the past. It is their loss."

" And the world's gain," I added.

Holmes's only answer was his familiar sardonic smile.

THE ADVENTURE OF
THE BLOODY STEPS

ARELY in my experience did one of Sherlock Holmes's cases start in such a way that gave no clue as to its unexpected and dramatic conclusion. It began with a letter addressed to Holmes at Baker-street, which arrived with the morning post one morning in 188–.

After opening the envelope and scanning its contents, he tossed it and the letter onto the table with an expression of disgust.

" Pah ! These constant requests for investigation of matters that more properly pertain to the profession of fabulist than detective will be the ruin of me," he exclaimed.

" Why ? What is it ? " I enquired.

" See for yourself, and tell me what you make of it," he invited me. " Pay no attention to the contents at present, but simply tell me what you see in the letter and envelope themselves."

I picked up the envelope and letter and started to examine them, employing such of Holmes's own methods as I could. " The postmark is from Rugeley, a town with which I am personally unfamiliar, although the name has some resonance," I started. " The address has been written in a hand which appears to be of one unaccustomed to writing, but differing from the educated hand in which the letter has been written, even though the pen and ink appear to be the same. There is a large dirty fingerprint on the back of the envelope, presumably imprinted when the envelope was sealed."

" Excellent as far as it goes, Watson, though you have omitted the most important points. Rugeley is a coal-mining town in Staffordshire, as can be confirmed by the particles of coaldust adhering to the thumbprint – not made by a finger, incidentally, as you will admit if you take the trouble to examine it a little more closely. The reason that the name may be familiar to you is that Rugeley was the town from which the infamous poisoner, Palmer, hailed. He was hanged in 1856, following a trial at the Old Bailey. The aforementioned thumb was used to spread the glue that was used to seal the envelope, and the print, carrying the grains of dust, actually appeared before the envelope was sealed. The thumb, by the way, bears the marks of two cuts or scars which have yet to heal, indicating that the man – for this is undoubtedly the thumbprint of a man – is engaged in a manual occupation, maybe as a miner.

" As you rightly remark, the handwriting of the envelope and the letter differ. The envelope was addressed, we may assume, by the man who provided us with the thumbprint and who sealed the letter, and consigned it to the postal services. The letter on the other hand..." Holmes took the letter back from me, and scrutinised it with one of his lenses, bringing it close to his face before handing it back to me. " Ah, yes. A left-handed female writer. Educated, as you say, quite probably privately, by a French governess."

" How can you say such things ? " I asked, astonished.

" The left-handedness is elementary. The sex of the writer is easily deduced from the aroma of lilies of the valley emanating from the paper."

" And the French governess ? "

" The shapes of the 'a' and 'f' closely resemble the way in which our Gallic cousins are taught to represent them. It is, of course, not impossible that the writer is herself French, but the quality of the language used in the letter would seem to preclude that as a possibility. Read it to me, if you would."

I started to read. " 'St. C____ Rectory, Rugeley, Staffs.' Dated yesterday. 'Dear Mr. Holmes, I feel I must turn to you as my ONLY hope. Once more there is BLOOD upon the Bloody Steps, and poor Christina Collins has been seen once more. My husband, the Reverend Ezekiel Thornby, REFUSES to believe what I have seen WITH MY OWN EYES, and which has been witnessed by MANY OTHERS, and will not allow me or anyone to report this to the police. I URGENTLY require your assistance, and your assurance that I am NOT MAD, and that there is something that threatens us all from beyond the grave. Yours, Anna Thornby, (Mrs.).'" I put down the letter. " What does all this mean ? Who is Christina Collins, and what are these Bloody Steps ? Yet another message from a lunatic, I fear, Holmes."

" Certainly the work of a disturbed mind. And yet she possessed the wit to write to me, and to have another address and post the letter, thereby evading her husband's scrutiny. If this be lunacy, it is of an uncommon intelligence. As to the Bloody

Steps and Christina Collins, I have an inkling that I have heard of this in the past. Have the goodness to pass me the volume by Beardson entitled *Notorious Crimes in the Midlands of England*. I fancy you will find it on the second shelf to the right of the fireplace, between Norton's *Fishes of the North Sea* and Holtzen's *Beobachtungen über Kohlenteer-Derivate*".

I discovered the work in the place that Holmes had described and passed it to him. He flicked through the pages rapidly until he reached the point for he was searching. " Hah ! This is it. In 1839 a young woman, Christina Collins by name, was travelling as a passenger on a canal barge to London. Somewhere close to Rugeley, the bargees, who had been paying her unwelcome attentions throughout the course of the journey, were found to have assaulted and killed her, throwing her body into the canal. They were tried and hanged in Stafford."

" And these ' Bloody Steps' ? "

" The body was found near a flight of steps which lead down from the road to the canal, which is raised above the Trent valley at that point and crosses the river via an aqueduct. It was said that the blood from the body stained the steps when it was carried up them, and no matter how many times the steps were cleansed of the blood, it would always re-appear."

" It seems to be a common superstition when it is a question of old castles and the like," I commented, " but it is interesting that it has survived into this modern age."

" True. I wonder," Holmes mused, " whether we should visit Mrs. Anna Thornby and investigate the matter ? "

" I see no reason to do so,"I objected. " Why should you concern yourself with the fancies of a hysterical woman living in a provincial town ? "

" There is something here that intrigues me," Holmes answered slowly. " I cannot at present put my finger upon it, but beneath the hysteria, there may well be a seed of common-sense and reality. The fact that these visions have been seen by others may well prove to be the divide between imagination and reality. At present, I will not inform Mrs. Thornby of our movements, if for no other reason other than preventing further discord and dissension between husband and wife."

For my part, I suspected Holmes of seeing himself as being

under-employed, and regarding this trip as a diversion which would yield little, if anything, of importance or interest. Nonetheless, I packed my Gladstone with the basic necessities, and on a whim, added my medical bag to my baggage. We set off from Euston, and alighted at Rugeley Trent Valley station where, after a little difficulty, we secured transport to the Talbot Inn, which Holmes informed me had formed the venue for the inquest on the unfortunate Christina Collins.

The evening meal we were served was passable, but the beer, hailing as it did from nearby Burton upon Trent, was excellent. I attempted to follow the conversations of the others drinking at the bar, but found it impossible to follow the heavy accents.

"It is a difficult turn of phrase for outsiders," commented Holmes. "I fear we are less than welcome here."

Indeed, this seemed to be the case. Some of our fellow-drinkers were casting suspicious looks in our direction, and I had no doubt that they were more than somewhat curious as to our reasons for being in Rugeley. One of the fellows made his way over to us, and asked us roughly what we thought we were doing.

"Why, we are here to find out more about the Bloody Steps and the woman who was killed there. We're writing a story for one of the London newspapers," Holmes said easily. "Would you know anything about this story?"

"Not me," said the man, "but Jim over there'll tell you more. It was his granddad, so he says, who carried the poor lass up those steps. London, eh?" He seemed impressed by the mention of the capital, but it was noticeable that there was no deference in his words to us or in the manner of his speech – factors that marked almost all of those with whom we conversed in this town of independent-minded individuals.

The man whom he indicated came over to join us, and Holmes offered to buy another round of drinks for the whole party, an offer which was readily accepted.

"Your health," said 'Jim', raising his glass to my friend. "Aye, it was my father's father who helped lay the poor lass to rest. And he walked across the Chase to Stafford to see them boatmen hang. She's in the churchyard now, you know. Some of the folk here took pity on her and took up a subscription to give her a decent burial and a stone."

"Not that that put her to rest," said the first man. "You tell them what your granddad told you, Jim."

Jim took a look around the room and dropped his voice before continuing. "What he told me was that she kept coming back to the Steps after her killers was hanged. Many folk saw her just standing there. And the blood that dropped on the steps when my granddad and the others carried her – why, it never went away. They tried cleaning it, scrubbing it, but nowt worked. The blood was still there, and it would stay there till Doomsday, that's what they said."

"And is it still there?" Holmes said. It was the first man who answered.

"Now, it's funny you should be asking that. It's been quite a few years since Christina Collins was seen by the steps, and since the blood was seen on them, but for the past month or more—"

"Going on for three months now, Jack," Jim interrupted.

"More like two," Jack countered. "Anyhows, there's been blood on the Steps, so they say, and there's been the figure of a woman seen at the top."

"And have either of you two seen anything?" Holmes asked.

Both men shook their heads. "Haven't been up that way for some time. Now, the rector's wife, she's a strange one anyway, but she was one of the first who said that she'd seen something, according to my missus, who heard it from the cook at the rectory."

"How did she come to be there? The rector's wife, I mean. 'Tain't as if it's on the way to anywhere," asked Jim.

"I'm only telling you what my missus told me was told her by Betty. She said that Mrs. Thornby had been taking some soup or summat to old Lydia Yardley, that being Betty's husband's aunt, and was coming back the short way to the rectory when she saw this figure at the top of the steps. A woman's figure, she said, and she couldn't see the face, but she could make out that it was probably a young woman by the way she held herself."

"And then?"

" She called out to her, but there was no answer, and according to Betty, Mrs. Thornby could see through her. I mean, she could see the trees and all through her. And then she vanished, so she said."

" Interesting, to say the least," Holmes remarked. " Has anyone else seen this apparition ? "

" Just a load of women, and you know how daft they can be at times. They say so, but I dinna believe them. But then there's the blood."

" Ah." Holmes sat forward in his chair. " Tell me more."

" Well, Betty said that Mrs. Thornby felt the steps go slippy-like when she went down them back home, running away from the ghost or whatever it was she thought she saw. The next morning she told Arthur Machin, who does the rectory garden, and he went to look. There was blood there, sure enough."

" Not red paint ? " Holmes enquired.

" Arthur Machin knows blood right enough. He's slaughtered enough pigs in his time to know what he's talking about."

" And the blood is still there ? "

" So they say. Haven't been there myself."

" We should be going there tomorrow," Holmes announced. " Another glass of beer, gentlemen ? "

Despite Holmes's best efforts, it seemed that there was little more to be learned from these men, but, as I could not help remarking to Holmes as we mounted the stairs to our room that all seemed to be based on hearsay.

" Indeed so," he answered me, " but there is hardly ever some smoke without a fire underneath it."

" But surely," I protested, " there can be no such thing as a ghost, and the story of the blood is too preposterous to be believed."

Holmes smiled. " I am sure that Mrs. Thornby is completely sincere in her belief of what she has seen. As to exactly what she has experienced, we will discover more on the morrow."

The next morning saw us walking up the path to the front door of the rectory, following a wretched breakfast at the inn. As we neared the house, I was surprised to see the angry face of a man gesticulating at us through the window of one of the front rooms. Suddenly, the face vanished, and a few seconds later the door burst open to reveal a red-faced middle-aged portly man in clerical dress.

" Be off with you ! " he shouted at us. " I want none of your sort here. My wife is not to be disturbed. Now go, before I call for the police to remove you ! "

" An invitation it would seem churlish to ignore or refuse," remarked Holmes, as we turned and retraced our steps to the gate that took us onto the road. " Let us make our way to the famous Steps. I obtained directions from mine host this morning."

However, we had not gone a few yards before we were accosted by a giant of a man, whose black beard framed a friendly smile. " You'll have been to the Reverend's, then ? "

I nodded agreement.

" He's none too friendly these days, since his wife saw Christina Collins and the blood on the Steps."

" And why would that be ? " asked Holmes.

" Well, he's a queer one, the Reverend. He doesn't seem to understand us at all. Well, I suppose that's not too unusual with them Church folk, especially one like that who only came here just over a year ago. Most round here are Chapel, anyway, like me. But he does like to keep himself to himself. Now take me, I'm the gardener there, and—"

" Ah, you are Mr. Arthur Machin, then ? " Holmes asked.

" You'll have got my name from Jim last night, then ? I met him this morning, and he told me about you two. Newspaper gents from London, come to see the Steps."

" We were just on our way there," I explained.

" Then I'll take tha. Maybe I can tell a few things tha's not heard."

Machin told us more grisly details of the original crime that had led to the blood on the steps, as he had heard them as a boy from his uncle. It appeared that the unfortunate young woman had been on her way from the North to meet her betrothed in London, and had unaccountably decided on canal barge as her means of transport. The bargees at that time were considered to be a wild and lawless section of society, and some claimed to have heard a woman's cries from the barge

as it passed through locks a little to the north of the town. She
had even complained to agents of the company that owned the
barge, and to lock-keepers about the language of the boatmen,
and the unwelcome attentions they had shown to her. There
was little doubt in anyone's mind, it was said, that the bargees
had violated the poor woman, and killed her.

" And these latest doings ? "

" Well, that's a funny one, to be sure. The Reverend Thornby
is a strange one, like I said. Hardly goes out of the house, unless it's to take services in his church, though some say they've
seen him out late at night doing God knows what. Not that I've
seen that, anyway."

"And his wife ? "

" Now she's a poppet, she is. Married the Reverend six
months ago, but they didn't have the wedding here. Somewhere
down south in her town, I heard. Pretty as a picture is that one,
and sweet-tempered with it. Not two things tha sees together
that often, I reckon." Holmes nodded in response. " It was her
what took me on as the rectory gardener only a week or two after she came here, which I do for her when there's not so much
work down the pit, and I have to say I couldn't be working for
a better mistress. Always a please and a thank-you, and there's
never any trouble about money."

" And was it you who posted a letter to London for her the
other day ? "

Machin started. "Why, yes it was. Bist tha the gent she
wrote to ? Mr. Sherlock Holmes ? "

" That is myself," Holmes acknowledged.

" I've read of tha in the papers, then. Tha's the one what
solves those mysteries where the police can't manage it
themselves."

" That is one way of putting it," Holmes smiled.

" Aye, she wrote a letter, but she didn't have an envelope to
put it in without asking himself, and she didn't want him to
know that she was sending it, so she gave me the letter and an
address and the money for the stamp and an envelope."

" I see," said Holmes. " I had deduced that it was something
along those lines, but it is always gratifying to have one's con-
jectures confirmed. And did you read the letter ? "

The other was indignant. " No, I did not. I know better than to read a lady's private letters."

" But did she tell you what it was about ? "

" She did that. It was all about the Steps, which we're just coming to, here on the right, and what she had seen there. The Reverend said to her that she was going mad when she told him about what she had seen, and she didn't want him to know she was writing to you."

" Would you say that she was frightened of her husband, then ? Is he a violent man ? "

" Violent with his fists, you mean ? No, not that. But he has a temper on him, that one. He's not one you'd want to cross."

" We saw something of it just now."

We had reached a point in the pathway where a flight of worn stone steps led upwards. They appeared to be covered with some dark stains.

" This is the blood ? " Holmes asked. Without waiting for an answer, he bent to examine it more closely.

" Aye, it's blood right enough," Machin said.

" I agree. But human blood ? "

" That I couldn't say."

" Nor I," confessed Holmes. " Now, did Mrs. Thornby tell you what she had seen ? "

" Aye. It was a figure of a woman, but it was dark, so she couldn't see the face. Just there, she said to me that it was," he added, pointing to a spot on the bank. " She called out, but there was no answer. And what really worried her was that she could see through it, she said. You see that farmhouse over there ? " and he indicated a building some half a mile distant. " She said the lights was on there, and she could see the lights through the figure."

" And then ? "

" She ran back to the rectory."

" Natural enough in the circumstances, I would have said. And then ? "

" She told me her husband had gone out to visit the work-house. The only person in the rectory was the man they keeps to look after the horses and some of the work around the house, Tom Leighton. He came in from the stables a few minutes after

Mrs. Thornby had come back from the Steps. She told me that she told him what she had seen, and he laughed at her."

Holmes shook his head. " Tut, tut. Most distressing. What manner of this man is this Leighton ? "

" He's not from around these parts. He's from somewhere south of here. Keeps himself to himself most of the time, and we never see him in the Talbot or anywhere. Just doing some of the marketing. Women's work," he added in a tone of some disgust.

" They don't employ a maid for that ? "

" No. Mrs. Thornby has a maid, but that's what they call a lady's maid, who just looks after herself, and don't do that much around the house. Janet came with Mrs. Thornby. Pert little thing she is, though she must be forty if she's a day. And then there's Betty Malpas who cooks for them. And then there's Tom Leighton, who calls himself Thomas because Tom's not grand enough for him, I reckon, does some of the things that maids do, like the marketing, like I said. He worked with Mr. Thornby before he was married, they say, as some kind of secretary, but he does other things around the house as well."

" And what manner of man is he ? "

The other laughed. " Some would hardly describe him as a man. All dolled up in fancy clothes and with his hair just so, even though he's meant to be taking care of the horses and such. Not a man's man, if you take my meaning."

" Most interesting," Holmes answered. " His age and appearance ? "

" He's not that young," was the answer, after some thought. " Perhaps thirty or thereabouts. Not a tall man, perhaps a little shorter than your friend there," indicating me, " and thin as a waif with it." He picked at his thumbnail for a few seconds, and looked up. " What's tha thoughts on the ghost, then ? " Machin demanded.

" I have never seen a ghost," Holmes answered, " but I know those who have claimed to do so. However, on further investigation, I have come across little in the way of evidence to support those claims."

Machin appeared to consider this for a moment. " What

about this here blood, then ? " he asked Holmes. " That's real enough, ain't it ? Tha canna deny that, can tha ? "

" I certainly agree that it appears to be blood, but there is no way for me to determine whether it is human blood or not. It could be pig's blood, for example."

At these last words, Machin started. " Tha's not saying I did it, is tha ? " he exclaimed, with a tone of menace in his voice.

" My dear fellow," Holmes replied easily. " Why in the world would I ever suggest such a thing ? It is true that I remember one of your friends in the public bar last night telling us that you have some experience in slaughtering pigs—"

" That's true enough," replied the other. " I've been doing that since I was a lad of thirteen."

" —but that is hardly a sufficient cause for me to accuse you of playing a trick like that," Holmes continued, as if Machin had not spoken. " After all, you have expressed a warm regard for Mrs. Thornby. It would hardly seem consistent that you would attempt to frighten her with such a childish trick."

Holmes's words appeared to mollify the Midlander, who sullenly nodded his head. " Well, them's the Bloody Steps," he told us, " and you must agree that they have been named right."

" Indeed so," I agreed. I waited for him to leave us, as he seemed anxious to do so, but still remained near us. However, it was soon borne upon me that he was waiting for some sort of financial reward for his actions as a guide, and I pressed a florin into his hand.

" Why, ta," he said, with an air of simulated surprise and what seemed to be a slightly ironic air. " That's most generous of you."

Out of the corner of my eye, I could see Holmes was amused by this exchange. Again, it might be that one who was unacquainted with his moods might be unaware of this, but to my practiced eye, it was unmistakable. As Machin made his way back up the steps to the footpath leading to the Wolseley road, Holmes's face broke into a broad grin.

" Well done, Watson," he said to me. " Now we can examine all of this in a little more detail with no further interruptions." His attention seemed to be focussed on a thorn bush at the bottom of the steps. He examined it carefully, and using a pair of forceps, took something from a twig, and placed it in one of the envelopes he habitually carried with him for occasions such as this. He bent to examine the ground, and again picked up some almost invisible object which he placed in another envelope.

" It is fortunate that it has rained quite recently, making the ground soft and amenable to footprints," he remarked. " Maybe the trifles I have just observed will be of some use."

" Then you believe that Mrs. Thornby saw something ? " I asked.

" Indeed I do, but I am positive that there was nothing in the least supernatural about what she saw." He walked to the steps. "And now for the blood." He pulled a small wooden spatula from his pocket and used it to probe the stains on the stone steps, peering at the result through his lens.

" See for yourself, Watson," he invited me. " It is evident that the blood has been applied on more than one occasion. There are several layers here which are clearly visible."

I took the lens and indeed, it seemed that there were several layers of the dark red stain, indicating that the liquid had been applied at different times.

" What do you think might be the object of this ? " I asked.

" It is reasonably clear to me that the blood, and the 'ghost' that have been seen here are intended as deterrents to prevent investigation of this area. Something is amiss here, and I have my suspicions that the answer lies in the rectory."

" Why on earth should you suspect anything to be amiss there ? "

" I have my reasons," he answered, with a shrug. " Come, I have seen all I need to see at present. Let us make our way up the Bloody Steps."

As we approached the rectory, we could see in front of us the figure of what appeared to be Thornby, the rector, walking away from us in the direction of the town.

" Excellent," commented Holmes. " We may yet meet Mrs. Thornby, and this mysterious Leighton while the ill-tempered rector is away."

We walked along the road, when I suddenly stopped.

" What is this ? " I asked, bending to pick up a glove that was lying by the side of the road. "Someone will be sorry to have lost this." It was a dark kid man's glove, and it hung strangely from my fingers before I passed it to Holmes, who placed it in his coat pocket before we walked on. We entered the rectory garden, and rang the front bell, which was answered by a young man, who from his appearance could be none other than Leighton, who had been described to us earlier. His manner and general clean-shaven appearance could best be described as "unmanly", and his voice when he spoke was one which would not have seemed unduly out of character if it had issued from a woman's mouth.

On our enquiring after Mrs. Thornby, he regretted, with many polite evasions and flourishes, that she was currently engaged in some charitable errand in the town, and she had not informed him when she would be returning.

"Who shall I say has called on her?" he asked us.

Holmes dismissed the question with a negligent wave of his hand, instead withdrawing from his pocket the glove that I had observed him pick up earlier. "Does this belong to anyone here?" he asked, extending the object before him, explaining that we had found it by the side of the road only a few minutes earlier.

The effect on the other was surprising. His pale face drained of whatever colour it had previously possessed, and he stammered as he declared it to be his property. Holmes handed it to him, a faint smile on his face.

We made our farewells, and turned back towards the road, Holmes chuckling quietly to himself. "Well, at least we know the identity of our ghost, do we not?"

"You mean that young milksop?" I asked. "Why, you have hardly set eyes on him," I exclaimed, "and yet you are already accusing him of complicity in some nefarious scheme."

"Complicity indeed, but he is not the guiding spirit, of that I am sure." He chuckled quietly. "However, it is possible that he may be acting as a spirit of some kind."

"I can hardly guess at your meaning," I answered.

"Come, Watson, you do not believe that the spirit of the poor girl who died some fifty or more years ago continues to haunt this place, do you?"

"With so many witnesses, there must be some truth to the story, surely."

"Indeed there probably is some truth. But why do you believe that it must have some sort of supernatural explanation ? This world is strange enough without us bringing the next world in to fill the gaps in our understanding."

"Then you believe that someone is impersonating the ghost ? Leighton ? "

"Precisely."

"And he is spreading blood, maybe pig's blood, using the story of these Bloody Steps for some purpose of his own ? "

"Exactly."

We walked on in silence, when we were accosted by a man whom I recognised as having been one of our conversational partners in the public house the previous evening.

"I didn't want to say anything back there last night," he told us, jerking his thumb backwards in the direction of the hostelry where we had talked. "But there's summat funny going on with that Arthur Machin," referring to the gardener of whom we had so recently taken our leave.

"And what might that be ? " asked Holmes.

"Well, I was telling you last night that he slaughters pigs. It's one of the ways he makes his living, along with the gardening and such like, and he does it for all the folk around here. Now, what he does is to save the blood to make black puddings, and Arthur Machin, well, he's a generous sort of man, and he just gives this blood away to anyone who asks him for it. Well, my missus went round to his house just the other day to ask him for some of the blood, and he told her that he didn't have any. Now that was queer, because he'd killed Bill Stubbins' pig just the day before, and he wouldn't have used all that blood in one day, would he now ? "

"I lack your experience in these matters," said Holmes, but I am sure you are correct. Did he give a reason to your good lady for the absence of the blood ? "

"No, he did not."

"And your conclusion ? "

"Well, I don't like to speak ill of a man like Arthur who I've grew up with since I was a lad, but I reckon he's the one putting the blood on the steps, like."

"It is a theory that certainly has something to recommend it," my friend answered gravely. "What about the ghost that some claim to have seen?"

"Now that's not going to be Arthur Machin, is it now?" replied our informant.

"Why do you say that?"

"Well, he's a big man, isn't he? There's no one in this town who'd ever mistake him for a young lass, even in the dark. Mind you, there's one round these parts who you might take for a girl."

"You are referring to Thomas Leighton?"

"Aye. You've met the b____, then? You'd agree that he'd make a fine figure of a woman?"

"There is definitely something in what you say," Holmes agreed.

"I'll be leaving you with that thought," our interlocutor said to us before turning away.

"Our friend has just stumbled upon the truth, has he not?" Holmes remarked as we walked towards the town. "Leighton does indeed make a perfect substitute for the shade of Miss Collins, does he not? In the dark, with the right draperies, I am sure that he achieves a fine impersonation of a ghost."

"To what end?"

"Ah, it would be premature of me to reveal my thoughts as of now, while they remain as mere suspicions. We must investigate a little further. But halloa! I feel that we are about to meet Mrs. Thornby."

Indeed, a lady was approaching us, whose dress and general demeanour seemed to be other than that of the usual inhabitants of the place.

As she drew near, Holmes tipped his hat to her, and addressed her as " Mrs. Thornby".

"You have the advantage of me, sir," she replied, clearly startled by Holmes's words.

"I am Sherlock Holmes," he explained, "and this is my friend and colleague, Doctor Watson," indicating me.

She gave a little start of surprise. "I do not remember that you informed me that you would be visiting this Godforsaken place."

"In what way can you level that charge at the town, madam?" Holmes asked her. "Your husband is in charge of what appears to be a fine church, and we have spoken to your gardener, Mr. Machin, who seems to be a regular attender at Chapel, from what I could gather. Surely the Almighty has not entirely deserted this place?"

She smiled thinly. "After my previous life in rural Hampshire, I am afraid that this is hardly a desirable location for me. But may I invite you to come into the rectory? The street is hardly a suitable place to hold this conversation, I feel."

"I am afraid that your husband was somewhat emphatic in his expression of his wish that we leave, telling us that you were not to be disturbed."

She smiled, but there was little humour in her expression. "Indeed I have been greatly disturbed by what I have experienced here lately, and I hardly think that your presence will inconvenience me more. In any event, my husband has gone to Lichfield for the day. Allow me to invite you to our home."

We turned towards the rectory for the second time that day, and were conducted to a room which presumably did duty as a sitting-room, meagrely furnished. Mrs. Thornby rang a bell, and requested the maid to bring us tea.

"I must apologise," our hostess told us, "for the state of the place. A parson's stipend is not great, and I have not been long enough here to furnish the place to my liking."

"You are recently arrived here, I take it?"

"Not six months ago," she agreed. "I came here following my marriage to Mr. Thornby, not knowing precisely what to expect. Though I admit that the people here are kind enough in their way, this is not a place I would choose to live of my own volition."

"May I ask how you met your husband?"

She paused. "You may consider me a foolish woman, but to tell you the truth I hardly knew my husband when I married him. I am not as young as my appearance might suggest to you, and I had a horror of being left on the shelf, as the saying has it.

" He visited my parents' village for a week's holiday, and paid his attentions to me. I was naturally flattered, and when he proposed marriage to me, I accepted, without being fully aware of what this might entail.

" I suppose that most would term him a good husband, but oh, this place..." Her voice trailed off before she resumed her speech. " The town is filthy with coal dust, I can hardly understand what the people are saying, and there is no society here worthy of the name. And then, to add to all this, there is the apparition of the Bloody Steps."

" May I ask you about that ? "

" Of course. This was my original reason for inviting you here, was it not ? " Holmes nodded, and she continued, " I had been visiting one of my husband's parishioners, a Miss Yardley, taking her some hot soup, and I decided to take the path by the canal—" Here she made a gesture in the direction of the place from which we had come. Holmes assured her that we had been there ourselves, and we were familiar with the location.

" Very well, then," she continued. " It was dusk, and I was approaching the steps – that is to say, the ones that they term the " Bloody Steps" – I saw a slight figure standing at the foot of the steps. It was dressed in a black cloak or some sort of wrapper. Though the face was partly obscured by the cloth, a breeze blew the cloth aside, and the face was revealed briefly."

" A woman's face ? "

" It was visible for only a short time, and the light was dim, but yes, I believed it to be a woman's face."

" And what led you to believe that the figure you saw was in some way supernatural ? "

" Mr. Holmes, I do not consider myself to be unduly imaginative, or in any way fanciful, but I had an impression of pure evil when I saw that face. Furthermore..." She paused, and Holmes invited her to continue. " Furthermore, it was my distinct impression that the figure was – how shall I say this ? – transparent. I distinctly remember seeing the steps and the bushes through the figure. I turned away, perhaps to see if there was anyone there who would be able to confirm what I believed I was witnessing, but there was no one. And when I turned back, the figure was gone."

" Did you approach the place where you had observed the figure ? "

" I confess that I was too frightened to do so. I stood, rooted to the spot, for what seemed an eternity, but in truth was probably no more than a minute. When I examined the place where I had seen the figure, there was no trace of anyone's having been there."

" And then ? "

" I raced up the steps to the rectory. When I entered, I called out to my husband, but he was not present. His secretary, Leighton, was also absent, but came into the house from the stables some fifteen minutes later, and I told him what had occurred."

" His reaction ? "

" I am sorry to say that he simply laughed at me, and regarded my tale as a foolish woman's fancy."

" Indeed, most distressing," I commented.

" Upon his scornful dismissal of my fears, I took myself to my room, and told the tale to my maid, who was more sympathetic than Leighton. She administered some sal volatile and I recovered myself somewhat. When my husband returned from his duties, I told him all that had passed, but he refused to credit my words, and brusquely informed me that I must have been mistaken."

Holmes's next question to Mrs. Thornby came as a surprise to me. " What did Machin have to say to you when he heard about this ? " he asked.

" Why, I never told him anything, but my maid Janet talked to our cook, Betty Malpas, and she must have been gossiping with her, and that is how the story will have reached Machin's ears.

" I met him the day after I had seen the— whatever it was that I did see that night, and he was kind enough to tell me the grisly story of the poor young woman who was assaulted and murdered there. I may add that he is one of the members of this community who shows the most kindness and friendliness towards me, though he is not a regular worshipper at my husband's church. I had never heard the story before, which makes it more unusual that I saw the figure of a young woman, not knowing the history of the place."

" Indeed," agreed Holmes. " And the blood on the steps ? "

" I had never noticed it before, to tell the truth. It was dark when I saw the figure, and it was impossible to distinguish any details. The only detail I can add is that it felt slippery under my feet."

" I see," commented Holmes. " May I turn to another subject, that of Thomas Leighton ? "

She made a slight *moue* of disgust. " If you must, though I hardly see what he has to do with this matter."

" It is my habit to gather as much information as possible on the circumstances and the people surrounding an incident. It is impossible to ascertain at the start of an investigation exactly which matters will prove trivial, and which vital. What can you tell me about him ? "

" He acts, as I am sure you have been informed, as secretary to my husband, though I hardly feel that the demands of the parish here justify such a position. He also does some other work around the house, such as would be expected of a female domestic, which may be considered an eccentricity on my husband's part to employ him in this way. Although, as I have mentioned, the stipend here is far from generous, it is my husband rather than the Church who is responsible for his board and keep, and his salary. He had joined my husband's employment here a little time before our marriage, though he behaves with a familiarity that would suggest a longer association."

" I see. And your feelings towards him ? "

She leaned forward and lowered her voice to an almost inaudible level. " There is something about him that makes my flesh creep. He is, in a word that we used as girls at school, ' sneaky'. One never knows where he will be, listening at doors, or peering through windows. To be frank with you, Mr. Holmes, I detest the man. "

As she concluded her speech, Holmes rose from his chair and silently made his way to the door, putting his finger to his lips. With no warning of what he was about to do, he flung open the door to reveal Leighton on the other side, bending down, seemingly having had his ear applied to the keyhole.

" I... I was simply retrieving a handkerchief which I had dropped," stammered the secretary, and indeed, there was a square of white cloth in his hand. He appeared to recognise Holmes and myself, and started. " What are you doing here ? " he demanded of us, but Holmes remained silent. " I swear to you that I heard nothing," he protested.

" Why, no one was accusing you of anything," said Holmes, smiling at him. " However, to avoid any such suspicions in the future, I would strongly recommend that you take yourself away from here." We watched Leighton remove himself and move down the passageway, and Holmes closed the door. " I begin to understand your problem," he said to Mrs. Thornby. " And I believe that it has a material, not a supernatural, cause. With your permission, we will leave you now, and I trust I will be able to supply you with a satisfactory explanation of the situation within twenty-four hours. For now, I can assure you that your imagination is not playing tricks – though I have a strong suspicion that there are tricks being played of a very corporeal nature."

" Why, thank you, Mr. Holmes,"said our hostess. " You have already relieved my mind immeasurably. My one fear is that the Leighton creature will inform my husband of your presence here, and that he will become angry with me."

Holmes's face took on a look of concern. " You fear your husband's anger ? " he asked.

" He dare not strike me," she answered. " He knows full well that my money and property are mine and mine alone, and I have the power to deprive him of their use."

Holmes and I resumed our seats. " This would seem to add a new angle to the problem," he commented. " You have not said so in so many words, but you would appear to imply that your husband married you primarily on account of your money."

She bowed her head. " I did not want to say this, but I fear it to be the case. As I say, I was impetuous in my affection for him, and perhaps I failed to perceive his true motives in marrying me."

" Would you describe him as an affectionate spouse ? " I asked her.

" Hardly that, I fear. Indeed, you might well describe me as a neglected wife. I have attempted – oh, how I have tried – to be a good rector's wife. I visit the sick, I attend the services and offices at which he officiates. I provide him with as comfortable a home as our circumstances allow, but still I wait in vain for a sign of his affection. Why, I believe that he thinks more of that Thomas Leighton creature than he does of me." She buried her face in her hands, and appeared to be weeping silently.

"My dear Mrs. Thornby," I said to her, rising, and placing a hand on her shoulder. "You must be strong, and place your faith in Sherlock Holmes here. If there is one man in England who can unravel the problems that you currently face, it is he."

She raised her face to me with a look of gratitude. "It is good of you to say so, Doctor Watson."

"In the meantime," I continued, "you may find this cordial to be of value in settling your nerves." I reached in my bag for a bottle that I handed to her. "Three drops in a glass of water to be taken after meals."

She received it from my hand with a suitable word of thanks, and we rose once more to leave the house.

Once we had left the premises, Holmes turned to me. "I trust that the sedative you gave to her will have no adverse effects."

I laughed. "I will be most surprised if it does," I answered him. It consists of a little vinegar, and some caramel dissolved in water. I find it to be most efficacious with women who are undergoing emotional upheaval, such as Mrs. Thornby is suffering at present."

"Excellent, Watson. Your oath to do no harm is obviously well observed in this case. Now," rubbing his hands together, "tell me what we have learned today from Mrs. Thornby, when we combine it with the information we have received from other sources."

"We appear to be dealing with a marriage of convenience," I answered. "She complains of a lack of attention to herself, while the Leighton creature, as she terms him, appears to occupy a closer place in her husband's affections. I do not wish to make assumptions here, but—"

"Quite so," Holmes cut me off short. "Let us not turn our speculations in that direction. We can assume, however, that

Thornby and Leighton were acquainted with each other prior to the former's removal to this town, can we not ? Our next task is to discover where they might have met, and under what circumstances. I wonder," he continued, " if there might be a library in this town with a copy of *Crockford's* ? "

We enquired of a passer-by and were informed that the Free Jubilee Library was situated in Bow-street. It proved to be relatively well-stocked, and after hearing Holmes's request, the librarian directed us to the shelves where the clerical directory was located.

Holmes turned the pages, and with a grunt of surprise, looked at me. " Watson, how old would you guess the Reverend Thornby to be, based on our brief meeting earlier ? "

" I would not put him above forty years of age," I answered.

" Not sixty-eight ? " Holmes asked, smilingly.

" By no means," I retorted.

" See here," my friend told me, pointing to an entry in the book. I looked, and beheld the name of the Reverend Thornby, and a date of his birth which would indeed make him sixty-eight years old.

" There is more than one Reverend Thornby ? " I suggested, but Holmes shook his head.

" There is but one."

" Then the man in the rectory is not the Reverend Thornby, it is clear. Who is he, then ? "

" I believe his name to be William Brooks."

I was taken aback by this assertion. " How in the world can you say that ? Do you know the man ?."

" It is true that we have never met face to face," Holmes answered me. " On the other hand, it may be that I know a great deal about this man whom we met so briefly earlier. If I am correct in my suspicions, and I fully believe that I am, he is one who has proved most successful in his profession, which is that of 'fence', or one who disposes of stolen goods. I had my eye on him two years ago, but he suddenly dropped out of sight, and I was unable to determine where he had gone. Obviously he took on this new identity, and moved himself here, where there were few checks made on his antecedents."

" It seems incredible that he should be able to pass himself off as a clergyman," I said. " Could a common criminal such as he convince a congregation that he was an ordained minister of the Church ? "

" Not as difficult for him as it might be for some," Holmes said to me. " He has had the advantage of a University education, though he never took his degree, being sent down for a series of petty thefts from his fellow-students, according to my sources."

" I can scarcely credit it. But how do you come to suspect this Brooks of this impersonation ? And what is his purpose here ? "

" One question at a time, my dear Watson," Holmes admonished me. " As to his identity, that hinges on the glove that we discovered in the road, and passed to Leighton at the rectory. I must send a telegram to Hopkins at the Yard. His answer will confirm my suspicions. Come, to the post-office."

Holmes sent his reply-paid wire, with the answer to be delivered to the Talbot, where we repaired to await the answer, and to take our midday meal.

As we sat over the roast pork that mine host had provided for us, the pig from which it was taken probably having been slaughtered by Machin, I asked Holmes about his further conclusions regarding the ghost that Mrs. Thornby claimed to have seen.

" I do not deny that she must have seen something. She appears to me to be a sensible woman, unlikely to imagine something entirely. However, I do consider that her imagination has caused her to misinterpret various natural phenomena." Here Holmes reached in his pocket, and extracted an envelope, which I recognised as one which he had used to store something that he had picked up from the Bloody Steps. " What do you make of this ? " he asked me, laying the scrap of cloth before us on the table.

I examined the item as minutely as possible under the circumstances, but was unable to provide any answer, other than to reply that it seemed to be a piece of dark gauze.

" Precisely, Watson," was Holmes's reply to me. " At most times of the day it would appear to be part of a solid cloak, but in the flickering gloom of the evening, it would at times appear to be transparent. Hence, Mrs. Thornby would perceive it at times as being a solid figure, and at other times as a ghost."

" And the feminine face ? What woman would play such a trick ? "

" It was no woman that Mrs. Thornby saw," Holmes said meaningfully. " As you know, we have encountered the 'ghost' twice today already, and I expect to have further dealings with him again before the day is out. See here." Upon his saying this, he extracted the second envelope from his pocket, and placed the object that he had removed from the steps on his plate. " See here," he invited me, passing his high-powered lens.

I looked, but could see little. " I see a seed-like object embedded there, but I fear I do not recognise it."

" It is a seed of the tree *Araucaria araucana*, commonly known as the monkey-puzzle tree."

" Is there anything strange about it ? The area is surrounded by trees."

" Indeed so, but there were no trees of that genus to be seen in the area. Indeed, there is only one such tree that I have observed in this town. It is in the rectory garden."

" Is it not possible that Mrs. Thornby unwittingly carried it from the garden and deposited it there ? I cannot see this seed as proof of anything."

" I would agree with your conclusion, Watson, were it not for the fact that the seed has been partially embedded in the dried blood coating the step, thereby implying that it was dropped there when the blood was still in a liquid state, probably by the man who spread the pig's blood on the steps."

" Arthur Machin ! " I exclaimed. " He is the rectory gardener, and he is the one man in this town who seems to have access to the pig's blood and the tree."

" Why do you not assume that the man who impersonated the ghost is also the one who spread the blood ? "

" I do not consider it likely," I told my friend. " Leighton seems to me to be too much of a milksop to engage in some such practices."

Holmes said nothing in reply, but merely smiled, and reapplied himself to his food. We had nearly finished our meal, when the landlord approached us, bearing a telegram, which he handed to Holmes, who tore it open with a grunt of satisfaction.

" Excellent ! " he commented. " I have always maintained that Hopkins is, together with Gregson, one of the rising young stars in the firmament that is Scotland Yard. He has risen to the occasion admirably. Here, read this."

He passed the telegram to me and I read the following, " BROOKS LEFT HAND TWO SMALLEST FINGERS MISSING." I paused. " I understand the meaning of this, but who is William Brooks, and what is he to us here ? "

" Ah, there I believe my professional knowledge puts me at an advantage over you. As I was saying to you earlier, William Brooks is well enough known in his trade, which is that of ' fence', or receiver of stolen goods. Perhaps I should say that he was well-known, as he disappeared from sight somewhat above eighteen months ago.

" Now, it is important not to draw conclusions before all the facts are known, but since Brooks' disappearance, within this last year, there have been several robberies recently in provincial cities, where the purloined items have been offered for sale in London a matter of weeks later, all through the same agency."

" Then the police have simply ignored this ? "

Holmes shook his head. " Naturally, they have questioned the owner of the shop where the articles were for sale, but were unable to prove that the purchase was anything other than legal, even though the items were indisputably those which had been stolen in Manchester, Liverpool and Birmingham. All attempts to locate the supposed vendor of the items have failed, invariably leading to a false address. Without further proof, the police have been unable to act."

" If I remember correctly, the Reverend Thornby has been rector here for just over a year, according to what we read in the library."

" Indeed."

" But pray, why did you ask Hopkins about the missing fingers ? "

" Because Leighton has all his fingers still."

" I fail to understand you."

" You remember the glove that we picked up in the road and we presented to Leighton ? "

" Naturally."

" Was it a left-handed or a right-handed glove ? "

" I cannot remember."

" It is these little matters, Watson, that may send a man to the gallows, or allow him to prove his innocence and walk away from the dock as a free man. In this case it was a left-hand glove, made by Mercer's of London. Also, as you may have noticed, the two smallest fingers of the glove were packed with cotton-wool, such as might be used to disguise the fact that the wearer was missing those fingers from his hand.

" When we presented Leighton with the glove, I took care to examine his left hand, and it transpired that none of his fingers were missing. There is, to our knowledge, only one other adult male in the household, Thornby, so I concluded that the glove was his. This deduction was also partially confirmed by the confusion displayed by Leighton on receipt of the article."

I turned over these facts in my mind. " And the connection with Brooks ? "

" I had heard it mentioned that Brooks was missing some fingers, but I had not heard which fingers, or on which hand. The story is that he lost them as the result of a bloody dispute with an Amsterdam jeweller over the price of some diamonds that he was attempting to sell. I knew that he had been arrested in the past, and that Scotland Yard would have a record of his physical characteristics, including any missing fingers, and I therefore telegraphed Hopkins to obtain that information."

" I believe I am beginning to see the plan," I said. " Somehow, as you suggested earlier, this Brooks has taken on the identity of a genuine priest who was appointed as rector here, in order to carry out some nefarious scheme. Where is that priest who was appointed here ? "

Holmes shook his head. " I fear the worst. Brooks and his operations are, I believe, controlled by a man who sits in the centre of the criminal life of this country like a spider in his web, pulling a thread here and spinning another trap there. He and his organisation will stop at nothing to achieve their foul ends. I fear that the murder of a priest would mean little or nothing to them. I have yet to make my final reckoning with this man, but I believe that our paths will collide sooner or later."

" Surely," I objected, " those making the appointment of the rector would have noticed some discrepancy between the man who presented himself as Thornby, and the man whose description we read in *Crockford's* ? "

" It is quite possible that this is not the case," Holmes said. " According to what we read, the Reverend Thornby was previously the incumbent of a remote parish in Northumberland. It is extremely unlikely that anyone here would have personal knowledge of the man. In any case, it is a simple matter to add or subtract a decade or two from one's age. I have done it myself, you may recall, with some success."

" But why should Brooks choose to make his home here, of all places ? " I asked. " And who is Leighton ? "

" As to the first, consider," my friend said to me, " the location of this town, and its nature. We have here a station on a direct line which takes us to the south directly to London and to the north to Crewe, and hence to Manchester and Liverpool. We also have a line into Birmingham, and some of the major towns to the north of that city. It is not too far from the Great North Road or from Watling Street, which passes close to Lichfield, less than ten miles from here. Consider also the canal which we have just visited. From there, it would be a simple matter to transfer the proceeds of a robbery, for example, from any part of the country to any other part."

" One would hardly suspect this small Midlands town to be the nexus of the traffic in the country's criminal proceeds, but I can well believe it now that you make the case. And you believe this to be so ? "

" Stanley Hopkins was kind enough to lay the little problem regarding the proceeds of the robberies that I mentioned earlier before me, and I was of the opinion that there existed a central point at which the goods were collected, and then sent on. Little did I suspect, however, that in coming here I would discover this to be the central point.

" As to the second question, there have been rumours concerning a certain indelicacy associated with Brooks' private life. I have little doubt that Leighton, or whatever his true name may be, along with whatever other moral failings he may possess, has links to the criminal organisation to which I alluded just now, and acted as Brooks' accomplice in the past, prior to their removal to this place."

" I guess we may take it that Thornby, or Brooks, as I suppose we must term him, took a wife on account of her money and her property ? "

" Of that, I am sure. The marriage would also provide a cover of respectability for his operations. An unmarried man living alone with one such as Leighton, would be certain to set tongues wagging in the town."

" The purpose of the ghost and the blood on the steps was to deter visitors to the place ? "

" Of course. It is almost certain that the proceeds of the burglaries were transported by canal to this place, prior to distribution to other parts of the country, or to ports. For example, diamonds could easily be sent to Amsterdam for disposal."

" A truly ingenious scheme. Who would ever dream of searching canal barges for stolen goods ? "

" Who indeed ? Their lack of speed would actually prove an advantage in this capacity. By the time they reached this place from their point of departure, the hue and cry would have died down."

" And the booty would be taken to the rectory, and stored there before being passed on ? "

" We may assume so. Again, a perfect hiding place. What police agent would dream of searching the home of a man of the cloth for jewellery purloined from a house some seventy miles distant ? "

" And what are we to do ? We have no warrant for his arrest or to search the house."

" We must wait by the Bloody Steps tonight and take our chances. There was a robbery in Sutton Coldfield not a few nights ago which bears all the hallmarks of the others. It is quite likely that the proceeds have been transferred to a nearby canal and will be making their way to this point, either tonight or in the next few days."

" And Machin's part in all this ? "

" Machin is implicated, to be sure. But I do not consider him to be guilty. My belief is that the blood was stolen from him, and that he might have had his suspicions as to the guilty party, he was unwilling to make a definite accusation without more definite proof. You may have remarked some bloody footprints at the Steps, which can only have been left when the blood was still in liquid form, meaning that they were the prints of the person who had spread the blood ? "

" I did notice them."

" When we were talking to Machin, I took the liberty of directing him, without his being aware of the fact, to a soft patch of ground. While you were rewarding him for his services as a guide, I examined the prints that he left there, and compared them with the footprints on the Steps. It is impossible that he is the one who left those prints, meaning that it was another who was responsible for the blood."

" Then how is he implicated if he is not responsible for the blood on the steps ? "

" I am sure that the blood came from his stores, and he knows it, even if he did not give permission for it to be removed. Surely you must have noticed his unease when we talked to him, and his genuine concern for Mrs. Thornby's welfare."

" Very well, then, I am your man. At what time should we begin our vigil ? "

" A little before it turns to dusk, which at this time of year is about seven o'clock."

Accordingly, we waited at the inn until that hour, Holmes being of the opinion that there was little to be done until that time, and we set off once more for the Steps. Holmes had, with his customary foresight, located a suitable hiding-place for us on our previous visit, and we concealed ourselves, none too comfortably, behind a thick bush through which it was still possible to observe the canal.

We had waited for perhaps an hour in the gathering gloom before a horse-drawn barge appeared, and was moored by the bank. The horse was turned loose from the boat, though still tethered, and immediately began to graze on the rich grass of the bank by the tow-path.

I felt Holmes nudge me in the side with his elbow, and

looked in the direction in which he was pointing. A dark shadowy figure had appeared on the Steps, and though I knew it to be Leighton clad in a cloak of dark gauze, I realised how Mrs. Thornby had believed that she was able to see through the figure. The slight breeze ruffled the cloth, and my hair stood on end, as I perceived the bushes behind the figure through it.

Leighton, for it was certainly he, made his way slowly down the Steps, and I could now discern another more solid figure at the top.

" It is Brooks," whispered Holmes almost inaudibly. " He is waiting for the 'ghost' to disperse any onlookers."

Leighton slowly approached the barge, with an almost gliding gait, with his impersonation of a supernatural spirit calculated to inspire fear in any observer.

One of the bargees, who had been lounging in the stern of the boat, smoking a pipe, addressed Leighton, but the words were unintelligible at this distance, being spoken in a dialect that was unknown to either Holmes or myself.

Leighton replied, and again we were unable to make out the words, but the boatman stood up, holding in his outstretched hand a small bag.

Leighton took it, and after opening it and apparently examining the contents, reached in his pocket and pulled out what appeared to be an envelope, which he handed to the boatman.

" It is time ! " Holmes said to me, and sprang from our place of concealment with a wild shout. I followed him, adding my own version of a Pathan war-yell to his cries.

As we approached Leighton, the barge's horse, seemingly startled by our noise, appeared to panic, and moved rapidly away. In its haste, it kicked up its hooves, striking Leighton on the head and sending him, seemingly senseless, into the water.

The bargee who had received the money from Leighton instantly threw a rope towards him, but it appeared that the unfortunate man was in no state even to recognise that assistance was being offered, let alone to take advantage of it.

I made as if to strip off my coat and enter the water to save the drowning man, but Holmes restrained me.

" Leave him be," he instructed me. " It will save the cost of a rope and a hangman's fee."

I was somewhat shocked by the callous nature of these words, but could appreciate their sense, and refrained from further action.

A wild cry came from above us. "Thomas ! " wailed Brooks. "Will no one save him ? " He rushed down the steps, and stopped short when he recognised Holmes and myself.

"What are you doing here ? " he demanded, but did not wait for an answer, rushing to the waterside. "Save him ! " he demanded, pointing at the floating body. " I cannot swim. It is you who must rescue him. For God's sake ! "

Holmes stood impassively, still gripping my arm, and restraining me, against all my instincts, from saving the life of a fellow human being, no matter how foul his character.

Having done what he obviously saw as being his whole duty, the boatman sat back, relit his pipe, and placidly regarded the sight of Leighton's body floating in the water.

"You ____ ! " screamed Brooks at the impassive bargee, letting forth a string of invective which I will not bother recording here. "And you ! " indicating Holmes and myself. Without warning, he reached inside his coat and pulled out a revolver. "Take that, you ____ ! " he screamed, loosing off all six chambers in our general direction, though fortunately, his shots all went wild, missing us by several feet at least. The sound of the gun startled the horse, which bolted, tearing out the stake which had tethered it, and it went cantering along the towpath. At the same time, the rooks roosting in the trees were awakened by the noise, and soared into the sky, their hoarse cries almost deafening us.

With a snarl of rage, Brooks hurled the revolver towards us in apparent disgust before fleeing up the Steps at a run.

"And that, I fancy," commented Holmes, " is the last we or anyone will see of the Reverend Thornby. I will wager that we discover his clerical clothing discarded in a ditch on the way to the station. Naturally, the Yard will continue to keep a sharp lookout for William Brooks. And as for you, my lad," turning to the stupefied boatman, " I think you had better come with us to the police."

"You can't make me come with you," objected the other.

"Very true," admitted Holmes. " However, we do have the

name of your boat, and a watch may easily be set up and down
the waterways of England. And without a horse, I do not think
you will be travelling very far."

"All right," agreed the bargee. "But I've done nothing. You
wait till I tell them."

He shouted to someone inside the boat, and a woman
emerged. "I'll be back soon," he informed her. "The horse has
gone off again. Best get Jem or Lizzy to go after her." With
that, he stepped onto the shore and took up a position between
Holmes and me.

"What was in the bag you passed to him?" Holmes asked
him as we set off up the steps.

"God's truth, I don't know. That bag was sealed, and I was
told it was more than my life was worth to open it. All I knew
was that I had to deliver it to that nancy-boy who you saw just
now and I'd get paid. No one told me about any b____ parson
coming along, firing a b____ great gun at me, though."

"How much did they offer you?"

"Twenty pounds is what they told me. I'm hoping that they
got it right."

Holmes let out a low whistle. "Good pay for a few minutes'
work," he said.

"That's what I thought to myself when they asked me," the
boatman told us.

"How many times have you done this, then?" Holmes asked
him.

"That's the first time, honest."

"And it will be the last, I am sure," Holmes commented,
grim-faced.

At the police-station, Holmes explained the facts of the matter to the sergeant on duty, who promised to keep an eye open
for Brooks, and dispatched two of his men to the Steps to recover Leighton's body.

"Though if what you say is true, sir, the Reverend, or whoever he might be, is on his way to London or beyond by now,
and there's not a lot we can do about it."

The boatman continued to protest his innocence, but upon
opening the envelope which he believed to contain the twenty
pounds he had been promised, it was found to hold only four

slips of paper of the same general size as five-pound notes. Upon this discovery, he soon changed his tune, giving a full description of the man who had approached him near Sutton Coldfield with the sealed bag. " I knew he was a wrong 'un from the start," he whined, " but I needed the money. Business has been bad these past few months."

We left him in the police-station, giving what appeared to be a full family and business history for the past two years.

" I fear that the Countess' emeralds, for that is what I believe the bag to contain, are lost for ever," commented Holmes. " I hold out little hope for their recovery from the mud of the canal bed. And now, before we leave the fair town of Rugeley, we have one more duty to perform."

We bent our steps in the direction of the rectory one more time.

" I do not think that Mrs. Thornby will find herself seriously inconvenienced by our visit, despite the lateness of the hour," smiled Holmes.

We were received by Mrs. Thornby in the same room as before, and Holmes explained the events of the evening, and the thoughts and deductions that had led up to them, which she received in silence.

At the end of it all, she leaped up abruptly, and exclaimed, smiling, " Then I am free of him ? The marriage was null and void ? "

" I believe so," said Holmes. " I think that no one could force you by law to remain in a relationship with that man."

She clapped her hands in an expression of pure delight. " Then you have done me a great service, Mr. Holmes. Not only have you set my mind at rest regarding the ghost that I believed I had seen, but you have released me from a bondage that I had come to detest." She suddenly assumed a graver aspect. " It is wicked of me, I know, but I cannot help feeling in some sense glad that Thomas Leighton has met his end."

" I cannot find it in me to altogether condemn your feelings," said Holmes. " But the greater villain who, I believe, is responsible for the death of Thomas Leighton, is Brooks, whom we will quite possibly never see again."

There was silence in the room for a while, which I felt it incumbent upon me to break.

"What will you do now, Mrs. Thornby?" I asked, curiously.

"Oh, do not call me by that name. It was never mine, I see now, and I am glad to revert to the name I had before I contracted that false marriage. I am now once again, from this day forward, Miss Anna Kingsland. And to answer your question, I shall return to my parents, who, I may add, were never approving of my union with— with that man."

"And I trust that this experience of matrimony will not dissuade you from attempting the experiment in the future," I smiled.

"I make no promises in that regard," she said. "I must be content with what Chance will bring me."

"Come, Watson," said Holmes. "We must leave this good lady to herself. Madam," he addressed her directly, "I pray that all will proceed smoothly from now, but should you find yourself in any difficulties vis-à-vis your marital situation, please do not hesitate to get in touch with me, and I will use what powers I have to expedite matters on your behalf."

"Thank you, Mr. Holmes," she answered him, taking his hand. "And thank you, Doctor Watson, for all your care and concern." Her small cool hand lay in mine for a moment, and I considered that it would be a lucky man who could persuade this woman into matrimony.

We left the rectory, and walked some half a mile in silence before Holmes spoke. "There is, I believe, a milk train which leaves here in the early morning and will allow us to arrive in Baker-street in time for one of Mrs. Hudson's excellent breakfasts. In the meantime, let us repair for the last time to the Talbot Inn, and refresh ourselves with a glass or two of that excellent Burton ale and whatever fare we can find there before taking ourselves to the station."

"An excellent idea," I agreed. "I do not think I could face another one of the Talbot's breakfasts."

THE ADVENTURE OF THE HOLLOWAY GHOSTS

Note: This was written as an audio play, hence the lack of stage directions other than sound effects. Also, the characters address each other by name far more than they would if the adventure was being told as a traditional story.

Originally read by the late Steve White, and still available as an audiobook distributed by MX Publishing.

CHARACTERS

Mr. Sherlock HOLMES
Dr. John H. WATSON
MRS. HUDSON
Inspector LESTRADE
Unnamed POLICEMAN
MRS. BAXTER
PC RUDDOCK
Otto SUSSBINDER

SCENE 1: BAKER STREET

[SOUND OF VIOLIN BEING PLAYED
COMPETENTLY BUT TUNELESSLY]

WATSON: Holmes, will you stop that infernal scrap-
            ing? You have been at it for some fifteen
            minutes now.

[VIOLIN STOPS PLAYING]

HOLMES: My apologies. I was considering the case of
            The Countess of Westmererland's rubies.
            The only possible explanation remaining
            is that the maid, Laforge, passed them out
            of the window to the chimney-sweep, her
            accomplice.

WATSON: But he was taken up by the police later that
            afternoon, and his person and his equip-
            ment were searched most minutely. Nothing
            was found.

HOLMES: What the police failed to remember was
            that in the hours between his work on the
            chimneys at Westmereland House, and his
            subsequent detention, he had visited sever-
            al other houses, in which he had ample op-
            portunity to secrete the jewels in locations
            where he knew they would remain undis-
            turbed until his next visit. Possibly he was
            intending to leave them there for up to a
            year. Where the police, and, I confess, I my-
            self, were in error, was in the assumption
            that the gems were purloined for immedi-
            ate disposal. Those directing the operation
            were obviously playing a long game, allow-
            ing the scent to grow cold.

WATSON: Then you do not suspect the maid of being
            the instigator of the theft?

HOLMES: By no means. Despite her chequered past, with which my friend le Villard of the *Sûreté* has been kind enough to provide me, her history shows her to have been more of a cat's paw than a cat, if you will forgive the expression. The sweep himself was no doubt offered a considerable inducement to play his part. I shall send a telegram to Lestrade and inform him of my— [BREAKS OFF] Halloa ! I see the man himself arriving at our front door.

[PAUSE. KNOCK AT THE DOOR]

MRS. HUDSON: [OFF] Inspector Lestrade to see you, Mr. Holmes.

HOLMES: Show him in, Mrs. Hudson.

[DOOR OPENS. FOOTSTEPS]

HOLMES: Ah, Inspector. Come in. Take a seat. Cigar ?

LESTRADE: Good day to you, Mr. Holmes, and to you, Doctor. Thank you, but not so early in the morning. I have come to you today, because we at the Yard are faced with a mystery, and I have to admit to you, sir, that we are baffled.

HOLMES: [LOW] Not for the first time.

LESTRADE: Have you read the newspapers today, Mr. Holmes ?

HOLMES: I am afraid not. I have, however, solved the problem of the Westmereland House robbery. There is no urgency, however.

WATSON: Inspector, are you referring to the incident in Holloway that was reported in the *The Morning Post* ?

LESTRADE: Indeed so, Doctor. The facts of the matter are, briefly, Mr. Holmes, that at half-past eleven the night before last, our constable on the beat was approached by a man who claimed to have heard screams and the

	sound of blows issuing from a house oppo-site his in Lowman Road, which is a quiet residential street—
HOLMES:	—off the Hornsey Road. I am familiar with the area. [BEAT] Pray, proceed.
LESTRADE:	Our man was further informed that this house was apparently unoccupied, and had been so for several months. However, he was told that a light was visible through the windows and, as I mentioned, sounds of an altercation could be heard.
HOLMES:	I take it that he did not enter the house ?
LESTRADE:	He reported that all means of entry were locked. The man who originally informed the constable—
HOLMES:	He has a name, I take it ?
LESTRADE:	Allow me to consult my notebook. [BEAT] The constable recorded his details as Mr. Josef Meyer, widower, originally from Bohemia, aged 54, clerk, resident of Number 18 Lowman Road, which is almost immedi-ately opposite Number 46, which is where the alleged incident took place.
HOLMES:	Thank you. " Alleged", you say ?
LESTRADE:	Indeed. Upon visiting the address in ques-tion, the constable observed that the house appeared to be deserted, and all doors and windows were securely fastened, as he had been told. No sound issued from the house, and there were no lights visible. Meyer, as I was saying, had previously informed our man that this was not the first time he had seen lights in the house from his room in the house opposite, but had assumed that it was the result of tramps having broken into the house and set up camp there for the night. On this occasion, the sound of shouts and screams, and what sounded to his ears

	to be some sort of fight, was sufficient to send him out into the street to seek assistance from our man.
HOLMES:	And I take it that there has been no evidence of tramps using the house in the way suggested by this Josef Meyer ?
LESTRADE:	We have yet to enter the house to determine the truth or otherwise of this assertion.

[HOLMES LIGHTING AND DRAWING ON PIPE]

HOLMES:	Tell me. What was this Josef Meyer wearing when he approached your constable ?
LESTRADE:	I have no idea. You would have to ask Constable Ruddock for the answer to that question.
HOLMES:	I intend to do so, if you wish my assistance in this matter. I also intend speaking to Mr. Meyer and to visit Number 46, in company with you and your men.
LESTRADE:	Thank you, Mr. Holmes.
HOLMES:	There is no time like the present. Come, Watson. Lestrade, let me while away the time on our journey to Holloway by informing you of the location of the Westmereland rubies.

SCENE 2: LOWMAN ROAD

[OUTSIDE NUMBER 46. HORSE-DRAWN TRAFFIC]

LESTRADE: So here we are, Mr. Holmes. Number 46, where the ghostly lights and sounds were observed, is just over there.

WATSON: You surely do not believe in ghosts, Inspector?

LESTRADE: In cases like this, I do not know what to believe. As Mr. Holmes has remarked to us on more than one occasion, when you have eliminated the impossible, whatever remains, however improbable, must be the truth.

HOLMES: Ghosts, my dear fellow, are impossible. Therefore we may eliminate them from our enquiries from the start. I have neither the time nor the patience to provide you with my reasoning on the subject. Come.

[DOOR HANDLE RATTLES]

HOLMES: As you said, Lestrade, it is locked. And the windows all appear to be securely fastened. There is no sign of entry from the front. Let us proceed to the rear of the house.

[THREE SETS OF FOOTSTEPS ON PAVEMENT AND GRAVEL. DOOR HANDLE RATTLES]

HOLMES: Again, locked. Lestrade, you have no objection to my picking the lock, I take it? Excellent. [GRUNTS]

[LOCK SNAPS. DOOR OPENS]

HOLMES: Enter, gentlemen.

[THREE SETS OF FOOTSTEPS ON WOODEN FLOOR]

LESTRADE:	I am glad you are on the side of law and order, Mr. Holmes. I believe that even the most skilful housebreaker in London could not match you in this matter of opening locked doors.
WATSON:	Lestrade, you said that this house is reported to have been unoccupied for several months ?
LESTRADE:	That is correct.
WATSON:	The floor seems suspiciously free of dust and grime for a building that has been empty for so long.
HOLMES:	Very well observed, Watson. Indeed, there is a little dust, but it has been swept, and recently, by a broom, almost certainly that which is standing in that corner.
WATSON:	I do not believe tramps would be so fastidious when it came to the place where they sleep.
HOLMES:	Indeed so. Nor ghosts, Inspector. I have never heard of ghosts that keep their surroundings clean.
LESTRADE:	I confess that the idea of spirits seems more unlikely, given this fact.
HOLMES:	And what of the light that was observed ? Let us see if the gas is still connected. [PAUSE] No, there is no gas here. Did Meyer mention what kind of light he had seen ? No ? We must interview Mr. Josef Meyer soon, before his memory fades.
LESTRADE:	Indeed so. [PAUSE] There is a spot of candle-grease on this table, Mr. Holmes.
HOLMES:	And the table has also been cleared of dust, which means that the candle, wherever it might be now, was lit and placed here relatively recently. I am guessing that it would

be visible from the street if the door to the hallway was open as it is now. Shall we move into the front room ?

[THREE SETS OF FOOTSTEPS ON WOODEN FLOOR. THEY SUDDENLY STOP.]

WATSON: [GASPS] My God, Holmes ! Look there, in the corner !

LESTRADE: Is he dead ?

[ONE SET OF FOOTSTEPS ON WOODEN FLOOR]

WATSON: [OFF] Garrotted, poor soul. The ligature, some sort of leather whip or lash, is still embedded in the flesh of his neck. You can see it just below the beard. He is a big man. I cannot see that it would be easy to beat him in a fair fight, but with a weapon such as this . . . .

HOLMES: There is the argument that was reported to your man, Lestrade.

LESTRADE: Aye. I must call in the constables.

[FOOTSTEPS LEAVING THE ROOM. SOUND OF POLICE WHISTLE (OFF)]

HOLMES: Quick, who is he ? Let us search his pockets before Lestrade and his myrmidons come in with their boots and disturb whatever evidence remains. Aha ! A letter, in German, no less, addressed to Tómaš Kiska. A Bohemian name, if I am not mistaken. Let us see his boots. Ah yes, from that part of Europe, to be sure. The little distinctive touches, Watson, that help determine a man's origin. A man may change his clothes in order to appear as a native of another nation – see how this man's coat and trousers are distinctively English – but he will invariably fail to change his boots, which will always bear the mark of his native country.

WATSON: See here, Holmes. Look. Below the right ear, where the beard stops.

HOLMES: Your powers of observation are coming on apace. That star-shaped tattoo is the mark that allows members of one of the most vicious and depraved group of European anarchists to identify each other. We seem to have stumbled upon a deep mystery, Watson, very deep.

[FOOTSTEPS ENTERING THE ROOM]

LESTRADE: Here he is, constable. Discovered anything more, Mr. Holmes ?

HOLMES: For your ears alone, Inspector. First, though, we should examine the rest of the house before we go over the road and visit Josef Meyer.

POLICEMAN: What are we looking for, sir ?

HOLMES: Anything that strikes you as being unusual.

POLICEMAN: The whole blooming thing seems a bit queer, sir, if you don't mind me saying so. This is my beat, and I know this house has been empty for several months now. Never seen or heard anything, and then this turns up.

LESTRADE: Any idea how long he's been dead, Doctor ?

WATSON: Rigor is passing. Given the recent weather, I would say that death occurred some time within the past forty-eight hours. However, I cannot say with certainty. Nonetheless, I can be reasonably sure that this is the place where death occurred, as can be judged by the lividity of the body, and the fact that the garrotte drew blood, which has dripped into the beard onto the body, and not onto the floor below it.

LESTRADE: So this man was killed here, at the time that Grimsley reports that he saw the lights and heard the noises ? Who is he ?

HOLMES: A letter in his pocket is addressed to Tomáš Kiska, and I have reason to believe, thanks to Watson's observation of a distinctive tattoo, that he is a member of an anarchist gang, sworn to exterminate the aristocracy and royalty of Europe.

LESTRADE: I admit that you sometimes see things that escape my notice, Mr. Holmes, but I would very much prefer it if you were not to meddle with the evidence before the police have examined it. Constable, you are to forget anything that you hear today between Mr. Holmes and Doctor Watson here and myself.

POLICEMAN: Very good, sir.

HOLMES: [SNORTS] Come, let us search the rest of the house.

[DEPARTING FOOTSTEPS. [FADE OUT.
FADE UP] FOOTSTEPS ARRIVING]

LESTRADE: Nothing. The whole place is clean as a whistle.

HOLMES: Really, Inspector ? You failed to mark this ?

LESTRADE: A minute speck of cigarette ash ? Hardly of importance.

HOLMES: On the contrary, my dear Lestrade. You are aware, are you not, of my monograph on the subject of the different types of tobacco ash ? This is the ash of a certain type of German tobacco, of the kind generally rolled into cigarettes. To the best of my knowledge, it is unobtainable in this country, meaning that the person who smoked this tobacco brought it into England.

LESTRADE: We are dealing with foreigners, then, it would appear.

HOLMES: Indeed so. And let us recall that His Serene Highness the Grand Duke of Hohe-Saxburg is due to visit this country in the next week. Any attempt on his life made here could seriously damage the relations between this country and the other great powers.

LESTRADE: It seems that we must interview Meyer now, as a matter of some urgency, in that case.

HOLMES: Precisely. Come.

LESTRADE: Constable, you are to remain here and to admit no one, do you understand, without my permission, other than myself, or Mr. Holmes and Doctor Watson here.

POLICEMAN: Very good, sir.

[FOOTSTEPS LEAVE. FADE TO FOOTSTEPS OUTDOORS. DOORBELL RINGS, FOLLOWED BY VIGOROUS KNOCKING ON DOOR]

HOLMES: [CHUCKLES] Enough to wake the dead, Lestrade.

[SOUND EFFECT : DOOR OPENS]

MRS. BAXTER: Yes ? Who are you, then, and what do you want ?

LESTRADE: My name is Inspector Lestrade of Scotland Yard, and my friends and I wish to speak to a Mr. Josef Meyer, who we believe lives here. You are Mrs. Meyer, I take it ?

MRS. BAXTER: Certainly not ! My name is Elizabeth Baxter, and Josef Meyer is one of my lodgers.

LESTRADE: I beg your pardon, Miss Baxter.

MRS. BAXTER: Mrs.

LESTRADE: Sorry ?

MRS. BAXTER: *Mrs.* Baxter, not *Miss.*

HOLMES:	Be that as it may, Mrs. Baxter, we would like to speak to Mr. Meyer.
MRS. BAXTER:	Well, you can't.
LESTRADE:	Why not ?
MRS. BAXTER:	Because he's not here, Mr. Clever-dick Scotland Yard.
HOLMES:	He's at work ?
MRS. BAXTER:	I don't know where he is. He went out two nights ago and hasn't come back. Leastways, his bed hasn't been slept in last night, or the night before, as I could see when I went in there this morning. And he hasn't been taking his meals with the other lodgers. And he likes his food, he does. He's a big man. He'd have all the eggs in the dish at breakfast and leave none for anyone else if I didn't put a stop to it.
LESTRADE:	I see. Then may we see his room ?
MRS. BAXTER:	Not without a warrant, you can't. I know my rights – and his, even if he is a foreigner who can hardly speak English. You've no right to go poking your noses into his business. If he's done something wrong, I want to know what it is, first.
HOLMES:	I'm afraid we can't answer that question at the moment, Mrs. Baxter. Can you tell me if Mr. Meyer smoked ? A pipe, maybe, or cigarettes ?
MRS. BAXTER:	Not in this house, he didn't. And not out of it, as far as I know.
HOLMES:	Thank you for your help, anyway.
MRS. BAXTER:	I won't say you're welcome, because you're not. Now clear off, and come back with your warrants if you want any more out of me.

[DOOR SLAMS]

HOLMES: Charming ! Will you make arrangements for the body to be removed ?

LESTRADE: I have already done so, when I summoned the constable. Indeed, I believe this is the hearse coming towards us now.

[HORSE-DRAWN WAGON APPROACHES AND STOPS]

WATSON: There is no coffin.

LESTRADE: I requested none. Let me inform the constable on duty of their arrival and allow them to be admitted.

[DEPARTING FOOTSTEPS]

HOLMES: This is a strange business, Watson. Who is this Josef Meyer ? Where has he disappeared to after informing the policeman of the disturbance in the house last night ? As for the letter we discovered on the body....

[PAPER RUSTLES]

WATSON: You retained it after removing it from his pocket ?

HOLMES: To be sure I did. Lestrade may have it when I am done with it. My German is a trifle out of practice, Watson, so you must bear with my impromptu translation. Hmm . . . Yes, here we are. *"Be prepared for the visit next week. Ample supplies will be provided via the usual source. Visit Abigail from Hamburg. Three then four and reply with three."* Signed " *Gustav*".

WATSON: And who in the world is this Abigail ?

HOLMES: I do not know at present, but she may prove to be the answer to this riddle. Ah, they are bringing the body now.

WATSON: I fail to see why Lestrade did not order a coffin or at least a shroud. Whoever that man might have been, it hardly seems decent for his corpse to be carried in that way with no covering.

[DOOR FLIES OPEN]

MRS. BAXTER: [SCREAMS] There he is !

WATSON: Who, Mrs. Baxter ?

MRS. BAXTER: That's Josef Meyer that they're carrying there. I just saw him from the front window.

HOLMES: I beg your pardon ?

MRS. BAXTER: The man you've been looking for. I can see his face from here. It's him. He's dead, isn't he ? I can tell.

HOLMES: Excuse me, madam.

MRS. BAXTER: What ?

[SCUFFLE.]

MRS. BAXTER: Ouf ! How dare you break into my house like this ?

[FOOTSTEPS GOING UP STAIRS. A DOOR OPENS AND CLOSES]

MRS. BAXTER: I don't know who your friend is, but he's going to be arrested for trespassing, he is.

WATSON: My friend is Sherlock Holmes. You may have heard about him.

MRS.BAXTER: Oh. Then you are Doctor Watson, I take it ? I've heard about you two. Read about you in the papers.

WATSON: I am, madam. Could you tell me something about the house opposite ?

MRS. BAXTER: It's stood empty this past three months or more.

WATSON: And you have never heard any sounds come from there or seen lights ?

MRS. BAXTER: I told you, it's empty.

[FOOTSTEPS COME DOWN STAIRS]

HOLMES: I have it, Watson. It is all here in this news-paper. Apologies, Mrs. Baxter. You have done this nation a great service. Greater than you will ever be allowed to know. Accept the thanks of a grateful nation. Watson, let us meet Lestrade, inform him of what we have just learned, and make our way to Scotland Yard, where we can inter-view the constable who met the purported Josef Meyer last night.

WATSON: [CLOSE] " Purported" ?

[MUSIC: LINK]

SCENE 3: SCOTLAND YARD

LESTRADE:	I still find it incredible that the man who informed us of the lights and the argument taking place in an empty house should be found strangled inside that very house.
HOLMES:	You are making one very elementary mistake, my dear Inspector.
LESTRADE:	That being ?
HOLMES:	That the man who reported the incident to your constable is the same man whose body we discovered.
WATSON:	Is it not possible that after he left the constable, he entered the house, where he was set upon and killed by those whom he had noticed earlier ?
HOLMES:	I doubt it very much. The house did, after all, appear to be empty and deserted when the good constable examined it. Ah, but speak of the Devil...
LESTRADE:	Constable Ruddock, this is Sherlock Holmes, who has been good enough to give us some small hints in the past regarding some of our more difficult cases, and his friend Doctor Watson.
RUDDOCK:	Pleased to meet you both, sirs.
HOLMES:	You are the constable on duty who was addressed the other night by a Mr. Josef Meyer regarding a disturbance in an empty house on Lowman Road ?
RUDDOCK:	That is correct, sir.
HOLMES:	And when you examined the house, was Mr. Meyer with you ?
RUDDOCK:	He was, sir.
HOLMES:	And what did you see in the house ?

RUDDOCK: Well, I couldn't see nothing, sir. All the doors and windows was locked, and when I looked through the windows, all I could see was black, sir. The house is a fair way off from the nearest streetlamp, and my lantern wasn't strong enough to see more than a yard or two inside the rooms.

HOLMES: So what did you say to Mr. Meyer when you had discovered this ?

RUDDOCK: Well, sir, it's a funny thing, and somehow I forgot to put it in my report. When I had finished trying to look in through the back window, I turned 'round, and I was going to say to Meyer that he was imagining things. Well, blow my eyes, he'd scarpered. He wasn't there anymore.

LESTRADE: Blow your eyes indeed, Ruddock ! Why did this not go in your report ?

RUDDOCK: It sort of slipped my mind, sir.

LESTRADE: We will have words about this.

HOLMES: Later, Lestrade, later. Anyone can make a mistake. Now, Constable, can you describe this man to us ?

RUDDOCK: Well, it was only by the light of the streetlamp, sir, and I didn't get that good a look at him, but he had fair hair, cut very short. A small man, much smaller than you or me, sir.

HOLMES: Moustache ? Beard ?

RUDDOCK: Clean-shaven except for a small moustache, sir. Fair, like his hair.

HOLMES: And how was he dressed ?

RUDDOCK: Now that is something that did strike me, sir. Half-past-eleven at night, most folks in that area are in bed. It's not like it's the

	West End, where the toffs have parties and come home half-seas over at all hours. Begging your pardon, sir.
HOLMES:	Granted.
RUDDOCK:	Well, he wasn't drunk, I'd take my oath on that. But what struck me was the fact he was fully dressed – shoes, socks, collar and tie, and all. And yet he told me he'd been watching from his window in the house opposite and seen the lights and heard the noises from there. Would you expect someone to dress themselves up in that way if they were going out to look for help from the police on something like that, sir ?
HOLMES:	I agree, it seems unlikely. So he was wearing a collar and tie ?
RUDDOCK:	Yes, sir. I remember it most distinctly. That and the patent-leather boots. And the way he spoke – it wasn't quite right. Something queer about it. Sort of foreign.
LESTRADE:	We want you to identify a body, Ruddock. Go to the mortuary in Holloway and ask to see the body of Josef Meyer.
RUDDOCK:	He's dead, sir ? The man I talked to the other night ? I can't believe it.
HOLMES:	Neither can we. Which is why we need your help in identifying him.
LESTRADE:	And when you return, Ruddock, we will have words on this importance of making a complete report.
RUDDOCK:	Sir.
	[DEPARTING FOOTSTEPS]
HOLMES:	Don't be too hard on him. Even without his identification of the corpse, we know that the body is not of the man who identified himself as Josef Meyer to your man. Slight build, heavy build; fair hair, dark hair; small

| | moustache, full bushy beard; patent-leather shoes, hobnailed boots; slight accent, can hardly speak English. |

WATSON: The two men seem to be exact opposites of each other.

HOLMES: No accident there, I am sure. These contradictions, seemingly pointing in opposite directions, may actually be a signpost pointing to a solution of this mystery.

LESTRADE: One of your theories, Mr. Holmes ?

HOLMES: As yet, no definite theory, but a multitude of ideas. In the meantime . . . .

[PAPER RUSTLES]

LESTRADE: What is that ?

HOLMES: A letter, in German. Tell me, does the name "Abigail" from Hamburg mean anything to you ?

LESTRADE: I have never heard of her.

HOLMES: Now see here.

[PAPER RUSTLES]

HOLMES: This newspaper dated two days ago. Column four. The list of ships arriving at the East India Dock.

LESTRADE: *S.S. Abigail*, Hamburg. Arrived on Tuesday, and will sail this evening. Why is this important ?

HOLMES: I strongly suspect that this ship is the bearer of the infernal machine or whatever means of destruction the dead man was meant to use in the assassination attempt on the Grand Duke. He would be unable to bring it in as a traveller, but as part of a ship's cargo, it would be relatively easy for it to arrive in this country and be delivered – or, as I believe in this case, collected by the recipient.

WATSON: But how did you make the connection with the ship, Holmes ?

HOLMES: Later. For now, let us make haste to the East India Docks. Lestrade, bring along several of your stoutest constables, and you may want to alert the River Police in case the *Abigail* tries to give us the slip.

[MUSIC : LINK]

SCENE 4: EAST INDIA DOCK

[SOUNDS OF GULLS, WATER, MACHINERY, ETC.]

HOLMES: There we are, the *Abigail*. She may not look like an impressive vessel, but I believe she carries the seeds of destruction. Consider the international situation should an attempt on the Archduke's life be made in this country, whether it is successful or otherwise.

WATSON: It would be war in Europe, for sure, and we here in Britain would not escape it.

HOLMES: Indeed so. Lestrade, I feel that I may have more success here than the uniformed police. Watson here is armed with his revolver, and I myself am carrying my loaded riding-crop, together with my swordstick. Should it become necessary, however, I will use my whistle to summon you and your men. [BEAT] And have no fear, Lestrade. When all this is over, should it come to the attention of the press, Inspector Lestrade will have all the credit, and Sherlock Holmes none.

LESTRADE: Most generous of you, Mr. Holmes. God speed. We are ready and waiting should you need us.

HOLMES: Come, Watson. Let us make our way to the *Abigail*.

WATSON: (LOW) Holmes, I do not have my revolver with me.

HOLMES: (LOW) I am aware of that. Nor is the stick I am holding my swordstick.

WATSON: (LOW) Then ... ?

HOLMES: We proceed.

[FOOTSTEPS]

HOLMES:	We are close enough.
WATSON:	What are you doing, Holmes, holding up three fingers in that way ?
HOLMES:	I am waiting for the countersign of four fingers. Ah ! You see it, Watson ? On the poop. The master of the vessel, if I am not mistaken. I raise three fingers in reply and now...
SUSSBINDER:	[OFF] Come aboard !

[FOOTSTEPS UP GANGPLANK]

HOLMES:	*Guten Tag, Herr Kapitän.*
SUSSBINDER:	Ah, you speak German, Inspector ?
HOLMES:	*Ein bißchen.* A little. However, I am not a policeman, let alone an inspector. My name is Sherlock Holmes, and this is my friend and colleague, Doctor Watson.
SUSSBINDER:	*Zufrieden.* Otto Sussbinder at your service. Delighted to make the acquaintance of such a distinguished detective. And of you, Doctor. I have enjoyed your accounts of the cases which Mr. Holmes has undertaken in your company. Now, how may I assist you gentlemen ?
HOLMES:	I must ask you to return to Germany, carrying back to there the infernal machine which was to be collected by Tómaš Kiska.
SUSSBINDER:	(LAUGHS) Mr. Holmes, there is no infernal machine. There never has been any infernal machine.
WATSON:	But surely, Kiska was an anarchist ?
SUSSBINDER:	He was.
WATSON:	And he was in contact with an anarchist group who would supply him with the means to destroy the Archduke on his visit here, to be delivered on this very ship ?
SUSSBINDER:	That is what he believed, yes.

HOLMES:	(PAUSE) What rank do you hold in the police force of Hohe-Saxburg, *Herr* Sussbinder ?
SUSSBINDER:	Ah, you have guessed my little secret, Mr. Holmes. My congratulations. I am a captain in the police of the Archduchy of Hohe-Saxburg, with a special responsibility for thwarting the plans of anarchists.
HOLMES:	And Kiska was in fact in contact with you, believing himself to be taking orders from a group of nihilists ?
SUSSBINDER:	Indeed so. You have it precisely. We had previously placed him in that room in Lowman Road opposite the empty house, to which we had keys – you do not need to know the details of how we obtained them, but I can let you know at some other time if you require the full story. One of our agents in this country used this empty house for meetings with Kiska at night.
HOLMES:	A smaller man, fair haired, with a moustache, well-dressed ?
SUSSBINDER:	Indeed, that is a fair description of the man I will refer to as Gustav. Last night, he met Kiska to discuss the final details of how the supposed infernal machine was to be collected, and an argument ensued over money, as you might have expected. Kiska – you have seen the man's body, yes ? – was a strong and powerful man, but Gustav, despite his size, is an extremely tenacious and skilful opponent, and was able to twist his riding-crop around Kiska's neck, and thereby kill him.
WATSON:	The trachea was crushed. Death must have been swift.
SUSSBINDER:	Having left the body where it fell, Gustav proceeded to take the sole candle which had illuminated the evening's proceedings,

and decided upon a risky course – that of alerting the British authorities to the existence of Kiska. He therefore gave his name as the alias being used by Kiska, and told one of your English policemen that he had witnessed a suspicious happening in the empty house. As the policeman attempted to examine the interior of the house, the supposed Kiska, that is to say, Gustav, escaped into the night.

HOLMES: And you intended us to discover that the man who had alerted the police was not who he said he was, and that we should discover the true identity of the dead man ?

SUSSBINDER: Indeed so. There are those in your Government who are aware of the existence of Kiska, but were not aware of his presence in this country. I decided to make you a gift of him. We could, of course, easily have disposed of the body, and the man known as Josef Meyer would simply have disappeared.

HOLMES: And the whereabouts of the man you call Gustav ?

SUSSBINDER: That, I am afraid, I will not tell you. He is, of course in strictly legal terms, a murderer, and has killed on English soil, but I ask you to ask yourselves, Mr. Holmes and Doctor Watson – are you really so anxious that he should face the gallows ?

WATSON: For my part, I am ready to let him go free, given that he has likely saved Europe from war.

HOLMES: Good old Watson. The voice of England has spoken through you. We will make no further enquiries regarding this Gustav.

WATSON: One question, Captain Sussbinder. When we entered the empty house, the floor, the table, everything was clean and swept. Why?

SUSSBINDER: Must you ask? We are Germans, and as you know, we Germans like everything to be just so. It was impossible for Gustav to be in a place as dirty as that house had become. (PAUSE) Now, if there is nothing further that you wish to know, I will bid you farewell. We sail on the tide.

HOLMES & WATSON: Farewell.

WATSON: How will you explain this to Lestrade?

HOLMES: Despite appearances, he is no fool. He will understand.

[FADE]

SCENE 5: BAKER STREET

WATSON: Holmes, I can understand most of your reasoning, but how did you deduce that *Abigail* referred to a ship and not a person?

HOLMES: When I made my way into Mrs. Baxter's house, I was able to go straight to the room where Kiska had been lodging. Remember, we were told that the lights had been observed from his window, so it must have been one of the rooms at the front of the house on the first floor. One of them was locked, and Mrs. Baxter had told us that she had been into Kiska's room. That door was unlocked as I expected, and, by good chance, there was the newspaper, on the bed, open at the shipping page.

WATSON: Wonderful.

HOLMES: Elementary.

WATSON: And the deduction that his killer was no criminal, but an agent of the law?

HOLMES: Everything was too perfect. The man who talked to the constable, pretending to be Meyer, was the complete opposite of the Meyer lodging in Mrs. Baxter's house. The letter addressed to Kiska – had he been killed by one of his fellow anarchists, that letter would have been removed. The letter itself, though addressed to a Bohemian, presumably from a Bohemian group of nihilists, was written on German paper from a manufactory in Hohe-Saxburg. The very fact that the body, together with the incriminating weapon, and more importantly, the mark identifying its wearer as a member of a criminal society, was left for us to discover. The fact that there was no sign of forcible entry to the house. And, as you remarked, the cleanliness of the place. All this pointed to an operation conducted with Teutonic thoroughness. I therefore had no hesitation in approaching the *Abigail*, though I confess to deceiving Lestrade to the extent of requesting constables for assistance.

WATSON: It could have turned out otherwise.

HOLMES: A possibility, true, but a remote one. And now, I must consider how to inform brother Mycroft of these happenings.

[THE VIOLIN STARTS AGAIN, TUNELESS, BUT PLAYED WITH BRAVURA AND CONTINUES FOR A FEW SECONDS BEFORE IT STOPS]

HOLMES: [CLOSE] That is, of course, unless he already knows all about them.

[THE VIOLIN STARTS AGAIN]

THE ADVENTURE OF
VANAPRASTHA

HE relationship between Sherlock Holmes and the supernatural would appear to have been one of mutual disdain. With his firm belief in reason and logic as the dominant features that distinguish the human race from other animals, the doings of " ghoulies and ghosties and long-legged beasties and things that go bump in the night" held little interest for him.

Likewise, those aspects of the world that are more than are dreamed of in our philosophy seemed to give him a wide berth. While others might discuss their experiences of having established communication with their deceased loved ones, or recount terrifying tales of rocking tables and flying crockery, untouched by human hand, no events of this nature ever seemed to come near to Sherlock Holmes.

" The affairs of human beings are complex enough, Watson," he remarked to me once, " and the world of experimental science still holds enough mysteries without adding the addled hallucinations of the feeble-minded to the list."

" But surely," I replied, pointing to the article in the *Morning Post* that announced the arrival in England of a famous ' medium', which had sparked the discussion, " Sir William Keighley is a well-known scientist, indeed, a member of the Royal Society, and he defends the effects produced by Signora Galliani as being genuine."

Holmes snorted. " Sir William is a fool," he retorted. " Eminent he may be in his chosen fields of light and heat and electricity, but when it comes to exposing the tricks of a conjuror, he is a babe in arms."

I forbore from making any further comment on the matter, but held my peace. For my part, the Highland blood of my maternal ancestors had provided me, I believed, and continue to believe to this day, with the gift of perceiving those things that are hidden to many others. I have, for example, a very clear recollection of my mother sitting in her favourite arm-chair and conversing with me on the subject of my future career as a doctor. This is hardly remarkable, you may say, but this dialogue occurred some two years after her death. However, were I to mention this, or other similar incidents, to Sherlock

Holmes, I have no doubt that he would scoff and dismiss such matters as merely the product of an over-active imagination.

It was with some amusement, therefore, that I anticipated Holmes's reaction to the somewhat bizarre story being related to us by Inspector Alec MacDonald of Scotland Yard, who had visited us one day.

" By all accounts, it is a strange case, Mr. Holmes," he confided, leaning forward in his chair, " the like of which I have never seen for myself, and I would be grateful for your help when I visit the scene." Inspector MacDonald, as always, was sufficiently aware of the level of his own, albeit considerable, abilities, to feel no embarrassment at requesting advice and assistance from one who was acknowledged to be the foremost practitioner of his art in Europe.

" Proceed, Inspector," Holmes answered him, languidly filling his pipe. " There is whisky in that decanter, should you feel it will help you recall the facts of the matter."

" A wee nip would do no harm," MacDonald replied, with a faint smile, and I hastened to splash a little of his native spirit into the Scotchman's glass. " The facts as relayed to us at the Yard are clear in my memory," MacDonald continued, with a slight shiver. " The case concerns a certain Colonel Richard Cardew, formerly of the Westmorland Regiment. He had served with some distinction in India, including some gallant actions in one of the native uprisings in the area of the North-West Frontier–"

" Your old haunts, Watson," smiled Holmes.

MacDonald continued. " While serving there, he took a ball in the shoulder and was invalided home. He lived in Eastbourne, alone except for two Indian servants, a cook and a manservant, the latter having accompanied him since the time he was in India, and an English housekeeper who did not, however, reside on the premises.

" He appears to have been well liked enough by his neighbours, insofar as he seemed to provoke no quarrels or friction, and though he did not attend any Christian place of worship on a regular basis, he was an occasional contributor to good works. From what I can gather, he worshipped some sort of heathen idol that he had encountered in his service overseas."

"There were one or two of those in my regiment," I remarked. "Stout fellows for the most part, though they took little part in Mess activities."

"Indeed ?" MacDonald nodded politely in my direction. "It is the first such case that I have encountered. In any event, the business may now be described in the past tense. Colonel Cardew was found dead in his bed this morning by his manservant, Jayant Singh. The sheets were described as being soaked in blood, and the body was almost drained. The wounds–"

"More than one wound ?" interrupted Holmes, who had been puffing away at his pipe without comment up till that time during MacDonald's recital.

"That, Mr. Holmes, is the horror of it all. The body had been slashed all over. No weapon was visible, and the room was locked, with the key on the inside of the door. According to the local constabulary, who relayed these facts to the Yard by telephone, so says the cook, Anil Bannerji, for that is the fellow's name."

"The Death of a Thousand Cuts," I murmured to myself.

"What was that, Watson ?" Holmes asked sharply.

"It is an Oriental form of punishment. A gruesome protracted form of execution, reserved for those who have offended the morals of their country."

Holmes raised his eyebrows. "Is that so ?" He turned to MacDonald. "And I suppose there is no chance that it is this Jayant Singh who discovered the body who may have carried out the deed ?"

"It is possible, I suppose, but the facts would seem to argue against it. Cardew clearly did not repose a great deal of trust in his Indian servants, though Singh had been in his service for some time, since he had been his batman, in fact. Bannerji is a more recent addition to the household, having arrived some months ago. It was Cardew's custom each night to lock the two Indians in a small stone shed located in the grounds of the property, and allow them their liberty in the morning, either by unlocking the door himself, or ensuring the housekeeper performed that duty when she arrived each morning."

"Inhuman !" I exclaimed. "To treat fellow human beings in such a fashion."

The police inspector nodded in agreement. "It would seem that Cardew was something of a tyrant in his domestic affairs. I believe these poor wretches were kept without money, meaning that even were they able to escape, they would be without the means to travel. In this instance, Mrs. Bryant arrived at the house, and discovered that Cardew was still abed. This was not an unfamiliar circumstance, and she went to the parlour, fully expecting to find an empty decanter and a glass there, as she had done in the past. However, there was no evidence of any such indulgence on the previous night. She then proceeded as usual on these occasions, however, and took the key of the shed from where it was hanging on a hook behind the kitchen door to release the cook and Jayant Singh."

"But this Jayant Singh, or the other, the cook, could well have escaped the prison in the night and returned himself to captivity," I pointed out.

MacDonald shook his head. "I trust Mr. Holmes and you, Doctor, will come to Eastbourne with me," he said, "and you will then confirm for yourselves what the local police reported to us, that such a thing would not be possible."

"The cook," broke in Holmes. "What can you tell us of him?"

"Oh, Anil Bannerji is reported as being a puny little shrimp of a man," laughed MacDonald. "The idea of his being a murderer is patently absurd. Even so, both he and Singh are now being held in custody."

"Then we must look for a housebreaker who is prepared to kill in pursuit of his loot," I said.

Once more MacDonald shook his head. "According to Mrs. Bryant, nothing is missing, and there is no sign of any disturbance."

"From the little I know of this torment," I said, "it is excruciatingly painful. Surely the poor man's cries must have been heard by others?"

"I have yet to visit the place," MacDonald said to us, "but according to the local constabulary, the bungalow is somewhat set apart from others, at the end of a long drive, and is surrounded by a tall yew hedge, which would tend to muffle any sounds."

" It appears to me as though this could be an intriguing puzzle which should afford us some gratification in the solving," Holmes commented.

" I was rather hoping you would say something along those lines," smiled MacDonald. " I may take it that you would not be averse to accompanying me to Eastbourne ? "

" Not in the least," said Holmes. " I would positively welcome a break from the confines of the metropolis. May I assume that you intend starting immediately ? If that is the case, pray allow me a few minutes to prepare myself for the journey."

" Naturally," replied the police agent.

In a very short space of time, we were on the train to Eastbourne, Holmes audibly sniffing the air like a bloodhound on the trail of its quarry. It was a habit I had noticed in the past when he was engaged on a case, and on the occasions when I had brought it to his attention, he claimed to be unaware of his action.

"Though I had far sooner you had not remarked on it," he had told me. However, Sherlock Holmes was in many ways one of the least self-conscious of men, and this habit of his almost certainly passed unnoticed, save by those, such as myself, who knew him well.

On arrival at Vanaprastha, for such was the name of the late Colonel Cardew's residence, we were greeted by Inspector Jowett of the local constabulary.

" This one's a bit beyond us, sir," he said to MacDonald, after the introductions had been made, " and we've left everything very much as we found it. And we've heard of you, sir," as he turned to Sherlock Holmes, " and very glad indeed we are to have you with us."

" Would it be possible to see the room where the body was discovered ? " Holmes enquired.

" In good time, sir, if you don't mind. We have the two Indian servants in custody and I would be obliged if you would ask them some questions now. I've tried to get straight answers out of the pair of them, and all I can get is a load of Oriental superstition that makes no sense from the one of them, and nothing useful out of the other. We've set up shop, in a manner of speaking, in Cardew's study, so if you could follow me there, please, gentlemen, I would be grateful."

" And the housekeeper ? " Holmes asked.

The police inspector laughed. " It's the other way round with that one, sir," he called over his shoulder as we moved along the passageway. " The problem with her is getting her to stop talking."

Holmes smiled. " We'll take the Indians first, then. Watson," he remarked, turning to me. " This is your chance to shine."

" I ? " I asked.

" Indeed so. I take it you still remember some words of your Hindustani, and when these gentlemen find themselves addressed in their own language, we will find them much more receptive to our questions."

" Well now, that's a canny wee trick," exclaimed MacDonald.

For my part, I was conscious of the fact that my knowledge of this Indian language, never profound at the best of times, had almost evaporated from my memory, but I determined to do my best.

Our first subject for interview was the Sikh, Jayant Singh. He was heavily bearded, and dressed in the style demanded by his religion that I remembered from my time in India, with a dark blue turban and a metal bracelet. His scowl was ferocious as he faced us across the table.

" *Namaste*," I greeted him, placing the palms of my hands together and bowing slightly.

His swarthy face relaxed a little as he recognised the word, and he returned my greeting.

In my half-forgotten Hindustani, I explained Holmes's identity and reputation, and attempted to make it clear that all we required from Jayant Singh was the truth of the matter regarding his late master. I added that my command of his language was less than perfect, and if possible, we should conduct the business in English.

" Certainly," he answered in English, a smile lighting his face. " Though my English may be better than your Hindustani, Doctor, it is not perfect, so I hope that you will be forgiving me for any mistakes that I may be making."

Both Holmes and I assured him of this, and Holmes proceeded with his questions.

"When did you last see your master alive?" he asked.

"At eight last night. He locked the door of the small house where I and the cook, Bannerji, and I sleep." He betrayed no visible resentment at having been confined as a prisoner by his late employer.

"And then?"

"I slept," he replied simply. "I am sleeping when it is night. I wake when it is light."

"And you heard nothing in the night?"

The Indian shook his turbaned head. "I heard nothing. I slept, I am telling you."

"And in the morning?"

"Mrs. Bryant unlocked the door to allow Bannerji and me to leave our sleeping place and enter the house."

"Was this usual? That the housekeeper and not your master unlocked the door?"

"Several times in a month. More often at the time of the full moon, when Colonel Cardew had drunk too much on the previous evening, and was unable to rise." He shook his head in what appeared to be sorrow.

"It was a full moon last night," Jowett reminded us.

"And yet Inspector MacDonald told us that according to you, there was no evidence of Cardew's having consumed alcohol to excess last night."

The Indian shook his head. "That is being the case," he told us. "There was no glass or bottle in the sahib's sleeping room, or in any other room."

"And when you opened the door to Colonel Cardew's room, what did you see?"

"I did not open the door."

"I was told that you discovered the body."

Again he shook his head. "You are most correct in what you believe, sir."

"Then how was the door opened?" I asked the Indian.

"It was locked, and it was not my place to open it."

Holmes appeared somewhat exasperated by this answer. "Then who was it who opened the door?"

"The local constable," Jowett told us. "According to Mrs. Bryant, there are two keys to this lock. One of them was in the lock on the inside of the door, and she was unable to locate the other in its usual place when Singh here called to her that he was unable to unlock the door. After a number of fruitless attempts by Bryant, Singh and Bannerji to rouse Cardew, Singh went to the police station and called the constable on duty to investigate. It was he who forced open the door."

"That is being absolutely correct, sir," said Singh, shaking his head.

"Well, I'm happy to have you confirm it at last," said Jowett, sighing. "Mr. Holmes, are there any further questions you wish to ask this man?"

"None at present," Holmes answered him. "Thank you, Mr. Singh, for your help." He bowed slightly towards the Indian, and the courtesy was returned.

"Inspector?" asked Jowett, turning to MacDonald. "Do you have anything further to ask?"

"Like Mr. Holmes, I have nothing I wish to add at this point."

"Off with you, then, my lad," Jowett addressed the Indian.

"I am free, sir?"

"At present, yes. But I must ask you not to leave the house until I give you leave. Ask Constable Hawker to send Bannerji in here, will you?"

"Very good, sir."

When he had left, Jowett spoke. "A capital idea of yours to break the ice with Doctor Watson here, Mr. Holmes. Many thanks to you both for your assistance."

"I do not see that we are much further forward, though," grumbled MacDonald. "It seems that all we have is confirmation of Mrs. Bryant's word on the matter. And the two of them could be in cahoots."

Jowett laughed. "The idea of those two getting together is somewhat absurd, sir, as you will discover when you meet Mrs. Bryant."

MacDonald started to speak, but he was prevented by the entrance of the cook, Bannerji, who had been rightly described as a shrimp of a man. He was darker in appearance and smaller and slighter in stature than his compatriot, and positively cringed as he approached.

"May I sit, please?" he asked us in English. I noticed the tremor of his hands, and the somewhat livid cast to his face, which bespoke a somewhat agitated state of mind. Jowett wordlessly motioned towards a chair, and the Indian gratefully took his seat.

Holmes, following a nod from the two police agents, opened the questioning. "What meal did you serve your master last night?" he asked, in a gentle tone.

"Why, a curry made with vegetables, as usual," answered the cook, in a low but pleasing tone of voice.

"As usual?" enquired Holmes.

"Why, yes. Colonel Cardew would never eat the flesh of once-living things, since he began to follow my Way of Truth."

Holmes shrugged silently, but I observed Jowett and MacDonald exchange a glance.

"And what did you and Singh eat that evening?"

"We took our meal in the kitchen, and it was the same as I served to the Colonel. This was the usual practice. The Colonel had told me that he had found English food to be bland and tasteless since his return from India. Accordingly he preferred to eat the dishes of my country, and when I suggested to him that I should prepare a larger quantity of his meals for consumption by Singh and myself, he voiced no objection."

"Would there be any of that dish still remaining?" Holmes asked the cook.

"There is none remaining," was the reply, "but the pans in which I cooked the meal and the dishes in which it was served are still unwashed. That would usually be my first task of a morning, but I am sure that you can understand that matters are somewhat in disarray following this morning's discovery."

It was evident to me that the man's manner of speech and command of our language was significantly in advance of that of his compatriot. The same thought had obviously entered Holmes's mind. "Have you always been a cook, or did you at some time follow some other trade?" he asked, politely.

The Indian smiled, it seemed a little ruefully. "Indeed, no. Before I met Colonel Cardew, I taught English at a university in Calcutta. The story of how I came to be in my present position is a complex one, but let me simply say that Colonel Cardew once saved me from a most unpleasant fate at the hands of some religious fanatics who were opposed to my beliefs. Upon reflection, I sensed that my life up to that point had been wasted, and I therefore resolved to start a new life, dedicating myself to educating at least one Englishman – that is to say, Colonel Cardew – in my beliefs. To do this, it was necessary for me to enter his service."

"And you succeeded in educating him?" half-smiled Holmes.

"Oh yes indeed I did," came the eager answer. "But there was one matter on which he proved most obstinate, and I could not persuade him to change." Holmes said nothing, but leaned back in his chair, his eyebrows raised.

"He had removed from one of our temples a most sacred image of one of our gods. This small statue is of great antiquity, and is considered to be most holy by the wise men of my religion. Many times, I entreated with him to return it to its rightful place. Many many times," he repeated sadly, "but it was to no avail. He continued to possess this image, which I and the other followers of my Way, regard as being sacrilege."

"It is of some value, then?" asked MacDonald, addressing Bannerji for the first time.

"It may be of some value in itself," replied the other. "Some gold and jewels were used in its manufacture—"

"Aha!" broke in MacDonald.

"Pardon me, sir," said Bannerji. "The true value of this image is not to be measured in terms of money, but in the sanctity and the veneration with which it is regarded. Furthermore, there is a legend attached to this image. That is to say, that if it is removed from the temple where it is meant to be, he who removes it will suffer a painful and lengthy death. The revenge of the gods may not come quickly, but it will come. It will come," he pronounced with an air of finality.

"Cardew removed this statue from a temple, then?" asked Holmes. "How did he come to do that?"

"It was at the time that he saved my life," came the answer. "I had fled from my pursuers, who seemed intent on killing me, with my only crime being that I was, in their eyes, a believer in false gods. I fled into my temple, assuming that they would not dare to follow me in there, but I was sadly mistaken. The Colonel, though he wore but the uniform of a Major at that time, saw the chase, and followed my attackers, arriving as they were about to beat my brains out with a cudgel, whereupon he drew his pistol, and drove them away from me. I perceived that he was about to shoot them then and there, and I begged him not to spill blood within the holy precincts of my temple, whereupon he forced them outside, and shot them through the head, one after the other, in full view of the crowds in the street.

"As you may imagine, I was astounded that an Englishman would do such a thing on my behalf, and it was then that I made my vow to change my ways. However, on returning to my temple, the Colonel's eyes lit upon the image I have described to you, and before I could utter a word, he had seized it and placed it in the knapsack that he was wearing. I was thunderstruck, and unable to protest. There also may be a part of me that believed that he deserved to retain the image as some sort of reward for saving my life.

"But before I had fully realised what had occurred, he had disappeared. I rushed into the street, thinking that it would be easy to discern the Englishman in the crowd, but to my astonishment, I could not find him. I returned to my temple, and as I gazed at the empty spot where the image had stood, I wept for the sacrilege that had been committed.

"Despite my anguish at the lack of respect that he had shown to my religion, this Englishman had saved my life. I prayed earnestly that I should seek him out, and repay the man who had saved my life, by serving him, and working to convert him to the Way of Truth.

"It took very many months of diligent enquiries before I was able to establish the identity of my saviour, by which time he had left Calcutta. I traced him then to Lahore, but by the time my enquiries were complete, he had returned to England. I was able to establish that he had been promoted since the time when I had seen him, and held the rank of Colonel when he left India.

"I thereupon determined to follow him over the oceans, to make myself known to him and to enter his service, and there were several reasons for my doing so." The man's face became animated as he lifted up one finger of his left hand. "Firstly, I wished to repay my debt to him." Another finger was raised. "Secondly, I wished him to understand my religion and to accept the Way of Truth that we follow."

"And how did he take to that, may I ask?" enquired MacDonald.

"He was not receptive at first," smiled Bannerji, somewhat ruefully. "However, in the fullness of time, he accepted the truth of my words, and became a believer of our ways. But, sir, you have not heard my third reason." The third finger was raised. "I wished him, as a result of his acceptance of the Way, to return the image to its rightful owner."

"And how did he respond to your requests to return the idol?" asked MacDonald.

"Sir, I would respectfully ask you not to refer to the image using that word," retorted Bannerji quietly, but firmly.

"Very well," answered a somewhat discomfited MacDonald. "What has become of the image that Cardew removed from the temple, if you prefer?"

"It is in his bedroom, I believe, together with other similar images which he acquired through more regular means. Often and often I attempted to persuade him to return it to its rightful owners, but he was not to be persuaded. And now," a strange light entered the eyes of the Indian as he pronounced these words, "the god has struck him down. His folly in retaining the image of the god, despite the earnest entreaties of me, a devoted disciple, has caused the wrath of the Destroyer of Worlds to come down upon him."

"Did you see the image earlier, when you entered the room?" asked McDonald.

"I did not enter the room, sir," came the simple answer, calmly spoken.

"Indeed?" asked MacDonald. "You had no curiosity regarding the fate of your master? I find that very hard to believe, Mr. Bannerji."

"Of what are you accusing me?" protested the Indian.

"I am accusing you of nothing," said MacDonald. "I merely expressed my surprise that you were incurious regarding your late master."

"Hardly that, sir. Indeed I was curious, but the tenets of my religion forbid me to gaze upon a dead body unless I thereupon go through a lengthy process of purification, which would involve secluding myself for seven days. Since I was aware that the police might well wish to question me, as you are doing now, I felt it was better if I remained uncontaminated by the sight of a body."

"Very praiseworthy, Mr. Bannerji," commented Holmes drily. "For now, as I mentioned earlier, I would be obliged if you could keep the dishes and pans from last night's meal unwashed for future examination."

"It shall be done," answered the other. "Do you have any more questions for me?"

"At present, no," Holmes told him. "Gentlemen?" he enquired of MacDonald and Jowett, who both shook their heads.

"You are free to leave, Mr. Bannerji," Jowett said. "Do not leave the house, and send Mrs. Bryant to us."

"A cool customer," remarked Holmes, when the door had shut behind him. "The face seems strangely familiar, but I am unable to place it at present. There is more to this man than he has told us, I am convinced."

"Do you believe his story?" I asked.

"Which one? The tale of his rescue from death at the hands of his religious enemies? That of the mysterious stolen idol? His sudden obsession with finding his benefactor? Or his transformation from a university professor to humble servitude overseas in the household of a stranger to his land? Or his aversion to viewing a body?"

"Fanciful twaddle, the lot of it, if you ask me," said Jowett. "Why have you asked for last night's dishes, Mr. Holmes?"

"I believe that the meal may have contained something other than the usual spices," Holmes replied, and would say no more on the subject, despite further questioning from the police officers.

"It does seem to me, though," I remarked, "that nothing short of a supernatural agency could be responsible for the death of Cardew, since the door was locked on the inside and no sound was heard, even following what must have been an excruciating death."

MacDonald shook his head. " I dinna like what you say one whit, Doctor, but I fear we have the Devil himself at work here, in the shape of one of these heathen demons masquerading as gods." I wish that print could reproduce the fine rolled Scots ' r' that gave full force to the word ' masquerading'.

Holmes smiled. " The Devil, if it is indeed he who is at work here, always acts through human agents, in my experience. I do not anticipate any difference in his *modus operandi* in this case."

"Whisht, man ! Dinna speak of the Devil in that fashion," said MacDonald in a fearful tone of voice.

At this point, Mrs. Bryant made her entrance. A woman with whom it would be foolish to argue, I told myself, as she took her seat facing us without asking permission, a determined expression upon her face.

Her account of the events and corroborated for the most part what we had been told earlier by Jowett. She confirmed that she had been at the scene of the death from the time that the door was broken down and the body was discovered, to the time when Jowett had called, and that Bannerji had not entered the room.

" And it was Singh who went in first ? " asked Holmes.

" That it was, sir. Him having being a soldier and all, he would have been used to sights like that, I would have thought, but he went as pale as any of his kind can go pale when he saw the master lying there in his blood, all cut up like he was."

" And Colonel Cardew was dead at that time ? "

" Lord bless us, sir, how would I know that ? I leave that sort of thing to the doctors and them that know about such matters."

" But were you not somewhat overcome ? You didn't feel faint or anything like that ? "

" Well, sir, it was a shock, I confess. But my late husband, Norman Bryant that was, he was a butcher, and I kind of got used to that sort of thing, I suppose. In any event, I'm not the fainting type, though there was one time twenty years ago—"

" We are only concerned with the events of this morning," Jowett reminded her sharply.

" Did you notice anything missing from the room ? " asked Holmes.

" No, sir. I went in there, but it was the first time I'd ever been in that room. Usually it was that Singh who looked after the master, and I stayed well out of that place. Gave me a turn, it did, though, to see all of them heathen idols and pictures up there. I knew the master was a bit strange-like in his beliefs since that Bannerji arrived here, and live and let live is what I always say, but even so..." Her voice trailed off.

" You are certain that no one other than Singh and yourself entered the room ? "

" I am sure of it, sir. If you give me a good Christian Bible, I'll take my oath on it, if you like."

" That will hardly be necessary," smiled Holmes. " Would you say that Colonel Cardew was a kind master ? " Holmes asked her.

She considered for a minute. " To be honest, sir, no I wouldn't say that. He was hard on them two darkies, locking them up each night the way he did. Not that I'd trust them myself, you understand, but I wouldn't shut them in like that. He paid my wages on time and without complaining, but I wouldn't say he was a friendly soul."

" And did he have friends who visited him ? "

" Nary a one, sir. In the years I've worked for him, there has been no place set at the table for any but the master, and no visitor has ever spent the night here, to the best of my knowledge."

" Did he receive many letters or telegrams ? " Holmes asked.

" It wasn't my job to collect the post and deliver it to him, but from what I could see, he hardly ever received any letters or messages. He kept himself very much to himself."

" Well, what do you make of it, Mr. Holmes ? " MacDonald asked when the housekeeper had left us.

" Much depends," answered Holmes, " on the condition of last night's curry."

MacDonald laughed outright. " I dare say you may be correct there, but I am dashed if I can see how. Mr. Holmes," he explained to the smiling Jowett, " often comes up with these fancies, which appear strange and improbable at first sight, but he has this uncanny way of proving to be right in the end."

" There is nothing uncanny about it, Inspector," Holmes remarked. " It is merely a matter of intelligent observation and then putting two and two together to make four. A simple process."

" Ah, Mr. Holmes, you are too modest in your own self-judgement. False modesty is as much of a sin as pride, as we learned in the kirk when I was younger."

" All very interesting," commented Jowett, " but what do you gentlemen wish to do next ? "

" We should view the body, and the scene where it was discovered."

We made our way to the door of the death chamber, which had been forced open, as was evident by the splintered wood of the frame, and the state of the lock.

Holmes said nothing, but raised his eyebrows as he bent to examine the lock with his ever-present lens for the space of a minute, after which he stood upright, with a thin smile on his lips.

We then entered the room, which presented a gloomy aspect, the curtains being drawn shut against the light. The almost naked body of an elderly man lay face downwards on the blood-stained sheets that covered the bed. The corpse was painfully thin, almost in a state of emaciation, and the skin of the back was covered with cuts, which were filled with congealed blood, and which seemed to cover the whole body, but were concentrated around the torso.

" The curtains were drawn shut like this ? " Holmes asked Jowett, pointing to the window.

" Yes, sir. We haven't touched anything in that sort of line," came the reply.

With a quick gesture, Holmes twitched the curtains open, and the wan winter daylight flooded the room as he closely examined first the windowsill and then the lock on the window.

" It is clear that this window has not been opened for some considerable time."

" With the door locked, that leaves only the chimney as

a possible means of entrance for the burglar," remarked MacDonald.

"And of exit," Holmes shrugged. "There are no signs of entry or egress through this portal, any more than through the window." He turned to examine the principal feature of the room – the wretched cadaver of Colonel Cardew, which he gently turned over, exposing the face, set in an expression almost of serenity, in contrast to the lacerations covering the flesh of the body. The sight drew my horrified gaze for a minute or more, until I could tear my eyes away and look around the room, which was furnished conventionally enough, but with almost every surface covered with Oriental knick-knacks, such as incense burners and pagan idols, and the walls hung with pictures of the same pagan deities. The one striking exception to the Eastern paraphernalia that filled the room was a service revolver that stood on the small table beside the bed.

"Seems like a right little heathen temple in here, sir," remarked MacDonald, with more than a touch of Scotch Presbyterian censure in his voice.

"From what we understand from Bannerji, and what Mrs. Blyth told us earlier, sir, that's not too far off the mark," Jowett answered.

On looking closer at these *objets*, my time in India helped me to recognise, if not by name, some of the idols that decorated the room, some with elephant heads or heads of other animals, and featuring multiple arms and heads. Holmes was busy examining the revolver, which he picked up and smelled, before flicking open the cylinder and moving on to the Eastern images. He stopped short at a console table which was bare of any ornament.

"Nothing has been moved, you say?" he asked Jowett.

"That is correct, sir," answered the police agent.

Holmes said nothing in reply, but bent to the surface of the table and examined it with his lens, finally standing straight with a grunt of satisfaction before dropping to his hands and knees, and peering under the bed. "Aha! What is this?" he exclaimed, reaching under the bed and producing an extraordinary object, which he held delicately by the extreme tip.

It was a whip, similar to a cat o'nine tails, with knotted

lashes. I shuddered as I beheld it brandished in Holmes's hand. On closer examination, I noted that the lashes were encrusted with a dark substance, and I withdrew with disgust.

"Yes, Watson," said Holmes calmly. "It does indeed appear to be dried blood."

"Surely he did not use that monstrous device on his servants?" I whispered in horror.

Holmes said nothing, but merely pointed to the lacerated body of Cardew that lay on the bed.

"You believe that these cuts were caused by this whip?" Holmes nodded. "But that would be immensely painful," I objected. "Surely someone would have heard his cries? And who would do such a thing, and why?"

"The answer to your last two questions lie before us in this very room," was my friend's only enigmatic reply. "Come, gentlemen, let us examine the servants' quarters."

Jowett led the way through the kitchen door to a small stone shed at the bottom of the garden. There was one small window, high above our heads, which was barred by a trellis of iron bars, spaced some six inches apart. The door was a thick oaken portal, reinforced with further iron bars, and locked with a heavy lock.

Sherlock Holmes once more dropped to one knee as we approached, and examined the lock minutely through his lens. On entering the somewhat cold and damp cheerless chamber, he repeated the process of examining the lock, but from the inside.

The room was furnished with two beds, similar to the charpoys with which I was familiar from my time in India, and it was obvious from the military style in which the bedclothes had been folded on one bed, compared to the other, which one had been occupied by the Sikh, and which by Bannerji. Holmes moved swiftly to the cook's bed, and thrust his hand under the mattress, where he appeared to be searching for something. After a few seconds, he withdrew his hand, a look of triumph on his face.

"Hoots, man!" exclaimed MacDonald, as he examined the object that Holmes held out to him, his Scots accent coming to the fore in his astonishment. " 'Tis nobbut but a wee picklock, Mr. Holmes, is it not ? "

" Precisely," said Holmes. " And, I fancy, this is not all I will discover in this little Aladdin's cave here. His hand plunged under the mattress, and emerged again holding a small phial, which he held out to me. " What do you make of this, eh, Watson ? " he asked.

I took the bottle carefully in my hand and inspected the contents through the glass before removing the stopper and taking a cautious sniff of the yellow liquid contained in it. " It has a strangely familiar odour which reminds me of the more unsavoury quarters of the bazaars of India, but I fear I am unable to put a name to it." I passed the small bottle over to Holmes, who passed his nose over it, and replaced the stopper without, however, making any comment other than to remark to Inspector Jowett, " Before we make any further moves, I strongly suggest that your constables secure Bannerji. I have a strong suspicion he is about to attempt to give us the slip."

" If you say so, Mr. Holmes," replied the inspector, and left us.

" Then Bannerji killed Cardew ? " I asked, somewhat incredulously.

" Yes and no," answered Holmes. " As I have said earlier, much depends on the contents of last night's meal. It is unlikely, but it is within the bounds of possibility that I am following a false scent."

We made our way to the kitchen, where Bannerji was writhing in the arms of a burly constable, Inspector Jowett standing behind them. The utensils and dishes used for last night's meal were lying unwashed beside the kitchen sink, but the shattered remains of at least one dish were lying on the floor. The smell of Indian cooking filled the air.

" He was trying to get to them and break them, sir," the constable said to MacDonald.

" Whose dish was that ? " Holmes enquired sternly of the Indian, who had not ceased his struggles, and pointing to the shards of crockery.

As he gazed at Holmes, the Indian seemingly appeared to realise that he had met his match, and his attempts to escape the constable's grasp ceased. " That was Singh's," he muttered. Holmes stooped, and, using a wooden spatula, scooped some of the remains of the food adhering to a fragment of the plate into a test-tube which he had drawn out of his pocket together with the spatula.

" Be so good as to mark that as ' Singh'," he told me, " and sign and date it. Now," turning to Bannerji, " which was Colonel Cardew's plate ? "

" The one on top," said the Indian, nodding vigorously.

To my astonishment, Holmes shook his head smilingly as he picked up the second of the two plates, and transferred a sample into a test-tube which he requested me to mark ' Cardew', then repeating the process with a sample from the top plate which was marked by me as 'Bannerji'.

'Take him to the station,' Holmes directed the bewildered constable.

'Is he under arrest, sir ? "

The question was directed at Jowett, who looked at Holmes before shaking his head and replying, " No, he is to be held for questioning."

" At least at this stage," added Holmes.

The terrified Bannerji was led away, leaving the two police inspectors and myself alone with Holmes.

" I have a verra strong suspicion," said MacDonald, smiling, " that Mr. Holmes here is about to tell us how Colonel Cardew met his death, and who is responsible."

" Quite correct, Inspector," said Holmes. " And it is not your Devil who is responsible, at least in his horned and hoofed incarnation. Let us move outside. I am in need of fumigation, and I fancy that even the coarse tobacco that is all I seem to have with me will not be improved by the addition of Oriental spices."

He led our party into the small area behind the kitchen door, and leaning against the wall, languidly lit his pipe and commenced his disquisition.

" First, the wounds inflicted on Colonel Cardew which lead to his death were self-inflicted."

I could not contain my incredulity, and Jowett emitted an audible snort of laughter.

"You have out-done yourself, Mr. Holmes," said MacDonald, smiling. "You are asking us to believe that the man cut himself to ribbons, and in complete silence, what's more. Furthermore, the man had a revolver beside his bed. If he wished to kill himself, a bullet would have been more merciful than the horror of whipping himself to death. In the name of God, man, you are asking us to believe the impossible."

"I am telling you to believe what I tell you because it is the truth," said Holmes. "I will endeavour to reconstruct the events for you. First, let us look at Colonel Cardew's life and habits. We know little enough about them, to be sure, but they are enough to give us some vital clues.

"First, we have the testimony of the admirable Mrs. Bryant that no visitors were ever entertained here at Vanaprastha. Not only that, but no servants stayed the night in the house. What does that suggest to you, Inspector MacDonald ? "

"That any noise of a struggle would pass unheard."

"True," Holmes admitted. "But there is more."

"It suggests that Cardew was afraid of some kind of retribution ? " I ventured.

"Bravo, Watson ! Indeed. It is clear to me that Cardew was indeed frightened of something or someone. And it is my deduction that the man who calls himself Anil Bannerji is none other than the pandit of the temple from which the statue was stolen, and the man of whom Cardew lived in fear. Consider that Bannerji constantly talked about ' my temple' and ' my religion'. I have every reason to believe that he was not a mere member, but the leader of a sect which incurred the jealous opposition of rival sects. One of the chief reasons for this rivalry may be the value of the image that Cardew abstracted from the temple."

"Ridiculous ! " exclaimed Jowett. "Pardon me, sir, but wouldn't Cardew recognise the man whose life he saved as soon as he offered his services as a cook ? "

"Consider," Sherlock Holmes went on, "that Cardew saw the man only briefly in extraordinary circumstances several years previously. I think it is highly unlikely that he would recognise him."

MacDonald continued to shake his head. "Mr. Holmes, I

still cannot follow your reasoning here. That wee picklock that you discovered shows that Bannerji is no stranger to the art of opening locked doors. From the way you examined both the door of the room, and the door of the servants' quarters, I conclude that your opinion is that Bannerji picked both locks, entered Cardew's bedroom, killed Cardew, abstracted the idol, and returned, careful to re-lock all the doors behind him."

" Excellent, Inspector," smiled Holmes. " Other than one or two minor details, that is indeed my opinion, based on the evidence, of what happened."

" Those details being ? "

" First, Bannerji did not kill Cardew. As I said earlier, he killed himself, or, to be more precise, he inflicted those injuries upon himself that led to his death. He may not have intended to kill himself, but in his weakened state – you could see for yourselves that he was malnourished as a result of his refusal to eat meat – his wounds proved too much for him."

" But why, in the name of all that's holy, would he do such a thing ? " exclaimed Jowett.

" You have hit the nail on the head," Holmes told him. " It was indeed in the name of all that's holy, or rather, what he regarded as holy. Bannerji, we know, had been attempting to convert Cardew to his beliefs. Within that conversion, we may assume that Bannerji stressed the importance of remorse and of returning the stolen image. With Cardew drugged—"

" Drugged ? " I asked.

" Naturally. You all saw the phial I retrieved from under the mattress. Analysis will prove the content, which I am certain will result in its being identified as some sort of opium derivative, a soporific, a pain-killer, and a way of weakening the victim's mental resistance, so that he will be more likely to follow suggestions. It was clear, from the plates that we were shown in the kitchen, that the two servants used utensils which were of a lesser quality than those used by Cardew. It was obvious that Bannerji was lying when he identified the plates, and I have no doubt that chemical analysis will reveal traces of the drug in Cardew's food. The spices of the curry would, of course, conceal any taste of the drug."

" My God ! " ejaculated a visibly shocked MacDonald.

"Your God," said Holmes, " but not Cardew's or Bannerji's. You must have noted that the arrangement of the objects beside the bed was that which only a left-handed man would have considered rational, and the wounds on the body likewise could only have been self-inflicted by a left-hander. The pain-killing properties of the drug would have dulled the senses, Bannerji is, as no doubt you noticed, right-handed, but there is no doubt in my mind that he never inflicted any wound upon his master."

I cast back in my mind to the image of the horribly mangled corpse, and nodded in agreement.

" By the way, in larger doses, such as we may assume were administered to Singh, the soporific effect would be enough to keep the larger man unconscious while Bannerji did his deed. Now let us imagine the frightful scene," Holmes went on. " Cardew takes himself to bed, feeling somewhat light-headed and confused, maybe from the drug which he unwittingly consumed in his evening meal of curry. He drifts into a light sleep, from which he is awakened by the sight of Bannerji, standing by the bed, holding a vicious scourge, and bidding him rise and lash himself in order to purify himself of the theft of the image. His resistance weakened, in his diminished mental state, Cardew simply did what was requested. I have no doubt that Bannerji also possesses some skills in the art of mesmerism, as is common among such fakirs and pandits. We can imagine him standing there, coolly watching his master inflict hideous damage on himself until he collapsed in the blood-soaked heap that we found on the bed."

" The devil ! " MacDonald exclaimed.

" Did I not tell you," Holmes answered him, " that the Devil works through human agencies ? After collapsing, Cardew died either from shock to the heart – we may determine later whether he suffered from a weak heart – or from loss of blood, or from a combination of factors. In any event, I have little difficulty imagining the smiling Indian watching his master expire. It was then the work of a moment to abstract the image – you all remarked the empty space on the table, did you not, where a prized object might be expected to take pride of place – and exit the room, locking the door behind him and re-entering his sleeping quarters, which he likewise re-locked."

" It is the most abominable thing that I have yet encountered ! " cried Jowett, in shocked tones.

For my part, I had been considering Holmes's words. "You mentioned that Inspector Macdonald's account had one or two missing details. You have mentioned one such – the death of Cardew. May I suggest that the other is the hiding of the image. After all, we did not discover it in the servants' quarters, did we ? "

Holmes laughed. "Watson, you never fail to amaze me. You are completely correct. The idol is indeed missing, but not for long. Come." He led the way back into the house, and to the study where we had conducted our interviews. " Here," he said, opening the bottom drawer of the very desk where we had been seated, and retrieving from it a golden figure, about twelve inches high.

" Did you not remark Bannerji's gaze constantly returning to that place as we spoke to him ? " he said, in answer to our unspoken queries. On closer examination, the gold proved to be inlaid with precious stones – chiefly emeralds and rubies. A large diamond of at least five carats, by my estimation, had been set in the forehead. Despite its exquisite workmanship and the obvious value of its materials, the object seemed to exude an evil which could not be described in words.

" Hoots ! " exclaimed MacDonald, with a low whistle. " That bonny wee mannie must be worth more than a few bawbees."

" But how shall we charge Bannerji ? " asked Jowett.

" That, my dear Inspector, is a matter for you to decide. I merely point you in the direction of the true quarry. It is then your responsibility to determine that he shall not escape you," Sherlock Holmes told him.

But in the event, Bannerji never faced trial or punishment – at least, not in this world. Following committal to the Assizes, he was found dead in his cell one morning, the victim of some unknown poison, which it was assumed had remained hidden from the authorities during his arrest and subsequent detention.

" We can only hope," I said to Holmes, when I read the account of his death in the newspapers, " that the torments he suffers in the next life are commensurate with those he inflicted on others in this."

"And though I am neither by nature revengeful nor religious," said Sherlock Holmes, " I will add my Amen to that."

THE ADVENTURE OF THE CHOCOLATE POT

HERLOCK Holmes was a man of many interests – indeed, I do not recall ever making the acquaintance of any man whose breadth of vision and intellectual scope extended so widely. Nor were these interests of a superficial nature, but in the majority of cases the knowledge that he acquired was of such a depth that he might have passed as a professor of the subject, employed in one of our Universities.

Sometimes these interests were of a passing nature, lasting for only a few months, but in that short space of time, he would have become an expert in that field, and the comprehension thus obtained would remain with him, often to be used in the solution of a case many years later.

An example of this was his interest in the markings of bullets which had been discharged from a firearm. Holmes was of the opinion, which he attempted to verify, that the rifling within the barrels of guns, though theoretically identical, being of the same model and sourced from the same manufacturer, nonetheless exhibited individual characteristics, much as do the whorls and loops of our fingerprints, as theorised by Faulds in his paper of 1880, with whom Holmes was in later communication.

However, to Scotland Yard, Holmes's theories on the individuality of bullets remained an unproven theory and he was unable to convince even the officer whom he considered to be the finest of the official force, Inspector Stanley Hopkins, of the validity of his suppositions.

Another of Holmes's multifarious interests in which he displayed an uncommon skill was acting. He informed me once that he had entertained a notion to become an actor, but that his family had disapproved of his choice of future career.

" However," he informed me one evening as we were sitting in our chairs following dinner, " I took part in several amateur productions at University, and secretly took some instruction in the dramatic art from a professional actor. Much of what I learned, principally that relating to the stage and the theatre, was of little interest to me in my present profession, but some of the fundamental principles of the thespian art, such as how to inhabit another's character, and the mechanical aspects of disguise and so on, have never left me, and indeed have proved of the greatest value to me in my work."

I had many opportunities to witness the skill with which he made use of this past instruction, and to my mind, the case I am about to describe is one of the finest of such incidents, as well as demonstrating his ability to acquire a high degree of expertise in a subject at short notice.

The case had its beginning one spring morning when London was covered by a fine grey mist, rather than the yellow fogs that had plagued us all winter. Though it was not actually raining, it was a day that a Scotchman would describe as " dreich", and the coat of the client who sat in the chair by the fire, telling us of his problems, was pearled with a thousand shining beads of moisture. His hat had not entirely protected his head from the weather, and he gratefully accepted my offer of a towel to dry his longish silver hair.

" No, thank you," he had said when I had offered to relieve him of his outer garment and have it dried. " Even in a room such as this, which is admirably heated, I find myself to be cold. At my age it is hard for me to keep warm, and the coat will dry very satisfactorily by the fire."

Sir Barnabas Elkinstone, as he introduced himself, had come from Hampshire to visit Holmes. Since my friend was at that time not currently engaged on any case that he considered of any importance or interest (though any of the three cases on which he found himself employed would have furnished a Scotland Yard detective with a firm foundation on which to build a future career), he consented to see Sir Barnabas and to listen to his story.

" I live a quiet life in Elkinstone Manor, a little outside Winchester," he told us. " The house has been in my family for generations, but my wife died childless some years ago, and on my death the estate will now pass to a distant cousin living in Australia. What will become of it then, I do not like to imagine. But," and he seemed to recover himself from a sad reverie, " that is hardly to the point of what I am about to tell you."

" It is never certain," Holmes answered him, " what may or may not be to the point of a case. But please proceed, sir."

" Very well, then. My hobby – indeed, you might almost

consider it to be a passion," and here he gave an embarrassed tittering laugh, " is the collecting of antique silver. I am considered by some to be an expert on the development of fluting in the ornamentation of silver tableware during the later years of the last century, and my thoughts on the matter have been published in several places. Perhaps you have seen them ? " he enquired hopefully.

" Alas," Holmes replied with a faint smile, " they have so far escaped my notice."

" No matter," said our visitor. " I fear that I sometimes expect the whole world to share my hobbies. In any event, my nearest neighbour shares my interest, and if my interest is to be described as a passion, his may almost be described as a mania.

" He is immensely wealthy, and a good portion of his wealth has been spent on his collection of Jacobean and Stuart silver, which is acknowledged to be one of the finest in the land. He has occasionally made use of my services as a judge of the authenticity and quality of a piece when he has been contemplating a purchase to add to his collection. The pieces that he has selected are usually of the finest quality, and are often priced beyond the reach of my more modest purse.

" However, to the best of my knowledge, some of these pieces have not been offered for sale by auction – at least in this country. I receive the catalogues of all the major auction houses who deal with these things, and I would know immediately if they were for sale.

" Now, in my collection are several pieces which have been in my family for a few hundred years and are reckoned by experts to be the finest examples of their kind. When he has visited the Manor, my neighbour—"

" May we know this neighbour's name ? " Holmes asked.

The other sighed. " I was hoping that I could give this account while preserving his anonymity. It is not a pleasant story that I have to tell, and I have no wish to besmirch a man's name unnecessarily."

" Without a name," Holmes told him firmly, " I am unable to discover any relevant facts, and without such facts, I am unable to proceed with my investigations. The name, sir, or I shall be forced to decline your case."

"Very well, then. The man in question is a Mr. Samuel Berenson." Holmes made no reply to this information, but merely raised his eyebrows. " He has, as I said, visited my home on a number of occasions, and has admired many of the pieces, which may best be described as heirlooms. Indeed, his interest goes far beyond admiration, and would be better described as covetousness. He has on more than one occasion offered me a considerable sum of money for some of these pieces. I have, of course, refused in every case of this nature."

" Was the sum offered a fair price, in your opinion ? "

" Oh, very much so. Indeed, I would say that it is nearly double the price one would expect to pay a dealer for such a piece – provided always that such an item found its way into the market. However, while being nowhere as wealthy as Berenson, I am in no urgent need of the money, and refused emphatically. Besides this, there is also the matter of the historic and family value of the silver, with many of the pieces being stamped with the Elkinstone arms. There are indeed three separate occasions on which he has offered me money for a particularly delicate Queen Anne chocolate pot, which is said by some to be the finest of its kind in existence, and each time I have declined to accept his offer."

" And his reaction when you refused ? "

" He appeared to be angry, Mr. Holmes. It was, perhaps, not readily apparent in his face, but I was able to mark the workings of his hands, as they clenched and unclenched into fists."

" And has that anger been expressed in other ways ? "

" Not outwardly, at least. He continues to be a good neighbour who seems to desire nothing but friendship, but the other day my butler, Widdenthorpe, informed me that he had been approached by Berenson with a request to purloin the chocolate pot, and present it to Berenson in consideration of a fee. Naturally, the good fellow refused."

" It would seem a somewhat clumsy way to accomplish his ends," remarked Holmes. " Unless your Widdenthorpe has some skills in these matters, such a robbery committed from the inside of a household almost invariably leads to the detection of the culprit, and in the case of the robbery having been instigated from the outside, as in this case, to the detection of the prime mover in the affair."

"I can assure you that Widdenthorpe lacks these criminal skills," we were assured. "He has been in the service of the family since he was a boy, and is as honest as the day is long."

"In that case, Sir Barnabas, I am unsure as to what action you wish me to take on your behalf."

"But do you not see, Mr. Holmes?" exclaimed our visitor, in a state of great excitement. "Berenson now appears to be determined to lay his hands on my silver, by fair means or foul. I may, of course, forbid him my house, but I consider that he would treat that as a hostile act, and I fear that it would spur him on to greater outrages. I wish you, sir, to appeal to Berenson's better nature, and to persuade him of the futility of his quest."

"Do you not think that this matter would be better handled by the police than Mr. Holmes?" I asked him.

"Other than the report by Widdenthorpe that he has been asked to commit a felony, I cannot see that any crime has been committed, and it is merely my word against that of Berenson. No sir, I do not see that the police would wish to be involved in this affair. I consider that the words of Mr. Sherlock Holmes would have more effect than an official warning."

"You do me too much honour, sir," Holmes remarked, with a self-deprecatory smile. "Allow me to look into the matter at more length, and I will let you know whether I decide to carry out your wishes."

Our visitor left us, and Holmes turned to me with a faint smile on his face. "Well, Watson, what do you make of all this?"

"The collector's mania is a strange one, to be sure. I feel that Sir Barnabas was correct in describing it as a passion. I take it that we may take the butler's account of affairs as being correct?"

"Let us do so for the moment," Holmes agreed. "What are your impressions of our visitor?"

"I would take him to be a typical country gentleman, with a consuming interest in his hobby."

" Quite so. And for the moment, let us regard him in precisely that light until we have sufficient cause to do otherwise. But what of the neighbour, Berenson ? What do we know of him ? "

" The name is familiar, but I am unsure why."

" Let us look in the Index." Holmes searched out a languid hand towards the shelf containing the scrapbooks in which he collected information about those members of society in which he had an interest – that is to say, those who were in one fashion or another, breakers of the law. " Here we are. Berenson, Samuel. Though he has never been prosecuted in a court of law, rumours regarding possible sharp practice in his business affairs have continued to circulate."

" Now I seem to remember some details," I told Holmes. " Was he not the man who owns a number of flour mills ? If I recall correctly, he was accused of bribery when his company purchased a rival, against the wishes of a majority of the directors, but the case never came to court."

"You have it correctly, Watson. Bravo. He was, I believe, recommended for a knighthood immediately prior to the incident you just mentioned, but this was withdrawn following the scandal. It is still unclear why he was not prosecuted, but it is more than likely that while he was skirting the limits of legality, no law could be proved to have been broken."

" And this case to which we have just been introduced would seem to be another example of such an act which, while not strictly illegal, would appear to be at the very least highly immoral. Do you intend to take up the case and perform the task that Sir Barnabas requested ? "

" Given the *dramatis personæ*, I may well do just that. As it happens, I have had my eye on Berenson for some time, in connection with some other little affairs connected with antique silver. He is a sly one, and nothing could be proved, but there have been too many coincidences for my liking."

With these words, Holmes retired to his bed-room, and emerged some fifteen minutes later, to all intents and purposes a different man.

"You know my methods, Watson," he said to me in a voice which lacked much of the refinement with which I usually associated it. " Pray, tell me what you see of the man in front of you."

I examined Holmes carefully. " I would mark you as a man who has come down in the world. Your boots, for example, are of good quality – not of the best handmade type, to be sure, but were still quite expensive when new. They have been allowed to grow old and shabby, however, and, together with the rest of the garb, display a once prosperous state which sadly, no longer exists. A tradesman, I would say, with a predisposition to drink, as witness the hip-flask protruding from your pocket, and this failing may be the cause of your current distress. As to what sort of trade, I could not say."

Holmes clapped his hands. "An excellent summary," he said in the accents in which he had first posed his question to me. "You behold before you Mr. Ezra Littleboy, once of Jellicoe's, the Bond Street jeweller, but as you rightly observe, brought low by drink." His voice reverted to its usual accents. " However, I am sadly ignorant of some of the details relating to antique silver, and I must therefore request you to acquire the following volumes, which are out of print, but should be available from second-hand booksellers. You may find Cecil Court to be the most promising area." He handed me a list of some half-dozen titles, all dealing with antique silver. " It is better that I as Sherlock Holmes, or in my present character, not be seen in pursuit of these volumes."

" And where will you be ? " I asked.

" Oh," he replied airily, " making discreet enquiries among some distant acquaintances – that is, I know of them by reputation – regarding Mr. Berenson. Pray inform Mrs. Hudson that I expect to return in time for dinner. A beefsteak would be welcome, I think."

With a tip of his battered bowler, he was gone. I passed on his message, and made my way to Cecil Court, where I was able to purchase five of the six requested volumes, from four different shops. The sixth appeared to be unobtainable, though one of the booksellers expressed an opinion that a friend of his in Edinburgh might be able to oblige in the matter.

I returned in some triumph to Baker-street, to await the

return of Sherlock Holmes, who arrived some thirty minutes after me. He, too, wore a look of satisfaction.

"I perceive your day has also been well spent," he greeted me, indicating the pile of books on the table beside me. "To be frank, I had not expected more than three of these titles to be available. To have discovered five of the six is good work indeed."

"And may I ask how you have progressed?"

"In a few minutes, Watson. Allow me to restore myself to my proper state."

Some time later, Holmes was seated in his favourite arm-chair, smoking his pipe as he recounted the day's adventures.

"I had some notion of where I might find these men whom I sought. They frequent the public houses at the fringes of the City – appropriately, perhaps, since these men are on the fringes of respectability and legality. It was a relatively simple matter for me to gain their confidence regarding Mr. Samuel Berenson. He is, in their expressive phrase, ' a wrong 'un', though they freely admit that no legal proceedings against him have ever borne fruit. I also dropped heavy hints that I had access to some valuable antique silver to which I had few claims of rightful possession, and it does appear that from time to time Berenson has been known to make purchases in the past without enquiring too deeply into the legality of possession by the seller."

"Outrageous!" I exclaimed. "That a man in that position should encourage theft and larceny!"

"The world of art is a murky one, Watson. Were we to make a close examination of the provenance of many of the works in our National Gallery, we would, I am sure, be more than a little surprised. And now," he added, as Mrs. Hudson entered bearing a tray, "for our beefsteaks."

The next day saw us at breakfast when a telegram was brought to us by the page, Billy. Holmes ripped it open.

"Bradshaw, Watson. The next train to take us to Winchester, if you would. Billy, take this to the telegraph office." He scribbled a few words on a piece of paper and handed it to the page.

"What is it?" I asked as I turned the pages of Bradshaw.

" Murder ! " exclaimed Holmes, his eyes gleaming. " See for yourself."

He held the telegram in front of me, and I read, " ESSENTIAL YOU COME AS SOON AS POSSIBLE STOP SHOCKING MURDER HERE STOP ELKINSTONE."

" Who would have thought, that on the very day after he visited us, that there would arise such an opportunity ? The train, Watson ? "

" There is an express leaving Waterloo in a little over an hour."

" Excellent. I must dress and prepare for the journey." He had barely emerged from his room when Inspector Lestrade of Scotland Yard was admitted.

" If you are not too engaged, Mr. Holmes, I would appreciate your accompanying me to the scene of a dastardly crime that was committed last night. On several occasions, I confess that you have observed some signs which escaped my notice, and enabled me to deduce the identity of the perpetrator."

" Impossible, Lestrade. Watson and I are on our way to Winchester."

" The crime of which I spoke has been committed near Winchester," Lestrade said in some astonishment.

" At Elkinstone Manor ? " Holmes asked him, a sly smile on his face.

Lestrade started. " How in the world did you know that, Mr. Holmes ? "

By way of answer, Holmes reached in his pocket and pulled out the telegram we had received that morning. " I will acquaint you with my knowledge of the case while we are travelling to Winchester," he told Lestrade, " and you, for your part, may explain all that you know."

As the express sped us towards our destination, Holmes told the police agent of our visitor of the previous day, and Lestrade in his turn informed us that the victim of the murder was the butler, Widdenthorpe, of whom Sir Barnabas had spoken to us. His body had been discovered early in the morning by one of the maids who had come into the room to lay the fire. The room itself was the one in which Sir Barnabas kept his collection of silver, and with one exception, the cases were locked. One item of the collection was reported to be missing.

"I think we will discover the missing item to be a Queen Anne chocolate pot," Holmes told Lestrade.

"Very likely so," answered the police detective, and continued with his account. The dead man's skull had been nearly crushed with a blunt instrument, the nature of which was unknown, as there was no trace of it to be found. The French windows leading to the garden were opened, and faint traces of footprints had been found leading across the flowerbeds.

"But by now, they will have been washed away," Lestrade remarked regretfully, indicating the rain, which was falling steadily.

At the time that the murder had been discovered, Sir Barnabas had been absent from the house, but had returned within thirty minutes of the discovery, having spent the night at his London club, and returned to Winchester by the earliest train.

"The main suspect must be Samuel Berenson," I said. "Living close by, and knowing the house, and indeed, the collection, he must have seized his opportunity to purloin the silver. It is quite possible that he observed Sir Barnabas leaving the house yesterday, maybe even taking his chance with the knowledge that the master of the house would be absent."

"I think you have hit upon it, Doctor," Lestrade told me. "Putting together what I have been told by the Hampshire Constabulary and what Mr. Holmes has been telling me, I am certain that you are in the right here."

"Let us not jump to conclusions, Inspector. I agree that at first sight Mr. Berenson would appear to be the thief, but I can see one major flaw in this otherwise admirable theory."

"That being?" I asked.

"I credit you and Lestrade here with sufficient intelligence to deduce it for yourselves," Holmes said, and lapsed into silence.

On arrival at Winchester station, we discovered that the local police force had already ordered an open trap for us to carry us to the manor. Happily the weather had cleared a little, and it was no longer raining. We were escorted by a local constable, who seemed to be in awe of the great personages with whom he was travelling, and hardly opened his mouth for the first fifteen minutes of our journey, save to offer conventional greetings.

" Are you a local man ? " Holmes asked him, obviously attempting to put him at his ease.

" Why, yes, sir. Born and bred in the shade of Elkinstone Manor."

" So you are acquainted with the inhabitants of the Manor ? "

" Hardly that, sir. I wouldn't be knowing the family, now would I, sir, with my father being only an under-keeper on the estate ? And the inside servants keep themselves to themselves very much. I might sometimes meet some of the footmen in the Red Lion on their days off, but not to speak to beyond passing the time of day."

" I see," said Holmes. " And what of Mr. Berenson ? "

" Well, sir, Mr. Berenson is a different kettle of fish as you might say, sir. If you meet him in the lane, he's willing enough to give you a good morning or a good afternoon as it might be, but I wouldn't call him a friendly soul for all that. Hard to say why," continued the young policeman. " And then there were stories of what he'd done in London in his business."

" Very interesting, is it not, Mr. Holmes ? " Lestrade commented to Holmes. " The case against Berenson seems to be tightening." He addressed himself to the young constable. " Have you any idea why your Inspector has not arrested Mr. Berenson yet ? "

" No, sir. I'm afraid my Inspector doesn't tell me that sort of thing, sir."

" And quite right too," said Holmes. " These things can lead to hurtful gossip."

In a few minutes, we had turned off the main road up a drive leading to a handsome mansion, which had a look of the seventeenth century about it.

" Elkinstone Manor," announced the local constable. " Inspector Crashaw will be meeting you."

As we stepped from the trap, a broad, ruddy-faced man in tweeds introduced himself as Inspector Crashaw. " Inspector,

Mr. Holmes, Doctor Watson," he greeted us. " Shall we go in and see the body ? "

" If you have no objection," Holmes answered him, " I would much prefer to see the garden first, particularly the area outside the scene of the crime."

Crashaw looked at Lestrade enquiringly. The latter shrugged. "Mr. Holmes has had some good luck when we have worked together and he has followed his own nose. I strongly recommend that we allow him this freedom in this case."

" It has hardly been a matter of good luck, Lestrade,"Holmes commented acidly, " but I thank you for your support." Crashaw led the way to a set of French windows, and Holmes stooped to examine the ground.

" Dear, dear, Inspector," he remarked to Crashaw. " Your men have trampled the ground like a herd of elephants. There is remarkably little to be seen here other than the marks of official police boots."

The other appeared only slightly discomfited. " I do not see what you might expect to see here, Mr. Holmes, given the amount of rain that has fallen in the past few hours."

" Tut, man," my friend exclaimed. " While a little rain may obscure some of the more obvious clues, there is always something to be learned from the examination of the ground in the first hours following an event. However," and here he bent to retrieve something from the ground, and slip it into an envelope that he retrieved from his pocket, " we may now enter the room, following the supposed path of the killer. These windows were locked, I take it ? "

" Yes, sir. According to the servants, they were locked last night."

Holmes bent to examine the lock, using his lens to do so. With his eyes firmly fixed on the ground, he led the way into the room, where the body of the unfortunate butler still lay, the head surrounded by a ghastly halo of scarlet blood.

Holmes regarded the gory scene with equanimity. " Yes," he murmured, as if to himself. " A blunt instrument, such as a club or a life-preserver."

" One of my constables discovered what we believe to be the weapon, sir," Crashaw told him with some pride in his voice.

"A poker, covered with blood and hair, which has been identified as one belonging to the Manor. It was found on the path leading to Mr. Berenson's house."

"Indeed?" said Holmes. "That is well done."

He turned to the display cabinets, which held a glittering array of antique silver. One of the cabinets was open, and it was clear from a conspicuous gap in the arrangement that a piece was missing. "Aha," Holmes continued, moving to the cabinet in question. "No doubt this once contained a Queen Anne chocolate pot."

"So we have been led to believe," said Lestrade.

"Have you no theories on the case, Mr. Holmes?" asked Crashaw.

"At present, none, until we meet Berenson."

"Then you suspect Berenson of committing this murder?" Lestrade asked him.

"I did not say that," Holmes answered him. "It is essential that we meet Berenson as soon as possible."

"Where is Sir Barnabas Elkinstone?" Lestrade asked Crashaw.

"He appears to have been overcome by the events of the previous night," replied the Hampshire policeman. "The doctor is presently attending him."

"And we shall no doubt be attending him in the near future," remarked Holmes. "In which direction is Berenson's house?" Having received an answer, he started to stride off across the parkland, not bothering to look behind him to ascertain whether we were following him or not.

I immediately started off in his wake, and Lestrade shrugged and followed suit. The country inspector, though obviously mystified by the actions of my friend, had no option but to do the same.

I caught up with Holmes, and asked him, "Do you really intend Lestrade to arrest Berenson on the basis of what you expect to discover at his house?"

"On the contrary, Watson," Holmes smiled. "However, I must see for myself what I have only so far heard by rumour."

Another ten minutes' walking brought us to the stately Georgian mansion which had been purchased by Samuel

Berenson following his retirement from business. Holmes rang the bell, and gave his name to the servant who answered it, not bothering to mention the names of his companions.

" If you gentlemen would care to wait in the library, I will see if Mr. Berenson is available," we were told. " May I enquire the subject of your visit ? "

" Certainly. It concerns his neighbour, Sir Barnabas Elkinstone."

" Very good, sir." He retired, and we were left to examine the room to which we had been conducted, which was named as a library, but in truth seemed to act as a museum, housing a collection of antique silver which to my eyes outshone even the collection that we had just left at Elkinstone Manor.

While we were examining these *objets*, a strange creaking sound could be heard, and as our eyes turned towards the door, where we beheld a frail elderly figure, seated in a bath-chair pushed by the footman who had admitted us.

" Mr. Holmes, I believe ? " the old man enquired of my friend in a quavering voice. " I have long enjoyed the accounts of your cases as written by your friend. And you must be he," he added, turning to me. " Doctor Watson. A pleasure to make your acquaintance. And these two gentlemen are... ? "

Holmes introduced the two police inspectors.

" Dear me ! I hope you have not come to arrest me ? " Berenson, for this was indeed he, started to laugh, but his laughter was soon replaced by a fit of coughing. " Forgive me," he requested when this had subsided. " It is simply that I find the idea somewhat amusing. Now, you mentioned that your business was with my neighbour, Sir Barnabas. Perhaps you would care to enlighten me."

Holmes informed him not only of the murder which had been committed, but also of the visit that Sir Barnabas had paid to Baker-street on the previous day.

Again, the old man burst into fits of coughing laughter, at which we stood astonished at the reaction of a man whose response to the news of a murder was laughter. " And so you believed that I would rob my neighbour of his prized chocolate pot, and kill his butler while I was about it ? " Lestrade had the grace to stand abashed and mutter something that might have been taken as an apology. " No, my dear fellow, I freely admit that I coveted that piece, and I offered Sir Barnabas a handsome sum for it on more than one occasion. However, in my present condition, I could not even make my way unattended to Elkinstone Manor, and the idea of my taking a weapon against the admirable Widdenthorpe must surely seem absurd to you."

" But you offered Widdenthorpe money to purloin the item, did you not ? " I asked.

The old man regarded me with a fixed gaze. " I did indeed," he replied. " However, I was under no illusion that he would be tempted by my offer, and my main purpose in making it was to display to Sir Barnabas the strength of my interest in the piece." He sighed. " Believe me, Sir Barnabas would have done well to accept my offer. He no doubt omitted to tell you, sir," addressing himself to Holmes, " of the fact that he is deeply in debt as the result of the investments in his collection. The sum I offered him would have gone a long way towards paying off that debt, and I would be happy to pay it. For all the words that may have passed between us in the past, I am sorry for his misfortune."

" I see," said Holmes. " May I ? " He produced a cigarette case.

" I must implore you not to use tobacco in this house, sir. My lungs are particularly delicate, so much so that no servant of mine is permitted to smoke, either inside or outside the house. Is that not so, James ? " he asked the footman who had been standing silently behind his master's bath-chair.

" Indeed so," came the reply. " There is no one in this household who touches tobacco in any form."

" Of course," went on the old man, " even though it is clear that I cannot be the murderer of poor Widdenthorpe, one of my servants may well have committed the crime, either on his own initiative, or at my behest. Is that not so, James ? " addressing the footman once more.

" From what you have told us, that is not possible," Holmes retorted smartly, saving the servant the embarrassment of answering. " I am sure that James and his fellow-servants will be delighted to learn that they are not objects of suspicion."

The footman allowed a faint smile to cross his face. "Thank you, sir. That is indeed most gratifying."

"We may pay you a further visit," Holmes informed the old man, who had fallen into a half-laughing, half-coughing fit once more. "But for now, I must thank you for your help, and will bid you adieu."

"Why," Lestrade asked Holmes as we made our way across the fields to Elkinstone Manor, "do you not wish to question the servants ? "

"Because of this," Holmes produced the envelope into which he had placed his find from the garden. "A cigarette end, of an unusual type. You are aware, Lestrade of my contributions to the detective art with relation to such matters ? "

"Very well, but I do not see that this will help us catch the murderer."

"On the contrary, it is the noose round his neck."

On our return to the Manor, Holmes made his way to Sir Barnabas's room, where the baronet was still recuperating from the shock of recent events.

"I have only a few things to ask you," Holmes told him. "May I ask whether your collection, specifically the missing piece, was insured ? "

"Naturally. I shall be making a claim for the theft of the chocolate pot."

"And the amount for which it was insured ? Would that be equal to the amount offered to you by Berenson for the piece ? "

"Slightly in excess of that," was the answer.

"And finally, apart from Berenson, were any other offers made for the pot by any other collector ? "

The baronet frowned in thought. "Lowenstein of California once wrote me a letter offering to buy it, I recall. Mathis of Basingstoke expressed an interest, and McPherson of Edinburgh likewise. Lord Goring and the Duke of Shropshire have at times expressed a mild interest. Other than that, I cannot recall any others. There are very few who would have the knowledge to appreciate the piece, and the purse to afford it."

"Thank you." To my great surprise, and that of the two police officers, Holmes proposed an immediate return to London.

" I believe I will have the murderer for you in forty-eight hours," he told the astonished Lestrade. " I will send for you when it is time to make the arrest."

On the train returning to London, Holmes opened one of the books on antique silverware that I had previously purchased for him, and immersed himself in it. On arrival at Waterloo, we took our leave of Lestrade, and made our way to Baker-street, calling on the way at Leahy's in the Strand, where Holmes replenished his stock of pipe-tobacco.

Once returned, Holmes ensconced himself in his chair, pipe to hand, and a pile of books by his side, which he proceeded to devour. A call to dinner failed to rouse him.

" I must study," he told me. "At this moment, it is more important than food." However, at half-past ten he rose from his chair, clamped a thick slice of roast beef between two slices of bread, and ate it hungrily.

" I am for bed," I told him, as he returned to his chair and picked up the next volume. He replied by means of a wordless grunt without even looking up, and I took myself to my bed-room.

In the morning, the air was blue with the fumes from Holmes's pipe. He himself was nowhere to be seen, and an inspection of his room showed it to be empty, and the bed unslept in. Mrs. Hudson had not seen him that morning, but I assured her that Holmes was unlikely to be in any danger.

A little before luncheon, Holmes returned, dressed in his previous disguise of Ezra Littleboy, the former jeweller's assistant, and in a high good humour.

" We have our man, Watson," he exclaimed. " I lack the final proof that will send him to the gallows, but I expect to be able to obtain that readily enough."

Following our meal, Holmes once again disappeared into his room, and emerged in a different guise. " And now ? " he asked me.

Before me stood the very image of a servant in a good house – a senior footman, perhaps, whose honesty might be in question. His whole deportment and manner proclaimed it, and I said as much to a delighted Holmes.

" Exactly the impression I wish to give. Now, I must be off.

Pray request Lestrade to be at the King's Head public house in Shoreditch at seven o'clock this evening, in the saloon bar, together with a couple of stout constables to be stationed outside in case of trouble. I trust you will accompany Lestrade."

"I would not miss the *dénouement* of this case for the world," I smiled. "You have succeeded admirably in shrouding what at first seemed to be a simple case in an impenetrable mystery."

As Holmes had required of me, I took his request to Scotland Yard, where Lestrade received it with a smile.

"And whom does he suspect?" he asked me. I was forced to reply that I had no conception of the course that Holmes had been pursuing.

"Your Mr. Holmes does enjoy his little secrets, does he not? I was sure that we had Berenson by the heels, but it is clear that even if he is the mind behind the crime, it could not possibly be he who committed the murder."

I spent the afternoon at Scotland Yard, passing the time in conversation with one of the police surgeons with whom I had come into contact in the past, and discussing various ways in which our profession might be developed to be of further service in the apprehension and conviction of lawbreakers.

At a little after six, I rejoined Lestrade, and in company with two constables, as requested, we set out for Shoreditch, where we soon discovered the King's Head public house, the saloon bar of which we entered, leaving the constables outside, with instructions to keep out of sight as far as possible, but to be on the alert for the sound of Lestrade's whistle.

It was immediately obvious that we were far from being the usual type of customer who frequented the establishment. Our fellow-drinkers appeared to be those on the far side of the cusp of respectability, and indeed, Lestrade was able to identify several by name, as those with whom he had had professional dealings in the past.

At two minutes past seven, Holmes entered, dressed as I had seen him earlier that day. His disguise was so complete that Lestrade failed to recognise him, and I was forced to surreptitiously identify him for the policeman's benefit.

After a few minutes, another man entered and joined Holmes

at his corner table. It was clear that the beard and moustache that he wore were false, and that the shabby coat that he wore was not his usual wear, to judge by the state and the quality of his boots.

Holmes was smoking his briar pipe, and the stranger in his turn pulled out a silver cigarette case. In a short time, the distinctive smell of Turkish tobacco wafted over to us, as Holmes and his companion discoursed in low voices.

Lestrade and I naturally strained our ears to discern the content of their conversation, in as unobtrusive a manner as possible, and I repeat here what I was able to make out.

Stranger: Your note to me this morning was most disturbing.

Holmes (with a slight smile): It was intended to be.

Stranger: No jury will believe you. My word against yours. They will never send me to prison.

Holmes: You are correct there. You will be hanged for what you did.

Stranger: It was never my intention to kill poor Widdenthorpe. I entered the room, the doors being [here there was a rattle of glasses from the bar, and I was unable to make out the following words]. I must have made a noise, and the poor man entered, gripping a poker. Presumably he considered he had discovered a housebreaker at work.

Holmes (amused): So he had.

Stranger: It was him against me. In the brief struggle, I was able to wrest the poker from his grasp, and somehow I struck him over the head with it. He fell senseless.

Holmes: Whereupon you beat him savagely many times on the head, did you not ?

Stranger: I panicked. I did not know what I was doing. Then I came to myself and realised that I still did not have the item for which I had come. I opened the case, removed the chocolate pot and left the house.

Holmes: Lighting a cigarette as you did so, no doubt in an attempt to calm yourself.

Stranger: How do you come to know that ? And what do you want of me ?

Holmes: Justice, Baron, justice.

At this point Lestrade leaped to his feet and blew his whistle.

He made a move towards the clearly petrified companion of Sherlock Holmes, as the two constables entered the room, to the consternation of the clientele, many of whom started towards the door.

Holmes leaned forward and tugged at the other's false beard, which came away in his hand to reveal a face well-known to readers of Society magazines.

Laying his hands on Holmes's companion, Lestrade declared, " I arrest you, Baron Dowson, for the murder of Charles Widdenthorpe. Will you come quietly, or must I use these ? " He produced a pair of handcuffs from his pocket. At this, the other customers of the King's Head quietly moved as far away from our little circle as possible, a proceeding that Holmes regarded with amusement.

" I will come with you," said the Baron, for it was he, despite his advanced age, one of the most photographed men about town, and the doyen of many glittering *soirées*. " But," turning to Holmes, " since when have the police used a man's domestic servants as spies and tattletales ? "

" I am no servant," Holmes replied calmly. " My name, Sherlock Holmes, may, however, be familiar to you."

" Oh, well. In that case..." the Baron grumbled.

" Let's have you down at the Yard," Lestrade told him, with little more ceremony than he would have used had he been arresting one of the " regulars" who stood around the edges of the room, wide-eyed.

When we had returned to Baker-street I asked Holmes how he had managed to track down the murderer so quickly.

" There were one or two clues that Lestrade and that good country inspector completely failed to take into account. First, we had the fact that although it was reported that the French windows to the room had been locked, there was no sign of forced entry. We can only conclude that they were in fact unlocked when he entered. As we walked to those windows, I could detect no other obvious signs of footprints or forcing at any other window, which implies that the perpetrator knew that the doors to the room where he would find the silver pot would be unlocked.

" Then there were the footprints on the ground outside.

Though, as I remarked, the local police had done their best to destroy the evidence, there were still signs of a pair of shoes, as opposed to police boots, entering and leaving the room. On the way out, the creator of these footprints had smoked a cigarette of a very distinctive type. I instantly recognised the tobacco as being of Turkish origin, and the maker's name, Leahy's, was printed on the paper. As you know, I called at Leahy's and they identified that type of cigarette as being specially made for only a few customers – a half-dozen at most.

" Of those half-dozen, who was the most likely candidate ? From my conversations as Ezra Littleboy, I had established the names of the foremost collectors of antique silver. I also obtained such a list, as you heard, from Sir Barnabas. One name was on my list but not on the list of Sir Barnabas – that of Baron Dowson. Why ?

" On learning from Berenson that Sir Barnabas was in financial difficulties, and from Sir Barnabas himself that his collection was insured, I was able to tie together two threads, and conclude he had arranged for Baron Dowson, known to at times undertake proceedings of a somewhat adventurous nature, to purloin the prize of Sir Barnabas's collection, so that the insurance might be collected, without Sir Barnabas having to expose his financial difficulties to the public, which would otherwise have been the case were the chocolate pot to be offered for sale, no matter how discreetly."

"And the Baron would perform this dastardly deed himself ? "

" It would appeal to his nature, as well as having the added advantage that the fewer who know of this plot, the closer the secret.

" Following my identification of the thief, whom I might justifiably assume was also the murderer, I determined to convict Dowson out of his own mouth. By posing as a servant of Sir Barnabas, and leaving a note for him, together with some very heavy hints that I knew all, I lured him to a place where he was expecting to pay money in exchange for my silence. With a few facts based on my deductions, as you saw, he was convinced that I was an eyewitness to the murder. The pattern of the bloodstains on the floor told me how the murder had been committed – with a single blow to strike the victim down, and then with a flurry of frenzied violent strikes to the head, shattering the skull and indicating a sense of panic on the part of the murderer, rather than the more dispassionate approach of a hardened criminal. I have no doubt had I persisted with the conversation, Dowson would have been willing to part with a large sum to keep my mouth closed."

" But did you not suspect Berenson at first ? "

Holmes laughed. " There is one excellent reason, other than Berenson's physical condition, why I knew it could not be he. The man is a collector who loves display. He is far from being the secretive miser of legend. A rogue in business, perhaps, but an honest rogue, if you take my meaning. If he acquired that bauble, he would wish to display it. No, there is no way that he would be the thief."

Dowson was sent for trial, where he pleaded guilty to murder, and was sentenced to be hanged, there being no extenuating circumstances. Following Holmes's report to Scotland Yard, Sir Barnabas Elkinstone was arrested and charged with insurance fraud, but was found dead in his bed the morning that he was die to stand trial. A verdict of accidental death was returned.

Sherlock Holmes visited Baron Dowson in prison the night before he was hanged, and on that occasion, the condemned man paid Holmes that handsome tribute to his thespian powers that I have mentioned elsewhere.

The Adventure of the Murdered Medium

HE years immediately following the Great War were in many ways even more challenging than the war years themselves. I, along with many of my profession, found ourselves ministering to the spirits as much, if not more so, as to the bodies of our brave boys who had returned from France, who had witnessed horrors beyond our imaginings. Added to which, the pernicious influenza that ravaged our population cast a constant gloom over the whole population, myself included.

Although I had intermittently been in contact with my friend Mr. Sherlock Holmes, the intimacy of our earlier friendship was missing, and this was an additional cause for a sense of despondency which grew on me by the day.

One of the patients at the military hospital where I was practising was a former captain of the Grenadiers who had been wounded while serving with his regiment at Arras. As it happened, I discovered through conversation with him that I had served with an uncle of his in India, and this happy coincidence cheered both him and me.

One day he mentioned to me that he was anxious to be discharged from the hospital as soon as possible. This in itself was not unusual – many of our patients were impatient (if you will pardon the play on words) to return to what they trusted would be a normal life. What stuck in my memory were the words he used to describe his wishes.

" My family, though of an ancient lineage, is afflicted by poverty, though this was not always the case. One of my ancestors was a sea captain, with rumours that he was a buccaneer, and that he came home from the sea laden with treasure, which, on account of his not trusting others, he buried in the grounds of the family home, intending to dig it up should he ever be in need of the money. Sadly, he died before he recovered the gold and jewels, and the secret of their location was lost with him."

" Many such stories exist in our older families," I laughed. " Usually they are legend without any substance."

" This may be the case here," Captain Groves ruefully admitted to me. " It is, however, a very strong item of faith within our family, and indeed many of us, my late father, Sir William included, have attempted to locate the treasure and restore the fortunes of our house, but to no avail. Indeed, our family was reduced to being forced to sell some of our land to a neighbour about a hundred years ago, in order to clear some debts."

About a month following this conversation, I pronounced Captain Groves to be sufficiently cured for him to be discharged from the hospital, though I feared he would walk with a pronounced limp for the rest of his life.

The story of the buried treasure continued to work on my mind, as I suppose it must with any man possessed of an imagination, and I cast my thoughts back to the time when Holmes and I had chased a boat, supposedly laden with a similar treasure, down the Thames. On that occasion, we had lost the jewels to the mud of the river's bed, but I had gained a greater treasure, Mary Morstan, who condescended to become my wife, for alas ! too short a time before her death.

My work at the hospital continued to occupy most of my time and energy, however, and it was with some surprise that I received a letter from Captain Groves.

" My dear Doctor," the note read. " I very much dislike presuming on your good nature in this way, but I would very much appreciate your assistance in a matter which is causing me considerable concern. As I mentioned to you while I was your patient, my younger brother was lost in the Somme. He was always the darling of the family, loved by all, myself included, and I fear that his loss has sent my widowed mother into a nervous decline. She has recently taken up with a younger man, a certain Lucas Klopstock, of whose antecedents I am unsure, but I suspect him to be from a nation in the east of Europe. Certainly he is not British, but that should not be any cause for concern. What troubles me are the beliefs of this bounder. He has persuaded my mother that he is able to communicate with my deceased brother's spirit, and that, given time, he will be able to summon the spirit of Black Jack, my supposed pirate ancestor, and reveal the secret of the buried treasure. While he is making these preposterous claims, he is staying with us, living the life of Riley at my family's expense, as my mother denies him nothing. I have caught him on more than one occasion looking through our family papers. I dare not throw the blighter out on his ear, dearly as I would like to do so, for I fear for my mother's very sanity were I to carry out my wish. I am aware that at one time you worked with the consulting detective Mr. Sherlock Holmes. Would it be possible for you to pay a visit to Kidlington Hall, with or without Mr. Holmes, and discover exactly what it is that this rogue is after. You may, if you choose, care to make this a medical visit. My lower leg, despite your expert attention in hospital, is still giving me some discomfort."

As it happened, I was due some leave, and the prospect of spending a few days in Oxfordshire was a pleasant one. I dispatched a telegram to Holmes, inviting him to join me, if he was free to do so, and hinting at the prospect of a mystery to be solved.

Within the hour I had received a reply from him.

"DELIGHTED TO JOIN YOU. WILL ARRIVE SATURDAY AFTERNOON STOP SEND DETAILS OF MYSTERY TO ME C/O ADMIRALTY STOP SH STOP"

It was news to me that Holmes was still engaged in work for the Government – I had privily been made aware of the nature of his work during the War with the group known as Room 40, who had been responsible for breaking the codes of the Kaiser, including that infamous telegram which hastened our American friends into joining us against the Teutonic hordes. However, I had imagined that Holmes had by now severed his links with that section of the British government, and the requested address caused me to exercise a little curiosity.

Nonetheless, I assembled the few facts that I had at my disposal, summarised them, and passed them on to Holmes addressing the letter as directed.

I journeyed down to Kidlington on Friday morning, and as arranged by telegram, was met at the station by Captain Groves himself, driving a dog-cart.

"Glad to see you, Doctor," he greeted me. "The bounder Klopstock is still with us, I fear. Still, you will have an opportunity to see him in action for yourself tonight. My mother has invited some of her more feeble-minded friends to dinner tonight, and arranged for Klopstock to perform his trickery afterwards."

"A *séance* ?"

"Yes, that's what he calls these sessions. And not cheap, I can tell you. He demands a fair few guineas each time he summons these spirits of his."

We drove on in silence for a while, our dog-cart accompanied by the sound of cheerful birdsong and the scent of the wild flowers along our way. At one point, Groves halted the cart and pointed with his whip through a gap in the trees to our left towards a handsome well-proportioned building in the Palladian style. " Kidlington Hall," he announced, with a touch of pride in his voice.

" A handsome building," I answered him, which was indeed nothing but the truth.

We drove on and arrived at the gate lodge in a few minutes before driving up the avenue of elms towards the Hall. A servant took my cases, and we entered the hallway to be greeted by an elderly lady who was introduced to me as my friend's mother, Lady Groves.

" I am so grateful to you for taking such care of Lionel," she said to me. " He wrote such nice things about you in his letters from the hospital."

" No more than my duty, madam," I answered her. " Though I could hardly have wished for a more cooperative and good-natured patient."

She smiled, and turned to her son. " Dear Lucas is resting," she informed him. " He is reserving his energies for this evening." She turned back to me. " I am referring to Mr. Klopstock who is currently staying with us." She paused, and Captain Groves leaped into the conversational breach.

" I was telling Doctor Watson about Mr. Klopstock as we drove from the station," he said in a tone that effectively precluded any further discussion on the subject.

" Indeed, that is the case," I confirmed.

" Very well, then. Lionel, why don't you show Doctor Watson to the Green Bedroom so that he can make himself ready for luncheon at one o'clock ? "

Groves spoke to me in a low undertone as he led the way up the stairs. " Resting, indeed. I'll bet the wretch is ransacking my father's papers at this very minute."

" For what purpose would he be doing that ? " I asked.

" Searching for a clue to my ancestor's treasure is my guess. Trying to discover exactly what we own, where it is, and how he can get his filthy paws on it." His face corrugated with rage and I feared that he might suffer an apoplectic fit. I was concerned for him, given his recent medical history, which included shell-shock.

" Steady on, old man," I said, laying a hand on his arm. " Don't get over-excited about this."

Instantly he seemed to become quieter and more composed. " My apologies," he said in a calm voice. " There is something about this man and his business that upsets me beyond all reason."

We arrived at the top of the stairs, and I caught at his arm. " Tell me, where does this Klopstock sleep ? "

" Why, in this room just here," he answered me, pointing to a door.

" Might I trouble you to stand guard outside the room while I make a quick search. If, as you say, he is engaged in some nefarious activity downstairs, there will be no danger of his interrupting me."

" What are you hoping to discover ? " Groves asked me.

" I have some ideas," I told him, but I was reluctant to say more. It was not my intention to be secretive for the sake of producing mystery, but I felt it was as well for as few people as possible to know what I was about.

In fact, Sherlock Holmes had replied to my letter informing him of the doings at Kidlington Hall with a letter of his own, in which he enumerated many of the tricks that were employed by fraudulent mediums in their trickery.

I slipped through the door that Groves held open for me, and started to search the bottom drawers of the dressing-table. There were one or two items of interest, corresponding to those of which I had been informed by Holmes in his letter. I left them undisturbed, but made a list of them in my notebook.

The whole operation took me a little less than five minutes, at the end of which time I left the room, closing the door behind me.

" Did you find what you were looking for ? " Groves asked me.

" Indeed I did," I answered, and I confess that at that moment, I felt a sense of satisfaction, as of a job well done. The room to which Groves showed me was large and comfortable, with a splendid view over the fields towards the dreaming spires of Oxford.

After an admirable lunch, Groves proposed to show me some of the estate, and I put on my ulster to join him. He was carrying a shotgun under his arm, and I looked at it curiously.

" It's not the season for pheasant, is it ? " I asked him.

" No," he laughed, " but I might get a shot at some rabbits."

The estate, such as it was, was not particularly large, and a walk of only a few minutes brought us to the boundary where the Groves estate marched alongside that of the Earl of Doncaster.

" A grouchy old so-and-so," Groves chuckled, referring to the earl. " Good enough in his own way, I suppose, but too quick off the mark when it comes to defending what he sees as his rights, in my opinion."

" Now," Groves told me as we turned back, " I will show you something of interest." A few hundred yards past a small copse brought us to the brink of a circular crater, some three yards across, and two deep.

" We saw enough of these in France, I can tell you," chuckled Groves. " But this one isn't the work of the Boche. This was all my father's doing. He was convinced that this was the site at which Black Jack had stowed his loot." He shook his head. " Clearly, he was mistaken." He stopped suddenly, and pointed with the barrel of his gun to a spot on the other side of the crater. " Halloa ! What have we here ? " He indicated a spot of bare earth which by all appearances had been disturbed recently, probably within the past few days.

" Moles ? Rabbits ? A badger, perhaps ? "

" Nonsense, my dear doctor. You have spent too long in the consulting-room and not enough time in the open air. The animal that created that excavation was of the species *homo sapiens*. Look, you can even see the blighter's footmarks."

It was true enough. There was a trail of imprints, as of a square-toed shoe or boot. From my time with Sherlock Holmes, I was also able to deduce that the wearer of those boots walked with a slight limp, the left foot being slightly twisted inwards. I said nothing, but stored away the fact for future reference.

"Most intriguing," were my words as we started to turn back towards the hall.

"Damned if I'm going to let him get away with this," my companion muttered.

"Why did your father dig there ?" I asked, seeking to change the subject.

"Oh, some poppycock foolishness about 'when the Chittering spire shows between the hills, and St Michael's tower to the west is aligned with the House'. Some nonsense of Black Jack's. See." He pointed in one direction, where the tip of a steeple was visible through an indentation in the low hills, and then in another direction , where a square church tower stood prominent in the landscape, almost lost in the slight mist that still clung to the land. "Take my word for it, on a clear day, the tower of the cathedral at Christ Church College, which as you no doubt know is often referred to as the House, is in line with this tower at this point."

"It seems clear to me," I said. "And yet your father found nothing ?"

"A false scent," Groves admitted ruefully.

On our return to the Hall, before dressing for dinner, I wrote an account of the day's events, and addressed it to Holmes before leaving it in the post-bag in the hall to be carried to the village post-office. After making myself presentable for dinner, I made my way downstairs to the drawing-room, where Groves had told me the dinner guests were to assemble.

Imagine my surprise as I viewed the entrance hall from the stairs as I descended, to see a figure in evening dress take up the post-bag, and remove a letter from it. It was too distant for me to discern the identity of the letter, but somehow I was certain that it was my epistle to Holmes that was in the miscreant's hands.

By the time I had reached the bottom of the stairs, the letter and its taker had vanished into the drawing-room. I could only assume that the unknown was also staying in the Hall – it was most unlikely that one of the dinner guests would engage in such activity – and I had no reason to believe that Groves would examine his guests' mail.

I entered the drawing-room, and Lady Groves introduced me to some of the guests. Most of the women were wearing black, and many of the men sported mourning bands. I guessed that all these had lost sons or other relatives in the War, and were here to attempt to make contact with their departed loved ones.

Lastly, I was introduced to the infamous Klopstock, and a young lady, described by Lady Groves as his secretary. Lucas Klopstock himself struck me with a powerful feeling of unease. It was difficult for me to state precisely on what grounds I experienced this sensation, but neither his limp handshake nor the over-broad smile disclosing teeth that seemed too regular and white inspired confidence. His voice, when he spoke, betrayed more than a trace of a European accent. As for his secretary, though she was demurely dressed, to me it appeared that her pretty young face held more than a hint of mischief. As was the case with her employer, there was something that was indefinably un-English about her speech.

Elena, for that was her name, immediately attached herself to me, and began a conversation which indicated that she had an extensive knowledge of Sherlock Holmes and my association with him.

" How I would like to meet him," she sighed, laying her hand upon my sleeve.

I thought to myself that if my suspicions regarding her employer were correct, a meeting with Holmes would not be entirely to her taste, and might result in a somewhat different outcome to the one she clearly had in mind.

At dinner, I found myself seated next to her, and for the first course, she managed to chat away in a seemingly innocent manner without, however, providing me with any significant information about either herself or her employer. My other neighbour was the wife of a local dignitary, who proceeded to provide me with an exhaustive account of how her eldest son had been reported as missing, presumed dead, after that terrible third battle at Ypres, which had claimed so many young lives.

Quite frankly, it was a a relief to me when the signal came for the ladies to retire, and the men to light their cigars and pass the port. To my intense disappointment, this did not take place.

Klopstock addressed the company before any of us had even removed our cigar-cases from our pockets, or laid a finger on the decanter. " The spirits will be offended if the air is polluted by tobacco smoke," he announced in his curious accent. " Nor will they manifest themselves if alcohol is allowed to befuddle our brains."

There was an audible sigh from many of the assembled company, but no one seemed inclined to challenge Klopstock on this matter. Conversation was desultory, and lasted only a matter of a few minutes before Groves rose and led the men to join the ladies in another room, where a circle of chairs had been placed around a round table, draped with a purple velvet cloth. Lady Groves invited us all to take our places and, as at dinner, we were seated alternately men and women. The secretary, Elena, was not part of the circle, but remained outside it, presumably to manage the ' business' of the *séance*.

I found myself between my companion of the dinner table and Lady Groves, whose small dry hand clasped mine as Elena dimmed the lights, and the *séance* began.

I had attended such gatherings before, and the show played out in a familiar fashion. Cracks and knockings were heard from the table, no doubt produced by the mechanical hammer that I had observed on my visit to Klopstock's room. Klopstock himself produced a variety of voices delivering the usual vague inanities, and the fine muslin I had seen in the drawer upstairs made an appearance as ectoplasm.

These phenomena were all received uncritically by my two female neighbours, who kept muttering phrases such as " How marvellous ! " and uttering sighs of satisfaction as messages, supposedly from the spirit world, reassured them that after death there was nothing but peace and light, and that there was no pain on " the other side".

After what was probably about three quarters of an hour of this, Klopstock, using his usual voice, announced that he was fatigued, and requested that the lights be turned on.

" I will need all my strength for this next manifestation of the Unknown," he proclaimed. "Through me, the great spirit Desistra will manifest herself. And to prove that she has visited us, she will place her manifested hand into this container of molten paraffin wax," pointing to a container on the sideboard under which Elena had lit a spirit lamp, from which she poured a large amount of liquid wax into a smaller container, about six inches in diameter and about a foot deep, " before dematerialising, leaving a vacant space in the wax, accessible only through the small aperture formed by her wrist when she placed her hand in there. It would be impossible for any material being to perform what is about to happen, and it should convince any of you who still, despite all the proof, harbour doubts regarding the reality of the spirit world and life beyond the grave."

Once more the lights went down, the mechanical hammer did its work, and the cheesecloth made its appearance once more, this time topped by a luminous mask. The grotesque charade made its way to the pot containing the wax, whose spirit lamp had previously been extinguished. There was a hushed silence for a few minutes, at the end of which the apparition vanished abruptly from view, and Klopstock gave a low groan, as if in pain.

" My dear Lucas, are you unwell ? " asked Lady Groves, breaking the silence in the darkness.

" Merely exhausted with the effort of acting as the vessel for Desistra's manifestation," Klopstock replied in a weak voice. " Elena, the light, if you would."

In a matter of a few seconds, the room was once more flooded with light. Elena was standing by the switch, seemingly having been there for the whole period of the *séance*, but I noticed a scrap of muslin protruding from her sleeve, which I was positive had not previously been there. If my suspicions had not already been aroused, I would have taken it for a handkerchief or the cuff of a blouse.

Klopstock motioned to her, and she brought the container of solidifying wax to the table. There was a deep depression in the centre, which might conceivably have been made by a wrist.

"We will wait for a while," said Klopstock, "until the wax has become more solid. Perhaps some coffee might be in order, my dear Lady Groves ? "

The servants brought in coffee, and we partook. I remained where I could keep an eye on the wax.

After about fifteen minutes, Klopstock clapped his hands together, and announced that it was time to prove that the spirit of Desistra had indeed visited us. "And the proof will be provided by the eminent doctor, John Watson, of whose exploits in conjunction with the equally eminent Sherlock Holmes we are all no doubt aware," he announced, handing me a large scalpel. "If you will be good enough, doctor, to perform a dissection that will prove to us all the undeniable truth of the spirit world."

I was naturally reluctant to proceed, but I had no option but to accept the offer with a good grace. There was a strong temptation to destroy any supposed proof of the spirit visit, but I confess to having been intrigued by the problem.

As I removed the wax around the impression, I saw that what Klopstock had predicted had actually come to pass. There was a cavity within the wax which was the shape of a hand. The only connection to the outside was a wrist-shaped tunnel, along which I was satisfied that almost no human hand, no matter how contorted, could pass.

I had had occasion to examine Elena's hands previously before dinner, and her hands, though small, would be unable to pass through the narrow opening. Furthermore, the hand that had left the impression in the wax was considerably bigger than her hands, and she was the only person who had been near the wax, as far as I had been able to ascertain.

"Puzzled, doctor ? " Klopstock's tone verged on mockery. "Remember what William of Ockham said about unnecessary multiplication of entities ? Or what your friend said about when the impossible has been eliminated, whatever remains, however improbable..."

"...must be the truth." I completed the sentence.

"Indeed so." He spread his hands. "Lady Groves, ladies and gentlemen, surely this must convince even the most hardened sceptic. But now, let us to the drawing-room. Gentlemen, I believe we may now enjoy our port, and those of you who in-dulge in the weed may step onto the balcony and enjoy their pleasure."

He had taken control of the gathering, and it seemed that Lady Groves had no objection to his doing so. However, I glanced over to Captain Groves, whose face bore a thunderous expression, and from what I could discern, was grinding his teeth with rage.

I swiftly moved over to him. " I fully agree with you," I said before he could utter a word. " Come onto the balcony with me. I have some fine Havanas here," tapping my cigar-case. " Believe me, he is not worth bothering with. The time to un-mask him is not now. Think of your poor mother if we do. She will be made to look weak and foolish in front of her friends. We will act later."

" By God, we will ! " he exclaimed. He regarded me. " Thank you, doctor. Without your intervention I would have made a fool of myself, and my mother too." He smiled. " Come, let me sample one of these Havanas."

A little diplomacy was enough for me to keep Groves and Klopstock apart for the rest of the evening until the guests departed.

I said goodnight to my host and hostess, and made my way to bed, where I fell asleep almost instantly, and remained un-conscious of any events until I woke at the unreasonably late hour of half-past eight.

I made my way downstairs to the dining-room, where the only other person was the secretary, Elena, breaking her fast with porridge. I greeted her, and helped myself from the sideboard.

" Mr. Klopstock ? " I enquired.

" Out for his usual morning constitutional," she answered. " He usually arises early and walks for a few hours before breaking his fast."

" Most praiseworthy," I answered.

Our repast was interrupted by the entrance of Kerrigan, the butler, clearly flustered.

" Have you seen Captain Groves, sir ? " he asked me.

" No, not this morning."

" Or Lady Groves ? " His tone was almost hopeful.

I shook my head. " Excuse me, but are you feeling un-well ? You appear to be shaken. Come, sit down." I pulled out a chair for him. Indeed, he was ashen-faced, and sweating pro-fusely, despite the coolness of the morning.

"Thank you, sir, but no. It's just that—" he broke off, and looked at Elena. " Excuse me, Miss, that I'm the one who's breaking the news, but your Mr. Klopstock..." His voice tailed off. " Well, he's dead, like. Shot in the head. Harry Jacobs – he's the keeper – came in just now and told us."

" Oh my God ! " Elena screamed. Her face turned as white as a sheet, and she simply sat unmoving, with unfocussed eyes gazing at nothing.

" I have a sedative in my bag in my room," I told the butler. " Stay with her till I return. If I see Captain or Lady Groves, I will inform them of the news."

As it happened, I did not meet anyone on my journey to and from my room. As I administered the sedative to Elena, her eyelids fluttered and a little colour came to her cheeks. I turned to Kerrigan, who was still standing, clearly still in a state of some shock.

" Find a maid," I ordered him, " to take this lady to her room. She needs to be in bed, resting."

"Very good, sir." He left, and returned within two minutes with one of the chamber-maids. I repeated my words to her, and she left with my patient (for I now regarded her as such) in her charge.

"Who has called the police, Kerrigan ? " I asked him.

"Why, no one, sir. We have been waiting for orders from Lady Groves or the Captain."

I let out a snort of exasperation. " Then I shall make the tele-phone call myself."

"Very good, sir."

I was led to the instrument, and there connected to the police station, where I explained that I was calling from Kidlington Hall, and that I was calling on behalf of the Groves family, the members of which seemed to be currently unavailable.

" A dead man, you say, sir ? "

" I believe so. I have not as yet seen him. I will do so as soon

as I have finished this conversation with you. His name is
Lucas Klopstock. He is— rather I should say he was – a guest
of Lady Groves."

" And your name, sir ? "

" My name is Watson. John Watson. I am a doctor, and I will
be happy to act as the medical examiner in the case, should
you require a police surgeon."

" That's very kind of you to offer, sir, but I'm afraid that
might look like some sort of conflict of interest, if you take my
meaning, sir." There was a pause, and what sounded like an
embarrassed cough at the other end of the line. " Doctor John
Watson, sir ? The gentleman who wrote about the cases of the
detective Sher—"

" The same," I interrupted him.

" Honoured to have you on the case, sir. I'm sure there will
be no problem with your assisting us. We will have men at the
Hall within the hour. Thank you for your cooperation, sir."

I smiled to myself as I replaced the receiver. Even after
all these years, and a great and devastating war, the name of
Sherlock Holmes still seemed to inspire respect.

I knew that Holmes was meant to be arriving in the afternoon, but considered that it would be of some advantage if
he were to arrive earlier, so scribbled a brief note: " Come to
Kidlington at once if not sooner. Murder may have been done.
JHW", and handed it to Kerrigan, with instructions that it be
dispatched immediately as a telegram to Holmes at his London
address, where I guessed he would be staying.

The mention of murder would be sufficient to draw him, I
felt, given the enthusiasm he had always displayed at the mention of such crimes. To me, it was simply an excitement generated by the anticipation of his being able to exercise his
intellectual powers, but to others, it seemed to be a morbid
fascination.

I took up my bag, and was met at the door of the Hall by
the keeper, Jacobs, who had been informed that I would be in-
specting the body.

" This way, sir," he said, leading the way towards the copse
that Groves and I had passed the previous day. " I warn you,
sir, that he's not a pretty sight, but I reckon as you'll have seen

worse in the past few years, seeing as how you're a doctor and all that."

" Where did you serve ? " I asked him.

" Mesopotamia, sir. And hell it was, sir. I was right glad to be back in Blighty where there's a nice spot of rain and the sweat's not pouring off a man's back the whole bloody day, if you'll pardon the language, sir."

" I've heard worse," I chuckled. " I've been known to use worse as well."

We trudged on in silence for a while. " He's over there, sir," I was told.

" Have you touched him ? "

" I felt his neck, like, for a pulse. Otherwise, no, sir. He's just as he was when I saw him first. Unless someone else has been here in the last half-hour or so."

I went forward. Jacobs was right. Half the back of the man's head had been blown away. It was clear that this was not self-inflicted. No weapon was visible, and death from such a traumatic wound would have been instant, meaning that there would have been no possibility of disposing of the weapon.

It was clearly superfluous for me to check for signs of life, but I did so, anyway. The word of a doctor would carry more weight at an inquest than that of a gamekeeper, and it might become necessary to prove that life was extinct at the time that I first saw the body. It appeared that the only injury, to the back of the head, had clearly not been caused by a blunt in-strument, but to my eyes, which had seen many such wounds in the previous few years, appeared to be the result of a fire-arm, almost certainly a shotgun, discharged at close range. A further cursory examination confirmed the identity of the vic-tim as Lucas Klopstock, and that on the body's feet were the same strange square-toed boots that matched the prints seen by Groves and me the previous day.

As I straightened up, I noticed that the ground was dis-turbed, and blood was present on some of the vegetation which had been flattened. Clearly Klopstock had not been killed in the place where his body now rested. I followed the trail, care-ful to disturb the scene as little as possible, and after a few yards found myself in a small clearing, in the centre of which was a shotgun, which seemed to me to be the one which I had seen in Groves' hands the previous day.

As I pondered the significance of this, I heard footsteps and voices approaching. I turned back, and saw the keeper accompanying a uniformed constable and a man whom I took to be a plainclothes police officer, who introduced himself with a hearty handshake as Inspector Hardwicke.

" Delighted to have you here, Doctor Watson. I suppose that there is no chance of Mr. Holmes joining us ? " he enquired, with a hopeful expression on his face.

" As it happens, he should be with us today."

" Excellent. I confess that we do not have many deaths like this in our part of the country, and competent assistance is always welcome. Now," turning to the body at our feet, " this is shocking. Do we know who he is ? "

" The name I knew him by is Lucas Klopstock. He was a medium, staying as a guest at the Hall, and he performed a *séance* for us last night. The tricks he played were all fraudulent, I am sure."

" Make a note of all this, Collins," Hardwicke ordered the uniformed constable. " One of these spiritualist johnnies, eh ? A guest of Captain Groves ? "

" Of his mother, I am sure. Captain Groves had no time for the man."

" I see. And you are quite sure that he is dead ? "

I nodded. " Death would have been instantaneous."

"You would swear to that in the witness-box at the inquest ? "

" I would certainly do so. I would add that it would be impossible for a man with that type of wound which has effectively broken the spinal column to have crawled twenty yards." I indicated the trail of broken branches and crushed vegetation.

Hardwicke gave a somewhat puzzled look but said nothing, and I continued. " There is a gun at the other end of that trail, in a small clearing."

" Let us see. Collins, cover the body with the sheet," he ordered. " Jacobs," he told the keeper, " come with us."

I led the way to the copse, where the gun lay prominently on show.

" Do you recognise that gun ? " the inspector asked me.

" I cannot be sure, but it appears to me to be the one that Captain Groves was carrying yesterday when we walked together."

Jacobs had bent and was examining the gun. " It's the Captain's, all right. I've seen it often enough."

Hardwicke turned to me. "And how, precisely, are you acquainted with Captain Groves ? " he asked. " If he is a friend of yours, I may have to ask you to step aside from the case."

Slightly stung by the unspoken implications of this, I explained that Groves had been a patient of mine, and that to the best of my understanding my invitation to the Hall had been partly for the purpose of unmasking Klopstock as a fraud.

" I am unsure of whether I should be asking you this, sir, but were there any symptoms of, shall we say, disturbance, in Captain Groves when you treated him as a patient ? If you do not answer this question, I will not take it amiss."

I was torn between my desire to see the law take its course, and my feelings, such as they were for the man who was my host. " At present, I prefer not to answer that."

" I see. And where is Captain Groves now ? "

" I do not know."

Hardwicke asked the same question of Jacobs, who likewise was unable to provide an answer.

" In that case," he said, " we must return to the Hall, and send two men to bring in the body. That is unless, doctor, there are any further investigations you wish to make *in situ.*"

I answered that I believed there was nothing more to be seen as far as the body was concerned, though I added that the area should be disturbed as little as possible once the body had been moved. I also suggested that photographs should be taken of the body and the surrounding area before it was moved.

Hardwicke grunted in seeming approval. "You may be right," he admitted. " I will arrange for this to be done."

On our return to the Hall, Kerrigan presented me with a telegram. " It arrived some ten minutes ago," he explained. I read it, and exclaimed, " Sherlock Holmes is on his way here. He expects to be here before midday."

"Excellent news," said Hardwicke. To the butler, "Have you seen Lady Groves or Captain Groves this morning, my man?"

"Lady Groves is in her room resting, sir. She suffered a severe shock when she was informed of Mr. Klopstock's death, and retired to her room."

"Is she in need of medical attention?" I asked.

"I believe she would welcome a visit from you, sir."

"And Captain Groves?" Hardwicke asked.

Kerrigan shook his head. "No one seems to have seen him today."

"Has his bed been slept in?" I asked.

"It appears so, sir, and his walking outfit is missing."

"I shall ask you later to provide a description of Captain Groves and this walking outfit," Hardwicke told him. "Doctor, you may attend to Lady Groves. I will telephone for a photographer."

Kerrigan coughed. "If you will excuse me, sir. Photography is a hobby of mine. I have a camera and film in my room, and if you are in need of photographs, I will be happy to assist in any way possible."

"Good man," Hardwicke told him. "Would you be prepared to take photographs of the body of Mr. Klopstock, and the surrounding area?"

"I cannot honestly say that it would give me great pleasure, sir, but I am happy to assist the law. I'm sure I have seen worse in my time when I was serving in South Africa. If you will come this way, sir, and inform me of what is needed, I will prepare the appropriate equipment."

They went off, and I took myself to Lady Groves.

"Has my son been found?" she asked me. I shook my head. "And Lucas Klopstock? He is dead, isn't he?" Her tone almost seemed to hold a touch of relief.

"I'm afraid so. I am sorry."

"I am not." Fire flashed in her eyes. "He was a foul beast of a man, and I am glad he is gone. There! I've said it, and I will say it at the inquest if they ask me to."

I remained silent, and she continued.

"He was blackmailing me. He knew things about my late husband that would spell ruin for us if they were made public.

Oh, he was not blackmailing me for money. God knows we have little enough of that, but he wanted the chance to find Black Jack's treasure. He was certain it was here, and he was determined to find it. He spent hours in my late husband's study and in the library. Of course, I never believed that he was a genuine medium. I knew all about the tricks he got up to in the dark, and he knew that I knew, but he saw the chance to make money from my friends, and he took it."

I must have appeared thunderstruck.

" Now, tell me honestly. Do you believe my son killed him ? I have heard the facts from Kerrigan and the other servants. Now I need your opinion."

" The facts argue against him."

" But I can tell from your expression that your heart tells you that he is innocent. My boy would not hurt a fly."

I coughed. " I must tell you that he won his Military Cross for killing seven Germans with an entrenching tool. There is no doubt in my mind that he is capable of killing. As to whether he would murder a man in cold blood, I cannot say. It is more than likely that he was overcome by a fit of rage, and did not know what he was doing."

" I believe he is innocent." Her face was set in a determined expression, and it was clear that I would never be able to convince her otherwise.

" One last question. Did your son know of the blackmail ? Or indeed of the secret regarding your husband ? "

She shook her head emphatically. " No. It was my secret, and mine alone. I had no wish to encumber the poor boy with any more trouble."

I remembered the errand on which I had originally come, and enquired if there was any medical assistance I could render.

" Thank you, no," she smiled. " I am perfectly in control of myself and my faculties. I do, however, trust that what I have just told you will remain as confidential information, as shared between a patient and her medical adviser."

I was slightly taken aback by this, and was forced to make some kind of non-committal answer.

" Never mind," she said. " I suppose all will come out anyway, with or without you. The police these days seem to have no respect for breeding or family. Indeed, I believe it gives them great pleasure to drag us down to the level of common criminals." She waved a languid hand. " You may go."

I left the room, and descended the stairs, just in time to see the front door open, and Sherlock Holmes admitted. Older and greyer he may have been, and moving without the spring in his step which had marked him in his younger days, but the tall lean figure was still unmistakable. I confess that the very sight of Sherlock Holmes transported me back twenty years or more, to the extent of a lump forming in my throat, even before he spoke.

" My dear fellow," he exclaimed as he caught sight of me. " I came as soon as I received your telegram. No baggage, as you see," spreading his empty hands.

"You must have wings to arrive here so promptly," I smiled.

" Hardly that. Though I fear that my chauffeur exceeded the legal speeds for most of our journey. But here I am. Where is the body ? Who is the officer on the case ? And tell me all you know."

" Inspector Hardwicke of the Oxfordshire constabulary is assigned to the case."

" I have no knowledge of him. Sound man ? "

" Inexperienced, but sound, I would say. At least he listens to what I have to say, and he seems to be what the Americans term a ' fan' of your work."

" He is more likely an admirer of your elegant half-fictions," Holmes smiled. " And who and where is the body in this case ? "

" A Lucas Klopstock. Fraudulent medium, and fortune hunter."

" Ah. There is a woman in the case ? "

" There is, but not in the usual way. I will explain later."

" And the cause of death ? "

" Gunshot wound to the back of the head." I indicated on my own person the location of the wound.

" Weapon ? "

" There is a shotgun belonging to my former patient some dozens of yards from the body."

" Hmm. Hardly suicide, then ? "

" Impossible, I would say."

" Very well. Let us go and examine the *corpus delicti*. I take it the inspector is there ? "

" I believe so. He is with the butler."

Holmes raised his eyebrows.

" The butler is an amateur photographer," I explained, " and volunteered to take photographs for the police."

" Most public-spirited," Holmes commented sardonically. " Now," as we made our way to the copse, " tell me all that has happened since you arrived here yesterday."

" I wrote you a letter, which never reached you, on account of its having been purloined before it entered the postal system."

" By whom ? "

" By the murdered man. I trust that the letter is still in existence."

By now, we had reached the copse, and Inspector Hardwicke introduced himself to my friend. I noticed that the butler was engaged in packing away his photographic equipment, presumably having completed his task.

" Delighted to see you, Mr. Holmes," said the police officer, extending his hand in welcome.

" And I you," Holmes replied. " This here," indicating the shrouded body, " is the deceased, I take it ? May I examine the gun that has been discovered ? " he asked.

The inspector showed a little surprise. " Not the body ? " he asked.

" All in good time." We made our way to the gun, and Holmes, having obtained permission from the inspector, used a hand-kerchief to pick it up by the barrel. " You will note, I hope, that I am doing my best to preserve any evidence in the form of fin-gerprints that may exist," he told the inspector, before applying his aquiline nose to the muzzle.

" I do not believe this has been fired since it was last cleaned," he said. " There is no smell other than that of min-eral oil. I believe that when you break the gun, you will either find an empty chamber, or an unfired cartridge. At any event, the hammer is cocked and the safety is still on. If this had been used as the murder weapon, I do not believe the murderer would have recocked the hammer and carefully placed the safety on after firing the fatal shot."

"It has, however, been identified as Captain Groves' gun, and the Captain is nowhere to be found," the inspector pointed out.

"Tush, man. That hardly constitutes proof, as I am sure you are aware." He stopped and looked around him.

"What is through there ?" he asked, pointing to a gap on the trees on the opposite side of the clearing to that where we had just entered.

"That's the edge of our estate, sir," said Kerrigan, who by now had joined us, having packed away his camera. "That on the other side of the fence you can see is Lord Rathbroke's land – that's the Earl of Doncaster, sir."

"Thank you. Now to the body. Have you examined the pockets ?"

"Not yet. We were going to wait until the body had been moved into the Hall."

"Very well." Holmes turned to me. "Have you seen all that you want to see here, Watson ? Do you feel there would be any advantage to delaying the removal of the body ?"

"I do not."

"That is a satisfactory answer."

Hardwicke gave orders to the butler to appoint two servants to carry the body, and to prepare a room in the Hall to act as a temporary morgue.

We slowly made our way back, and awaited the arrival of Klopstock's corpse. Kerrigan, with what might have been a sense of irony, had prepared the very room and table around which we had sat the previous evening for the *séance*.

When the body arrived, the inspector methodically went through the pockets. Other than a few keys, an empty silver cigar case with the initials 'W.G.', small change amounting to seven shillings and four pence, an Ordnance Survey map of the area, some miscellaneous papers, and four 12-gauge shotgun cartridges, there was nothing.

"I'll wager that the shot that caused the fatal wound does not correspond to that in these cartridges," Holmes remarked. "May I be permitted to look at the papers ?"

As he took the papers, I noted that one of them was the letter I had written to Holmes and which had been purloined by Klopstock from the post-bag. The envelope had been opened.

I drew Holmes's attention to this, and he requested permission to read it, given that the letter was addressed to him. He scanned it quickly, and turned to me. " Excellent, Watson. This is of great assistance." He paused. " Where is Elena ? " he asked me.

" Who is that ? " asked the inspector.

I smote my brow. " My God ! I had forgotten all about her. She is Klopstock's secretary – at least, that is how she was introduced to me last night. I do not know her other name. I met her at breakfast this morning, and the discovery of Klopstock's body was announced while we were still eating. She was overcome by a fit of the vapours and I prescribed a sedative and ordered her to bed."

" We must speak to her," said the inspector. " As her doctor in this case, you must go to her room and bring her down here, or obtain her permission to be questioned while she is in bed."

Burning with shame for my omission, I made my way upstairs and knocked on the door of the bedroom where I had been told Elena was staying. There was no answer. One of the maids passing spoke to me.

" There's no use knocking, sir," she told me. " About twenty minutes after she'd gone in there after breakfast she came out again in her walking-dress, carrying a small bag. She said she was going to walk into the village."

I cursed under my breath, angry with myself that I had failed to pay due attention to a woman who might at the very least prove a source of valuable information, and at most might prove to be directly implicated in the crime.

I shamefacedly returned to my companions and informed them of the news.

" We all make mistakes, Doctor," the inspector consoled me, but I remained downcast by my failure.

In the meantime, while I had been upstairs, Holmes had been examining the other papers that had been found on the body.

" I believe I now know the place where Klopstock was killed," he said, " and who was responsible for his death, even if he was not the actual killer."

Hardwicke and I looked at him in astonishment. " It is all here," he explained. " Remind me, if you will, Watson, what Captain Groves told you about the location of Black Jack's treasure – a legendary treasure said to have been buried by an ancestor of the Groves family," he explained to the inspector.

I repeated the story of the alignment of the spires and towers that Captain Groves had told to me.

" Excellent," he said. " Now, look here." He spread out the map that had been discovered on the body, and pointed to a pencil line that had been drawn on it. " This line connects St Michael's tower and Christ Church in the city of Oxford. If there is any truth in the legend, the treasure is buried somewhere along this line."

" Where the Chittering spire appears between the hills," I said.

" Exactly so, according to what you were told. So here we have it," he said, pointing to another line which started at the spire of Little Chittering church, and passed between two sets of contour lines marking hills. " This line meets the other one here."

I examined the map. " That is where Captain Groves' father excavated and found nothing. So Black Jack's instructions are incorrect."

" No, they are perfectly correct," Holmes contradicted me. " See here. There are two villages with the name of Chittering. Little Chittering and Great Chittering."

" True," I said. " But look more closely. The church at Little Chittering has a spire, according to the map, and that at Great Chittering has a tower. The instructions as Grove repeated them to me definitely said the spire at Chittering."

" Very true," said Holmes. " But now let us take a look at this – a page torn from a book on the history of Oxfordshire villages. It says that the church of Great Chittering was struck by lightning in 1805, the year of Trafalgar, destroying the spire, which was never replaced, leaving only the tower. The village of Little Chittering, for its part, constructed a spire on its church tower in the year that Victoria came to the throne, 1837."

" And where does that place the treasure ? " Hardwicke was clearly fascinated.

" Here," said Holmes, pointing to where a third line which had been pencilled on the map, intersecting the line to Christ Church some few hundred yards from the first point.

" I do not believe that lies in the Groves estate," I said, after establishing the features on the map.

" It does not," Holmes agreed. " However..." He produced yet another paper, this time a bill of sale in which a certain Charles Groves made over all rights to a piece of land to a Joshua Rathbroke in 1823. " I cannot be certain, but I believe that this was part of the land sold to meet the family debts, which formed part of the Groves estate at the time of Black Jack, and it is on this land that the treasure, if it exists at all, is to be found."

We sat in silence for a while.

" This is all well and good," said the inspector, " and it is indeed fascinating. But—"

" But what has it to do with the gentleman here ? " indicating the body of Lucas Klopstock. " You were informed, were you not, Watson, that the Earl of Doncaster is very keen on his rights as a landowner. My belief is that Klopstock had discovered all these facts that I have just enumerated, and believed he had located the place where the treasure was buried. Unaware of the reputation of the Earl and his zealous crusade against trespassers on his land, or perhaps uncaring, or believing that there would be no one to hinder him, he crossed the fence. He was spotted by a keeper – possibly even by Lord Rathbroke himself, who knows ? and challenged. Somehow this led to his being shot fatally, maybe without the intention to kill, but killed he was."

" Incredible," I said. " But what of the gun ? Why is it there ? "

" Are we certain that Captain Groves took the gun ? Why might Klopstock not have taken it from the rack in the gun-room as he left the Hall ? "

" For what purpose ? "

" Maybe he did know about Lord Rathbroke's reputation. Self-defence ? Maybe as camouflage to disguise his true motives in going out that morning? It will be easy to discover whether his fingerprints are on the gun. In any case, once he died, the killer clearly decided that the body should not be found on the Doncaster estate, and dragged it to where we discovered it. There was a clear trail of broken twigs and crushed vegetation leading from the fence through that gap in the trees which I remarked, and which you appear to have overlooked."

" Our attention was held by the gun."

" As quite possibly was intended by the one who placed it there. The gun may have been left there as a red herring to distract you from the fact that the death took place some distance away."

" It all seems improbable," said the inspector. " I seem to remember something you once said, though, Mr. Holmes, about eliminating the impossible."

" Please, no." Holmes waved a deprecatory hand. " However improbable my theory, it fits the facts as we know them, supported by these papers. Were we to examine this area of land more closely, we might find ourselves in possession of a fortune."

" Or of a cartridge's worth of birdshot," remarked Hardwicke, sourly. " It does all seem rather far-fetched, Mr. Holmes, but I have to admit it works."

" But where is Captain Groves ? " I asked.

For answer, Holmes grinned broadly. " One last piece of paper. Read," he commanded me.

" Written in violet ink in a feminine hand. Dated last night at 11:30pm. 'It is addressed here to a 'Laszlo—'" I broke off. " The envelope is addressed to Lucas Klopstock."

" His real name. Almost certainly we are looking at what remains of Laszlo Korda, the well-known Hungarian confidence trickster and swindler. If it proves to be he, the world is well rid of him. Continue."

" 'I am leaving you. I have found the man I love, and who is a better man than you can ever aspire to be. You are not worthy to lace the shoes of this noble man. For the past month we have become ever closer, and we have now made our decision. We have made plans and you will not be able to find him or me under the names you knew us by. Nor will you be able to find the money that you stored under your mattress. It will go to repair the fortunes of a brave and honest gentleman. Farewell, E.' " I paused. "It seems to me that given this relationship between Groves and this woman, she would have informed him that Korda was far from being the spiritual guide that he claimed to be. I therefore fail to understand why he should ask you or me to expose him, given that he had the means to do the deed himself."

"I believe," Holmes replied, "that indeed he may have possessed the knowledge to expose Korda. However, I feel that he wished to have corroboration of this from an authoritative source in order to convince his mother, naturally unaware of the true relationship between her and Korda – and you, my dear friend, and possibly I, were to play that part."

Hardwicke had been listening open-mouthed to this exchange. "Let me expand on your theory, Mr. Holmes, if you will forgive my doing so. This woman wrote this letter late last night, and slipped it under this man's door," pointing at the corpse on the table. "He awoke early, read the letter, discovered that his savings had vanished – maybe she had taken them earlier in the day – and despaired. He could, of course, have waited and had it out with her later in the day, but he believed, thanks to these documents which you have linked together most ingeniously, sir, that he was on the verge of a discovery which would offset the loss of his savings."

Holmes had been nodding in agreement during this recital. "Excellent, Inspector. I find all this most plausible."

Encouraged, Hardwicke continued. "He took a gun with him, for whatever reason only he knew. Probably also a spade or some implement with which he could dig for this treasure. I am sure we will find a spade is missing if we ask the gardeners or the park keepers. And met his end, as you have described."

"Your problem now, Inspector," said Holmes, "is how you present the case."

"It is a ticklish business, to be sure," said Hardwicke. "I know that you are a man of the world, sir. How would you handle this if you were in my shoes?"

"Death by misadventure, my dear Inspector. The man went for an early morning lone walk, carrying a gun with which he was unfamiliar. He tripped, dropping the gun, which discharged itself, and it killed him. An open and shut case."

" That is outrageous ! " I exclaimed. " That would be a complete perversion of justice. Lord Rathbroke, or his retainer, cannot be allowed to escape his punishment."

" I have to say that I agree with Doctor Watson regarding this matter," Hardwicke said. " My duty is to bring those responsible before the courts to be judged."

" Your sentiments do you both credit," said Holmes. His face was grave as he continued. " Let us assume that Rathbroke has not discovered the treasure, the existence of which, I may tell you, I have serious doubts. Too many country families such as the Groves claim to have pirate or highwayman ancestors whose ill-gotten gains are secreted away. On a few occasions these romantic legends prove to have a foundation of proof. In most cases, they are simply that – romantic legends. If it transpires in the future that Rathbroke has suddenly acquired an unexplained source of wealth, then we may re-open the case." He paused and looked each of us in turn full in the eye. " What I am about to tell you now must be held in the strictest confidence, at least for the immediate future. As you are aware, Watson, much of my time is taken up with government affairs. Since the death of brother Mycroft, I have taken his place in some affairs of state. I am sure that you both are aware of Lord Rathbroke's position in the Cabinet ? Yes ? The position of this government is currently in a precarious state as the result of a number of factors, not all of which are public knowledge at present."

I nodded in understanding, as did the inspector.

" Very well," Holmes went on. " Should Lord Rathbroke, or even one of his servants, be arrested and prosecuted for their part in this death, it is quite likely that other sensitive matters will be revealed. We know that Korda was blackmailing Lady Groves. It is more than probable, though I cannot confirm this publicly, he had another ' client' in Rathbroke and maybe even more in the Cabinet. Any exposure resulting from a trial would bring about the collapse of the government."

" I see," said Hardwicke, thoughtfully.

" That would be a matter of international consequence. The

new naval treaty now being negotiated between the nations of the world depends for its success on the prestige and influence of the current First Lord of the Admiralty. Should he be replaced, as would certainly be the case..." Holmes shrugged.

"The naval treaty would never be signed, and the nations of the world would once more bankrupt themselves building unlimited dreadnoughts?" I suggested.

"Precisely so. And we might be plunged into another terrible global conflict."

There was a sombre pause, broken by Inspector Hardwicke.

"And Captain Groves and this woman?"

"I fancy that his mother will not be too unhappy if he believes he has found someone to love him," I said. "I have the feeling that she wishes his happiness, whatever that may be."

"One more thing," I said to Holmes as we were driven back to London in his official motor-car. "The hands in the wax. How do mediums perform that trick? I have been puzzling over it, and I cannot work it out."

"An old trick. Three words. Inflated rubber gloves. The rest you can surely deduce for yourself, having covered yourself with glory before my arrival. Save for a few major errors in judgement, of course."

I basked in this rare praise from Holmes, and sat back contented as the powerful motor devoured the miles on the road to London.

The Adventure of
the Dead Rats

Y friend Sherlock Holmes could never be described as one of the tidiest of men. Mrs. Hudson, our long-suffering housekeeper, was forced to endure a state of continued disorder that would have driven many other women into a terminal decline.

Quite apart from the presence of piles of paper covering almost every available surface, and the frequent presence of strange objects, often exhibiting clear evidence that they had been used in the commission of acts of violence, there was often an almost impenetrable fog of tobacco smoke which mimicked the London fogs outside the room. I confess that I was not entirely innocent as regards the last, but the emissions from Holmes's pipe far outweighed my more modest offerings.

Mrs. Hudson, however, no doubt mollified by the handsome sums that Holmes paid in rent, appeared to be largely unruffled, confining herself to mild remonstrations and clucking sounds.

For my part, I learned to tolerate most of the eccentricities that surrounded me, but towards the start of my acquaintance with Holmes, his occupation one morning as I entered the room after my constitutional tested the limits of my patience.

"What on earth are you doing?" I asked him, as I saw him stooped over the dining-table, on which the remnants of our breakfast had been pushed to one side. "Is that a dead rat?"

"Indeed it is," my friend assured me. "*Rattus norvegicus*, to be precise. A fine specimen, is he not?" He indicated the lifeless rodent, in the belly of which, judging by the bloodied scalpel lying beside the corpse, he had made an incision.

"This is intolerable!" I exclaimed. "The dining-table, indeed, our sitting-room, is no place for anatomical examinations. I demand that you remove this disgusting object to a more suitable location before Mrs. Hudson sees what you are doing, and throws us onto the street – an action that would be fully justified, in my opinion."

It was not often that I became angry with Holmes, but this latest exploit had, as I say, overstepped the boundaries of my tolerance.

Almost sheepishly, Holmes gathered up the rodent and surgical instruments.

" Would you have the goodness to move the bottles of prussic acid and strychnine from the laboratory bench and return
them to their places on the shelves ? " he asked me.

I did so, and he deposited his burdens on the space thus
vacated.

" Now tell me," I demanded. " Where did that rat come from,
and why are you so interested in it ? "

" To answer your first question, it was sent by messenger, in
the box you see there, a little after you went out. The answer
to your second question may be found in the note that accompanied it." He removed a paper from the top of the pile before
him. " Here, you may read it for yourself."

I took the paper, and read out loud, " 'The Fir Trees,
Artington, Guildford'. Dated yesterday. 'Dear Mr. Holmes,
Please excuse the contents of this package, which I assure you
I would not have sent had I not considered it necessary to do
so. As you will see, it is a Brown Rat, which I discovered deceaced outside the kitchen door of our house. This is far from
being the first specemin of its kind that I have discovered in
recent days'." I broke off. " This is more than a little ridiculous, Holmes. Does this man, for so I take the writer to be, expect you to behave like the character in Robert Browning's
poem and charm the vermin ? Surely there are rat-catchers in
Guildford ? "

" Read on," Holmes commanded.

" 'As you may imagine, I am angered by the fact that some
twenty of these rodents have been deposited outside my door
(for I cannot concieve how they all crept there to make it their
final destination in life) over the past week or so. I have hidden
the existance of these objects from my wife, and instructed the
servants not to mention them, as I am sure that she would be
upset by these events. Would you have the goodness to examine the enclosed in order to determine the cause of death ? If
I make so bold, the assistance of your companion, Doctor John
Watson, may be of value in this. Unless I hear from you otherwise, I intend calling on you this afternoon. Yours sincerely,
Mortimer Maberley (Capt., retd.)'."

" Well, Watson, a pretty little puzzle, is it not ? Twenty rats, all deceased in mysterious circumstances, all located at the same spot."

"And no obvious cause of death, I take it? No wound or injury?"

"Not that I can discern. Come, perhaps you would care to examine the *corpus delicti*? Captain Maberley seems to be under the impression that your professional expertise may be of value here, and I cannot say that I entirely disagree with him."

"Very well," I answered, "though my last experience of dissecting a rat was some years ago, in the early stages of my medical education."

It was the work of only a few minutes to confirm Holmes's observation that there were no visible wounds or injuries on the body of the unfortunate rodent. A few more minutes, during which I found myself praising Holmes's skill in dissection, revealed no obvious damage to the internal organs.

"Almost certainly poison, I would say," I declared. "Almost impossible to say when or where it was administered or what type of poison was used. Are you really intending to take on this case?"

"I will at least listen to what this Captain Maberley has to say to us. What do you make of the letter itself?"

I picked up the letter again and addressed myself to it, attempting to obtain information from it in the fashion which I had often observed with Holmes. "The handwriting definitely has a masculine flavour to it," I started. "And although the language is fluent and accurate for the most part, I do notice that there are one or two errors in spelling, such as ' concieve', ' deceaced', ' specemin' and ' existance'. I would say that this is the hand of a man who is unused to expressing his thoughts in writing."

"Indeed so. The paper, the ink?"

"I see nothing remarkable there."

"Both are of exceedingly poor quality. As you can see, this has been written with a steel nib, not a fountain pen, and one likewise of poor quality, moreover. The address on the package containing our visitor was written in a different hand, possibly feminine., but also using the same pen and ink, and also, by the appearance, unused to writing. The number of our house is missing, the package being simply addressed to Sherlock Holmes, Esq., Baker-Street, London. It seems that you are well enough known for the carrier to be able to deliver it," I smiled.

Holmes ignored my last, and continued. "The rat here was in a cardboard box, originally used for some other purpose. The remnants of a label saying '...nderby and Sons, Ltd., London SW' still adhere. I would venture that this is Enderby and Sons, the well-known suppliers of female apparel. The paper used in this package has previously been used for wrapping something else," he put his nose to the paper and sniffed, "I would say onions. The odour was quite noticeable when I first opened the box. Is our Captain Maberley one of the tribe of whom it is said that they have long pockets and short arms ? Even so, Enderby's is not the cheapest of emporia and the address would seem to indicate a certain level of prosperity. Perhaps we may deduce that Maberley has risen from humble beginnings to his present state, and still retains a certain caution in the way that he spends his money. And why, you may ask, would he ask the cook to write the address ? "

"The cook ? " I confess to being baffled by this last statement of Holmes.

"If the paper used to wrap the box was originally used to wrap food, then it would certainly have been left in the kitchen. Who better, then, to address the package ? "

"And why did he not address it himself ? "

"Perhaps he did not wish his wife to know of the existence of this plague of rats." Holmes's face took on that characteristic smile betokening the welcome of a problem to be solved. "There is something about this business that intrigues me. Let us welcome the Captain when he arrives this afternoon."

"In the meantime, I suggest that we remove all traces of this," I indicated the rat, "from the dining-table and elsewhere. Mrs. Hudson would, in my opinion, be perfectly entitled to turn us out onto the street if she were to discover that we were dissecting vermin on her furniture." I sniffed the air. "At least it is not producing an odour at present, but I fear that it will do so very soon, and we should take steps to dispose of it at the first opportunity."

"Very well," said Holmes. "In any case, I fear there is little more we can achieve with regard to a solution without more information from Captain Maberley."

Suiting our action to the words, we were soon able to make the room presentable to Mrs. Hudson. The rat was concealed in the coal-scuttle, to be disposed of in an alley by either Holmes or me, dependent on who left the house first.

Captain Maberley made his appearance at half-past two precisely. He was somewhat short in stature, with close-cropped greying hair, and a small moustache. I noticed a certain stiffness in one leg as he took his seat in the chair that Holmes reserved for clients. Remembering what Holmes had marked earlier about the Captain's spending habits, I remarked that the boots, though originally of good quality, had aged, and appeared to have been repaired, more or less skilfully, on more than one occasion.

" It's very good of you to see me, Mr. Holmes," were his first words, delivered in an accent which had more than a touch of the Midlands counties about it. " I told myself several times that such a great man as yourself would hardly be interested in such a trivial matter as this, but I assure you that this business has been a fair trial to me."

From my long acquaintance with Sherlock Holmes, I could tell that this speech caused him some amusement, but this would not have been obvious to any person who did not know him as well as myself.

" Pray continue, Captain Maberley," he invited our visitor.

" Perhaps I should tell you a little about myself. I was born in the city of Derby, and joined the Army as a boy. I fought as a sergeant with the Sherwood Foresters in Egypt, and would you believe, they gave me the Queen's Commission and a medal for something I did. The same business that gave me this," tapping his leg. " It still pains me in wet weather. Not that I'm one to boast about what I did, but it took me up in the world, it did. I married Mary, the widowed sister of one of my fellow officers, soon after my promotion, and I have to confess to you that there were words in the Mess about the match."

Holmes raised a quizzical eyebrow at this, which Maberley took as a request for further explanation.

"You see, Mr. Holmes, I wasn't of the same class as them. They'd been brought up all proper and knowing which fork to use at dinner and all that. And the idea of a former ranker sitting at the same table as them was not altogether to their taste, as you might say."

"It didn't seem to prevent you being promoted," I remarked.

"I was good at my job," he replied. It was not a boast, but a statement of simple fact. "But I knew that I'd never get past Captain, and that was good enough for me. I took my pension, and retired to the house in Guildford which had been left to my Mary by her parents." He paused. "I have to tell you that once again, those neighbours where I now found myself barely tolerated our existence. Indeed, if Mary's parents had not lived in the house before, I do not think we would have been tolerated at all. For myself, I do not mind too much, but it has broken my wife's heart to be shunned by those families with whom she grew up."

He spoke with a certain resignation, rather than with bitterness, and it was hard not to feel some pity for this man who had given so much for his country.

"You would not consider removing from there ?" I asked, and for the first time in his narrative, there was a flash of anger from Captain Maberley.

"I would not give them the satisfaction," he exclaimed. "In any case, Mary would never agree to leave her childhood home."

There was a silence, wherein we digested what we had just been told, broken by Holmes, who addressed himself to our client.

"May we talk about the rats ?" he asked.

"If we must," was the reply, accompanied by a shudder. "I have always hated the beasts, since I was a child. They disgust me more than I can say, and I have never made any secret of it to anyone." He paused. "About three weeks ago, as I was leaving the house for my morning cigar – I should perhaps explain that a cigar of a morning is a habit I developed as a young man, and I still continue to practice it, although Mary is somewhat worried about the effect of the smoke on the health of Douglas, her little boy from her first marriage, and for that reason I only smoke my cigars outside the house."

" Most considerate of you," Holmes remarked.

" Thank you. In any event, I noticed a dead rat just outside the front door," replied Maberley, shuddering once more at the memory. " It repelled me, but I forced myself to turn it over with the aid of a stick. Even so, I could discern no injury."

" How did you explain its presence to yourself ? " asked Holmes.

" It may be un-Christian of me, but my first thought was to assume that the rat had been killed by poison, and placed at my door by my neighbour, Sir Bertram Colton."

" You have a reason for ascribing this action to him ? " Holmes asked.

" Sadly, yes. He is a man who is known throughout the district for his bad temper and general dislike of almost everything. I fear that I am a special object of his dislike."

" Bertram Colton," Holmes mused. " The name is familiar. Watson, would you be kind enough to hand me the Index from the shelf behind you ? Thank you. Ah yes, my collection of C's. Colton. Ha ! Yes, indeed, Captain Maberley, you are correct in your report. He was bound over regarding a quarrel over a card game at the Albermere Club some years ago, and only escaped prosecution for assault on another occasion involving his carriage and that of another by buying off the case with a large sum of money. A man who is clearly a man of strong passions and of a temperament to put his thoughts into action. Pray continue," he invited Maberley.

" Well, Mr. Holmes, after breakfast I requested our gardener to dispose of the rat, after first informing Cook of our unwelcome visitor, and cautioning her to say nothing to my wife about the rat."

" Your wife shares your antipathy to the creatures ? " Holmes asked.

" She does, though I confess my dislike is stronger than hers. No, my reasoning was that she would be upset by the action of our neighbour, whose family were friends with her parents. Indeed, Sir Bertram and she used to play together as children."

" Indeed ? " murmured Holmes. " And I am to take it that these visitations continued ? "

" Indeed they did," was the answer. " One, two, or on one occasion, three corpses of rats have been left beside the door."

" Always in the same place ? "

" Indeed so. I had my suspicions, and one night I kept watch, intending to catch the villain in the act. I saw nothing, and yet, at my feet the next morning, I saw two of the loathsome creatures. It seemed a ridiculous affair to take to the police, and I feared they would simply disbelieve me, and take the word of Sir Bertram. I then remembered your name, which had appeared in one of the weekly papers, and fearing that my story would appear ridiculous to you without further proof, I requested the gardener to package the rat for dispatch to you, and—"

I interrupted his narrative. " Pardon me, but do you smell smoke ? "

" I smell nothing," our visitor replied, but Holmes indicated with a nod that he did.

" It appears to be coming from outside the room," I said, and rose to cross to the window overlooking the street. " It is indeed a fire," I reported. " It would appear that smoke is issuing from the house across from here which has remained empty for so long. I can now see the fire-engine approaching. It would appear that there is no danger to life from what I can see."

" Perhaps some tramp or idler has been lodging in the empty house, and an ember has fallen from his fire, and set alight the *débris* that accumulates in such places," suggested Maberley.

"Very likely," concurred Holmes. "Watson, perhaps you would be good enough to close the window. The smell is becoming quite strong."

" I confess that my sense of smell is rather weak," said Maberley. " Ever since I got that knock on the head in Jaipur. In fact, I really can't smell anything at all unless you hold it right under my nose."

" Is that so ? " I enquired. "Yours sounds like a most interesting case."

" If I had a sovereign for every doctor who has said that to me," he laughed, " I would be a tolerably rich man by now."

"You were saying?" Holmes invited as I closed the window and returned to my seat. "You were saying that you ordered your gardener to package the rat and address it to me?"

"Strictly speaking, it was not he who addressed the package. Lomax is almost unable to read or write and so it was Cook who addressed the package before passing it to the carrier."

"Not you?"

"If Mary had seen the package addressed to you, she would immediately wish to know why I was communicating with you, Mr. Holmes. Your name is hardly unknown. I fear I am very poor at dissimulation, and the truth, as I have said earlier, would cause her some considerable distress. If the writing on the outside of the package was not mine, she would express little interest in its contents. I wrote a letter which I requested be enclosed with the package, and – well – here I am."

"I see," said Holmes. "And what is it that you require of me?"

"Would it be possible for you to visit my house on Saturday? Mary will be visiting her sister at that time, so she will not know of your visit. I would like you to confirm my suspicions that Sir Bertram is at the bottom of this."

"And then?"

"I intend to bring him before the courts. It is intolerable that Mary and I should be subjected to this harassment."

"Perhaps I will take this case," agreed Holmes. "There is, however, the small matter of my expenses incurred in the matter, and my professional fee."

The other's face fell. "I am not a rich man," he said, "though if you were to see the house and style in which I live, you might fancy otherwise. The money is all my wife's, largely held in trust for young Douglas when he comes of age."

"No matter," smiled Holmes. "I have yet to demand a fee of a client that he or she cannot comfortably afford. In some cases, as Watson will confirm, I have been known to remit fees altogether. Art for art's sake."

"That is a weight off my mind," said Maberley. "Then you will come?"

"Indeed I will," said Holmes. "There are aspects of this case that present themselves as being of great interest."

Our visitor thanked Holmes profusely, and saw himself out, explaining that he was expected back before the evening.

"Well, what do you make of him?" Holmes asked me.

"As the Bard so rightly observed, 'some have greatness thrust upon them'," I answered. Poor Captain Maberley, I am sure, would have made an excellent sergeant-major. But giving him a commission, and forcing him to mingle with those who are his social superiors... I am all for giving others their due and recognising their achievements, but I fear that the mores of our society do not always permit such advancement to be a success for those involved."

Holmes chuckled. "Your views never fail to surprise me, my friend. So here we have a man from humble beginnings, living on the money supplied by his marriage, and disliked by those around him. Though," he mused, "being disliked by Sir Bertram Colton would seem to me to be more of a recommendation than otherwise."

"And what do you expect to achieve by visiting The Firs?"

"I do not know at present. No doubt all will become clear when we visit the scene of the incidents."

On Saturday, we took the train to Guildford, and took a cab from the station to the end of the road on which The Firs was situated.

"We are not going to see Captain Maberley immediately," Holmes replied in answer to my question. "First, let us pay a call on Sir Bertram Colton."

Sir Bertram's house proved to be an imposing red-brick building in the late Gothic style. As we neared the house along a winding drive flanked by yew hedges, Holmes appeared to be somewhat abstracted, his head bowed, and absent-mindedly using his stick to poke at and disturb the dead leaves and other vegetation by the side of the path.

Upon our approaching the steps leading to the front door, the door itself was abruptly flung open to reveal a tall bearded red-faced man clad in a crimson dressing-gown, brandishing a heavy blackthorn stick.

Seemingly unperturbed by this vision, Holmes mildly enquired if he was speaking to Captain Mortimer Maberley.

" Damn your insolence, man ! " came the furious reply. " My name is Bertram Colton and I have no connection with the man whose name you have just had the impertinence to utter."

" Why, what has he done ? " Holmes enquired.

" What has he done ? I will tell you what he has done. First, when offered the Queen's Commission, he did not have the common decency to know his place and refuse it. ' Captain' he styles himself. I refuse to recognise that title. Next, he had the temerity to seek the hand in marriage of my childhood playmate and sweetheart, Mary Upton. And lastly, with the Devil knows what lack of respect and propriety, he moves into the house next to mine," pointing with an angrily shaking finger. " I tell you that the man should be horsewhipped, and his very existence is an affront to the whole neighbourhood."

" Thank you," Holmes replied in a mild tone. " Can you tell me," smiling, " if there is a path that leads between this house and that of Maberley ? "

" Your impudence knows no bounds, sir. Would I allow such a path to continue to exist, given what I have just told you ? Now be off my property forthwith, before I set the dogs on the pair of you." As if in answer to this threat, the sound of baying dogs arose from within the house.

" Thank you," Holmes replied, tipping his hat in salute, a gesture that seemed to infuriate Sir Bertram still further.

We turned and walked down the yew-tree avenue.

" I believe he was on the point of apoplexy," I remarked when we were out of earshot of the house. " From a very superficial observation just now, I fear that I do not give him long to live."

" A most illuminating discussion, nonetheless," was Holmes's answer.

We reached The Firs, which, as its name suggested, was flanked by two magnificent specimens of the Douglas fir. The house itself, though undoubtedly handsome and of good quality, was on a smaller scale than that of its neighbour, but presenting a less gloomy and more cheerful aspect.

Maberley himself opened the door to us.

"Two this morning," were his first words to us. "I have left them where I discovered them. I will take you there."

"Excellent," said Holmes. "Lead on."

As we walked through the house, which was furnished in simple, but good, taste, Holmes mentioned that we had just called on Sir Bertram Colton.

"We found him to be as you described him," Holmes remarked.

"A singularly unpleasant individual," I added. "A few words from him were enough to confirm the opinion you gave of him earlier."

"He mentioned, however, that a path used to exist between the two houses," said Holmes. "What do you know about this?"

"I know that at one time there was a path, and that Mary and her family used to visit the next house using it. However, since we moved here, Sir Bertram has erected a stout fence between his property and ours. There is no path any more. Ah, here we are." We stopped in front of a door. "Please excuse me if I do not come any further. I explained my antipathy to these creatures, did I not?"

"You did," Holmes assented.

"Very well then. Gentlemen, if you could prove that it is indeed Sir Bertram who is responsible for this, I will be most grateful." So saying, he opened the door. "I will be in the drawing-room when you have completed your examination," he informed us.

We stepped outside, where, as we had been told, two dead rats lay before us on the bare earth. They were large examples of the type, and had they been living, one would have assumed they were in perfect health. A superficial examination was enough to inform us that they were deceased, and furthermore there were no wounds visible which might have been the cause of death.

I bent over to examine the corpses more closely. "Holmes, do you smell anything?" I asked him. "I believe there is an odour of which the source is something other than these unfortunate rodents."

With a look of distaste, Holmes stooped. "You are right. A

smell of coal-gas. I noticed that gas was laid on as we came through the house." He cast around and discovered a stout twig which, to my astonishment, he placed in the mouth of one of the dead rats, and used it to open the jaw, peering inside with the lens he held in his other hand. " As I thought," he exclaimed, as he repeated the process with the other corpse. " But here, why here ? "

He straightened himself and looked around. " Halloa, what do we have here ? " he asked, pointing to a small crockery dish beside the steps.

" I do not know," I said.

" It is the solution to the mystery, I feel. There are only two more links needed in the chain to complete the story." So saying, he strode off in the direction of the house of Sir Bertram Colton.

" Come here, Watson," he called. " See here." He was standing by a stout board fence, some six feet or more in height, through which it was impossible to discern anything. " Now," he said, " do you go this way," indicating the left, " and I will go the other. Call when you discover anything of interest."

" What do you consider as being of interest ? " I asked.

" You will know what is of interest when you see it," was his enigmatic reply.

More than a little irritated by the vague nature of this mission as it had been presented to me, I set off in the direction indicated. I had hardly taken a dozen steps, I suppose, before I heard Holmes's voice calling me.

" I have it," he said when I joined him. " See here, there is the remains of a track that was here in the past. Undoubtedly this is the path which the children used to visit each other. But more interesting still is this." He pointed to the ground at the foot of the fence. " A fence may be difficult to climb over, but for certain creatures, it is easy to go underneath it by digging a tunnel. And that is exactly what we have here."

" So the rats are not dead when they come into this garden ? "

" Indeed not."

" But why do they come here from the other garden ? "

"The cook will no doubt tell us," was his answer, as he led the way back to the kitchen door.

Maberley's cook, a Mrs. Danby, proved to be in the midst of creating an apple pie, a task she was happy to abandon when Holmes produced a half-crown from his pocket and displayed it to her.

"Tell me," Holmes asked. "Do you ever put out bread and milk or any other food for hedgehogs, or other animals ? "

"Not me, sir," she answered. "That would be the girl."

"The girl ? " I asked.

"Yes, sir. Little Jilly, the scullery maid. She comes in to give me a hand two or three days a week, though I have to say that she's that small, and quite frankly, sir, she's not all what she should be up there," pointing to her head, " so she's not as much use as you might think. Anyway, she came from the country somewhere, and she said that they always used to put out a little something for the hedgehogs – ' urchins' she called them – at night, and asked me if I minded. Well I didn't really, seeing as how it was only a few scraps of bread that had gone stale, and a bit of milk which like as not was already on the turn. So she used to use an old dish and put it out before she went off of an evening."

"Thank you, Mrs. Danby. That has proved most illuminating."

"Thank you, sir," she answered, pocketing the half-crown.

"And now for the drawing-room," Holmes said to me.

"Well ? " asked Maberley, rising to greet us.

"I am sorry to say, sir," Holmes told our client, " that Sir Bertram Colton, much as you, or indeed Watson and I, might wish him to be guilty of placing the rats outside your door, is innocent of that offence."

"Can you tell me more ? Specifically, how you reached that conclusion ? " Maberley asked. "Some brandy to refresh you and Doctor Watson ? " he offered.

"Thank you, no. I will be brief, as we must return to London shortly. First, let me remind you that there was no mark of violence or injury pertaining to these rats."

"They were poisoned, then ? "

"They died from poisons, yes. But that poison was not

deliberately administered. The drive to Sir Bertram's house is flanked by yew trees, as you have no doubt remarked."

" Ah yes. I was told as a child that the berries of the yew were poisonous," said Maberley.

" Interestingly enough, that is incorrect. The leaves are poisonous, to be sure, and so is the seed. The berries themselves are apparently edible, though I have never put this to the test. It is perfectly possible, indeed, it is likely, that rats, foraging in the undergrowth below the trees, ingested some fallen needles and perhaps also some berries and seeds. While a small amount might not necessarily kill them outright, it would certainly spell their eventual doom. Victims of the yew do not give up the ghost immediately, but will die within a few hours of ingesting seeds or leaves, even dead leaves, of the tree or bush. I discovered traces of yew foliage in the mouths of this morning's victims."

" I see. But how and why did they get into my garden over the fence ? And why did they die outside my kitchen door ? "

" As to the how, the cunning beasts had dug a tunnel under the fence at the point where the path had once been and therefore the vegetation was thinnest and it was easiest for them to dig. For the why, you must ask your scullery maid Jilly, who has been in the habit of leaving out food for hedgehogs. This almost certainly was a reason for the rats, having ingested a fatal dose of yew, to visit your garden on a regular basis."

" I see. But then, why would they die there ? "

" You remarked that you lacked a sense of smell," Holmes said. " You would therefore have been unaware of the fact that the gas pipe under the soil was leaking. The combination of yew poisoning and town gas proved fatal, The animals were rendered insensible and immobile by the gas, unable to steal away to die, and probably died without regaining full consciousness, but after a brief period of convulsions of the body and limbs, as was obvious by the marks on the ground around the bodies. In conclusion, other than the charge of maintaining poisonous material in the form of yew bushes, it is impossible to accuse Sir Bertram of anything. I am sorry if this is not the outcome you wished."

" Can I merely say that it is a most unexpected outcome ?

I thank you for your swift resolution of the matter, and I expect your account soon, which I will be happy to pay. It has not been pleasant to think of another man, even one such as Sir Bertram, as being guilty of what I had fancied him as doing."

"In this instance," smiled Holmes, "there will be no charge. This has proved a happy break from my usual routine, and I am sure that the change of air today will have improved my health. However, sir, I cannot speak for an improvement in your health if you do not arrange to have that leaking gas pipe repaired at the earliest possible opportunity. Come, Watson, let us away."

It was two weeks after the events recorded above that I observed in the *Morning Post* the notice of the death of Sir Bertram Colton from apoplexy.

"Your diagnosis when we met him was correct, then," Holmes said when I informed him of the news. "It is not often I say this of anyone, but the world will be a happier place without Sir Bertram in it. Let us hope that Captain Maberley and his wife are now able to lead a more peaceful life – one without Sir Bertram and without rats."

THE ADVENTURE OF THE NONPAREIL CLUB

N my experience of humanity, I have discovered that there are few forces as powerful as that of egotism. When I mentioned this to my friend Sherlock Holmes, the celebrated consulting detective, I was heartened to find him in general agreement with me on the matter.

"It is," he said to me when I had expounded my thesis, "a commonly held belief that the root of much crime is romantic passion. Though it is certainly true that a large number of crimes have this as their cause, it seems to me that injured pride is often at the root of the passion that supposedly prompted the commission of the crime. I would therefore have to agree with you that egoism and pride are the cause of much of the wrongdoing in this country."

Never, in my experience, was this more vividly demonstrated than in the case of Colonel Upwood.

"Sir Thomas Ridgson," Sherlock Holmes remarked to me in conversational tones one November morning as we sat at breakfast. The dense fog which enveloped London like a shroud had deadened the noise of the sparse traffic that made its cautious way down Baker-street, and I confess that I had become drowsy with the almost anæsthetic effects of the enforced solitude.

Holmes's words jolted me awake. "You were saying?" I asked.

"Sir Thomas Ridgson," Holmes repeated. "You are aware of him?"

"Of course. The famous African explorer, the first Englishman to explore the upper reaches of the Niger river, and the only white man to enter the city of Bamako. He was knighted two years ago for his achievements, was he not?"

"Indeed he was. He is also the president of the Nonpareil Club, and it is in that capacity that he intends to visit us this morning. A message was awaiting me as I awoke this morning, telling me that it is about this extraordinary society that he wishes to consult me." My bemusement must have shown in my face, for he added, "Perhaps Sir Thomas will be willing to explain the workings of this singular institution when he calls, if the details are unfamiliar to you."

I should perhaps mention here that the Nonpareil Club, the name of which was to become a household word as a result of the events that followed, was at that time virtually unknown to anyone who was not a member.

" Have you any idea of the matter on which he wishes to consult you ? "

" None. He is expected here at eight thirty."

At the appointed hour, Mrs. Hudson announced the arrival of Sir Thomas, and showed him into our sitting-room.

The famous African explorer presented a fine figure as he entered. Our doorway was scarcely tall enough to admit him, and his rugged frame seemed to fill our room with an impression of primaeval energy. His voice, rather than the booming tones that one might expect from such a man, was surprisingly quiet and weak.

" Thank you for agreeing to see me on this matter, Mr. Holmes," he greeted my friend. " I take it that you," turning to me, " are Doctor Watson ? "

I admitted my identity, and invited him to take a seat.

Once he was settled comfortably in an armchair with a warming and stimulating cup of coffee, Holmes invited him to explain his visit to us.

" It concerns the Nonpareil Club," he explained. " Since we are a somewhat private – some might almost call us secretive – group, it may be that you are unfamiliar with the Club and its conditions for membership."

" I have heard a little," Holmes told him, " but would appreciate hearing more."

" And for my part, I know nothing," I added.

" Very well then. I am the President of the Club, whose membership consists of those men who have achieved a unique success in life. Such a success may be similar to mine in being the only white man ever to have visited the African city of Bamako. It might be in the realm of science or medicine, such as being the only man to have brought about the cure of a patient suffering from a disease thought to be incurable, or in the world of music, such as having one's composition played by a famous European orchestra not usually given to playing works from outside its own country. Hence the name of the

Club, Nonpareil – all members are without equal in their individual fields."

" May I ask who determines what constitutes an achievement worthy of membership ? " asked Holmes.

" Certainly. A prospective member must be proposed by an existing member and the nomination seconded by two more. A ballot of all members is then taken to determine whether the prospective member and his achievements are eligible for membership. A quorum of half the membership is required for the vote to be valid, and a simple majority of those voting is sufficient to determine the result."

" This sounds like a remarkably parliamentary procedure," I smiled.

" Our membership does indeed include a few Members of Parliament and a few noble lords, who are members for reasons other than their political achievements. It was they who were responsible for this system."

" A question, if I may, Sir Thomas," said Holmes. " Your members are selected on the basis of having performed some sort of unique feat, are they not ? What happens if that event is duplicated by another ? "

" In that event, which happens frequently, given the pace of change in this modern age," replied our visitor, " a process similar to that of a new member's joining takes place. To take an example, should another man prove to have visited Bamako, any member of the Club could then call for my resignation, seconded by two members, and a ballot conducted along the same lines as I described previously. However... I should mention that a man may qualify for membership on account of more than one achievement. In my particular case, I may also lay claim to be the only man to have been made an honorary chief of the Soninké people – indeed, of any group in that region. There are other claims that I may make, which I will not bore you with at this time. Many of our members have some similar claim or claims, and so our membership is not as fluid as one might at first suppose."

" A very exclusive group of men, then ? " I remarked.

" Indeed, that is the case. And not only that, these men are jealously proud of their membership in the Club. Pride is a sin to which they are all – myself included on occasion, I confess – subject, and jealousy of others, particularly those they see as competitors in their field, forms another failing in many."

"Ah, Watson and I were speaking only the other day of such matters as being the cause of much crime," said Holmes. "Indeed, I gave it as my opinion that they were the primary cause of such wrongdoing. May I hazard a guess that it is in connection with this that you have come to us today?"

"Indeed, you are correct, Mr. Holmes. We are faced with a situation that is unprecedented in the seven years of the Club's existence. It concerns a certain Colonel Constantine Upwood."

"I have a recollection of that name," Holmes interrupted. "Watson, if you would be good enough to pass me the Index containing the letter 'U'. Ah, thank you." He received the appropriate scrapbook in which he filed any items of interest, and started to leaf through its pages. "Ah yes, my memory does not betray me. Formerly of the Greenjackets – that is too say, the Rifle Brigade – served in Afghanistan and North India – decorated for actions in the Battle of Ali Masjid – ah! this is why the name seems familiar – court-martialed for his part in the death of a native woman and her husband. Acquitted, but from my reading of the accounts of the case, there is no doubt in my mind that he was guilty as charged."

"That is the man, Mr. Holmes. I confess that I find the man's company to be distasteful, but by the rules of the Club, unless anyone can be proved to have duplicated the feat that gained him his membership, or unless he has been found guilty by a court of having committed a criminal offence, he cannot be expelled from the club."

"And the feat that gained him his membership?"

"The slaying of two tigers within seconds of each other with the use of a double rifle. Personally, I am against the taking of animals' lives simply to gratify one's vanity, but there was a sufficient number of members to secure his election."

"And now?"

"A certain Captain Vernon Pomeroy reports that he has achieved the same feat – however, claiming that he was on foot when he despatched the beasts, whereas Colonel Upwood was seated on an elephant howdah when his tigers were killed.

Pomeroy is also the only man known to have swum across the Hooghly River in Calcutta, and is for that feat that he was recommended."

" Then with regard to the shooting of the tigers, are these not different feats, then ? " said I. " Is there not a way in which both can be members ? "

" There are certainly those who believe that to be the case. On the other hand, there is a substantial proportion of the membership feel they have been insulted by Upwood, and would prefer to see his membership terminated. However, under the rules that I mentioned earlier, his membership cannot be revoked so easily as they would like. There is clearly bad blood between Upwood and Pomeroy – Upwood resenting the man he sees as a potential usurper who would deprive him of his membership, and Pomeroy regarding Upwood as a man who is unworthy to be a member of the Nonpareil Club since he, Pomeroy, has duplicated his feat.

" Matters came to a head two nights ago. Both men had been imbibing freely, and strong words were spoken. At one point, some witnesses claim that Upwood challenged Pomeroy to a duel with pistols. Upwood denies this, and asserts that his words were misinterpreted, claiming that he told Pomeroy that if these events had taken place at a different time in history, he would have challenged Pomeroy to a duel. In any event, both men were apparently extremely angry, and physical violence between the two men appeared to be a real possibility, according to some who were at the scene."

" Excuse me," interrupted Sherlock Holmes, " were you present while this was taking place ? "

" I was not present at the start of the argument. However, as matters became more heated, one of the senior Club servants had the presence of mind to dispatch an urgent message to me at my lodgings, which happily are only a few minutes away from the Club. I immediately made my way to the Club with the intention of acting as some sort of umpire or referee to settle the dispute."

" I see," said Holmes. " Pray continue."

" By the time I reached the Club, matters had cooled to the extent that the argument was to be settled, not with pistols, but with playing cards. As decided by other members of the Club who might be seen as acting in the role of seconds, there were to be eleven hands of *chemin de fer*[1], each man starting with a stake of one thousand pounds. At the end of the eleventh hand, the player with the most capital would be free to impose his conditions on the other: Upwood would retain his membership of the Club should he emerge as the victor, and Pomeroy would be able to claim that his tigerish exploit had invalidated Upwood's, should he come out on top, and Upwood would be forced to resign.

I confess that I was not in favour of this game, but I felt I had no authority to prevent it, and to be frank, little wish to do so, given the threatened alternatives. A coin was tossed to determine who should be banker, and Pomeroy won. He held the bank for three hands, and the bank passed to Upwood, who retained the bank until the end of the eleven hands. Over that period, he had gradually taken almost all of Pomeroy's thousand pounds, with only twenty-five pounds left on the table. He announced that he would wager one thousand on this final deal, and a murmur went up, as this went against the original agreement that only one thousand pounds should be the amount staked. However, Pomeroy coolly accepted this challenge, and seemed almost in a dreamlike state as the cards were dealt.

" Upwood triumphantly showed his hand – an eight and a king, but Pomeroy slowly turned his cards up to show a six and a three. Upwood's face turned black with fury, and he pushed over the counters representing the one thousand nine hundred and seventy-five pounds, together with five five-pound notes which he withdrew from his wallet, before storming out of the room, and indeed, out of the building.

" Despite his winnings, which had left him in sole possession of the field, as well as a wealthy man, Pomeroy was in a downcast mood. I drew him to one side, and as gently as I could, enquired if there was any way in which I might be of assistance to him.

" His reply was an almost tearful admission that his *fiancée,*

---

1   See Wikipedia (Baccarat) for an explanation of this game (basically a simplified blackjack with slightly different rules)

to whom he had been betrothed for the past two years, and to whom he was to have been married in two days' time – that is to say, today – had that very afternoon informed him of her intention not to marry him, giving no reason for this change of heart."

"Dear me," I said. "The poor fellow."

"He told me that he was ready to lose all his money, having already lost everything in the world that he held dear – that is to say, his betrothed."

Holmes sat in silence a while, his hands with the fingertips pressed together in that familiar steepled position which I knew betokened thought. At length, he spoke. "Sir Thomas, you have given us an admirable account of the facts, but I am unsure of what you require of me."

"I have not yet reached the point of the story, I fear. Last night at half-past ten o'clock, I was once more summoned from my lodgings to the Club. The messenger was agitated, but refused to tell me the reason for my summons. On reaching the premises, I was greeted by Sir Archibald Milton-Harbury–"

"The eminent surgeon ? " I asked.

"The same. He is a member of the Club following a unique surgical procedure which he and only he has been able to carry out successfully. He informed me that Captain Pomeroy had been discovered dead some thirty minutes earlier in one of the private dining-rooms."

Holmes sat up straight. "Dead, you say ? How had he died ? "

"According to Sir Archibald, it appeared that the poor man took his own life by cutting his throat."

I shuddered. "What a horrible method to choose."

"Indeed it is," Holmes agreed. " Of course, it has the advantage of being silent."

Sir Thomas and I looked at him in a silent entreaty for him to continue, but he simply asked, "The police were called, of course ? "

"Of course. A constable was on the scene within minutes."

"And which officer is in charge of the investigation, do you know ? "

"An Inspector Gregson. He specifically asked me to call on you."

" Ha ! Do you hear that, Watson ? I predict that Gregson will go far in his profession. A man, capable and competent as he is, who nevertheless knows and recognises his limits. Something must have seemed amiss to him, or he would not be asking for my assistance."

" You know him well, then, and you will be able to help us get to the bottom of this matter ? "

" Indeed I do, and I believe we will be able to work together to solve whatever mystery is involved. Do you know if the body has been moved ? "

" Other than Sir Archibald, I believe no one has touched the body, or indeed, anything in the room."

" Excellent," said Holmes. "We should strike while the iron is hot. Watson, you may bring with you whatever medical instruments you feel may assist us. For myself, if you will wait for a few minutes while I collect my impedimenta, Sir Thomas, we will travel with you to the Club. I fancy," he added, looking out of the window at the fog outside, " it will be more convenient and quicker to go on foot, as I perceive you did when coming here, rather than to entrust ourselves to the tender mercies of a jarvey."

Accordingly we groped our way from lamp-post to lamp-post through the London streets to the premises of the Nonpareil Club, a handsome townhouse on Lower Berkeley-street[2], where a doorman greeted Sir Thomas, and admitted us to the building.

Inspector Tobias Gregson was waiting for us in the hallway, and greeted Holmes and me with what appeared to be genuine pleasure.

" Very happy to see that you are available to help us on this one, Mr. Holmes and Doctor Watson. This is a strange affair, and no mistake," he greeted us, extending his hand. "You'll see what I mean. Follow me."

He led the way up the stairs to the first floor, where a constable was standing by a door. " Thank you, Jarvis," he said, as the uniformed officer stepped aside. " Now, take a look for yourselves, gentlemen," he proclaimed.

The scene inside was as shocking as any I have ever

---

2   Now Fitzhardinge Street

encountered. The body of a man sat in a chair at a table, both these pieces of furniture covered in congealed blood. Another chair stood on the other side of the table, and a piece of paper lay on the table beside the man's hand. But for the ghastly wound to the throat, visible even from the doorway, it might almost be thought that the occupant of the chair was dozing while in the act of composing a letter. A curiously-shaped blade lay on the floor beside the table.

" There are bloody footprints on the carpet, leading out of the room," I remarked.

" Indeed there are," Holmes confirmed. " Two sets that I can see, and if you will take the trouble," he continued, lying at full length on the floor, and looking over at the desk from that position, " you will notice several more distinct sets of footprints – three in this case, leading to the desk. Have you or any of your men entered ? " he asked Gregson.

" No. We have left the room untouched until now," said the police officer.

" Capital, Gregson. Then we may assume—"

" Excuse me," interrupted Sir Thomas. " Sir Archibald Milton-Harbury entered to examine the... the body."

" Then I will wish to see the boots he was wearing at that time, in order to compare them with these prints," said Gregson. " Sir Thomas, can you please dispatch one of the Club servants to Sir Archibald, so that we may confirm this."

Holmes clapped the Inspector on the shoulder. " Excellent, Inspector. If you continue in this way, I expect to see you at the head of Scotland Yard before too long."

Gregson flushed at the praise, but merely asked Holmes if he now felt it appropriate to enter the room.

" So long as we take the obvious precautions," said Holmes. As he and Gregson made their way along the edges of the room, keeping to the walls in order to preserve any clues that might lie in the path from the table to the door, I followed in their wake.

" Excellent," Holmes said. We proceeded to the grisly centre of the room, where blood seemed to cover every surface. The paper which we had remarked from the doorway lay on the table, its edges stained with blood, and an inkwell stood on one corner of it. A tumbler such as might be used for a whisky and soda was to the right of the paper. Holmes bent over and sniffed at it without touching it.

" Poor beggar," remarked Gregson.

" Carotid artery severed," I said, following a brief examination of the body. " Cause of death, shock following massive blood loss."

" Sir Archibald's conclusion also," remarked Sir Thomas from the doorway.

" And here we have the suicide note," said Gregson, pointing to the piece of paper.

" I think not," said Holmes.

" But look, man," expostulated Gregson. " Here it is, as clear as can be."

" Precisely my point," said Holmes. " Inspector, may I have your permission to examine this paper before it passes into the hands of the police ? I anticipate that it will not take more than half a day before I am done with it."

Gregson and I exchanged glances and shrugs as Holmes moved to the blade that was on the floor beside the chair on which the body sat.

" A *kukri*," I said. " The traditional knife of the Gurkhas of northern India. They are said to be able to remove a man's head with one stroke."

" Exactly the sort of knife one would expect a man such as Pomeroy to have in his possession following his time in India," remarked Gregson.

" I would remind you, my dear Inspector, that Pomeroy is by no means the only member of this Club who has spent time in India."

" Good God, Mr. Holmes ! " exclaimed Sir Thomas. " Are you saying that poor Pomeroy was murdered by another member of the Club ? "

" If, as I strongly suspect, he did not kill himself, he was killed by another. I believe we may accept this as being true, may we not ? This state of affairs hardly seems to be the result of an accident. And I am sure that no one except members and Club servants would be in the building at the time you mentioned, that is, ten o'clock in the evening."

" Our Club servants are all above reproach," Sir Thomas told us. " I will personally vouch for that."

" I notice," Holmes said in a low aside to me, " that he does not make the same claim concerning the members of the Club."

" Have you seen all that you need, Mr. Holmes ? " asked Gregson. " May we move the body ? I am sure that the Club will wish to clean this room and make it fit for use again."

Sir Thomas nodded his agreement, and Holmes also agreed. He turned as if to leave, but instantly stopped in his tracks.

" There ! " he exclaimed, pointing to a small grey object that stood out against the crimson of the carpet. He dropped to his knee, and used tweezers to transfer the item into one of his ever-present envelopes which he carried about his person for purposes such as this. " Cigar ash," he pronounced, " though at present I do not know of what kind." He continued to scruti-nise the carpet minutely, at times concentrating on individual tufts, which he probed with the tip of his mechanical pencil. After a few minutes of this, he turned to Sir Thomas, who was still standing in the doorway. " These rooms are cleaned regularly ? "

" Indeed they are. Once in the early morning, and once fol-lowing luncheon. We maintain a very high standard of cleanli-ness here."

" I had observed that," said Holmes. " Can you tell me wheth-er Pomeroy smoked cigars ? "

" Indeed he did. Trichinopoly. I assume he acquired the taste for them in his time in India."

" Thank you." Again, to avoid disturbing the clear footprints which marked the carpet, we made our way around the edge of the room. As we reached the door, the well-known figure of Sir Archibald Milton-Harbury appeared.

" I understand that you wish to view the boots I wore last night," he told us. " They are on my feet now."

" May I ? " asked Holmes, and without waiting for an answer, he once more dropped to one knee and proceeded to examine the boots through his ever-present magnifying glass and com-pare them with the footprints in the carpet. He thanked Sir Archibald as he rose.

" I think that has made matters quite clear," he told Gregson, who nonetheless appeared more than a little mystified. " Dear me," he added, patting his pockets. " I need a cigar to clear my nostrils of the smell of blood, but I seem to have left my cigar-case at home. Watson ? " he said to me, turning towards me and giving a wink together with an imperceptible shake of the head which would have been invisible to any other person. I took Holmes's silent hint and reported that I too had neglected to bring any of the weed with me.

" Allow me," said Sir Archibald, bringing out a cigar-case and offering a cigar to Holmes.

" Many thanks," said Holmes as the famous surgeon lit Holmes's cigar before applying the vesta to his own.

Sir Archibald turned to me. " You would concur, Doctor, with my diagnosis of the cause of death ? Severe shock following extreme loss of blood ? "

" Certainly," said I.

" Poor lad," said Sir Archibald, nodding towards the corpse in the room.

" Poor lad indeed," said Holmes. " Watson, we must be off. Thank you once again for the cigar, Sir Archibald. Sir Thomas, do you happen by any chance to have the name and address of Pomeroy's *fiancée* ? "

" I believe he signed her in as a guest on one of our social evenings, and her details should therefore be in our guestbook."

" Thank you. Gregson," he called as we moved away, " do not write your report until I have contacted you later today. I hope to have some more information for you by this afternoon."

After obtaining the name and address of Miss Emily Sallerton, and, with the permission of Sir Thomas, also examining some other papers pertaining to Pomeroy, we stood outside the portals of the Nonpareil Club. The fog of the night had partially lifted, meaning that we were able to hail a cab.

Holmes was in a sombre mood. " Murder is a foul thing," he remarked, apropos of nothing, as we jolted slowly through the streets.

" Murder ? " I said. " I was under the impression Sir Archibald and Gregson believe it to be a suicide."

" I have at least sown the seeds of doubt in the good Inspector's mind," he answered me. " As for Sir Archibald, he may be a famous and competent, even brilliant surgeon, but he lacks my extensive experience of investigating violent death. Let us take one trivial, but telling, example to illustrate my point here. Suppose you were to take it into your head to cut your own throat – an event that I sincerely hope will never come to pass, I may add – with which hand would you hold the knife ? "

" My right, of course, since I am right-handed."

" Naturally. And with which hand did Pomeroy supposedly cut his throat, based on the wound that you observed ? "

I had to reflect for a minute, but eventually answered, " With his right hand."

" Indeed that is so. Now tell me why a left-handed man should cut his throat with his right hand."

" How do you know that he was indeed left-handed ? "

" Tut, man. Think back to where the inkwell was on the table."

" To the right, if I remember correctly."

" You do indeed remember correctly. And the tumbler ? "

" To the left of the paper."

" Indeed. In a position where it would seriously inconvenience anyone attempting to write with their left hand. We have seen samples of his writing in the book at the club, as well as his signature and more of his writing on some bar chits. All exhibited the characteristics of a left-handed writer." He fell silent for a few minutes, and the cab stopped, with the driver informing us that we had reached our destination. Holmes paid him, and tipped him a half-crown to wait for us. " I fancy that this will not be a long visit," he said to me as we rang the bell.

A maid answered, and told us that " Miss Emily is with Colonel Upwood," and that if we cared to wait, she would let her know of our presence.

" Thank you, there is no need for that," said Holmes, and we turned and walked down the steps to the waiting cab. " I had marked Upwood as a cad," he remarked, " but this latest is quite a surprise to me."

" You mean ? " I asked.

" I think we may safely assume that Upwood has been

involved for some time in stealing the affections of Miss Emily Sallerton, detaching her from the unfortunate Pomeroy. It is quite possible that Pomeroy knew of this when she announced her intention not to proceed with the engagement."

"And now the scoundrel has the nerve to visit her on the day after her former betrothed's death? This is infamous, Holmes!"

"Indeed it is, but it is not the worst. This business is a foul one."

Once at Baker-street, Holmes placed the cigar ash that he had collected from the carpet under his microscope. "As I thought," he pronounced after about a minute's examination. "This is not ash from a Trichinopoly, such as we are informed that Pomeroy smoked, nor is it a Panetella, as enjoyed by Sir Archibald. Now, recall that the carpet showed us three sets of footprints entering the room, and two leaving. Your conclusions?"

"Given that we know Sir Archibald to have entered and left the room, we must assume that the footprints which enter and fail to leave are Pomeroy's, leaving another set unaccounted for."

"Precisely. And I was able to determine that the prints made by Sir Archibald's distinctively square-toed boots were made following the staining of the carpet with Pomeroy's blood, while those of the unknown were produced before that time on entry, and afterwards on leaving. We may therefore deduce that the unknown, who incidentally smokes a Havana Robusto, of a very different quality to that smoked by Sir Archibald, was present when Pomeroy lost his life."

"That would seem to be clear."

"Now we come to the letter that we discovered on the desk. In full it reads, 'I am in despair. I cannot go on. V. Pomeroy.' Short, sharp and to the point, and a clumsy attempt to divert us from the truth. We saw the register in which guests were entered, did we not, and where Pomeroy's signature was to be found. In the first place, that signature was not 'V. Pomeroy', but 'Vernon Pomeroy', and in the second, the formation of the letters differed significantly. In particular, the the capital P was formed in a completely different fashion. Furthermore, we agreed that Pomeroy was in all probability left-handed, and that supposition was borne out by the entry in the register. This, on the other hand, was written by a right-handed man."

" But how did you initially come to suspect the authenticity of the letter ? "

" Elementary. Do you remember Gregson's saying that it was clear as could be ? And so it was – clear of blood, when everything else on the table was saturated. It was obvious that it had been placed on the table after the death of Pomeroy. There is also the amusingly minor point that the ink in the ink-well appeared to be blue ink, while this is written in blue-black ink. And you may also recall the pen on the table."

" I saw no such item."

" There was none. Now, it is just possible that Pomeroy wrote the note in blue-black ink, using his own fountain-pen which will be discovered on the body, with his handwriting and signature being made less than typical by the emotion of the event, and placed the finished note on the table following the cutting of his own throat–"

" So improbable a sequence of events as to be impossible," I interrupted.

" Exactly. I think we must therefore conclude that our smoker of Havana Robusto cigars penned this short missive before entering the room, and dropped it on the table following the death of Pomeroy."

" And how was that death accomplished ? "

" As a medical man, you may be in a better position to give me the details."

" Very well, then. The carotid artery was severed. I would say that, given the angle and depth of the wound, the head was bent back at the time that the wound was inflected."

" Good. And ? "

" The depth of the wound was excessive. It did not appear to me to be a wound inflicted by an action usually inflicted in the cutting of a throat." I shuddered. " In my time in India, I saw enough such, inflicted on our brave lads by their Afghan captors. This wound seemed to be more in the nature of an attempted decapitation. A swinging slashing cut, rather than the slicing action whose results I have seen in the past."

" Such as might be expected from the wielder of a *kukri*, such as we saw by the body ? "

" Just so. The design of this weapon makes it suitable for such an attack." I paused. " Are you suggesting, though, that Pomeroy allowed his unknown assailant to attack him in this manner without putting up any resistance ? "

" There is another piece to this puzzle which I have not yet explained to you. You remember the tumbler on the table ? "

" Naturally. I had assumed that it had contained a whisky and soda, or similar."

" Indeed it had, but there was also a faint, but yet distinct smell of chloral hydrate, which as you probably know, forms a powerful sedative when mixed with alcohol and water.

" Let me reconstruct the scene for you as I see it. The murderer – I think we may now both agree that Pomeroy's death was no suicide – arranged a meeting with Pomeroy in that private room. Pomeroy arrived first, and brought with him a whisky and soda which he had previously ordered from one of the Club servants. When the murderer arrived, already armed with a concealed *kukri* and the forged suicide note, he managed to distract Pomeroy's attention sufficiently to add the hypnotic to the drink unnoticed. Once the chloral had taken effect, he pulled poor Pomeroy's head back, out came the *kukri*, and–" Holmes brought his hand down in an energetic gesture.

I shivered. " And the weapon itself ? "

" I think the *Army List*, or maybe *Who's Who* will provide us with the answer." He stretched out a lazy arm towards the bookcase, and pulled out the latter volume. " Upperby, Upton, ah ! Upwood. Here he is. Yes, indeed, Watson, here it is. Seconded to the Fourth Gurkha Rifles for a year some time back. I am sure that ghastly weapon is a souvenir of his time there."

" What do you intend doing ? "

" We will go and see him now. And if he is not at home, we will wait for him. You may care to bring your revolver and one cartridge."

I did not question this extraordinary request, but did as I had been bid.

We arrived at Colonel Upwood's rooms at three o'clock, and

were informed by his valet that the Colonel was expected to return at half-past the hour.

On our informing the valet that we would wait for his master, we were conducted to a small sitting-room, furnished with Oriental knick-knacks, including various native weapons. A space on the wall clearly indicated where one such ornament had been removed and not subsequently replaced. I silently indicated this to Holmes, and he responded with a nod.

At length we heard the sound of the front door being opened, and shortly thereafter, Colonel Upwood fairly burst into the room.

" Dobbs informs me that you two have been waiting for my return. Infernal impertinence ! Why could you not have left a card ? "

Holmes, still seated, responded. " This is an urgent matter that requires your personal attention."

" Very well. I will give you two minutes of my time to state your business, Mr...? "

" The name is Sherlock Holmes, and my friend here is John Watson."

" The nosey-parker busybody ? The police spy ? "

" I am no spy for the police, Colonel. If I were, you would now be handcuffed and in the cells. I am giving you a chance to clear a man's name, and at the same time to restore a little honour to your own."

" Damn you, you miserable meddler in other men's affairs ! You and your friend may leave instantly." He pointedly held the door open, and stood by it, but Holmes remained seated. " Are you going of your own free will, or shall I make you go ? " he shouted as he advanced upon my friend with a look of fury on his face.

There was a flash of steel, and Holmes was on his feet, his swordstick unsheathed, with the point at the Colonel's throat. " You would do well to sit, and to listen to what I have to say to you. No, do not consider calling for assistance. It will serve no useful purpose. Sit." He moved the swordstick in a meaningful fashion, and Upwood half-fell into the chair behind him.

" There is little point in denial," Holmes told him. " I have been informed of the circumstances surrounding this business at the Nonpareil Club. I have investigated the matter, and can now present enough evidence to convict you many times over in a court of law. Did you really think that your clumsy efforts could persuade even our Scotland Yard police to believe that Pomeroy killed himself? Your efforts at forging a suicide note were laughable in the extreme. And the carelessness with which you left a clear clue as to your identity in the form of a half-inch of cigar ash is almost unparalleled in the annals of crime. My only question to you is why you behaved so abominably?"

The fight seemed to go out of Upwood's body as Holmes spoke, but his eyes burned. "My reputation, Holmes. As a member of the Nonpareil Club, I was accorded some respect. Should I lose that membership, my creditors would come flocking around like vultures to a Parsee Tower of Silence." He paused. "Young Pomeroy would have seen me out of the Club, and I would have been ruined. His *fiancée*, young Emily Sallerton, would have brought with her some ten thousand pounds upon her marriage to him, and with that money, he could have easily bought the votes to expel me from the Club.

"I therefore determined to woo her away from his side, and was successful to the extent that she broke her engagement to him and entered into an understanding with me. And that same evening, we had words."

"I heard about that and about the card game."

"That thousand pounds that I paid him when he won that final hand – that was money I did not have. I would be ruined even more thoroughly in the eyes of society. So... I knew he was in low spirits over the breaking of the engagement. I suggested that we talk together over the tiger business – you know of that. He was in the room, waiting at the table. I brought two whisky and sodas with me, and I had added a few drops of chloral to the glass I gave him. In a few minutes he was practically asleep, and I– I am ashamed to describe what I did."

"I think we know," Holmes said, almost gently.

"I never imagined there would be so much blood. My God! I have seen men die in battle, and I have seen the inside of a surgeon's tent, but..." He paused and drew a deep breath. "I arranged the glass and the inkwell and hurriedly placed the note I had written in his writing on the table."

"You neglected to notice that Pomeroy was left-handed," Holmes remarked, almost negligently, "when you placed those items, as if for yourself. Furthermore, it was clear that they had been placed there after the blood had been shed. You also, by the way, neglected to leave a pen with which the supposed suicide note had been written."

"Maybe I did make a few mistakes," said Upwood, a new strength in his voice. "But it does not really matter, does it?" He held out his left hand, a small revolver pointed at Holmes held in it. "You will drop that stupid pigsticker, and if you believe in a God, you will say your prayers before I dispose of an intruder whom I discovered in my rooms."

He seemed to have forgotten my existence. I was seated in a position invisible to him as he faced Holmes, and it was the work of a moment for me to use the butt of my revolver to knock him senseless with a blow under the ear.

"Good work, Watson," said Holmes, removing the unconscious man's revolver from his hand, and removing five of the six cartridges. "Do you think you can guard him while I get the servants out of the house?"

I agreed to this, and Holmes left the room. Our adversary stirred, and moaned as he opened his eyes to find himself staring down the barrel of my pistol.

"Do not move," I told him. I have no doubt that I would have shot and killed him, unarmed as he was, had he attempted to make any resistance. He was a dangerous man, and had threatened my friend with death.

After a few minutes, the sound of the front door opening and shutting reached us, and Holmes re-entered the room.

"Now, Colonel, I wish you to sit at that bureau and to write to my dictation."

"The devil I will."

Holmes clapped the revolver he was holding to Upwood's temples. "Very well, then. I shall be forced to take you to the police."

"Damn you, I'll write."

He struggled to his feet, and seated himself at the desk while

Holmes dictated a detailed confession of how he had arranged Pomeroy's death.

" My congratulations. You are the devil himself to know all this, even given what I have told you already," said Upwood when he had signed the document and placed it in an envelope.

" Some have said so," smiled Holmes, pocketing the envelope.

" And what now ? " asked Upwood.

" I think you know what is expected of an officer and a gentleman," Holmes told him. " We will leave the room, leaving you with the revolver, which, by the way, has only one cartridge in it. There is therefore no point in attempting to attack us, armed with our own revolvers and my swordstick. If we have not heard the shot within five minutes, we will carry out the task that you have failed to do."

Holmes and I left the room, Holmes placing Upwood's revolver on the floor as we closed the door.

The sound of the shot reached us less than one minute later, and on opening the door, we beheld Upwood seated at the bureau, a bullet through his brain.

" Pride," said Holmes, looking at the ruined head. " Damnable pride. Come, let us to Gregson, and present him with this," waving Upwood's confession. " It will provide him with invaluable assistance in the writing of his report. And then to Sir Thomas."

Sir Thomas Ridgson listened gravely to the account that Holmes gave of events. " Shocking, shocking," he said, shaking his head. " And yet, I can hardly claim to be surprised. Our members, as I mentioned, are beset with that most invidious of the deadly sins. I can see it in myself, in the very founding of the Club."

It came as no surprise to either Holmes or myself when a few days later the daily newspapers provided a full account of the " Upwood scandal", as it became known, together with a full account of the card game that had preceded the killing of Pomeroy. Inspector Gregson was given the majority of the credit for the exposure of Upwood's atrocious conduct, and the same accounts also reported that following this scandal, Sir Thomas was dissolving the Nonpareil Club.

" A welcome move," I said as I read the story to Holmes over

our breakfast that day. " The fewer opportunities for these pea-
cocks to strut and display their feathers, the better for us all."

" I entirely agree," said Holmes. " How elegantly you phrase
things," he mused.

And then and there the Nonpareil Club became a nine days'
wonder, and then sank, as these matters invariably do, into the
marsh of history.

THE ADVENTURE OF
THE GREEN HORSE

"ou must help us, Mr. Holmes ! "

It would be a heart of stone that could resist such a plea, coming as it did from the mouth of one in such obvious distress. The name on the card that had been sent up to us was " Mrs. Frederick Lomax", and the bearer proved to be a young woman of about twenty-five years of age, fashionably dressed.

" Pray, calm yourself, Mrs. Lomax," Holmes reassured her. " Please take a seat here. Perhaps, Watson, you could arrange for Mrs. Hudson to bring us some tea ? "

I hastened to obey as Mrs. Lomax settled herself into the chair in which Holmes's clients typically unburdened themselves of their worries, and indeed, when I returned from my errand, she appeared more composed as she addressed Holmes.

" It is my sister, Mary," she began. " I call her my sister, but in truth she is my step-sister, the child of my step-father's first marriage. Mary Draycott is a little older than I, and I fear that nature has not favoured her in the matter of looks, nor the law in the matter of inheritance – her mother's estate was willed entirely to her brother, who now lives in Canada. She remains unmarried, and makes her living by acting as a nurse-companion to elderly gentlefolk in their last months of life. There is an agency which specialises in providing such services – I can provide you with the name if you wish."

" Later, later," Holmes murmured. " Please continue."

" As I say, she has been practising this profession for some years now without incident, until last week. The last patient she attended – that is to say, before her current post – died a month ago."

" The name of this patient ? "

" A Lady Fiona Pugsley, an elderly lady who lived in Portman Square, the widow of General Sir Archibald Pugsley. After Lady Pugsley's demise, the relatives came to settle the estate, and it was noticed that a valuable item was missing."

At that moment, Mrs. Hudson brought in the tea, and the conversation ceased momentarily. When she had left, and the door closed behind Mrs. Hudson, Mrs. Lomax resumed her story.

" The item in question was a small jade carving in the shape of a horse, which had always stood beside Lady Pugsley's bed. It had supposedly been brought back from China by the General, and was said to be very valuable.

" Upon the servants' being questioned, all denied any knowledge of the horse's whereabouts, and suspicion then fell on my sister Mary. Upon being asked about the horse, she immediately produced it, saying that she had been presented with it by Lady Pugsley as a gift in recognition of her services as a nurse and companion."

" Then it is merely a question of her word," said Holmes. " I confess that I am unsure of the problem facing you."

" If it were this alone," replied Mrs. Lomax, " I would agree with you. However, the relatives referred the matter to the police, and it was discovered that in six cases previously, some trinkets or small items, none as valuable as this jade carving, had been discovered as missing from the estates of the elderly patients for whom Mary had been caring. They confronted Mary with this, and she denied any knowledge of these pieces. Even so, they do not believe poor Mary, and she lives in constant fear of arrest of crimes that she denies, and I know in my heart that she did not commit."

" And you wish me to establish her innocence ? "

" Precisely that, Mr. Holmes."

" Very well. There would appear to be some elements to this case which provide some interest. The name of the agency that employs your step-sister ? "

" The Barnet Nursing Agency. It has offices in Chipping Barnet. The establishment employs about half a dozen nurse-companions in the same manner as they employ Mary."

" Indeed. Do you know the name of the police officer who is in charge of this case ? "

" Inspector Williamson of Scotland Yard, I believe."

" A name I have heard, but I have yet to have the pleasure of making his acquaintance. However, that will soon be remedied."

" One last question, Mr. Holmes. Your fee ? "

" We will discuss that when the time comes. Trust me, it will not be more than you can afford." Holmes smiled easily as he rose to his feet and extended his hand. "Thank you, Mrs. Lomax. I have your address on your card and will contact you as soon as any matter of import arises."

She seemed somewhat surprised at this rather abrupt dismissal, but rose, and took Holmes's hand. "Thank you, Mr. Holmes. Goodbye to you, and to you, Dr Watson."

"And what do you make of our Mrs. Lomax?" Holmes asked me, after we had watched her taking a cab from our window.

"If I were to deduce anything from her style of dress, which was fashionable, but not of the highest quality, I would hazard that Mr. and Mrs. Lomax are not in as favourable financial circumstances as they would like themselves to be."

"I agree. Excellent observation on your part. Did you notice her wedding ring?"

"I confess that I did not."

"Perhaps I should rephrase that. Did you notice the absence of her wedding ring? Perhaps its recent removal will prove significant." He paused, as if in thought. "I regret that you were here today to meet Mrs. Lomax."

"What can you mean?"

"If Mrs. Lomax had not met you, I would be sending you round to Chipping Barnet now to enquire about the possibility of hiring a companion for your elderly Aunt Amelia. I have a feeling about this. Since she now knows your name and face, that is impossible. Never mind, we will pay a visit to the Registrar of Companies, and then proceed to Inspector Williamson."

The police officer turned out to be a lean, almost cadaverous individual of gloomy aspect.

"I confess to you, sir, that we don't have a lot to go on here," he admitted when we introduced ourselves and explained our mission. "Miss Draycott seemed all too keen to show us the little gee-gee when we asked her about it, but we only have her word for it that it was a gift."

"Do you have the horse here?" asked Holmes.

"That I do, sir." Williamson opened his desk drawer, and extracted a small object which he passed to Holmes.

"Good Heavens, Watson," my friend exclaimed, letting out a low whistle. "Look at this!"

The carving, not more than two or three inches in length, was exquisitely worked in Oriental fashion. The material was a pale green stone, which almost seemed to shine with its own light as it lay in Holmes's palm.

"Inspector," Holmes said severely. "Your desk drawer is no place for this. Its rightful place is the British Museum, or, failing that, your office safe."

"It is valuable, then?"

"Almost priceless, I would say. It is fashioned from nephrite jade, the most prized and precious kind, and the workmanship is exquisite. I believe this dates from the Han dynasty, nearly two thousand years ago."

"Good Lord!" exclaimed Williamson

"If it were to be offered for sale, I am no expert in these matters, you understand, but I would estimate a price of fifteen thousand pounds to be not unreasonable."

"Good Lord!" Williamson repeated. "I shall follow your suggestion as to the safe immediately, sir."

"And the other items listed as having been stolen from her other patients. Where are they?"

The inspector spread his hands. "We searched Miss Draycott's lodgings, and a policewoman searched her person. There was no trace of them, nor any evidence, such as pawnbrokers' receipts, of their ever having been in her possession."

"I see. Do you have a list of these items listed as missing from the other occasions and their descriptions?" Holmes asked.

"Here you are, sir."

"Excellent," remarked Holmes, scanning the paper. "On the face of it, these would appear to be mere trinkets by comparison with our friend here," indicating the green horse, "worth perhaps fifty pounds or so each at the very most."

"Still a tidy sum, sir," Williamson pointed out.

"Indeed, but in a different class entirely. May I take a copy of this list?"

"I will have one made for you." He pressed an electric bell, and instructed the constable accordingly.

"Have there been any similar complaints from other clients of the agency employing Miss Draycott?"

" Not to my knowledge, sir. Mary Draycott is the only one of which I have any knowledge."

"You have talked with her, have you not ? How did she strike you ? "

" I have to confess that her appearance did not strike me very favourably. She does, however, have a pleasant voice, and a manner which I am sure her patients find relaxing and calming." He paused for a moment. " When she told me the details of how this here," indicating the jade horse, " was given to her by Lady Pugsley, I felt that she was telling the truth. I don't know if you ever have such a feeling, sir, but in my experience, the truth makes itself known through little things, such as posture, and tone of voice."

" Indeed it does, Inspector. And her denials of the other items ? "

" Again, it seemed sincere, but since she professed no knowledge of these items, other than to admit that she had noticed some of them while at work in the houses from which they were missing, there were no specific event or events to be verified or disproved."

" Excellent, Inspector. You have grasped the truth that absence of proof of innocence is not the same as proof of absence of innocence. Would that all juries could think the same. Where is she now ? "

"You may find her caring for Lady Beddesley in her house on Brompton Street."

" Excellent. I may pay her a visit at some point. But while we wait for your constable, perhaps you can tell me something about the Barnet Nursing Agency, Inspector."

" Not a lot to say, sir. Its offices are just one room on the High Street, above the fishmonger's, and the only employee, other than the nurses that it sends out, appear to be Mr. Lomax."

"You are aware, are you not, that Mr. Lomax appears to be married to Mary Draycott's step-sister ? Before visiting you, Watson and I paid a visit to the Registrar of Companies and discovered that a Mr. Frederick Lomax is the proprietor of the agency. The card of my visitor to Baker Street earlier today gave her name as Mrs. Frederick Lomax. I feel that there is more than a little coincidence here."

Williamson gave a visible start. "No sir, I did not know this. Why do you say that she ' appears' to be married to Mr. Lomax ? "

"When she visited us, I noticed that she had been wearing several rings, including her wedding ring. The marks were still on her fingers."

" I believe all this puts a fresh complexion on the case."

" It does indeed," Holmes smiled. " But as yet, I am unsure exactly what turn events will take. I take it that you would have no objection to my visiting Mr. Lomax in Barnet ? "

" None at all. To be frank with you, sir, I am pleased to have your opinions on the matter. Ah," as the constable re-entered, bearing papers. " Here is the list of items you requested. May I simply ask that you keep me informed of any developments as they occur ? "

" Naturally, Inspector. A very good day to you."

In the cab from Scotland Yard, I asked Holmes about his thoughts regarding the case.

" I have a theory," he answered me. "A theory which as yet lacks the foundation of a set of data to prove it. Ah, here we are." The cab had deposited us outside a house in Portman Square.

We descended the area steps and knocked on the kitchen door, which was opened by a girl in maid's uniform.

" If it's Mrs. Wallace the cook you're looking for, she left when her Ladyship died. There's just me and Mrs. Finch, the housekeeper, left here to look after the place all on our own."

" Excellent," Holmes smiled. " If you could answer a few questions for me, I'd be most grateful. Do you remember a Mary Draycott who nursed Lady Pugsley ? "

" Course I do. Not much in the way of looks, poor dear, but a good heart for all that. I couldn't believe it when they said she'd taken that little thing from her Ladyship's table without asking."

" Do you think her Ladyship might have given it to her, then ? "

" I'm sure she would, sir." The answer was given in firm

unhesitating tones. " Mary Draycott is a good kind person, and Lady P, as she liked us to call her, knew that as well as anyone. I do believe she could have asked for anything she wanted from Lady P, and she'd have had it."

" I see. Were there ever any visitors from the agency who sent Mary Draycott ? "

" A Mr. Lomax came to call before Mary came to join us. And he called again about a week before Lady P passed away. Came in happy enough, I seem to recall, but he left as if he'd just had a thundercloud sit on him. I only met him those two times, but I can't put my hand on my heart and tell you I cared for him one bit."

" And anyone else ? "

The maid shook her head. " Not that I can remember, unless they called on my day off. I'd be the one who'd let them in, see ? "

Holmes thanked her for her information. " And here's half a crown for your trouble."

" Why, thank you, sir."

" Where next ? " I asked Holmes. " Barnet, or Brompton Street ? "

" Neither," he said. "Ah, here we are." We had halted outside a handsome townhouse, the ground and upper storeys of which appeared to be empty. " This is one of the houses from which an item was reported as missing – a silver spoon, to be precise." Again, we descended the area steps and knocked on the door. This time, it appeared to be the cook who answered.

Holmes introduced himself.

" I've read of you, sir. But I haven't done nothing," our interlocutor protested.

" My dear lady, no one is accusing you of anything. I simply want to ask you a few questions if I may. Do you remember a Mary Draycott, who cared for Mr. Hammersley during his last illness ? "

" Mary ? I do indeed. Such a comfort to the poor gentleman she was. Nice as pie to us all."

" And do you remember something about a missing spoon ? "

" I do that. It was a silver rat-tailed spoon from the time of

King James, they said. It was the one that Mr. Hammersley used to take his medicine. It went missing after his death."

" And do you think Mary Draycott might have taken it ? "

She shook her head emphatically. " No, sir, I do not. Mary Draycott was an honest, good person."

" Thank you. One last question. Did anyone from the agency who sent Mary Draycott ever visit here ? "

"Yes, there was a Mr— Lucas ? No, Lomax, that was his name. He came to see if Mary Draycott was doing her job properly. That would have been a few days before Mr. Hammersley passed away. No," correcting herself. " I tell a lie. It was the day before he died. I remember Jane, the parlourmaid, took him upstairs to the sickroom so that he could see that all was being done proper. Jane told me that he didn't behave towards her like a gentleman should. I'll leave you, sir, to guess what she meant by that."

Again Holmes presented a half-crown along with his thanks.

" And what does all this mean ? " I asked. " How many more houses are we going to visit ? "

" To answer your last question first, I do not think it will be worth visiting any more. We have visited the last two where Mary Draycott worked, and the trail will have gone cold. The servants who worked with her will all have gone to other positions, and the houses will have passed into other hands. There is no more that we can do today in this regard. So let us take ourselves to the wilds of Chipping Barnet."

Once we had reached our destination, Holmes pointed to a fishmonger's shop. "Above there, if I am not mistaken, are the offices of the Barnet Nursing Agency." However, it was to a nearby pawnbroker's establishment that we took ourselves.

" I am interested," Holmes said to the shopkeeper, " to know if you have for sale any silver spoons of the time of King George II or earlier."

" I'd have to check the books, sir, but I think I have one or two here." After consultation, he arranged three spoons on the counter in front of us and held one up. " This one might be a bit early for you, sir. James the First, I believe."

" As you say, a little earlier than I was expecting, but the rat-tail design is exceptionally fine. The price ? "

"A guinea, sir."

"And while I am here, I am of the fancy that an amber-headed scarf-pin would be an excellent addition to my wardrobe."

"I know that I have just the thing for you here, sir. However, there is an insect trapped in the amber. I trust you have no objection to that."

The pin's head was as large as a walnut, and as described, the amber contained a perfectly preserved fly.

"Perfect," said Holmes. "The fly adds interest." He cocked his head enquiringly.

"I was going to ask fifteen shillings, but if you take this along with the spoon, I will sell this for twelve and sixpence."

"Excellent. One pound thirteen and sixpence, then, for the pair?"

"That's right, sir."

"I know that you have your professional secrets, but I would like to ask you if this spoon and this pin were brought in by the same person."

The shopkeeper looked at Holmes in amazement. "You're right, sir, but how in the world would you possibly know that? Yes, it's the same woman, and there are quite a few others that she has brought in from time to time."

"I won't pry further, other than to ask if she has brought in any rings recently?"

"Now, sir, I believe you are a true magician. You frighten me, sir. I refuse to answer that question."

"And your refusal provides me with that answer. Thank you. Thirty-three shillings and sixpence, we said? Here you are."

"Thank you, sir."

Holmes chuckled as we left the shop. "A moment, if you would, Watson." He paused to adjust his newly acquired scarf-pin in a prominent position. "And now for the Barnet Nursing Agency."

Mr. Frederick Lomax was a small man, whose round face was framed by black bushy side-whiskers. His clothes had once been of good quality, but were now sadly worn and threadbare in some places.

As Holmes and I entered, he rose to greet us, and gave a visible start as he beheld the amber pin at Holmes's throat.

"What— how may I help you gentlemen ? " he stammered.

" I believe that you supply nurses – companions, if you will – to provide comfort to those about to depart this life," Holmes said.

" That is so," the other acknowledged.

"Your agency comes recommended by the heirs of Mr. Augustus Barnstable, who passed away some two years ago. You supplied a nurse by the name of Mary Draycott, I seem to recall, who took care of him in his last hours."

Lomax's face had drained of colour as Holmes delivered his speech, and his eyes glared at us from an almost perfectly white visage as he replied through bloodless lips. " I do not know who you are, but I must tell you that Miss Draycott is unavailable. Indeed, at present we are unable to undertake any more engagements, and I must therefore bid you both a good day."

Holmes stood his ground. " May I trouble you for the answer to one more question ? "

" If you must." The permission was given grudgingly.

" Where is the jade horse ? "

I did not think it was possible for a face to grow any paler, but Lomax was by now literally as white as a sheet. " I have no idea what you are talking about," he told us defiantly.

" Then I will tell you. A nephrite jade horse of the Han dynasty is now in the possession of the Metropolitan Police. It is there because one of your nurses, Miss Mary Draycott, is under suspicion of having stolen it from her charge, Lady Pugsley."

" Haven't they arrested her yet ? "

" So you do know about it, then ? " Holmes answered smoothly.

" Damn your eyes ! " the other exploded. He bent and extracted a revolver from his desk drawer. " Unless you leave within five seconds, I shall fire."

" I would not do that if I were you. Watson here is a dead shot with the revolver you can make out in his coat pocket – yes, the one in which he currently has his hand – he is left-handed, you see. If I go down, you too will certainly fall, and Watson here will not shoot to kill. He will save you for the hangman."

The pistol dropped from Lomax's hand as he sank into the chair and broke into hysterical sobs. " I believe you know it all."

" Nearly all."

" It was Tabitha's idea to employ her."

"Your wife ? "

Lomax nodded. " Mary is a sweet and innocent soul, handicapped by her looks. Her mother's money was left to her brother in Canada. What Tabitha knows, and Mary does not, is that her brother is dying of consumption, and has left a considerable fortune to Mary in his will."

" And if Mary were to be no longer in circulation, under arrest or worse, your wife would then inherit as next of kin ? "

Lomax nodded again. " That was the idea. I had lost money on 'Change, more than I could afford, and this Agency," he waved his hand around the room, " by now had but one nurse on its books – Mary. By visiting the homes of the patients where she worked, I was able to abstract certain small but valuable items that, as you seem to have discovered, I took to the local pawnbroker's in exchange for cash. How much did he ask for that scarf-pin, if I may ask ? "

" Twelve shillings and sixpence."

" Oh, the rogue ! " Lomax exclaimed with a bitter laugh. " I only received seven shillings for it. Of course, there was no proof that Mary had taken these things, but they were small enough to be overlooked, but large enough to be noticed if a detailed inventory was ever taken. They would act as circumstantial evidence if Mary were ever to be suspected. But when I visited Lady Pugsley before placing Mary there, I caught sight of that little green horse that you referred to earlier. I do not have a detailed knowledge of such things, but I knew this was valuable. Its loss would prompt an enquiry. My aim was to remove the horse and place it among Mary's things so that it would be discovered there so that she would be arrested, charged, and sent to prison. How was I to know that it would form a gift from patient to nurse before my arrival, and Mary would be proud to acknowledge its possession ? " He broke off. " Have you any objection to my taking my medicine ? My heart," he offered by way of explanation.

Holmes shook his head, and Lomax extracted a glass into which he poured what appeared to be water from a bottle, adding some drops from a small phial that he extracted from his waistcoat pocket before draining the draught.

" Quick, Watson ! " Holmes shouted to me as Lomax slumped forward.

There was a smell of bitter almonds as I raised the unconscious body, feeling for his pulse. " Prussic acid, I fear," I said to Holmes. " We have lost him."

" I do not think it is the first time this phial has been used," Holmes said. " If we investigate, I am sure that many of Mary Draycott's patients died very soon after Lomax paid a visit."

" You do not suspect her of anything ? "

" I do not. But we must make haste to take the widow before she, too, escapes us." He opened the window onto the street and blew three loud blasts upon his police-whistle. A uniformed constable was with us within a matter of a few minutes, to whom Holmes explained the situation.

" If you wait here, sir, I'll bring my sergeant to go with you to find Mrs. Lomax, and I will stay here while you find her."

" If you are going to the station, please telephone Scotland Yard, and ask Inspector Williamson to join us at the station."

As the constable left us, I turned to Holmes.

" What in the world did you mean by saying I had my revolver with me, let alone saying that I could drop him firing left-handed from the hip ? You know very well that I do not carry my revolver with me unless specifically requested by you to do so."

Holmes laughed easily. " He was a nervous man and could easily have pulled the trigger of his own gun before being fully aware of any consequences. I had to provide him with a good reason why he should not do so."

It was only five minutes before the constable reappeared together with another policeman who introduced himself as Sergeant Jennings.

" I'll come with you, sir. What charges should I bring against her when I arrest her ? "

" I think, Sergeant, that we should simply ask her to accompany us to the station, and await Inspector Williamson's judgement on the matter."

" Very good, sir."

We set off for the Lomax house, which was known to Sergeant Jennings, and which proved to be a rather mean terraced house in a side-street. Tabitha Lomax's face brightened at the sight of Holmes and me, but her expression changed when informed of her husband's death and Jennings's request to accompany us to the station.

Once there and joined by Inspector Williamson she corroborated her husband's story, and confirmed Holmes's suspicions that some of Mary Draycott's patients had suffered unnaturally early deaths as the result of poison being added to their medicine by Lomax on his visits when he took the small articles.

When shown the list of articles that had been reported as missing, she laughed heartily. " This list," she said, " represents a mere fraction of the items that Fred took from Mary's houses. One spoon ? " She laughed. " He took at least six spoons and a cream jug. That jug alone paid the coal man for a week with what we got from that miser of a pawnbroker."

" Tabitha Lomax, I hereby arrest you on the charge of conspiracy to pervert the course of justice, and of being an accessary after the fact to numerous acts of theft," Williamson told her after she had made a full statement. " We'll also take in that pawnbroker. He is certain to have known that he was receiving stolen goods."

" And now, if you have no objection, Inspector," Holmes added, Watson and I would like to accompany you to Scotland Yard where I can collect the jade and return it to Mary Draycott."

" Certainly."

An hour or two later, we were knocking at the door of the room occupied by Mary Draycott in the Brompton-street house where she was currently acting as a nurse.

The door was opened by a woman, who, as we had been told, was less than attractive in her appearance. A large port-wine birthmark covered one side of her face, and the poor creature also suffered from a severe squint. However, there was a feeling of sincerity to her smile, and she invited us into the room which was neatly and comfortably furnished.

" Mr. Sherlock Holmes and Dr Watson. I am honoured," she said in a soft melodious voice. " No doubt you were sent here by Sister Tabitha ? "

" Indirectly, I suppose that may be true," said Holmes, and proceeded to relate the events of the day that had passed.

To our surprise, Mary Draycott burst out laughing. " I suppose that it is no laughing matter, really. I certainly believe that Fred was responsible for the deaths of some of my patients, but I could not prove anything, any more than he could prove that I stole any of the objects whose disappearance he wished to lay at my door. None of it would have worked, you realise. I could never be found guilty by a jury."

Holmes smiled. " You are right, you know. A jury would have to be satisfied beyond all reasonable doubt that you had stolen those things, and any advocate worth his salt could have implanted that doubt in their minds. They would be duty bound to declare you innocent, even if they felt you were guilty."

" The only evidence, such as it is, is this." She indicated the jade horse.

" Have you any idea what this is worth ? " asked Holmes.

" Han dynasty, nephrite jade. Probably carved for a member of the Imperial court. I think somewhere between fifteen and twenty thousand pounds."

I looked at her in astonishment. " How on earth.. ? "

" A hobby of mine, Doctor. Look." On the shelf above her bed was a row of volumes pertaining to antiquities, including some volumes on Chinese jade.

Holmes chuckled.

" I may not be a pretty face, Mr. Holmes, but the Lord gave me a good power of understanding. I always knew what Tabitha was doing and what Fred was doing at her bidding."

" But why would she call in Holmes to establish your innocence ? " I asked.

" Oh, that was never her intention. She believed that the evidence against me was strong enough to secure my conviction. And if even the great Sherlock Holmes could not save me, then..." She shrugged. " She always pretended to pity me, but actually despised me, and envied me for the fortune that will come my way when Gerald dies – oh yes, I know all about it, and I believe it is now only a matter of months now. And Fred ? " She laughed. " Fred's preposterous little Agency. He had no head for business. If it wasn't for me, that couple would have been bankrupted long ago – I acquired a good reputation and he was able to charge good money for my services."

" You were indeed good at what you did," Holmes told her. " All the servants with whom we spoke had nothing but praise for you and your character."

" It was work that I enjoyed doing, and I flatter myself that I did it well. I felt loved and appreciated, not just by my patients, but by the other servants whose lives I was easing by caring for their masters and mistresses."

" And so after all these years, you felt that you deserved – this ? " said Holmes, indicating the horse.

She said nothing, but looked Holmes in the eye and nodded.

" Holmes," I said. " What are you saying ? "

" I say nothing now, and I shall not say anything in the future about this."

Mary Draycott looked at Holmes, at the jade horse, and back again at my friend.

" Come, Watson. We are done here," said Sherlock Holmes.

" God bless you, Mr. Holmes," Mary Draycott said to us as we closed the door on this extraordinary woman and her green horse.

THE ADVENTURE OF THE
MURDERED MAHARAJAH

I T was one of those cold days in the early English spring that remind us that Winter has not yet completely departed. A light rain fell as I gazed out of our window at the passers-by in Baker-street.

"I do not think he will return to his wife," Holmes suddenly remarked to me.

"Who on earth are you referring to?" I asked, completely nonplussed by this statement, uttered completely at random, as it seemed to me.

"The cab-driver on the opposite of the road, talking to the flower-girl."

"She is remarkably pretty," I observed.

"I bow to your superior judgement in these matters," Holmes smiled.

I must suppose that I blushed a little at his words. "But how, in the name of goodness, can you make such an observation about the marital history of a complete stranger?" I asked him.

"Ah, but Jeffreys is far from being a complete stranger to me. He is by way of being a cousin of some sort to Wiggins, whom you have met in his capacity as the leader of the Baker-street Irregulars, and came recommended to me by that young gentleman as a discreet and resourceful driver should I ever have need of the same."

"I take it you followed the recommendation, then?"

"I did, and I have not had cause to regret it. His sole fault is that he will insist on talking – not at critical junctures in an investigation, mark you – but at times when he considers that I will enjoy his monologues. I am now in possession of more information regarding the home life of Mr. Arnold Jeffreys than I have ever considered necessary. However, his skill at following the vehicles of others, and at avoiding notice while so doing is, in my experience, unequalled by any jarvey in the metropolis."

"And he has an eye for the ladies, I take it, provided that their name is not Mrs. Jeffreys?"

"Indeed that is the case. That particular flower-girl seems to have caught his eye for longer than most. From the little I have seen of her, she would appear to be well-suited to him."

I laughed. "Holmes, I take it that you are not thinking of

taking up the profession of marriage-broker to the lower classes ? "

" By no means. I am currently engaged on an investigation that would not bode well for my future were it to go awry."

" The client is well-known ? "

" Very much so. One who holds a high position, and whose influence on others is considerable."

" And you fear that your art will desert you in this case ? "

Holmes sighed. " My dear Watson, painting is an art, music is an art, but my profession is a science."

" Very well," I smiled. " And I may suppose that those against whom you set yourself are also followers of a scientific profession ? "

" By no means," he contradicted me. " Among those few whom we may term professional criminals, given that most crimes are committed almost by accident, there are those who seem to regard the business of breaking the law as something of an art. In this instance, I would quote the example of a certain young man who is on the rise in his profession. I currently see him as the fourth smartest man in London. He is no stranger to imagination and daring." I knew that Holmes would place himself in the first three, but refrained from enquiry regarding the other two. " Then," Holmes continued, " there are those who would regard it as a science. We need merely examine the records of those who have taught at our universities, or those engaged in the professions – including yours, Watson – for such examples."

He paused, as if uncertain as to whether to continue. " There is a third category ? " I asked.

" There is indeed, and it is this category that is perhaps the most dangerous of all. These are the criminals who regard their deeds simply as a business. Such a one is the man known to the cognoscenti as The Deptford Assassin. Even I do not know his true name, but I do know that this man takes money in exchange for taking the life of one named by the payer. He is said to be without emotion, to work swiftly and efficiently, taking no pleasure in others' sufferings, and only finding satisfaction in a job well done, as he views matters. He sees these transactions as no more than a way of making a living."

I shuddered. "This does indeed appear to be as cold-blooded a criminal as one can imagine."

"Another such is Baron Maupertuis, but in his case, his business is the dissemination of lies and deception leading to his financial enrichment at the expense of others. There is, I will grant him, a certain artistry in some of his deceptions, but this appears to be merely a product of his ingenuity, rather than an example of art for art's sake. And it is he against whom I am presently set."

"He is set to defraud your client?"

"Indeed that is his intention. He is a most persuasive man, albeit that he usually works at at least two removes from his victims, employing others to act as his intermediaries. The whole business is diabolically organised, and even with the expenses he is forced to meet in order to pay his associates, I estimate he brings in a cool two or three hundred thousand pounds per annum for himself."

"What is his story?" I could not help enquiring.

By way of answer, Holmes fixed me with his steady gaze. "Watson, I have come to rely on you in many cases. May I entreat you to assist me in this case? No," and he held up a hand to prevent my speaking. "Do not answer hastily or glibly, but hear me out. This case is not a simple matter of tracing footprints to discover a thief or a murderer. It will present danger to those involved – Maupertuis is known to be utterly ruthless on occasion, and the number of police agents who have met untimely ends while investigating his affairs is now in the dozens. To trap Maupertuis and silence him is not the work of one or two men, but there is no one that I would sooner have at my side than you, my trusted friend."

"Can you doubt that I will be with you on this, Holmes?" I asked.

"I confess that I was expecting an answer along those lines," Holmes said to me. "Thank you. It is good to have my faithful Watson by my side." I was touched by the warmth of Holmes's tones, which were seldom, if ever, heard by others, and which belied his reputation as a cold calculating machine-like character, devoted only to his work and a few obscure hobby-horses and pastimes. He continued, "I should inform you now that

I am working alongside the official forces on this occasion. I believe you are acquainted with Inspector Hopkins, whom I believe to be one of the most intelligent and resourceful officers currently employed by the police."

"That is good," I replied. I had met Hopkins in the past, and had a very favourable opinion of the man.

"As it happens, I was on my way to the Yard to discuss the case with Hopkins. Will you accompany me?"

"With pleasure," I told him. Within ten minutes we were on our way.

I nspector Stanley Hopkins welcomed us into his office, and we sat facing him across his desk, which was piled high with papers and files.

"Maupertuis," he sighed. "Baron Gérard Louis-Philippe de Maupertuis, if you wish to refer to him by his full name, Doctor," he added to me. " Baron of some piffling little town in Western Germany, which formed part of France until the war of 1870. He was made Baron for his services to Germany following the war, although he is Belgian by birth."

"A man of many allegiances, then?" I suggested.

"Many, and none, I fear," Hopkins answered me. "He appears to be a man entirely without scruples, or loyalty to any, except himself."

"His associates would attest to that," Holmes agreed. "There are those who are in charge of criminal organisations – the Professor springs to mind, eh, Hopkins?" The police inspector nodded, and Holmes continued. "Such men, and the leaders of Italian gangs, such as the Neapolitan Camorra and the Sicilian Mafia, will take care of their subordinates should they be unfortunate enough to be taken by the authorities, providing legal assistance and so on."

"Not to mention outright subversion of the police and the judicial system through bribery," added Hopkins.

"The same is true of many American gangs," Holmes went on. "However, Maupertuis, as I mentioned to you earlier, sees his dealings purely in a business light. The rewards for his followers are generous if they succeed, but if they fail – that is, if they fall into the hands of the law – they are 'written off the books', to use an expression employed in business."

"Indeed, if they fail in their primary task, that of procuring money for the Baron, they are thrown to the wolves, as it were. The Baron does not tolerate failure within his organisation," Hopkins added. "I should also mention that the same ruthless-ness applies to those with whom he finds himself in competi-tion, as well as those with whom he finds himself in opposition. I would advise you, Doctor, as I have advised Mr. Holmes here, to go about your business armed. I do not say this to alarm you, but simply to advise you that I see it as a necessary precaution in this instance."

"You are implying that Baron Maupertuis or his henchmen may resort to violence?"

"It is more than an implication – it is a virtual guarantee," Hopkins said, shaking his head. "In the usual run of things, I would have more than a little hesitation in allowing amateurs to take part in this business, but I have sufficient knowledge of Mr. Holmes's experience and skills, and those of you, Doctor Watson, to be as confident, or even more so, in your ability to set yourselves against the Baron as I would of two of my own men."

"That is a most gratifying thing to hear," I said to him.

"Now, to the practicalities of the business," Holmes said. "Where, in your opinion, Inspector, do you feel we should start our investigations?"

"The Baron himself is rumoured to be in Recife in Brazil. According to my sources, he has plans to create a monopoly in the coffee trade of that country. If he succeeds, those who buy the coffee in the belief that they are making their purchas-es from many sources, will have no idea that they are in fact making their purchases from different aspects of the same many-headed Hydra."

Holmes chuckled. "I had not seen you as being one to turn such a poetic phrase, Inspector," he laughed.

"We all have our hidden depths," Hopkins replied, amused. "However, it is not that which is of immediate concern. We have reports – and do not enquire at present from where they have come – that the Baron, prior to moving on to his coffee scheme, has set in motion the wheels of the most elaborate and by most estimates the largest swindle yet recorded." He paused, as if for effect. " He has it in mind to sell an island to which he has no rights."

" A small one ? " I hazarded.

" By no means," Hopkins told us. He was smiling broadly. " The island in question is one of the Dutch East Indies – that of Sumatra."

" If I recall correctly," Holmes said, " that island has twice the area of England, Wales and Scotland combined."

" To a rough approximation, that is correct. I can provide you with the exact figures if you wish," Hopkins answered.

Holmes waved a negligent hand. " I do not need feel them to be necessary at present. But, as you say, this island is currently owned by the Netherlands. How can Maupertuis present himself as the owner ? "

" Maybe I misled you a little in my description," Hopkins apologised. " The agents of Maupertuis do not claim that he owns it. Rather, they claim to be acting for the Dutch government, which wishes to sell the island, or to be more precise, shares in the island's wealth, to a private consortium of some of the world's richest men. The money so raised, so they say, is to be used to fund Dutch naval expansion. When they talk to the French, naturally, the ships so purchased will be used to defend the Netherlands against the Germans, and when they approach German millionaires, they refer to the Gallic menace."

" And the Dutch government has been unable to act against these agents ? "

" As you can imagine, the whole affair is presented as being one of great secrecy. It is emphasised to the prospective buyers that the business is a closely guarded secret, even at the highest levels of the Dutch government. It is represented to them that this is a personal initiative of the Dutch Royal Family. Since those being approached are typically those who have made their money through trade, it is considered unlikely that they will ever come into contact with royalty."

I smiled. "Maupertuis would appear to know his fish well, and how to bait his hook."

"And how successful have these approaches been so far?"

"We know of at least one Frenchman who is rumoured to have purchased some thirty million francs' worth of shares. A Bavarian industrialist has purchased at least as many, and there are rumours that some American steel and railway magnates have been persuaded to take part."

"But as yet, no Englishmen?" Holmes enquired.

"No, nor Scotchmen or Welshmen or Irishmen for that matter," smiled Hopkins. "However, we are aware that one of the Baron's men is currently in London, attempting to take money from a man who is generally reckoned to possess one of the largest personal fortunes in the world. That man being—"

"—the Maharajah of Rajipur, who is currently visiting London with his entourage," I broke in.

"Indeed so," Hopkins said in some surprise. "You are familiar with the gentleman?"

"I once had the honour of treating one of his wives for a minor ailment. Though I never conversed with His Highness at any length, I did observe him at close quarters on more than one occasion, and we exchanged greetings."

Holmes laughed. "You never cease to amaze me, Watson. Why you will persist in chronicling my poor exploits, when you appear to have led a life of excitement and adventure, I do not know."

"I have had enough adventure and excitement for one life," I answered him, unconsciously rubbing the shoulder where a jezail bullet had left its mark. "I have no wish to relive it."

"Even so," Hopkins remarked, "this is a more than fortunate coincidence. If you think it possible to renew your acquaintance with His Highness, your help in preventing him from making the supposed investment will be invaluable."

"And meanwhile, I take it," Holmes added, "I will be following Maupertuis' agent, with a view to securing a lead to the man himself, and lure him to a place where he may be taken?"

"Indeed so," said Hopkins. "You are ahead of me, as always, Mr. Holmes, and it is a pleasure to be working with you. Now, with your permission, I would like to introduce to you a M.

Pierre Lejeune, who is a member of the French *Sûreté*, and who has been on the trail of Maupertuis for a number of years now. He has come to London to offer his assistance in this matter."

M. Lejeune, who was ushered into the office some minutes later by Hopkins, was a middle-aged man with little of the apparent alertness which marks our British detectives.

However, Holmes greeted him with apparent pleasure, speaking in his rapid and apparently fluent French. After a few exchanges in this language, during which Lejeune observed the expressions of bemusement on Hopkins' and my faces, he spoke in competent, albeit heavily accented, English.

" My apologies, gentlemen," he told us. " I was unaware that the private detective whom I had been informed by the good Inspector here was retained on this case was the famous Sherlock Holmes." He made a bow in the direction of my friend, which was returned. " And you," turning to me, " must be the equally famous Doctor John Watson." We shook hands.

" And for myself," Holmes replied, " I am more than happy to make the acquaintance of M. Lejeune, who covered himself with such distinction in the Abbeville double murder case."

The little French detective gave a start. " But you know of this case, Mr. Holmes ? "

" Naturally. I had come to the same conclusion as yourself, based on my reading of the newspaper accounts, but your capture of the postman was masterly, and may serve as an excellent lesson to all engaged in our profession."

" I am flattered and honoured," the other replied. " But now, let us talk about Maupertuis, and the danger he represents to your country and to mine, and to Europe as a whole. Has the inspector informed you of the latest fraud he is perpetrating, that of the Netherland-Sumatra Company ? He has ? Excellent. Now let me tell you of the Frenchman and the German who have fallen prey to his wiles. In Germany, it is Graf Friedrich von Heissen who has invested in this swindle. In France, it is

M. Thierry de Lantis. Do these names mean anything to you gentlemen ? "

I confessed that both these were unfamiliar to me, but Holmes spoke up.

" Both men are owners of large industrial enterprises engaged in the manufacture of arms. If I recall correctly, de Lantis owns a large shipbuilding company on the French Atlantic coast specialising in the production of light naval vessels. The von Heissen factory is noted for its naval guns."

" You are well-informed, Mr. Holmes."

" It is my business to be so," my friend smiled.

" Contrary to his usual practice, Maupertuis has not demanded cash as payment for the fraudulent Sumatra shares that he is offering."

" What, then ? "

" He has taken shares in these gentlemen's companies in lieu of cash. The paper value of these shares is less than the supposed value of the fraudulent shares he is offering."

I frowned. " This seems like a very strange way of conducting business," I said.

" Ah, but wait until you have heard the whole story, my friend," Lejeune told me, wagging his finger in my direction. " For some months prior to this, Maupertuis had been buying shares through proxies. As a result of his latest acquisitions, he now holds a controlling interest in these companies, though the supposed owners are unaware of this fact. And to what end ? you may be asking yourselves," he added, with a typically Gallic shrug.

" It can only be that he wishes to build his own fleet of warships ! " I exclaimed, " Ridiculous though the idea may seem."

" Indeed, Doctor, that is the conclusion which we in Paris have also reached."

" But he cannot put a navy to sea," I objected. " And to what end ? He cannot pit himself against the great powers of Europe or the Americas."

" Nor would he wish to," replied the Frenchman. " The goals of Baron Maupertuis have never been territorial, but rather financial."

" Piracy ? " suggested Holmes. " A small fleet of fast but

powerfully armed gunboats, acting as cruisers, and operating in remote areas of the globe, changing their base of operations at regular intervals, to attack rich merchant ships or even passenger steamers, holding the crew and passengers for ransom. Alternatively, he could simply hold the shipping lines of the world to account, letting them know that if they pay a certain sum of money to an agent, their ships and cargos will not be attacked. In any event, the possession of a fleet of small warships, specialised for the purpose of raiding the commerce of nations, would spell disaster to the world's economies."

" I think you have the correct solution, Mr. Holmes. At least, that is what many on the Quai d'Orsay believe."

" Such an enterprise would require a significant sum of money to implement," remarked Hopkins. " Even with control of the arms factories that you have mentioned, he is unlikely to be able to maintain a fleet of warships."

" Hence his approach to your Maharajah here in London," Lejeune told us. " Maupertuis is playing a very long game. You have heard from Hopkins here that he is in Brazil ? "

" For the purpose of making a 'corner' in the coffee market," I said.

" That may be one of his motives, but I can assure you that it is far from being the sole motive, or even the major one. We have good reason to believe that he is setting up a chain of coaling stations along the eastern seaboard of the Americas, with the most northerly being in the Caribbean, though we are unsure of the exact location, and the most southerly in southern Brazil. From there, he can potentially control much of the trans-Atlantic trade. He already owns, quite legally, several cargo vessels, which might be used as colliers, allowing any armed piracy vessels to stay at sea for longer than would otherwise be the case."

" Even given all that you have said, monsieur," I objected, " and I have no doubt you and your colleagues are correct in their surmises, I find it hard to believe that a man can take on the might of the navies of the world. The Royal Navy is one of the most powerful military forces ever known, as you are no doubt well aware–"

" –all too aware, I fear, Doctor." He grimaced slightly.

"Forgive me. I was about to add that the navy of France runs a close second, and of course neither the German nor the American navies can be said to be negligible."

"Doctor, your pride and confidence in your navy and that of others may be a little misplaced here. Notwithstanding Trafalgar and the other notable victories of your naval forces, many of them at the expense of my country, piracy is a difficult matter to counter with any effectiveness. I know you have served with the Army, Doctor Watson, but I take it you have never served on a ship? No? Then you may not be aware that it is possible to sail for weeks, even months at a time without coming into contact with another vessel. And if the hunted vessel is taking precautions to hide herself, well..." He spread his hands. "You may forget any hope of discovering her."

Holmes had been listening to this exchange, and broke in. "How much money does Maupertuis currently have at his disposal for the construction of this pirate fleet?"

"In terms of his possessions, he has more than enough to match the fleet of a smaller European nation – Denmark, for example. We are aware that he has a liking for works of art, some of which have been acquired legally through dealers, and some, we are convinced, are the results of thefts from galleries, though whether these thefts have been originated by him or not we are unsure. If these were ever to find their way onto the market, there is no doubt that he would have many millions of francs to his name. However, that hardly seems likely, especially in the case of the stolen artworks.

"In terms of ready cash, however, we are reasonably confident that he does not possess much at present. Many of his reserves were spent in building up shareholdings, not only in the companies that I mentioned earlier, but also in chemical works and producers of ammunition, etc. In this way, though, he has provided himself with the potential of a nation when it comes to the availability of weaponry."

"And the potential is there? I see," Holmes mused. "It would seem that our task here in London is to prevent his man from acquiring the cash that would allow him to set up his little scheme."

"Precisely, Mr. Holmes. And should he fail here in London,

as we sincerely hope he will, we must prevent him from attempting the same feat elsewhere, whether it be Rome, Constantinople, Moscow, Buenos Aires, or New York."

"And there is no time to lose," Hopkins added. "The first intended victim is the Maharajah of Rajipur, as I said, who is currently staying at the Cosmopolitan Hotel. His plans are to stay in London for the Jubilee later this year, but we believe he will be joined here in the coming months by many other Indian princes. If he is persuaded to subscribe to the Baron's swindles, we can be sure that his example will be followed by many others of his compatriots. If, on the other hand, he can be convinced that this is indeed a swindle, he may well be the cause of preventing others of his country from giving their money to this scheme."

"And the name of the Baron's agent who will approach him?"

"Alas, that is unknown to us," explained Lejeune. "We know him only as Number 17."

"I take it you have intercepted a written communication?" said Holmes.

"Precisely. All we know is that Number 17 is currently in London, and his duties are first to approach our friend at the Cosmopolitan, and to encourage him, once his money has been successfully taken from him, to persuade his Indian peers to disgorge their wealth in the Baron's direction."

"Was this letter written in French or English?"

"Neither. It was in the Italian language, and we have reason to believe that it was written by an Italian."

"So we are searching for a resident of London whose first language is Italian, but who also possesses sufficient fluency in English to persuade an Indian prince to part with a considerable sum of money?" I laughed. "Why, there must be several hundred such, in the guise of waiters, servants, barbers, and the like."

"Hardly so," replied Holmes. "In the first place, we can hardly imagine that His Highness will deign to listen to a financial scheme presented to him by a barber or a waiter. No, such a man would be of such a standing as to inspire confidence in His Highness. In the second place, why should we assume that the transaction will take place in English ? Would not the Maharajah be more receptive to a proposal couched in his own language, Hindustani or Urdu ? We may well be searching for a man in the Italian Embassy, possibly of noble birth, whose background includes time spent in India."

" These thoughts had not occurred to us," Lejeune remarked, " and it may very well be that you are correct on both these points."

" Hopkins," Holmes addressed the police inspector, " would it be possible for you to provide a list of all the Italian diplomats currently in London ? "

" I will have it sent to Baker-street at the earliest possible opportunity."

" My thanks. Very well," said Holmes, rising. " Monsieur Lejeune, you will be in London for some time ? "

" A matter of a few weeks only, alas, I regret."

" I would be delighted to see you at Baker-street for dinner some evening, should you find yourself at a loose end," Holmes invited him.

" I accept with the greatest of pleasure."

" There is no time like the present," Holmes said to me as we walked away from Scotland Yard. " We should visit His Highness as soon as we can. Do you think that he will recognise you ? "

" It is possible, I suppose," I answered. " However, you should bear in mind that our last brief meeting was several years ago, and in somewhat different surroundings."

" At any rate, there is a connection on which we can build," Holmes said. " We must use that for all that it is worth."

" Do you seriously believe those stories of Lejeune regarding Maupertuis' plans to set up and deploy a pirate fleet ? It all sounds so fantastical to me that I find it almost impossible to believe."

" I share your scepticism to some extent, but from what I hear and know of the Baron, there are few limits to his ambition. It may be, of course, that he is not altogether sane, even though he is intelligent, and his lack of judgement has caused him to take this path. However, I have faith in Lejeune and his organisation, and I believe that, unlikely as this scheme may sound, it is probably true to say that Maupertuis is pursuing it. Furthermore, given what we have heard, it is, sadly, more than feasible – it is practicable to a man of the Baron's resources, and could well be implemented sooner than we wish."

These words of my companion gave me pause for thought as we made our way through the London streets towards the luxurious hotel in which we were to meet Maupertuis' intended quarry. On arrival, Holmes presented his card to the *concierge*, with whom he appeared to be on familiar terms, and requested that a message be sent to His Highness, expressing Holmes's desire to meet him.

The answer arrived in a few minutes on a handwritten slip of paper, informing us that His Highness would be delighted to meet the famous detective and his friend, the accounts of whom he had read in the newspapers had generated the most keen interest, and inviting us to make our way to his suite.

On entering the room to which we were guided by a hotel porter, I was dumbfounded. The Maharajah of my memory was a portly elderly man whose English was less than perfect. The man who smilingly stepped forward and introduced himself as the Maharajah of Rajipur in response to our introductions was a trim figure of a young man with a luxuriant moustache, who spoke fluent English with a distinct Oxford accent. My surprise must have shown on my face.

"Doctor Watson? Is something the matter?" he asked, with an air of some concern.

"No, it is nothing. I merely remember meeting a rather different figure some years ago when I treated the wife of the Maharajah of Rajipur," I stammered.

"I believe you will have made the acquaintance of my father, then," the young man told me, "who passed away some two years ago, upon which I inherited the title, and indeed, the princely state of Rajipur. I flatter myself that in the short time that I have held my position, Rajipur has prospered thanks to a series of reforms I have initiated. One of these reforms," he said, turning to Sherlock Holmes, "is the establishment of a force of detectives to solve crimes. Should you ever be inclined, Mr. Holmes, to undertake the journey, I would be more than willing to recompense you handsomely for any instruction you cared to provide to my detectives."

"A most generous offer, indeed," replied Holmes, "and certainly one that I will bear in mind for the future."

"But I am sure that you did not make this visit merely for the sake of idle chit-chat. Pray, sit. And may I offer you some refreshment ? A brandy and soda for you gentlemen ? I generally partake of one at this time of day."

Holmes and I assented, and the Maharajah clapped his hands, giving orders to a turbaned bearer who entered from what was presumably the bed-room in answer to the summons.

"Excellent, Your Highness," said Holmes on tasting his drink.

"Please, no more of 'Your Highness'," protested the Indian. "Pray call me 'Jaimie'. It is not too far from my Indian name of Jaimal, and I became accustomed to it in my time at Balliol."

"We come to you on a rather delicate financial matter," Holmes said to him. " No," holding up a hand, " neither Doctor Watson nor I wish to borrow money from you or to take money from you in any way or under any pretext. Rather, I would ask you a few questions, if I may, and I would advise you that it will be in your best interests if you answer them as completely and sincerely as is possible."

"You intrigue me," smiled the young monarch.

"Thank you. First of all, may I ask about the finances of Rajipur ? You mentioned that you had instituted several reforms, and in my limited experience of such things, changes such as this cost money."

The Indian made a face. "You are correct, Mr. Holmes. Provision for my subjects in their old age, and other such changes to the society that I have instituted impose a strain on the state's coffers. I am unwilling to raise taxes, though my efforts to eliminate corruption have increased the annual amount paid to the treasury, while decreasing that paid to the collectors themselves."

"And your personal fortune ? Forgive me for my impertinence in asking, but these things are relevant."

" It is not my personal fortune, it is that of my family. Of my father, my grandfather, and those who came before him, and it is as much the fortune of my as yet unborn children and their children as it is of my ancestors. I may not diminish it, though I may increase it."

" And has anyone recently proposed to you a means of increasing it ? "

" Why, yes. Only two days ago, a Signor Pietro Andretti visited me here in this very room, and laid before me a way in which, although my family's wealth would be temporarily diminished, the loss would soon be recouped by the profits that would pour in from this investment."

" May I hazard a guess at the nature of the investment ? " Holmes asked. On receiving an affirmative nod, he continued. " This Signor Andretti informed you that he was acting on behalf of the Royal Family of the Netherlands who control the Dutch East Indies, specifically the island known as Sumatra. They are floating the island as a company, to be known as the Netherland-Sumatra Company, and you are invited to subscribe to shares in this company, which will pay handsome dividends, even from the start of the investment."

" You have it to a T, Mr. Holmes."

" And your answer to him ? "

" I asked for a few days to consider the proposition. The amount that he suggested that I invest in this venture was considerable – somewhere above one million pounds sterling. It is not a matter to be undertaken lightly, you understand."

" Indeed not," said Holmes. " May I ask you for a description of this Signor Andretti ? "

" Certainly. He is what one might term a " thick-set" man. Not as tall as Doctor Watson here, and with a mass of black curly hair. A waxed moustache, turned up at the ends, otherwise clean-shaven. A somewhat flattened nose which looked as though it might have been broken at some time in the past. Well-dressed in a way that would not invite notice."

" You would definitely believe him to be Italian ? " I asked.

" As far as I understand a typical Italian to appear, yes, though such stereotyping of races and nationalities seems to me to be a somewhat valueless exercise."

I blushed somewhat at this subtle rebuke.

" And one more question, if I may ? " Holmes asked him. " Was there any suggestion of, shall we say, a 'commission' to be paid to you in the event that any other of your fellow Indian rulers were to make a similar investment, based on your recommendation ? "

The young Maharajah flushed slightly. " Nothing definite was agreed in that area, but there were certain hints dropped that this might be the case."

" I feared that might be so."

"You advise against the investment ? "

" I do more than advise you, Your Highness." Holmes's use of the title added some force to his words. " I urge you in the strongest possible terms to have nothing more with this Signor Andretti or the organisation that he claims to represent. You are an intelligent man, Your Highness. May acquaint you with some of the facts as I have been given them ? "

" Very well." There was clear disappointment in the young man's words, presumably at the prospect of the proceeds of what had seemed like a profitable and welcome investment disappearing from his life.

Holmes proceeded to give a detailed account of what we had been told by Lejeune and Hopkins, with the Maharajah listening in horrified fascination.

" I believe you, Mr. Holmes, though I find it hard to do so. This Signor Andretti produced such convincing proofs of his veracity that I would not credit what you have just told me had they come from another. See here." He crossed to a table that stood by the window, and brought over some papers for Holmes's inspection. My friend took them, and examined several of them through one of the high-powered lenses that he always carried with him.

" These are excellently done," he pronounced. " This signature here would deceive anyone who did not possess intimate knowledge of the handwriting of the Dutch monarchy. See here, the shape of the 'e', and the tail of the 'p'."

" And you have such knowledge ? " the young man enquired.

" A case on which I was engaged a few years ago," Holmes replied negligently. " There is also the question of the paper. I find it hard to believe that the Royal Household has changed from the use of natively produced paper from Rotterdam to this product from Turin. One or two other details are suggestive, but to my mind, the points I have just mentioned are proof positive that these documents are forgeries."

"And your advice ? "

"To refuse to see this Andretti in the future, and, should any of your compatriots report to you any dealings with him, or with anyone representing this supposed organisation, to refer them to me immediately. From what I have told you, I am sure that you understand."

"I do understand. Indeed, I am due to receive Andretti later today. Should I cancel the meeting, do you think ? "

"As long as you are firm and persistent in your refusal of any offers he may make to you, I would think that there is little to be gained by cancelling the meeting."

"I thank you for the advice and the warning, and for your honesty and courage in informing me. Too often I am told the things that it is believed I want to hear, rather than what I should hear. My invitation to you should you ever decide to visit India is as open to you as it ever was. Good day to you, Mr. Holmes."

We made our farewells, and left the hotel. As we walked along the street, Holmes spoke to me, though without turning his head.

"Watson, do you think you could manage to trip and stumble over that paving-stone a few yards ahead of us ? Do not ask why, but simply do it."

"Of course," I answered him, and suited my actions to the words. As I recovered my footing, Holmes was at my elbow, assisting me to regain my balance, and we continued on our way.

"Excellently done, Watson," he told me. "Thanks to you, I was able to get a clearer view of the ruffian who has followed us from the hotel than I have been able to achieve from the reflections in the shop windows."

"We are being followed ? By one of Maupertuis' men ? "

"Indeed we are being followed, and I have little doubt as to the accuracy of your guess concerning the identity of the rogue's employer. I do not recall having seen him in the past, and he has a distinctly Mediterranean cast to his features.

However, I believe it is time to put him behind us." He hailed a cab, and we set off for Baker-street, Holmes confirming that we had left our follower standing helplessly on the pavement, unable to follow.

Once we had returned to Baker-street, we discovered waiting for us the list promised by Hopkins of those at the Italian Embassy. Hardly to our surprise, the name of Andretti was not among them.

Though our quarry's name did not appear in the list supplied by Hopkins, Holmes seemed to be undaunted. He took down the scrapbooks that formed his Index, and started to peruse them.

"It is possible," he said, after some fifteen minutes' study of these materials, "that Maupertuis has engaged some of the criminal elements of Italy to assist him. They are not all, by any stretch of the imagination, violent illiterate hooligans, though the leaders may employ men of that description to carry out their bidding. This 'Andretti' may be a leader of the Camorra or Mafia, hired to put us off the track. The description we were given does not give us many clues." He lit his pipe, and smoked for a few minutes in silence.

"I have sometimes thought," he said, "of a device that could be of value to the police. Have you ever considered how difficult it is to describe a face? Unless a person has a clear feature that is out of the ordinary, or a deformity, a description is difficult. And yet, presented with a range of images of noses, say, I am certain that most witnesses could choose a nose that corresponded to the face they had seen. And if not noses, why not eyes, mouth, chin, ears, and hair? It would be a mighty work to undertake, to be sure, but I am convinced it would bring positive results. In the meantime, however, we cannot examine the face of every Italian in London, in the hope that we will find our man that way."

"That is very true," I said. "However, is it not possible that at the Italian Embassy there is an official with links to the Italian police force, who might be of assistance ? "

"An eminently reasonable suggestion," Holmes said. "My compliments. I regret to inform you that I had formed the same idea myself not ten minutes before." He smiled at my crestfallen face. "But it is no less valuable for all that." He glanced at his watch. "However, I fear that we will have to wait until tomorrow before we can produce any sign of life at 25 Queen's Gate. In the meantime, I may profitably spend my time on the case of the Amersham jewels, whose simple solution still appears to elude the Berkshire police force, despite the hints I have dropped in my letters to the local paper. I think the time has come for me to spell out the whole solution in full, and present it as a letter to be delivered through Lestrade or some other of the Scotland Yarders. Heigh-ho."

The next morning saw Holmes up bright and early, penning his missive on the Amersham jewel case to Lestrade at Scotland Yard. Following breakfast, he and I set out together for the Italian Embassy in Queen's Gate, where we planned to determine the true identity of the man who had called himself Pietro Andretti.

On arrival at the Embassy, Holmes asked for the Italian Legal Attaché by name, and we were immediately shown into that official's office.

"My dear Signor Holmes," the diplomat exclaimed, rising from his seat and embracing Holmes warmly. "And your friend. Doctor Watson, may I assume ? " I was spared the intimacy of an embrace, Signor Rabello contenting himself with a warm handshake. "Coffee for you gentlemen ? I was about to order some for myself."

We accepted with pleasure, and an Embassy servant entered in response to the bell.

"Now, what can I do for you ? " Rabello asked Holmes. "I know that you are a busy man, and you would not come here purely for a social visit and chit-chat, as you English say."

" But it is always a pleasure to chit-chat with you, Signor," protested Holmes. " However, on this occasion, it is indeed a matter of business that brings me here."

" Aha ! Some mystery, perhaps ? "

" Indeed so. May I ask you if you have any knowledge of the doings of some of the criminal organisations of Italy in this country ? For example, the Mafia of Sicily, or the Camorra of Naples or the equivalents in Rome or Milan ?

The other shrugged. " There are some of these men here, yes. We know they are here, but as long as they break no laws here, there is little we can do about it. If we became aware that they had broken English law, then I suppose that we would in-form Scotland Yard of this, but so far that eventuality has not transpired."

" Then perhaps you would tell me if a man such as this is currently in the country ? " Holmes asked, giving a descrip-tion of the man who had proposed the Sumatra deal to the Maharajah of Rajipur. As he proceeded, I believed that I saw a flicker of recognition in the eyes of the other, but it might well have been an error of perception on my part.

" I am sorry, but that face and that name have no meaning for me. If you like, I can send a cable to headquarters in Rome, and discover if they have any records relating to this person."

" That would be most helpful. Thank you."

Holmes and Rabello exchanged a few more words on other matters before we took our leave and rose to go. Once outside the Embassy, Holmes looked around him before letting out a low whistle.

" I am saddened to see my friend in the clutches of those men," he said softly.

" Rabello ? "

" Indeed. He knows that man Andretti. I could see it in his face, and I could see the fear in his face as he believed I was going to press him further. Naturally, I expect nothing from the office in Rome, even if he makes the promised enquiry, which I very much doubt he will."

We walked on in silence, broken only by Holmes's monoto-nous whistling of some tune that I had previously heard him scraping on his fiddle.

Our progress was suddenly arrested by a police constable standing in our path.

" Excuse me, sir, but are you Mr. Sherlock Holmes ? "

" I am," replied my friend.

" Then I must request you and this gentleman here to come with me to the nearest police station," he informed us grave-ly. " If you will come quietly, there is no need for any fuss or bother."

Holmes held out his hands in front of him. " You wish to ap-ply the ' darbies', Constable ? "

" That won't be necessary, sir."

We walked in front of the constable a matter of a few hun-dred yards to the nearest police station, where the sergeant immediately recognised my friend.

" Sorry about this, Mr. Holmes, but Inspector Hopkins from the Yard has been looking for you, and didn't know where you was to be found, so he asked us all to go looking for you."

" There is no problem, Latimer," replied Sherlock Holmes. " No harm done, and Watson here was only a little embarrassed."

In truth, I had been more than a little embarrassed, but I deemed it best to hold my peace at this juncture.

" Fancy you remembering my name, sir," said the sergeant, wonderingly.

" One never forgets a man who does his work well," Holmes answered him.

" Well, be that as it may, sir, our orders from Inspector Hopkins was to get you to the Cosmopolitan Hotel as soon as possible."

" Why ? What has happened ? " I asked.

The sergeant shook his head. " It wouldn't be for me to tell you, sir, even if I knew, which I don't," he smiled. " I'm sure you will find out soon enough."

Once seated in the hansom that had been ordered for us, Holmes turned to me. " I fear the worst," he said in low tones.

I did not enquire further, but we sat in silence until we ar-rived at the hotel. Hopkins was waiting for us on the steps leading to the entrance.

" It is a bad business, Mr. Holmes," he warned us.

" What is the matter ? " I exclaimed.

" See for yourselves," Hopkins said to us, leading the way to the apartments where we had met the Maharajah the previous day. A uniformed constable was stationed outside the door, and saluted Hopkins as we approached.

" See for yourselves," Hopkins repeated, flinging open the door with a certain flourish.

On the carpet, beside a small escritoire, in a pool of blood which had spread out from the centre, lay the body of a man, face downwards, dressed in the same clothes in which we had seen the Maharajah dressed on the previous day.

" Death appears to have been instantaneous," Hopkins informed us. " A stab to the heart from under the ribs, using a long narrow blade, according to the surgeon who examined the body."

" A blade such as a stiletto, as used by Italian criminals ? " Holmes suggested.

" Precisely so. I believe we are thinking along similar lines," Hopkins answered.

" I am sorry for His Highness," I said. " He seemed to me to have the welfare of his people at heart."

" And he still does," came a voice from behind me.

I turned, and to my amazement, beheld the man to whom we had been speaking the day before.

" I am sorry for Ibraham, my servant," he said, indicating the body. " I would invite you to examine the face, and you will instantly see where the confusion has arisen."

I turned the body over and beheld a face that, while in many ways similar to that of the Maharajah, was nonetheless not the same. The eyes were open with a kind of horror in their expression. Clearly, though, the body was not that of the Maharajah. I closed the staring eyes, and returned my attention to His Highness.

" Let me explain the facts as they occurred to me," continued our host, if I may term him such. " After you had left me, Mr. Holmes, I got to thinking. I confess that not all my reading at Oxford was that which I had been assigned by my tutors, but I developed a taste for sensational literature, including stories in which Italian criminal gangs carried out their foul deeds.

"As we agreed, however, I admitted Andretti, who arrived some two hours after you left me. He was all smiles, expecting, I believe, a substantial cheque to be paid to him as a deposit on the investment he was persuading me to make. Without giving precise reasons, though, I told him that I was now unprepared to make the investment, and politely invited him to leave.

"Mr. Holmes, he was furious. I have hardly ever seen a man in the grip of a greater passion. He swore that I had given my word that I would pay him the money he was demanding. I angrily refuted this, and told him to his face that he lied. At this, he reached inside his coat, as if for a weapon—".

"Did you see such a weapon?" Holmes asked him.

"I did not. My servants, Ibraham here, and Abdul, who also function as body-guards, were also in the room at the time. They observed Andretti's move, and immediately leaped upon him, pinioning his arms to his side. I ordered them to remove him from my presence, and they did so, he spitting what I take to be Italian curses at me.

"Just before the door was shut, he thrust his face, contorted with rage, towards me, and spoke in English. 'You will pay for this,' he told me. Once he had been removed from the room, I rang the bell for the porter, and gave him strict instructions that Andretti was not to be admitted again, no matter what seeming proof of my welcome he might produce.

"Ibraham was far from satisfied, however. 'Highness,' he said to me, ' allow me to wear the clothes you are currently wearing, and to sit with my back to the door here at this desk. I fear that whatever orders you have just given regarding Andretti, he or one of his men will undoubtedly attempt to reach you for the purpose of killing you. Better for our people if I am the one who dies, rather than you.

"Reluctantly, I agreed to this proposal. I did not seriously expect that an attempt would be made on my life, but I waited, as Ibraham had suggested to me, in the bedroom through that door there. I remembered the tales I had read about Italian gangs, and I was ashamed of myself for having agreed to place my faithful servant in a position of danger. Indeed, I was about to enter this room and order him back to his duties, when I heard a knock on the outer door, and a voice announcing that the hotel was providing fresh towels."

"One moment," Holmes interrupted. "You say you saw nothing?"

"I was in the bed-room, as I told you. The door between here and the sitting-room was closed."

"And the voice? That of a man, or of a woman?"

"It was a deep man's voice, unmistakably. Furthermore, it was speaking with an accent which was not English. It may be merely my fancy, but I believed it to be Italian, even before what then took place.

"I heard Abdul opening the door, after he had instructed Ibraham to stay where he was. This was swiftly followed by a strangled scream, and the sound as of a chair being knocked over..." Wordlessly, Hopkins indicated the overturned chair next to the body. "And another sound – a gasp followed by a horrible kind of bubbling."

Here the Maharajah appeared to be overcome with emotion. It reminded me that although this young man was the ruler of several million souls, and the possessor of considerable presence and intelligence, he was still a young man, not long from University.

"I was petrified, Mr. Holmes. I cast about me for a weapon, but could see nothing, save the razor on the washstand, but before I could reach it, I heard the door to the hallway open once more. I dashed to the connecting door, and opened it, only to find my servants lying in their blood on the floor, and the back of a dark coat vanishing down the corridor. It was hopeless, I realised, to attempt to follow him, or even to call the hotel staff – he would have vanished long before any assistance could arrive. I bent to Abdul—-"

"Where is he?" Holmes asked.

"He is in the hospital," Hopkins told us. "He is wounded, but expected to survive."

"Ibraham, as you can see for yourselves, was not so fortunate, Having ascertained the state of things, I rang for the hotel staff, who arrived, and immediately contacted the police."

"I had given strict instructions that in the event of any disturbance of any kind at this hotel, whether or not it concerned

His Highness, I was to be immediately informed," Hopkins said. "Accordingly, I was on the scene very soon after the incident."

"I would say within twenty minutes," the Maharajah commented. "Remarkably prompt."

"You were expecting something of this nature to occur, then?" Holmes asked Hopkins.

"Not at all. However, His Highness is a most important guest, and with the link to the Baron's scheme that we had uncovered, I felt it best that I should be involved at as early a stage as possible should anything untoward occur."

"And you have nothing to add regarding the description of the man who did this?" Holmes asked.

"I saw nothing, as I told you."

"Very well. Hopkins, I take it the body here has not been moved?"

"I may have moved him slightly when I ascertained that life was extinct," confessed the Indian prince. "But otherwise, he is in the position that I discovered him." Again, he appeared ready to break down.

"Watson," Holmes ordered me. "Take His Highness into the next room and if you have anything about you that will help to calm his nerves, pray administer it. Inspector, I may require your assistance."

I gently led the Maharajah into the next room, and attempted to explain the situation to him.

"This is a hard thing for me to take in," he said. "Ibraham had been a companion since childhood, and even accompanied me to Oxford to serve me there. Such a man becomes much more than a servant – more than a friend, even. It is as if a piece of my own body has been cut out and discarded. I feel that I should leave London as soon as possible in order to make provision for his family. Two wives and three small children. They will be cared for, you may be sure, as if they were my own."

I couldn't help but feel for this young prince, who appeared completely sincere in his grief for the loss of his retainer.

"I am counting on you and Mr. Holmes to avenge this death," he told me with the greatest solemnity. "Swear to me that you will do so."

" I swear," I told him, " on behalf of myself and Mr. Holmes, that as far as it is in our power, this crime will not go unpunished."

" Thank you," he said. " Now leave me to my grief." It was a regal dismissal. Before I quitted the room, I administered a small dose of a sedative, having observed a bottle of a patent mixture by the side of the bed. I guessed that it had been prescribed by an Indian doctor, given the indication on the label. Once he had swallowed a few drops of the tincture, dissolved in a glass of water, His Highness appeared calmer, and acceded to my suggestion that he lie on the bed and repose himself. Immediately he did so, he appeared to fall into a deep sleep, occasioned, I guessed, by the recent expenditure of nervous energy as much as from the effects of the drug.

I passed as silently as I could into the other room, and closed the connecting door behind me. Holmes looked up from his kneeling position beside the Indian's body.

" How is he ? " he asked me.

I described my actions and the current state of His Highness. Holmes said nothing, but nodded, and went back to his work, quietly talking to Hopkins as he did so.

Suddenly, Holmes gave a sharp cry. " Aha ! " he exclaimed. " See here ! " He pointed to the dead man's right hand, in which a light gunmetal chain was grasped. He gently opened the dead man's fingers and extracted the chain, to which was attached a crudely stamped small medal, seemingly made of pewter or some similar material. " If I am not mistaken, this is a representation of the Black Madonna of Naples." He turned the medal over and examined the other side. " Interesting," he remarked, passing the medal to Hopkins.

" Indeed. With a Neapolitan connection such as you believe to be present here, we may well suspect that the Camorra has a hand in this. And if these prove to be the murderer's initials on the back, why we have him ! "

Holmes had continued his examination of the body, with a careful examination of the hands and the lower arms. " Look," he remarked. He pulled up the sleeves of the corpse's jacket and shirt. This is interesting, is it not ? " He indicated, on both wrists, marks as of a tight bracelet or armband, which had been removed.

"Interesting, yes," agreed Hopkins. "If we can catch the assailant, no doubt we will find the stolen items – the bracelets or whatever it may be that these Indians wear – in his possession. I believe with a little help from the Italian Embassy, we will have the killer in our power in a very short time from now."

"I am sorry to tell you that such assistance is unlikely to be forthcoming," Holmes told Hopkins. He informed the policeman of our fruitless quest earlier at the Italian Embassy.

"That is most disappointing," said Hopkins.

"Never fear, all is not yet lost. I have other sources of information on these subjects," said Holmes. "Our native homegrown criminals resent the intrusion of foreigners on their turf, and I may be able to use my contacts in those areas to discover more about our killer, and maybe even the mysterious Signor Andretti. The killer, I believe, may well be the man who followed Watson and me last night. In any event, it is possible that the staff of the hotel may be able to provide us with a description of the man, if he entered the hotel through the usual route."

"Very well," said Hopkins. "I take it you have seen all you need?"

"Almost," said Holmes. He picked up the dead man's other hand. "See here," he told us, displaying a shred of cloth. "I would lay odds that this once formed part of the killer's clothing, possibly his jacket. And here," he exclaimed. "A button. Once we obtain some sort of description, and we find a man who conforms to that description, we can easily prove or disprove his presence at this scene."

"I believe there is a book of recipes that begins its recipe for jugged hare with the words 'First catch your hare'," smiled Hopkins.

"Oh, we will catch him right enough, never fear," said Holmes. "And if we are lucky, he will lead us to bigger game than a hare."

"Andretti?" I asked.

"Indeed, and possibly even to the Baron himself."

"Then let us have the body taken up, and we should inform

His Highness of what we know. I will have a further guard set on the door," said Hopkins.

" However, for now, it may be useful to give the impression to the attackers that the attempt on His Highness' life was successful."

" I agree," the policeman answered him. " Given the rank of the supposed victim, a little secrecy in these matters may be expected, in any case." He gave the necessary orders to the constable at the door for the removal of the body, and I entered the bed-room, where His Highness appeared to be waking.

" Rum beggars, some of those Indians," Hopkins said, as we descended the stairs to the entrance lobby of the hotel after I had explained what had transpired. " But he's got a good heart, it seems, that one."

On approaching the concierge, Holmes enquired which of the staff had been on duty at the time when the murder had taken place, and they were brought to us.

One of the porters, an elderly man, claimed to have seen a man whose appearance suggested that he might have been the murderer.

" Sort of foreign-like, he was," he told us. " Dark skin, curly hair, and short. He'd only come up to my shoulder, I reckon, and I'm not that tall, as you can see for yourselves, gentlemen. I noticed how short he was when he walked past that potted palm over there."

" Excellent," said Holmes. " Anything else that you observed about him ? "

" Now you come to mention it, sir, there was something else. One of his feet – let me think now – yes, it was his left foot, was dragging a bit, as if he had something wrong with his leg. And did I say about his hair and his moustache ? Wild hair, you'd have to say. Black and curly. And a moustache on him that a Guardsman would be proud of."

" You are obviously a keen observer," Holmes said to him. " Did you speak to him ? "

" I did, sir. 'Where are you off to, then ? ' I asked him. He didn't look like one of our guests, see, so I didn't see the need to be that polite to him, like I would to a guest."

" Quite so. And what was his answer ? "

"Well, he just looked at me, with a sort of hard look, and told me he had a package for His Highness. I didn't need to ask who he meant, because at the moment we only have one Highness staying. We'll have a lot more come the Jubilee, of course, but right now, just the one."

"And he showed you the package?"

"He did that, sir. Small, wrapped in brown paper, it was. So I let him through and watched him go up the stairs."

"And when he came down?"

"Now you come to mention it, sir, I never saw him come down or go out of the door. That's bit queer, isn't it, sir?'"

"Perhaps the doorman might be able to inform you of that, Mr. Holmes," the concierge suggested.

"Perhaps," Holmes replied, "but I doubt it."

Holmes's prediction was proved correct. The doorman had a vague recollection of having seen the man enter the hotel, though his attention at the time was taken up with welcoming another guest, but he had no memory whatsoever of seeing him leave.

"Probably slipped out of the back entrance," Hopkins said.

"I am sure you are correct," Holmes told him, and thanked the staff of the hotel for their assistance.

"One more thing," Holmes asked the concierge. "Which members of the hotel staff would have been on duty in the doorway and in the hall yesterday evening?"

However, on questioning these hotel servants regarding the man who called himself Andretti, and who had been reported by the Maharajah as having visited him the previous evening following our departure, we drew a blank. None admitted to having seen a man such as had been described to us having visited the hotel at that time, though a porter and a doorman claimed to have seen him on the previous day, the porter actually having shown him to the Maharajah's suite.

"If he was aware that we were on his tail," Hopkins remarked, "it is likely that he would not wish to be seen here."

"If indeed he did visit the hotel at that time," said Holmes, enigmatically, but did not expand on this.

"There is no doubt in my mind," he told Hopkins, "that the man whom we believe killed the Indian servant is the one whom I observed following us last night, and who is, if the evidence of the medal found in the dead man's hand is to be believed, a member of the Camorra."

"I believe you should be concerned, Mr. Holmes, and you too, Doctor. Allow me to post some of my constables outside your lodgings to protect you against this man."

Holmes laughed. "I am indeed concerned, Inspector, but my main concern is that this man may not trouble to visit us. He may believe that London is too dangerous for him, knowing that we are involved in the business, and he may either lie low, or, as I believe more likely, he will attempt to slip out of the country."

"I will have the ports watched," Hopkins said.

As it turned out, Holmes's prediction was correct. Following Hopkins' prompt action in alerting the port authorities, a man corresponding to the description that we had been given was apprehended at Newhaven, attempting to board a ferry to Dieppe. His papers gave his name as Antonio Betteroni, and he was described as a cobbler and a native of Naples. He claimed that he had been visiting his brother, and gave an address in Whitechapel as proof of his veracity.

He was immediately arrested on suspicion of having killed the Maharajah's servant, and brought to London for questioning by Hopkins. Holmes was also present at the interview, and I was allowed to attend.

Hopkins wasted no time on preliminaries. "Your attempt to kill the Maharajah failed," were his opening words.

If this had been an attempt by Hopkins to trick the other into some sort of admission of guilt, it failed. There was little reaction.

"Come, now," Holmes told him. "We know that you speak English well enough to explain your presence in this country to the port authorities in Newhaven. Have you no answer to give the inspector here?"

"I do not know what you are talking about," came the sullen answer.

"Very well, then," said Holmes. "You are acquainted with the Cosmopolitan Hotel ? "

The Italian spread his hands. " I, a simple cobbler, should know about one of the most famous hotels in London ? " He realised what he had just told us, and attempted to rectify his error. " What I mean to say is that naturally I have heard the name. But to be acquainted with it ? You imagine that I can afford to sleep between silk sheets ? To drink champagne for breakfast ? You are a little *pazzo* – crazy, signor, if you believe that."

" The sheets at the hotel are linen, not silk," Holmes told him. " And I would expect a rough red to be more to your taste than champagne. I was not asking you if you had stayed there. I was asking if you were acquainted with it. Do you, for instance, know where it is located ? "

" I could not draw you a map, but yes, I know."

" And do you know where Baker-street is located ? "

A look of fear came into the other's eyes. " I know the name, yes."

Holmes glanced at Hopkins, who nodded almost imperceptibly, whereupon Holmes withdrew from an inner pocket the medal that had been discovered in the dead man's hand. " Is this yours ? " he enquired in an almost casual tone.

The Italian's hand flew to his throat, before seemingly remembering that the medal was no longer in his possession. " What... what is it, signor ? " he stammered, much of his previous bluster now gone.

" I think you know very well what it is," Holmes said to him. " Your initials are A.B., are they not ? The same initials that I see on the back of this medal." The other nodded. " It is not conclusive proof of your guilt, I agree, but it is strongly suggestive, is it not ? "

" Where did you find it ? "

" In the hand of the man you killed," Hopkins said drily.

" You said to me just now that I killed nobody, Mr. Policeman," protested Betteroni.

" I said nothing of the sort," said Hopkins. " I simply said that your attempt to kill the Maharajah had been a failure."

"*Dio*!" the Italian exclaimed. "I cannot understand what you mean here."

"What the Inspector is telling you is that you killed the wrong man. The man whom you left dead on the floor of the room at the Cosmopolitan Hotel was not the man you intended to kill."

"Then who was he?" came the answer. Immediately, Betteroni clapped a hand over his mouth. "What I meant to say was—"

"So you are aware of the murder at the Cosmopolitan?" Hopkins asked.

"Naturally. It was in the newspapers," said the Italian.

Holmes shook his head. "I am sorry to tell you that there has been no mention at all of the incident in the press. So where did you hear about it? Did a friend inform you of it?"

The Italian shook his head slowly. "I suppose you have me. Yes, I believed that I killed the Maharajah of Rajipur. But you tell me now that I did not."

"I must warn you," Hopkins told him, "that anything you say may be used in evidence at your trial. Do you understand?"

"I do."

"Did you kill at the orders of one Pietro Andretti?"

"At the orders of another. I do not know his name."

Holmes repeated the description of the man that we had been given by the Maharajah.

"That is he," said the other, "but I swear to you that I do not know his name or where he is to be found."

"How did you come to meet him?"

"A note pushed under the door of the room where I lodge, while I was at work."

"Your trade and place of work?" asked Hopkins.

"I am a waiter. I have no permanent place of work, but I assist at hotels when there is a banquet or some other big occasion where extra hands are needed."

"And I may take it that you have sometimes worked at the Cosmopolitan Hotel?" Holmes asked.

"I have."

"Then no doubt that would explain how you were seen entering the hotel, but not exiting. You entered through the front as a visitor in search of a guest, and you left from the back as a waiter, unremarked among the many hotel servants."

" My hat is off to you, Mr. Holmes."

"And you followed me and Dr. Watson back to Baker-street last night ? "

" I did. I was told that you were investigating the doings of the man who hired me, whom you call Andretti, and I was asked to discover how easy it would be to remove you from the investigation."

I was chilled at these words, realising how close Holmes and I had come to death at the hands of this assassin. Holmes for his part appeared almost sanguine. " Very good, then," he said. " Perhaps you will tell us more of the events surrounding the death of the man you believe to be the Maharajah."

" Oh, you think you are so clever, Mr. Holmes, with your ' the man you believe to be'. But yes, I will tell you of these events. The man who hired me – let us use the name ' Andretti', since that is the name you have, and I have no name – approached me a week ago, leaving a letter under my door. He told me that he was here to do a particular piece of business – to collect money from an Indian prince which was owing to his employer in Naples."

" How had he heard of you ? " asked Hopkins.

" My name is as famous in my circles," answered the Italian, " as that of Mr. Holmes is in his. To be sure, I do not seek publicity in the newspapers, nor do I have a Doctor Watson to record my doings, but when I have completed a job for one of my clients, it will usually be on the front page of the newspapers."

I was somewhat taken aback by the fact that this murderer appeared to show no remorse for his actions, but rather seemed to take pride in his foul deeds.

" Yesterday I accompanied him to the hotel and waited outside while he conducted whatever business was to be done. As he came out, he described you and Doctor Watson here, and told me to follow you to your lodgings."

" Can you describe his mood ? "

" He was in an excellent mood. Happy, almost to the point of madness, I would say."

" How did you report back to him once you had followed us to Baker-street ? "

" I did not. I was to wait for instructions. They came this morning, under my door. I was to go to the hotel, see myself up to the Maharajah's suite, and there to do him to death as swiftly and silently as possible. I was admitted by one of his servants, whom I felled with a blow from my dagger. The Maharajah was sitting at a desk with his back to me. He did not hear me approach, and I reached around and stabbed him through the heart, under the ribs. He fell to the floor, and I left the room."

" There was no one else in the room ? No-one attempted to stop you ? "

The other spread his hands. "Who would have stopped me ? The Maharajah was dying – I stooped to check his pulse, and his hands grasped feebly at my throat. At that time, I did not notice that the medal you hold there was missing. I then left the room, entered a linen room, and took off my overcoat, revealing the uniform of a waiter. You will find the overcoat at the bottom of a linen basket – that is, if one of the hotel servants has not already taken it for himself."

" And then ? "

" I had been ordered by this ' Andretti' to leave England as soon as I had completed my work. I was told that I would be paid when I returned to Naples. And that, gentlemen, is where you found me – preparing to leave the country."

" Is there anything else you wish to say ? "

" I wish an advocate."

" Do you have one in mind ? "

" Signor Rabello at the Embassy."

Holmes and I exchanged glances.

" I will see what can be done," Hopkins told him. " Though you had far better to plead guilty and maybe earn yourself a long sentence on the Moor rather than the hangman's rope." His words seemed to have no effect on the other, who sat stolidly until two constables answered Hopkins' summons and took him to the cells.

"My word," said Hopkins to us when the door had closed behind the prisoner. "What are we to make of all this?"

"That the murderer confesses to killing a man, but he claims to have murdered a man to whom we have just been talking? That his statements entirely contradict what we were told by His Highness?"

"Indeed, the confession that he made to us just now would be torn to shreds by any competent lawyer, when set against the word of the Maharajah of Rajipur," said Hopkins.

"I do not think that you will be able to present the word of His Highness as evidence."

"Why on earth not?"

"Because His Highness is dead."

Both Hopkins and I started to our feet in amazement. "Holmes," I ejaculated, "What in heaven's name do you mean? We were talking to him just now."

"Were we indeed? I wonder."

"You agree that the man to whom we talked earlier today, and the man with whom we spoke yesterday are the same man, do you not?"

"Indeed I do."

"And yesterday we spoke with His Highness, and ergo, we spoke to the same man, that is, the Maharajah of Rajipur. Is that not the case?"

"An entirely logical conclusion, my dear Watson, but you are basing your argument on a false premise."

"That being?"

"That we spoke with His Highness yesterday."

I was dumbfounded. "Then with whom did we speak?"

"My guess is that it was with the servant Ibraham, who we were informed today had been killed defending his master."

"Then where was His Highness when we talked yesterday?"

"I believe he was in the bed-room, sedated and bound, and probably gagged into the bargain. You mentioned that there was a bottle of some Indian sedative medicine near the bed? " I nodded. "You recall that the dead man's eyes were open when we turned over the body to examine the face?"

"I do," I shuddered.

" The pupils were like pinpricks, surely evidence of opium or some such substance having been administered. I would also draw your attention to the marks on the dead man's wrists. They were not the marks of bangles, or arm-bands or of any kind of jewellery. It was clear that these marks were the result of the arms being bound at the wrists."

" I will take your word for it," I said, and Hopkins nodded.

" And I take it that neither of you remarked the state of the hands ? Tut. The hands, my dear Inspector, can tell you more about their owner than the face ever will. These were hands that had never laboured for a living. The palms were soft, and it was unlikely that they had ever held any tool more effective than a cricket bat. The nails were smooth and polished, delicately manicured. These were not the hands of a servant, but of the master of a servant."

My mind was reeling with what Holmes had just told us. " But," I objected, " the man to whom we talked spoke excellent English, and talked about his time at Balliol."

" Remember what we were told today by the man, in his character of the Maharajah," Holmes reminded me. " He said that his servant had been his companion since he was a boy, and had even accompanied him to Oxford. Given that the man is as intelligent as the master – and there is no reason why this should not be the case – and given the continued intimacy of the relationship over many years, I think it is more than likely that the servant should acquire linguistic skills at least equal to that of His Highness."

" So we were speaking to a servant yesterday, when we believed we were talking to the Maharajah himself ? " Hopkins asked. " I can hardly credit it."

" I believe that part of the deception lies in the fact that the actors in this little game are not English. Should an English butler decide to impersonate his titled master, we could easily detect the difference. There are those little things that mark a servant as being of a different class. But when we are faced with a society and rules which are not ours, then can we rely on our instincts to distinguish the impostor from the real thing ? "

" What do you consider was the sequence of events ? "

Hopkins asked after a pause. " Whose initiative is this, do you feel ? "

" My feeling is that one of the servants was aware that vast wealth had been promised to those who would invest in the Baron's scheme. Now, we have no way now of knowing what the actual relations were between the Maharajah and his servants. Perhaps the matter was discussed between them, perhaps one of the servants in some way acquired and read a letter which pledged investment in the scheme, but the end result is the same.

" Again, we do not know the precise thinking behind all these actions, but I think it would be reasonable for us to assume that the servants conspired to impersonate His Highness. My feeling is that they wished to acquire this wealth for themselves. In any event, I think we may take it that Andretti, when he first met the Indians, did not speak to the man to whom he believed he was speaking. Rather, he was speaking to one of the servants, who promised to invest the money, which had been promised earlier by the Maharajah. I believe this to have been the case."

"And where was the Maharajah at the point ? " asked Hopkins.

"Why, as I said just now, he was sedated, and possibly bound and gagged, in the bed-room. Meanwhile, the servant Ibraham was dressed in his clothes, and was happily informing Andretti that the deal was forthcoming. He was still in this character when we came to visit. I am sure that much of what we were told was the truth – with regard to His Highness' time at Oxford, for example. It may even be that His Highness was proposing to make this investment for the good of the people of his state, but we cannot be sure of that.

" In any event, it is certain that the Maharajah could not be allowed to live following this impersonation. The servants no doubt were reluctant to perform the deed themselves, given their long association with him, and possibly a personal oath that they had sworn. It is impossible for us to know with any certainty. I have long held that the ways of the Oriental mind are not for us to understand. In any event, Andretti was informed by the servants that it was for him to ensure the demise of the Maharajah. Accordingly, the man Betteroni was dispatched to eliminate the Maharajah, who was dressed in his own clothes, drugged, and placed in the chair by the desk as a sacrificial victim. A fight was staged in which one of the servants was slightly wounded, in order to give some verisimilitude to the story, and the body of the Maharajah was then presented to us as that of one of the servants."

"If you are correct, Mr. Holmes, we must secure these servants immediately and confront them with all of this!" exclaimed Hopkins.

Holmes shook his head. "I fear we will be too late. I am certain that they will have flown the coop. If you were to search among the Lascars in the docks, there might be a chance, albeit a faint one, of discovering them, but I think we can assume that we will never more hear of them."

"And the Maharajah himself?" asked Hopkins. "Do we play along with the deception and simply regard him as missing, or do we accept the corpse as his?"

"I believe," said Holmes, after a moment's reflection, "that our best course of action will be to publicly accept what we were originally told, and identify the corpse as that of the servant who gave his life to save his master. We can give out that, as a result of this failed attempt on his life, His Highness has left the hotel, and is now in a secluded location prior to his return to India, which will be made incognito."

"That would seem to fit the bill," I said. "But what are the next steps in this case?"

"Why, we must discover how much money the Baron has received from this Sumatran source. If, as I fear, the funds are of a sufficient magnitude for him to begin the construction of his fleet of pirate gunboats, then our attentions must be turned overseas."

"To the German shipyards, and French steelworks?" I suggested.

"Indeed. Also to the financial institutions that Maupertuis uses to move his ill-gotten gains from one location to another."

"But cannot we – by which I mean the British government – alert the French and German authorities as to the Baron's intentions and thereby make them the cause of frustrating his plans ? " I enquired.

It was Hopkins who answered, shaking his head. "In the usual way of things, Doctor Watson," he replied, "that would be the way in which such a case would be handled, were it one simply of murder, or even embezzlement or theft. But in this case, questions of national defence come into play. Both the manufactories where Maupertuis now has a controlling interest are of vital importance to the nations in which they are situated. Alerting the governments of these countries would be seen as a ploy by Great Britain to weaken their defences. No, I fear that we must work outside government circles in order to frustrate the designs of the Baron."

It transpired that Sherlock Holmes was correct in his assumption regarding the Indians. We made our way to the Cosmopolitan Hotel instantly following the conversation recorded above.

We were informed by the manager that the Maharajah and his retinue had left the hotel about an hour previously, and had left no forwarding address. Although the porter remembered the number of the cab which had carried them from the hotel, and the driver was subsequently interviewed by Hopkins, it transpired that they had been taken to Liverpool-street station. Further enquiries there produced no memories of the Indians, and as Holmes remarked, any further attempt to trace them would be unnecessarily time-consuming.

My friend's attention therefore turned to the Continent, where Maupertuis was now operating.

"The devil of it is," he said to me, "that we have no idea how much money he has raised so far. The shares in the von Heissen and the de Lantis enterprises are a matter of public record, of course, but I am hoping that Lejeune will be able to provide us with more information regarding the amount of ready cash now available. I have hopes that the Pinkerton Agency in New York will be able to provide us with a little more information regarding the American side of the matter.

"But for now," he continued, "I feel I must take myself abroad."

"Do you wish me to accompany you?" I asked him.

"The offer of your assistance is greatly appreciated, as always, but at this stage of the case, I would prefer you to remain in London. Rest assured, though, that should I require your assistance, I will telegraph you immediately. And on the subject of money, I may inform you in the strictest of confidence that all our expenses will be met by Her Majesty's Government."

I could not help but feel a certain stab of disappointment at these words of Holmes, though I recognised that it would almost certainly be necessary for the success of Holmes's operations that there was someone in London on whom he could rely absolutely, and it was with some satisfaction to me that it was I who had been selected for that role.

"However," Holmes went on, "it will be necessary for me to make a few enquiries in the City before I set off, and it would ease my task considerably were you to assist me in this matter."

The next few days saw Holmes and me visiting stockbrokers in a vain attempt to discover any dealings in stocks and shares where the hand of Maupertuis could be traced. Not only did it appear that the shares of the Netherland-Sumatra Company had never been traded in London, but the very name of the company appeared to be unknown to the gentlemen of the City whom we visited.

"It was Lejeune who informed us of this Netherland-Sumatra business, was it not?" I asked Holmes one evening following a day of fruitless tramping in and out of offices. "Can we be sure that the information with which he provided us is correct?"

"I have known of Lejeune's work for some time," he answered me. "He has the reputation of being a most meticulous researcher – perhaps a little lacking in imagination, which is unusual for a member of the Gallic race, who are, as you know, prone to a certain amount of exaggeration, but that is all too common in the official detective forces. I believe that the facts as he related them to us are essentially true. It is merely that the shares in the company are not offered openly, but the deals are conducted in secrecy, given the ostensible and the true nature of the business."

In the end, Holmes was forced to leave for France without being in full possession of the true state of affairs, one which vexed him somewhat, and which proved to be more than something of a handicap in his subsequent endeavours.

AN UNNAMED CASE

A swirling fog envelops Baker-street,
And Sherlock Holmes lies, languid, in his chair.
The sound of cab wheels ceases, then –
A client's footsteps echo on the stair.

" Beyond the simple facts I can deduce;
You've been abroad and sailed the seven seas
Your wife has ceased to love you,
And that you're lame – I know no more than these."

" My goodness, Mr. Holmes, pray tell me how
You know these things before I've said a word."
A languid hand waves. " My dear sir,
These trifles are so simple, they are absurd.

" But tell me now, you come in haste
Without your gloves or stick. You even lack a hat.
The papers in your pocket have some bearing
On your query. Pray tell me more of that."

" The facts are very simple, Mr. Holmes.
And as you rightly say, it is my wife.
Her one time love for me has fled.
I cannot tell you why to save my life."

A silent pause hangs in the smoke-filled air.
John Watson's brows are raised in arched surprise.
The pipe goes out, and is relit.
And understanding shows in Holmes's hooded eyes.

" The answer to your problem, sir, is plain to see.
The papers in your coat are all to blame."
A puzzled frown, as Holmes replies,
" The papers, sir! What is their name?

" It is ' The Pink 'Un', is it not ?
That list of races, horses, and the odds
Which men who wager, such as you,
Employ to try to cheat the fates and gods.

" If you will cease to place these bets
On nags which never seem to win or place
I make my own small wager, that
Your wife will start to show a far more loving face."

" Why, thank you sir, I will begin
My life anew, and eschew these games of chance.
And pay attention to my poor, dear wife,
Perhaps we'll take a trip across to France.

God bless you, Mr. Holmes. You've helped a man
And woman find true happiness anew."
And so he took his coat and stood.
" I shake your hand, sir. Farewell. Adieu."

[in another hand]
> My Watson is an honest man and brave.
> As true a friend as any among men.
> But writing verse is not his forte.
> Let prose alone now flow from his pen.

OTHER BOOKS BY HUGH ASHTON

If you enjoyed these stories, please consider writing a review somewhere where it may be seen by others.

If you have not done so already, you may also enjoy some other adventures of Sherlock Holmes by Hugh Ashton, who has been described in *The District Messenger*, the newsletter of the Sherlock Holmes Society of London, as being "one of the best writers of new Sherlock Holmes stories, in both plotting and style".

Volumes published so far include :
Tales from the Deed Box of John H. Watson M.D.
More from the Deed Box of John H. Watson M.D.
Secrets from the Deed Box of John H. Watson M.D.
The Darlington Substitution (novel)
Notes from the Dispatch-Box of John H. Watson M.D.
Further Notes from the Dispatch-box of John H. Watson M.D.
The Death of Cardinal Tosca (novel)
The Last Notes from the Dispatch-box of John H. Watson, M.D.
The Trepoff Murder (ebook only)
1894
Without my Boswell
Some Singular Cases of Mr. Sherlock Holmes

Children's detective stories, with beautiful illustrations by Andy Boerger:
Sherlock Ferret and the Missing Necklace
Sherlock Ferret and The Multiplying Masterpieces
Sherlock Ferret and The Poisoned Pond
Sherlock Ferret and the Phantom Photographer
The Adventures of Sherlock Ferret

Mapp and Lucia stories, based on the originals by E.F.Benson:
  Mapp at Fifty
  Mapp's Return
  La Lucia
  A Tilling New Year
  The Tilling Smugglers

Short stories, thrillers, alternative history, and historical science fiction titles:
  Tales of Old Japanese
  At the Sharpe End
  Balance of Powers
  Leo's Luck
  Beneath Gray Skies
  Red Wheels Turning
  Angels Unawares
  The Untime & The Untime Revisited
  Unknown Quantities
  On the Other Side of the Sky

Full details of these and more at :
https://HughAshtonBooks.com

Printed in the USA
CPSIA information can be obtained
at www.ICGtesting.com
LVHW031348171023
761319LV00010B/1097